A KINGDOM OF SILVER SHADOWS

A KINGDOM OF SILVER SHADOWS

LILY RIAN

COUNTERPOISE
PRESS

First published in the United States in November 2025 by Counterpoise Press

Identifiers:

ISBN 978-1-962846-02-8 (hardback) | ISBN 978-1-962846-03-5 (paperback) | ISBN 978-1-962846-01-1 (ebook)

10 9 8 7 6 5 4 3 2 1

To find out more about Counterpoise Press visit www.counterpoisepress.com

Content Warnings

This book contains adult themes and is intended for mature audiences (18+). Reader's discretion is advised.

Anxiety, depression, and PTSD
    Blood
    Cruelty/abuse towards others
    Death
    Death of a parent
    Enslavement
    Explicit language
    Gore
    Heavy themes of grief
    Insinuation of attempted sexual assault
    Sexually explicit content (consensual)
    Torture (including a male character forcing a female character to undress, not for sexual purposes but for abuse purposes)
    Violence

Pronunciation Guide and Glossary

This story is based on Irish and Celtic mythology; therefore, you will find the Irish language utilized throughout the story. It is intended to highlight the beauty of the language and for the fun of learning new words. While some words have been used to fit the story, their origins remain true to their meaning. You can find their actual meaning listed here, along with their pronunciation and their connotation for the story itself. Please note that not all character names or words are of Irish origin, but their pronunciations are listed all the same. Keep in mind the author is not fluent in the Irish language, and there are different pronunciations for different regions in Ireland. The pronunciations listed below have been researched to the author's best ability.

Characters:

Ahlani—ah-lawn-ee
    Airi—are-e
    Aislinn—ash-lin
    Amon—a-mon
    Armond—are-mond
    Ceana—see-n-ah
    Cillian Aodhán—kill-e-an / ay-awn
    Enya—in-yah

Eoin Olcéad—o-in / ol-kade
Flore—flur
Kalee—kay-lee
Niamh—nee-v
Órga—or-ga
Petranella—petra-nel-a
Racenda—ra-sin-da
Reana—ray-na
Ronan Toirdelbach—row-nan / tar-lach
Saoirse Aíne Órlaith—sersh-a / awn-ya / or-la
Tara—tar-a
Zephyr—zeh-fuh

Creatures:

Aes sídhe—ah-shee ; Sometimes referred to as aos sí, the aes sídhe are known as the Fairy People that live in the mountains and forests of Ireland. In this novel, aes sídhe refers to the faie and fair folk as a whole.
Liliach— Lil-e-ack
Merrow—mare-oh ; Irish sea fairies aka mermaids.
Osnádúrtha—uss-naw-dhor-hah ; Supernatural. In this novel, osnádúrtha encompasses supernatural beings as a whole including (but not limited to) faie, fair folk, witches, merrows, etc.

Places:

Arundell—air-un-dell
Centra—sin-tra
Earrach—ehr-och; Springtime. In this novel, earrach refers to the Spring court of the aes sídhe.
Fómhar—foh-var; autumn or harvest season. In this novel, fómhar refers to the Autumn court of the aes sídhe
Geimhreadh—geev-ra; Winter. In this novel, geimhreadh refers to the Winter court of the aes sídhe,
Ilythia—ill-ith-ee-ah
Rúndaiaithe—rune-da-ee-de-he; Rúnda translates to mysterious and iaithe translates to land. In this novel, Rúndaiaithe encompasses Arundell, Ilythia, Sóngnahánn, and Centra.

Samhradh—s-ow-rahgh; Summer. In this novel, samhradh refers to the Summer court of the aes sídhe.

Sóngnahánn—s-oh-gna-hahn

Misc:

Anamchara—an-am-har-a; Soul mate or, more accurately, soul friend.

Malartaím—mal-are-ton; Exchange.

Samhain—sow-in; First observed by Celtic Pagans, Samhain is one of the ancient fire festivals in Ireland. Traditionally observed on the 31st of October and the 1st of November.

Taoiseach—tea-shah; leader, ruler, chief

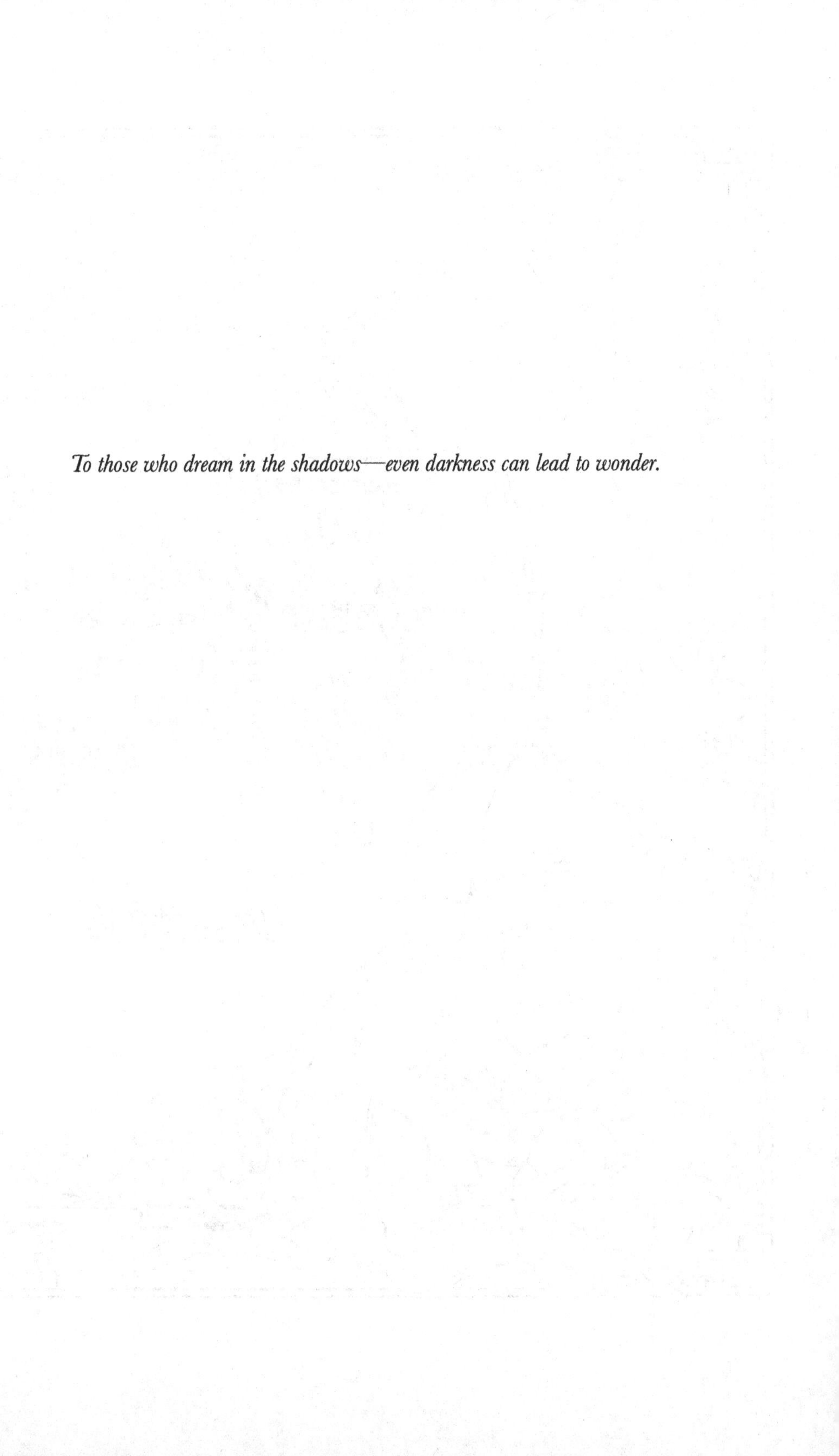

To those who dream in the shadows—even darkness can lead to wonder.

ENNISI MOUNTAINS
ILYTHIA
WILLOWMERE
AISLINN'S CHALET
HENFARROW
THE SEER'S COTTAGE
CENTRA

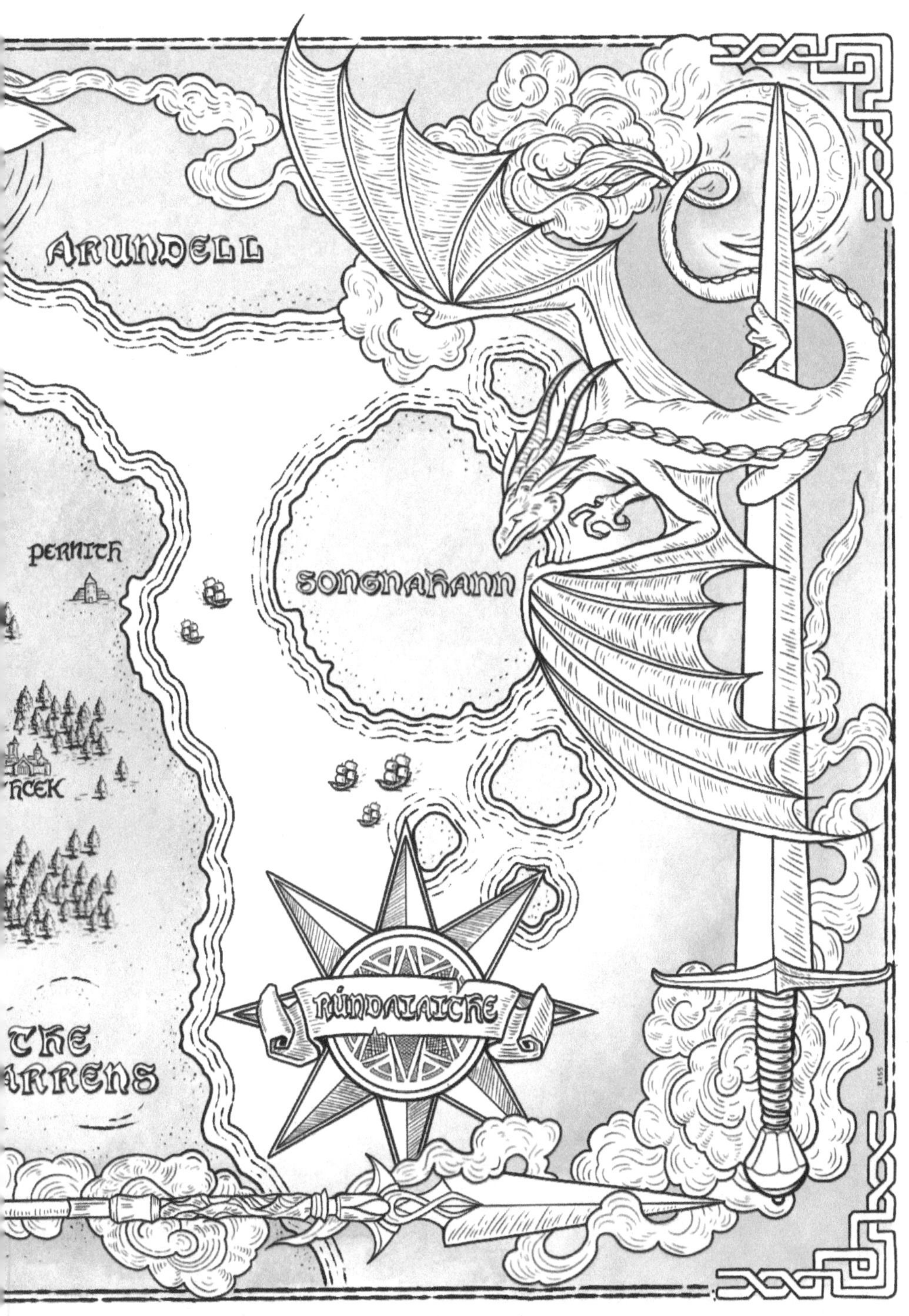

ARUNDELL
PERNITH
SONGNAHANN
HCEK
THE
ARRENS
RÚNDALAICHE

CHAPTER ONE

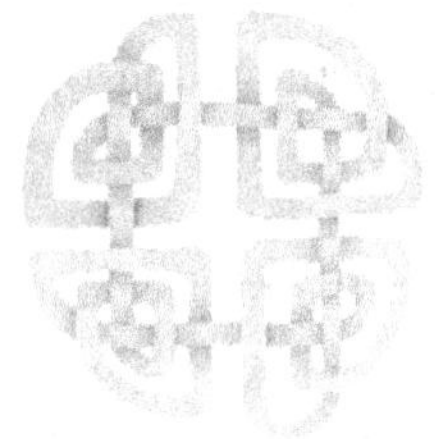

I bore no chains or shackles, but I was a prisoner all the same.

My will was not my own as I approached the villa under the cover of darkness. The Bond between the Conqueror King and me, or rather the leash he held on my soul, urged me on as snow crunched beneath my worn leather boots.

By now, the party would be in full swing. Guests would be too full of drink to notice what lurked in the shadows. Their host was too distracted to notice an uninvited guest.

Snowflakes clung to my lashes like fresh morning dew as I navigated the grounds, not caring about the trails of footprints left in my wake. The ongoing storm would erase them by morning. I longed to retreat to the warmth of my bedchambers, but my wants were irrelevant. They always were. There was no use in fighting against the Bond—I couldn't leave until my task was completed.

I had one objective tonight as the king's Informer: find and gather evidence against Lord Byrne.

The lord's multicolored brick house stood tall and wide compared to the other homes within sight. I clung to the side of the building, careful to keep away from the light casting from the windows.

Based on the map the Lord Chancellor gave me, I passed the foyer and greeting rooms, now empty aside from the occasional servant. The level above contained the party itself, as indicated by the guests who stood near the windows—the third level housed Lord Byrne's office.

Creeping toward the back gardens, I searched for the ladder. The chancellor assured that it would be placed next to the terrace, allowing me to reach the third floor unseen. Lord Byrne had been marked for death once the chancellor caught wind of his possible involvement in smuggling magic wielders out of Centra. The lord was too prominent to kill on the spot without question. Too human not to give him the benefit of the doubt. And so, I was sent to confirm his suspicions.

If Lord Byrne was indeed smuggling osnádúrtha out of Centra and the Bond forced me to bring back the evidence, it would mean betraying my own kind. Again.

I suppressed a groan when the terrace came into view with *no. Bleeding. Ladder.* There would have been some satisfaction that the chancellor wasn't as omniscient as he claimed if I weren't stuck in the biting cold looking for alternatives. I held up an obscene gesture to the rotted lattice, wondering if *this* was his idea of a ladder. Yeah, right. As soon as both feet were off the ground, I would come crashing down in a cascade of miserable glory, alerting everyone inside.

I cursed the chancellor for good measure. Of course, he wouldn't make it easy on me.

Puffs of hot air escaped into the night under my grumbled mutterings as I prowled the grounds. An unmarked door appeared a few paces away, and I almost kissed it. Almost. My ear pressed against the frost-tinged door, waiting, not needing to strain as my faie hearing could detect even the faintest of noises. Silence. This time, I kissed it.

The door opened up to what must have been the servant's stairwell. I toed the first step, testing for creaks before sneaking up the stairs. Echoes of hurried footsteps stopped my ascent. Moments later, the door to the second floor swung open and shut. I sucked in a breath, pulling the shadows closer to my hiding place, and pressed into the wall. A servant carrying a lantern rushed past. The lantern's light ricocheted off the stone, running right past me. Oblivious, the servant disappeared down the steps—the light with him. My heart raced despite knowing he didn't see me. He couldn't have, not unless he looked closer. But no one ever looked closer. Not with my magic concealing me.

The shadows didn't have a voice or a conscious thought, but they comforted and protected me all the same. Alive underneath the surface of my skin and identical in color to the silver of my hair, they were always with me. I never questioned why my features were tinged with silver when the shadows calling to me were deprived of light. If I wished, my silver swirls could pull from the surrounding shadows, claiming them as mine and shrouding me in darkness—a handy trick as a spy, but only useful if shadows were present.

Useful enough to become one of the king's Bonded.

The shadows might have camouflaged me, but they did nothing to conceal noise. I continued on near-silent feet. Muffled music buzzed through the walls with excitement as I traveled up the staircase. When I reached the third floor, I slipped into the dim hallway and let the door snick shut like a secret—quiet and just between the two of us.

The harmonies of the string quartet were louder here. Rising and falling. Reaching out, beckoning me forward. I squeezed my eyes shut, giving myself a moment to enjoy. The pluck of the strings thrummed in my veins, imploring me to move along with it. I'd never danced before, not formally. Not like the lords and ladies did below. But there was something magical about how music moved through the body, as if it was begging it to sway this way and that.

I fell victim to the music's pull. It was the only thing I enjoyed about living at the castle, and it was rare I was allowed within earshot, forced to listen through layers of stone. My stride quickened like the staccato of the violins, carrying me past the most exposed section of the third floor overlooking the lower level. Crouching, I concealed myself in the shadows and looked through the banisters, attempting a glimpse of the musicians. One of the marble pillars obstructed the band, but the scent of roasted boar wafted up the stairs. My stomach growled.

Below, members of high society preened to one another in the comfort of warmth as the party raged on. Indulging in gourmet foods and premium spirits, guests boasted about their wealth and successes. Most of them found their fortune on the backs of the osnádúrtha. When magic-wielders were stripped of their homes, their wealth, and their lives, the king dispersed everything to those he favored. Shops. Farms. Homes. Anything the osnádúrtha once called their own.

Centra was once peaceful and home to many magic wielders who roamed freely. Sixteen years ago, everything changed. A human king declared magic as the cause of the kingdom's ailments and the overabundance of osnádúrtha as an affront to the gods. His reign of killing, enslavement, and exploitation began—the Reckoning for our people. It shouldn't have been possible, but here we were. Those whose magic was useful were kept and later Bound to the Conqueror King, forced to do his bidding. Those who somehow managed to slip the king's grasp went into hiding with the hopes of fleeing the kingdom. Between paper checks, high ticket prices for ships, and the closure of Ilythia's border, an osnádúrtha's only chance of making it out of Centra alive was with the help of the smugglers.

Guests marveled at the osnádúrtha in the center of the room—faie by the looks of him, his pointed ears giving him away. The water wielder's fingers swayed in a rhythm known only to him as his magic manipulated the liquid from surrounding glasses to form scenes of galloping horses and flying birds. Nothing more than senseless party tricks. Was this what his life had been reduced to? Someone who used their gods' gift as entertainment for their oppressors? Still, it was a better fate than most.

Lord Byrne sat on a plush settee along the windowless back wall under his coat of arms: a shield surrounded by smaller symbols. As host, he held the attention of Crown Prince Ronan of Centra across from him. The prince sat with regal grace, his back as straight as one of Lord Byrne's marble pillars. Not a hair out of place on his blonde bun or a blemish on his pale skin, Prince Ronan's attire was immaculate as usual. Gold and crimson, his tunic flowed like the blood his father spilled for his throne. The shadows writhed beneath my skin. I didn't know the prince well and didn't need to. He couldn't be anything more than a replication of his father—a man of power, wielding it like a weapon over those whom he deemed less than him.

Twin sisters with rich brown skin in sage slips sat in the prince's lap. A man clothed in linen pants and an open vest stood behind him, running his broad hands along the prince's neck and over his shoulders. Prince Ronan stroked the sisters' arms in slow, lazy circles as he succumbed to the man's expert touch, leaning his head back into what was sure to be a firm torso—almost bored by what Lord Byrne had to say.

Did the prince know he listened to the words of a traitor? Perhaps he was sent here by his father to distract the lord while I gathered the evidence he needed. Or maybe he preferred to be surrounded by the lord's entertainment. Probably both.

Curiosity satiated, I moved to the study, following the map in my mind. Guilt weighed heavier with each footstep. Too often, I'd given over the names of innocent lives. Too often, my spirit withered away as the king used me against my people.

It was fruitless to outright rebel against the Conqueror King. If I had any sense, I wouldn't risk his wrath at all. But every time I encountered the name of an osnádúrtha to be brought before him, my mother's name was the only one I saw.

The odious mark signifying our forced magical Bond burned at the nape of my neck as if trying to berate me for such thoughts. *Shush,* I sent back down the Bond. Thank the Nine and the Mother herself it wasn't a direct link to the king. He would have killed me long ago if he knew what lay amongst my thoughts. I turned the handle of the study.

Locked.

I stuffed my gloves into the pocket of my cloak and removed two sharp pins from the leather pouch attached to my waist. I guided the pins into the lock with practiced ease until a familiar *click* sounded.

I let loose a breath, slipped into the office, and locked the door. Adrenaline coursed through me like a tidal wave. No matter how many locks I've picked, it was always the same, giddy feeling.

Well-loved books lined the shelves to my left, and an unlit hearth sat on the opposite wall. A mahogany desk took center stage, the focal point of the room. I inhaled deeply. The comforting smell of parchment settled my nerves. I searched through the books first, looking for any false tomes and checking between them for anything the lord might want to conceal. A few of the titles were familiar—others too dull for a second glance. *The Art of Preservation: A Guide to Keeping Your Fruits and Vegetables.* Who would read such a thing?

The bookcase provided no clues, except that Lord Byrne might be too mundane to be a traitor. Nothing significant stood out on the desk as I shuffled through the papers scattered across it: business accounts, ledgers, and other monotonous documents. Its drawers were too shallow to house a false bottom. The unlit hearth on the far wall was barren aside from a lone cigar box and an empty decorative vase.

I ran my hands along the wall behind the oil painting above the hearth and the tapestry next to the door. Nothing. Two potted plants sitting on either side of the window were just that: plants. Not a single thing in the room screamed 'secret documents here.' I pinched the bridge of my nose. It was unlikely, but perhaps the chancellor's information was wrong.

Despite my frustrations, I prayed it was true.

Any hope of a misunderstanding came crashing down, however, when I crawled underneath the desk. The hollow knock of a false panel reverberated into my knuckles. I fumbled more than once to insert one of my pins into the small keyhole, letting loose a curse when it didn't budge.

The unmistakable crash of glass shattered in the distance. My hands stilled. One breath. Another. When I was sure footsteps weren't rushing up the stairs, I resumed my lock picking.

Gears ticked into place the further I pushed the pin. With one final *click*, the panel popped open. I snatched the files within it and moved to the window, letting the light of the full moon aid me as I scanned the handwritten papers—all of which contained information to condemn the poor lord.

Illustrations of osnádúrtha wanted by the crown. Ledgers of supplies. Accounts dedicated to getting the osnádúrtha out of Centra. Merrows, faie, and witches' names—either true or false—were scattered throughout the files.

I traced along the likeness of a merrow. She was in her true form—half human and half fish. Even on parchment, the artist captured the mesmerizing pull toward her. The following illustration was of a faie, the higher beings of the aes sídhe. They, too, resembled humans, but they were *more*. The male in the drawing was tall and lean. His hair was sheared short, showing off delicately pointed ears. Subtle, sharp, tapered ends of his upper canines poked out beneath his shy smile. I rubbed my tongue over my own and resisted the urge to touch my tipped ears. My fingers lingered over the word *"deceased"* written on the bottom of the page. I didn't know him or his character, but grief washed over me none-theless. Did he have a family? Was he loved?

There were other drawings of the osnádúrtha—a few fair folk with wings or horns. Known as lesser beings of the aes sídhe, the fair folk all but disappeared from Centra since the Reckoning. My mother always made sure I understood that just because their smaller magic was often overlooked, it didn't make them any less. The king, however, didn't bother trying to Bond with them, deeming their magic as unimportant, and decided to rid the land of them instead. Those who survived hid within the land, waiting until they could make their escape.

I wasn't surprised to find there weren't any witches' portraits amongst the stack. It was odd for one to be caught outside of Ilythia, much less one willing to have their features recorded—they were known to be viciously private by nature. Probably why their kingdom still stood while others fell to their knees before Centra.

There were other pages filled with symbols I'd come to understand as some kind of code between the smugglers, listing people and places willing to help magic wielders. I separated them from the main stack, making sure any information damning others was kept to the side.

I allowed the ledgers to stay; none of them indicated they were coming out of another's pocket. The portraits were harmless enough, as no names were attached. Reading the correspondence letters from those who escaped, thanking the lord for his help was like a punch to the gut. Shepherding the man to his death was a knife to the heart.

Lost in thought, I almost didn't notice the footsteps shuffling down the hall. I took what I needed to satisfy the Bond and shoved the rest of the incriminating papers back into the compartment, locking the panel. Guilt weighed heavily in my heart, leaving the portraits behind. They deserved so much more than what the king and his men would do to them once they raided Lord Byrne's estate. Burn them, likely.

I stuffed the information I would hand over to the king in my innermost pocket, taking care to put the coded letters in my boot. The Bond demanded I gather evidence against Lord Byrne, but the king didn't specify to bring him *everything* I found. These little technicalities were the only way I could work around his commands.

Lord Byrne was beyond saving with the king's target on his back. But I could keep the other smugglers safe…for now. I had to help them as much as I could. If the smugglers were safe, so were the osnádúrtha they aided.

A key jiggled the lock. There was no escaping now. Heart hammering, I squeezed between the side of the bookcase and the darkest part of the room. I called to the shadows, letting their darkness surround me until I became it.

I clutched the locket tucked under my cloak like a lifeline. It was the last reminder I had of her. The last thing my mother ever gave me. Holding it reassured her I was trying my best to look out for our people, like she would have done. My name, etched in silver, had worn over the years, but my thumb still stumbled over the letters *S-A-O-I-R-S-E.* The motion calmed my thunderous pulse.

Lord Byrne's heavy stride stomped across the room. Flint struck steel, and the warmth of the fire in the hearth was almost immediate. The surrounding shadows thickened to counteract the soft glow of flames.

A series of knocks rapped at the door in quick succession. The shadows along the wall depicted the lord greeting his guest with a firm clasping of arms. I resisted the urge to peer around the bookcase to look at his face, too afraid the shadows would fail against the light.

"I trust you were able to slip away unseen," Lord Byrne said.

"It was no trouble," the man replied. His voice was somehow familiar, though I couldn't quite place it. "Any word on the recent shipment?"

"They were delivered to the North successfully." Arundell, I assumed if the shipment contained osnádúrtha. It was rumored my faie brethren in the North were offering refuge to all who could make it. Lord Byrne grabbed the cigar box on top of the hearth across from me, offering one to the man.

"Good," the man sighed. "For a moment, I thought they weren't going to make it."

"If it weren't for your help, they might not have."

There was a pause in conversation, as if they both had come to the realization that they had almost lost everything they worked for. A lump formed in my throat. They weren't out of the dragon's den yet.

"Were you able to find out any more information about the attacks?" The man asked, changing the topic.

My ears perked up. Attacks? Certainly not within Rothcek. Something soured in my stomach; I prayed the king wasn't sending more search parties for the osnádúrtha. Their presence was heavy soon after the Reckoning commenced, slowly dwindling once the osnádúrtha became more difficult to find, and the crown's focus shifted to the smugglers instead.

"Unfortunately, no," Lord Byrne said, his words mumbled. A match struck, its hiss sharp and quick. The gut-churning aroma of overworked leather and distant grassfire unfurled like a serpent, shoving its way down my windpipe until I could hardly breathe. "Only what you already know," he continued, "I tried talking to the king, but I was dismissed."

"I would assume as much. I haven't been able to make any headway with him either," the other man, presumably another noble, sighed. "I'll have my scouts keep searching, but so far, we haven't been able to find anything useful."

"Do you think it's him?" Lord Byrne asked, his voice barely a whisper.

"I don't know why anyone would attack their own subjects, but it hasn't stopped him before," the man spat, his disdain heavy in the air, mingling with the smoke.

The door opened with a low creak. "Sir, I—" the butler cut himself off. "Your Highness, my apologies."

The room spun, my world tilting with it. My eyes squeezed shut. Disbelief clung to me like a soggy shirt as Prince Ronan reassured the apologetic butler. I should have recognized his voice, but the son of the Conqueror King colluding with a smuggler was the last thing I'd expected.

"No need for apologies. Thank you again, Lord Byrne, for sharing your imported cigars. Truly spectacular," Prince Ronan said before taking his leave, all of my assumptions about the man leaving with him.

The prince couldn't be working with the lord. It was a disguise—a way to gather evidence and dismantle the smuggling ring from within. There was, however, no denying the disgust the prince harbored in his voice when he referred to his father's actions.

Lord Byrne followed his butler out the door, leaving me to stew in the deafening silence amongst the smog of tobacco and shattered expectations. I paused at the threshold, fingers brushing against the door frame. I'd nearly forgotten about the coded letters burning a hole in my boot. If anyone found them, more than one life would be destroyed. They needed to disappear.

The codes were a weight in my hand, the power they held insurmountable. I watched them dwindle to ash in the smoldering hearth and vanished into the night.

Chapter Two

Only a few servants, guards, and the Lord Chancellor of the Realm surrounded the king in his throne room. The chancellor was a stout man with a thick, ginger beard. The hair on his head conflicted with his facial hair—an exposed scalp peeked through thin streaks of strawberry-blonde. At first glance, his rosy cheeks might lead one to assume he was a kind man. The sinister light behind his bloodshot eyes suggested otherwise.

Those eyes skimmed my figure as I approached the throne placed upon a dais. Once. Twice. A third lingering glance made me thankful for my thick, unassuming cloak. I kept my gaze straight, repressing a shiver of disgust threatening to crawl down my spine. His attention almost made me forget the king seated on the throne.

Almost.

My footsteps echoed along the gray marble, passing pillars and shimmering curtains. The Conqueror King's dark leer narrowed as I approached. Hushed whispers from the chancellor slithered into his king's ear, but their gazes were trained on me like I was something to be watched and chaos could erupt at any moment. Despite his age, the king still appeared young. His hair was blacker than night save for a single white streak shooting across his temple—the only sign of his increasing years.

I bent into a strained bow as I've done many times in the last fifteen years, my eyes never straying from my mother's executioner. My captor.

My jailer. This was the man whose soldiers slaughtered my mother before abducting me. Yet, I kneeled before him.

Phantom touches from the hands of the guards who held me down as the king etched the Bond mark onto my neck ghosted my arms, my legs, my back. Flashes of what occurred in this room stole my vision. The soldier who kidnapped me wasted no time bringing me before his king with the spray of my mother's blood still staining his clothes. Did the paintings remember my screams? Aching and bleeding, I was forced to submit as the king forbade me from trying to end my life. Told me any attempt at escape was futile. The king's knee-length boots were polished to perfection today, as they were then, with not a speck of dust on them.

"Rise, Informer, and report," the king commanded, his voice deep and demanding. I did as he asked and kept my eyes on his too-clean boots. I was nothing more to him than my Bond. He would never say my name as I was not Saoirse, but only his Informer. Unfolding the paper from my pocket, I handed over the information that would sign Lord Byrne's death warrant.

"As the Lord Chancellor suspected, I found evidence to prove Lord Byrne a traitor."

The king examined the list. "This is it?"

"These are all the names Lord Byrne tried and failed to smuggle out of Centra, Your Majesty," I repeated, careful not to mention the coded letters. There were about fifty names on the list. Plenty to insinuate Lord Byrne a traitor and none other. It hinted that the lord, not an entire network of smugglers, was the one who orchestrated their failed escapes. I sent a prayer to the Mother. It needed to satisfy the king and prevent him from seeking more information.

The king stared at me for a long moment as if he could hear the thundering of my traitorous heart. "Is there any evidence he's working with others?"

"No, Your Majesty." Sweat beaded on my back as I pictured the pages filled with the codenames turning to ash in the flames. The Bond forced me to complete my mission, but it couldn't stop me from lying. My very nature as an aes sídhe prevented any lies from leaving my lips. However, this wasn't necessarily a lie. *Technically,* there wasn't any evidence of Lord Byrne colluding with others. Not anymore, at least.

If the king commanded me to report everything I found, however... I didn't want to think about what would happen. I hoped I had been obedient enough to earn a semblance of trust.

"Anything else you'd like to add?"

"I took only what I needed to avoid the lord's suspicion. You'll find other documents in the false panel under his desk if you conduct a search. There are ledgers and letters all indicating the lord is working alone."

"My king, there should have been more," the chancellor hissed. "My spies indicated he was colluding with others."

"Informer?" The king asked.

It was an effort not to gulp, to shake, to flee. Instead, I steeled my shoulders and said, "If you were to conduct the search yourself, you would find nothing else, Your Majesty." And because I couldn't help myself, I added, "Unless of course, the chancellor is concerned how the lord preserves his fruit."

My gaze stayed trained on the king, ignoring the chancellor's leer. I shouldn't have said that. Instead, I should have mentioned how the prince was conspiring with Lord Byrne. I didn't trust the prince. However, if there was a chance he was helping the osnádúrtha, I couldn't risk it. Not yet. Not until I knew for sure.

He's testing you, a horrible thought nagged. Gods, was I an idiot? I swallowed, thinking of all the ways Prince Ronan could be spying for the chancellor or his father—scrutinizing my every move, seeing how much of a loyal pet I was.

I'm still in compliance with the Bond, I reassured myself. Whatever Prince Ronan was up to, I was still compliant with the king's orders. It's not my fault the king wasn't specific with his commands.

Seemingly satisfied, the king didn't question me further. I let out a breath. The chancellor took the list from the king's outstretched hand and murmured in his ear—a cruel, cat-like smile stretched the corner of his thin lips. I knew I would regret my mouthiness. I always did. And yet, it didn't matter. Not really. The chancellor demanded respect and longed to wield power like his king. He wielded his authority by punishing me as he saw fit. According to the chancellor, there was always a lesson to be learned—*be more punctual, stand straighter, breathe quieter*. Whether I controlled my temper or not, I was to be punished. Hard and often. The king never resisted, of course. My compliance with his commands was inconsequential. To them, I was a dog to be beaten into obedience. Periodically put in my place so there was never a question as to where I stood—a reminder I was nothing.

Regardless of the excuse, the chancellor always punished me for the same reason: existing. For being an osnádúrtha, an aes sídhe—faie. For having magic and using it. My shadows were a part of me, as sure as the heart beating in my chest. Since the day they appeared, they've never left. Unlike other faie, my magic was a constant, visible presence, swimming under my skin like silk ribbons flowing in a gentle breeze. Like all faie, it was derived from the gods themselves. I prayed to them now, even though I knew they wouldn't listen. They hadn't in years.

"It seems you did not learn your last lesson in punctuality. The Lord Chancellor informed me you were late in delivering your report."

I wasn't.

"My apologies, Your Majesty," I acquiesced. Defending myself was futile and would only result in more lashes.

"You know what you must do."

I nodded and bowed at the dismissal. The faces of the guards who used to have to haul me away to the chancellor's office remained impassive as I followed the chancellor out of the throne room. With each step, I reminded myself there were others out there who kept other osnádúrtha from my fate. Humans were actively working to help my people, and because of me, because I burned those letters, they were still helping the osnádúrtha tonight and every night for as long as they could. The chancellor may punish me, but he couldn't touch the others, not if I could help it.

When we arrived at the chancellor's office, he didn't need to tell me to remove my cloak and shirt. Only in my thin undershirt, I kept my back to him as I laid the clothing over a chair quickly enough so he didn't think I was stalling and braced myself over the desk.

"And the undergarment."

I stilled. He usually let me keep my undershirt if the back was cut low. I cursed.

"Either you remove it, or I remove it for you," the chancellor said when I didn't comply.

My hands shook as I pulled the garment over my head. I kept my back to him and arms crossed over my breasts until I had no choice but to brace myself over his desk. It was humiliating to be bare before him. I tried to think of everything but my naked upper body and the lead cane he grabbed. It was his favorite, as minuscule pieces would break off into my wounds.

The desk was cold underneath my forearms, but it might have been my clammy skin. Gone were the usual trinkets and stacks of papers. Those had been pushed aside in preparation for our *lesson*.

Tuning out his vicious words, I took in the room's opulence—the ornate vases, gaudy tapestry, and other unnecessary finery. The Lord Chancellor benefited heavily when his king conquered most of the continent.

Without warning, a sharp, instantaneous slice of pain stung across my back at the first whack. My fingernails dug into the mahogany, adding to the menagerie of half-moon-shaped marks. The chancellor's words were muddled as if I was being held underwater. A second hit. This time to my right shoulder. My knees threatened to buckle underneath me, but I held as steady as I could. A third to my other shoulder. Another remark too muddied to make out. My arms trembled, struggling to hold myself up. If I collapsed, the chancellor would only hit me harder. My vision blurred, but I would not cry. Not anymore. I hadn't in nine years, not since I was fifteen. Instead, I drifted out of myself, leaving the world behind and focused on the tapestry in front of me.

Old and battered, the tapestry depicted an unfamiliar ancient battle. It clashed with everything else in the room. The colors were rich with deep reds, golds, and blacks. The woven threads called to me, depicting men clashing their swords with monstrous creatures from another world. I didn't know what they were and prayed I never would. Some resembled wolves or hounds, others of humans, but they were all wrapped in an ominous cloud of shadows, concealing most of their features. The piercing crimson eyes of the dark army's figurehead, insinuating death itself, were enough to fuel my nightmares. I favored the other half of the tapestry instead, where dragons scorched the monstrous figures and gods with ethereal beauty worked together to overpower the dark army.

My mother once told me a story about the bond between dragons and witches. Dragons were sacred to the witches. They protected one another because of it. What I wouldn't give to be a witch and for a dragon to protect me now. It was useless, though. I wasn't a witch, and the dragons were long dead.

By the time the chancellor delivered the final lash, I'd lost count. Blood trickled down my spine, a river of fire burning in its wake.

"We will see if you learn your lesson next time," the chancellor hissed. His scent of decayed roses clung to me like a recurring nightmare.

"Doubt it," I mumbled. The chancellor handed the cane to the guard and left without another word.

Sweat-drenched and blood-soaked, I forwent the cloak and tugged my shirt back over my head—trying not to wince as it passed over my battered back. I paused, noticing a new map of Rúndaiaithe pinned to the wall. Different colored pinpoints scattered throughout the once five, now four kingdoms. Centra was awash with red flags, concentrated more heavily in Rothcek and the surrounding villages. The Barrens to the south, now waving Centra's gold and crimson flag, were devoid of all pinpoints. Nothing lay amongst the sand and dust. The other kingdoms, however, held a singular black flag: Arundell, Sóngnahánn, Centra, and even the witch kingdom of Ilythia. Unsurprisingly, there wasn't much else in Ilythia —no pinpoints, city names, or even landmarks to distinguish the land.

It was difficult to decipher the map's meaning without an accompanying key. I was also too exhausted to care. The guard escorted me back to my room, and as much as I tried, I couldn't help the wobble of my knees as I trudged through the castle or the shake of my hand when I grasped the door handle.

Kalee, my handmaid and only friend, looked up from her book where she sat at the settee by my balcony window. Her chestnut hair was unbound—long, curly, and voluminous, nearly reaching her hips.

"Saoirse, I was wondering where you…" Her wide smile fell. Concern and something akin to pity swirled in her amber eyes. I looked away. Kalee rushed toward me and helped me to the attached bathing chamber. We replayed this scene often enough that she knew what to do.

My shirt stuck to the gashes and jutting bits of lead. Even Kalee's tender touch couldn't keep the burning at bay when she lifted my shirt overhead. Thanks to the magic running through my veins, the wounds themselves would heal fast as long as Kalee could pick all the lead out. Lead and iron were effective at counteracting magic, making it more difficult to heal. Oftentimes, the remaining shards of lead were too minuscule to get them all, leaving them to ooze and scar.

I sat there, silent in the warm water, while Kalee cleaned and dressed my wounds. With every inhale came a sharp sting, the pain more than physical. It traveled to my soul, festering like an unhealed wound—slow and creeping as it hollowed me out day by day. Something dark coiled inside me where happiness once stood. It waited patiently. Taking its time as it sought to steal every piece of me.

The weight of unshed tears lingered behind my eyes, but I still would not cry…not yet, not while Kalee was here. She couldn't see how badly the chancellor affected me, how weak and small he made me feel. How feeble and helpless I truly was.

She helped me dress, selecting a nightgown with a low back to avoid disturbing the area. The cool, soft sheets of my bed provided a minor comfort as I lay on my stomach.

Like me, Kalee was parentless—her mother died during childbirth, and her father passed before I came to the castle. But whereas I was Bound to the king for the rest of my life, Kalee was human and could do as she pleased. Though the position her father secured for her in the castle was the best she would ever have, it was difficult not to be jealous of my friend at times like these—when she could walk away and leave this place behind. Meanwhile, I was stuck here. Forever.

I hid my face in the pillow.

"I love you, Saoirse," Kalee whispered and kissed the top of my head. A gentle reminder that love could be found in this dark, odious place. That I was not alone. That she would stay if I asked. The offer was always there, but I couldn't burden her. Kalee left, and the darkness inside me took yet another piece. Tears streamed down my face the instant the door shut. I sobbed, not because of the pain, but because of the state of my life. Because of the monster I was Bound to. Because of my mother, whom I disappointed in the Otherworld.

I cried because I was so dangerously close to breaking and no one— not even Kalee—would be able to put the pieces together again.

CHAPTER THREE

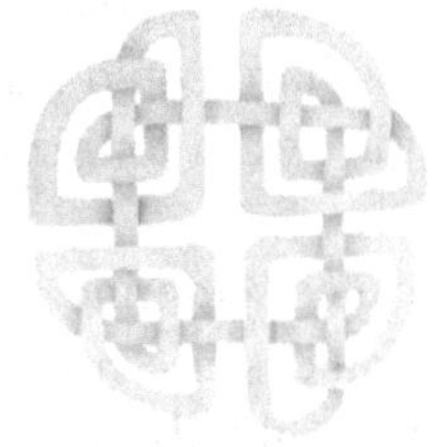

She would always visit me in the worst way.

Exhaustion had pulled me under swiftly, but then the nightmares took hold. I dreamt of my mother's broken body surrounded by a glinting red sea. Her hand stretched toward me, begging for help. I ran to her, but my nine-year-old body was too small, too slow, and too late as she took her last breath. Her soul escaped with her final exhale as her eyes dulled over—the brightness of her ice blue irises forever extinguished. My mother's wounds gushed with more, more, *more* until a tidal wave of crimson came for me. And then, I, too, was dying, drowning in my mother's lifeblood.

I clutched my heart. The air was too thick. *Breathe. Just breathe.* My chest rose and fell in quick succession, my lungs refusing to fill with air, choosing instead to wilt like flowers days departed from the stem. Midmorning sunlight peeked between the cracks of drawn curtains. Golden threads woven into the crimson comforter glimmered in the stream of light. I gripped it with shaking hands, reminding myself I was in my room at the castle and not in the field near the village.

"You're fine," I said aloud, my voice hoarse. "You're—" A sob worked its way out, sharp and quick. Twin rivers beyond my control fell from my cheeks. The edges of my vision blurred, and it took everything in me to stay upright. I focused on my surroundings: a corner wardrobe, a book-filled vanity against the wall, and two doorways leading to the dining area and bathing chamber. Eventually, the shaking stopped, and the edges of the nightmare faded, leaving me to face the torment of reality.

Breathe, I repeated to myself, using the pain in my back to ground me until the panic subsided and my lungs worked again. Shadows from the room's dark corners slithered across my body, caressing me with their inky tendrils in a soothing embrace.

I laid there until my thoughts drifted to Prince Ronan. The unknown was eating me alive. Any type of rest was obsolete until I knew if he was helping my people or hurting them. I've followed plenty of affluent people for the sake of the crown. How hard could trailing a prince be? I winced. If he caught me… Nope. I didn't want to think about those consequences. At least not before breakfast.

"Seerrrr-shaaaa," Kalee called, entering through my bedroom door, a food tray in hand as if she could sense my thoughts. Her chestnut hair dangled in a long plait, hanging right above the small of her back. Kalee's warm, brown skin glowed despite the cold weather and the lack of proper sunshine in recent weeks.

Sitting in my sweat-soaked bedding, my hair and night clothes clung to me. One wound on my back reopened during the thrashing. Blood mingled with sweat on my skin, clothes, and sheets. I might have been embarrassed if I wasn't so exhausted.

Kalee, the ever-loyal friend, offered a sympathetic smile before helping me discard the soiled sheets. "Another nightmare?"

I nodded and grabbed a spare set of sheets from a nearby closet.

"You can tell me, you know. You don't have to carry whatever burden you harbor on your own," she said, breaking the stillness.

A squeeze of her hand was my only reply.

Even though Kalee has witnessed the aftermath of my nightmares countless times, I never talked about what plagued me. It was hard enough to relive my mother's dying moment most nights; I didn't care to recall it in my waking hours, too. At least when I could help it.

"Eat," she commanded, nudging me to the attached dining area. Sausage, cheese, eggs, and assorted fruits were laid out on the oak table.

The monster housed inside my stomach made itself known with its needy growl at the sight of the spread. I obeyed its command by shoveling food into my mouth, barely breathing between mouthfuls.

"Gods, do you even taste your food when you eat like that?" Kalee asked, staring at me incredulously, despite seeing me eat with a ferocious intensity on many occasions.

I grinned, not bothering to swallow my food before replying, "I taste it just fine, thank you."

I couldn't help the vigor with which I ate. Faie expended an immense amount of energy every time we used our magic. Too exhausted to eat before bed, I was ravenous after last night. Already, my spirits lifted as I supplied myself with a second helping, this time chewing the food more thoroughly.

"I have your Midwinter gift," Kalee hummed, a mischievous smile spreading across her face. She pulled a neatly wrapped package from the pocket of her lace-trimmed apron and slid it across the table.

"Kalee, you shouldn't have. You know my gifts never compare to yours." The Bonded weren't allowed coin or access into most establishments.

"Hush. You know I love your gifts. Let me do something nice for you, Sersh, and just accept it."

Heat crept up to my cheeks, but I took the proffered gift nonetheless. With a tug of the ribbon, the paper gave way to a book titled, *Creatures of the Mist*.

"This sounds exciting," I said, thumbing through the pages.

"It has everything you like. Sword fights, bone-chilling monsters, and a dashing hero to save them all. It's all any of the ladies can talk about right now."

"Thank you." Excitement thrummed through me, though I didn't want to think about how much this had cost her, especially if it was popular. "I have your gift as well," I said, hopping up from my seat to rummage through the vanity.

Hers was not packaged with careful, well-placed folds of decorative paper. Instead, stolen, overworked plain paper, bearing the signs of too many re-dos, held her gift with a fragile tenderness. The blue ribbon, if it could even be called that, was a tangle of frayed silk sagging in a pathetic heap.

Kalee accepted it with a wide smile. "Oh, Sersh, I love it." She held up the ill-constructed page marker I crafted out of stolen fabric and mediocre needlework from blunted needles and leftover thread.

"It's nothing compared to your gift, but I thought it might be useful." I toed the leg of the table, looking down at my fraying slippers.

"It is exactly what I needed." She took out her own book, one of the many she always kept on hand, and smoothed out the recently folded corner, placing the page marker in its stead. "Perfect. Now, what should we do for Midwinter this year? Your orders are still on hold for today, right?"

"Yes, thank the gods, save for attending the ceremony later," I sighed, leaning back in the wooden chair. The best gift of the longest night of the year was a few hours of freedom. We usually spent the day together, but it wasn't likely I'd get another chance. "You know, I'm rather tired from last night. I want to spend the day lying in bed until the ceremony," I said carefully, speaking in half-truths, toeing the line with which my faie nature would allow me.

Kalee scoffed at the mention of the ceremony but didn't dwell on it. "Fine with me. We can crack open your new book and see what it's all about."

"I don't want to keep you on your only day off. You should spend it with your other friends. Take a break from me for once." I smiled, though I knew it didn't reach my eyes.

Her brows knitted. "*You're* my most cherished friend. I don't want to leave you."

I patted her hand. "Don't worry about me. I'd rather sleep the day away anyway. Go and enjoy the festivities."

Kalee pursed her lips but nodded all the same. My secrets piled up like unwashed laundry—unwanted and overwhelming, collecting more and more over time until I was forced to face them. This was for the best. I couldn't drag her into something dangerous. The risk of following the prince was high, but the potential dangers of what I might discover were far greater.

Chapter Four

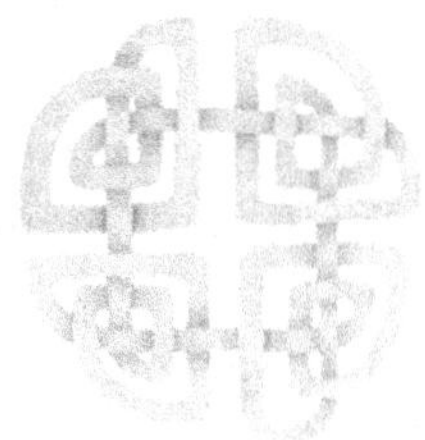

Prince Ronan emerged from the castle walls in the glow of early afternoon. He, like so many, was behind on securing Midwinter gifts—a suspicion proved true when the carriage headed to the heart of Rothcek. Centra's capital city was famed for its shops, fulfilling any and every need.

I blew hot air into my gloved hands, following the carriage through the streets. The crowd of people paid me no mind as I slipped within their ranks. Nothing more than a shadow amongst them. The wheels of the carriages clattered along the cobblestones, leaving little room for pedestrians as they weaved in and out of the narrow street, moving from one shop to another, seemingly unconcerned as they inconvenienced the riders. Four guards flanked the prince's carriage—only one stood out among them. He looked handsome from afar, the way any muscled, dark-haired man would. His face twisted into a scowl as he overlooked the crowd, only transforming when the prince blessed him with his presence. They exchanged smiles and laughs, talking through the side window every so often. The main guard carried an air of superiority that the others didn't have. One only second to the prince.

Lanterns hung in neat rows, travelling from shop to shop for the Midwinter holiday. Most shops stacked on top of one another, each building accommodating two or three different merchants. Windows displayed clothes, food, footwear, hunting gear, and jewels, beckoning their next victim. Prince Ronan fell prey to a small, standalone shop located at the far end of the market. A wooden sign above the door read *Precious Emblems* in a faded cursive font.

Concealed in shadows, I leaned against a building across the street. Through the glass windows, the prince perused the shopkeeper's selection, his guard close behind him while the other three remained stationed at the carriage. Unlike humans, I had no trouble seeing the details from this distance.

My sharp hearing was the only thing saving me from *him* creeping up behind me.

"I see you, little shadow," a husky voice whispered into my ear. I would have scoffed at the nickname if it came from anyone else. Goosebumps crawled down my arms like frost fracturing along a pane of glass, the hairs on the back of my neck raised in warning. Only he could detect my presence in the shadows. I didn't know what magic the Hunter possessed. His *talents* for capturing the king's enemies earned him the title of the king's most skilled hunter.

"Hunter." Voice clipped, I didn't turn to gaze at the face of evil. The Hunter was one of the few who Bonded with the king of his own free will. Like any other Bonded, he was compelled to hunt down the king's targets. But there were rumors of his wickedness long before he became entwined with the Conqueror King.

"Informer," the Hunter mocked.

I ignored the faie and watched the shopkeeper adjust the circular glasses perched on the tip of his nose as he talked with the prince, showing him varying degrees of gaudy necklaces. The man appeared to be in his fifties, with a round belly, a long, well-kept white beard, and a friendly face.

"What do you want?" I asked when the Hunter didn't move on. I didn't know his true name, only his title, as he did mine. The Bonded rarely spoke to one another, too scared to invoke the rage of those who commanded them. In the beginning, the osnádúrtha fought against the forced Bonds. Any resistance didn't last long, however, before they were forced into submission and secluded from potential allies. After what happened to the merrows in the East when Sóngnahánn's islands were burned to nothing but ash as retaliation for defying the Conqueror King, the osnádúrtha stopped fighting. But the Hunter had been brazen ever since our paths crossed two years ago.

"Will you not look at me when you speak?" he crooned.

My gaze stayed trained on the shop as I fidgeted with my locket while the prince settled on an emerald necklace. When it became clear that the Hunter refused to leave me alone, I turned to him. He always had a rugged look about him. Untamed like the wild itself from his fringed hair, black as a raven's feather, to his stubble-lined jaw.

"What. Do. You. Want?" I asked through clenched teeth, the muscles in my jaw aching. At least I was forced to betray our people. He was the true traitor as someone who chose this awful life, ushering other osnádúrtha to their deaths.

The Hunter's green eyes danced, loving every uncomfortable moment as he wormed his way under my skin. He enjoyed holding power over the other Bonded, knowing damn well he was favored above all else.

The hulking brute grinned, the light of the setting sun highlighting the sharp points of his faie canines, sharp enough to pierce flesh. He leaned forward, only a hair's breadth away, with those canines hovering over the soft part of my neck. Chills snaked down my spine.

"Only to see you squirm," he whispered in a tone a lover might use.

I held his gaze despite the sheer fear pulsing through me. His spiced juniper scent invaded my space, threatening to overtake my senses. He chuckled and straightened.

"So long, little shadow," he said, walking away as the prince bid the shopkeeper farewell, leaving me to my self–proclaimed task. Power pulsed through his steps—his stride even-paced and purposeful. The Bond Mark of the serpent with the knot in the middle peeked above the Hunter's shirt collar. My own mark slithered beneath my skin.

"Asshole," I muttered and pulled the hood of my cloak over my head, pushing the encounter with the Hunter from my mind. It wasn't unusual for him to torment me whenever our paths crossed, but in light of recent events, what if the king was behind it? I reinforced the shadows and stalked Prince Ronan's carriage down the crowded streets.

The carriage rolled to a stop outside an imposing yellow house. The outskirts of Rothcek were further than I expected the prince to travel, but he had been full of surprises lately.

With the sun having made its final descent, I found a dark, secluded area in the garden next to the home. It was plentiful in large concealing shrubbery and blessedly unoccupied thanks to the miserable weather. Through the windows, the prince enjoyed himself. Laughing and drinking, capturing the attention of everyone at the party. My stomach grumbled—

an audible demand. I pressed a firm hand to my abdomen to silence the sound, wishing I'd brought something to eat.

An hour passed, and doubt weighed heavily on me as the grumbling in my stomach turned into an absolute riot, screaming for sustenance. Prince Ronan must have been playing spy for his father the other night. Or he was spying on *me*, which meant I was delusional for thinking I could follow him and discover some sort of secret identity. But his exchange with Lord Byrne turned over in my mind again and again. The prince sounded deeply concerned about the shipment making it to Arundell. And if the shipment involved the osnádúrtha…

As hard as it was to believe, what if Prince Ronan *was* helping the osnádúrtha? What would happen then? If the king were even a bit suspicious and demanded information pertaining to his son, I would be forced to turn him in. The osnádúrtha would lose a powerful ally. I flexed my frozen toes within my boots. I should go—protect him and myself. And if he were spying for his father, well, then I would stay out of his way.

I turned to leave when a sizable, shadowed figure caught my eye. It was no ordinary shadow, but one of a man scaling down the side of the building from the second-floor window. I crooked my head as the cloak of the guard billowed in the wind.

"What are you doing?" I whispered. Why would Prince Ronan's guard scale down the side of the building instead of taking the front door? What would the prince think of his guard now? The breeze picked up, blowing back the hood of the guard's cloak.

A chill that had nothing to do with the weather washed over me as Prince Ronan finished his descent and took off, jogging away from the party. His blonde hair gleamed in the moonlight before he readjusted his hood. My head swiveled between the prince and the window from which he came. Before I could think better of it, I ran after the prince, unable to resist the pull of curiosity.

The prince went to the edge of Rothcek, stopping in front of a cottage partially secluded by trees. My legs burned from the quick pace. I blended into the surroundings—mindful of stray twigs and low-hanging branches. The air was crisper here compared to the heart of the capital—cleaner with the stench of the bustling city far away from the undisturbed area.

Even the cottage hid from onlookers. Vines obscured the front of the quaint building, winding in thick, twisting strands, their tendrils reminiscent of the way the shadows wrapped themselves around me. Soft, warm light streamed from the inside, and a feminine silhouette took shape behind the curtains. The prince approached the door with the familiarity of someone who had done it a million times.

And maybe he had.

As soon as the door cracked open, a slender woman with glowing, brown skin wrapped her arms around him—bringing the prince in for a long, passionate kiss. I only recognized her when the woman pulled away.

It was Kalee.

CHAPTER FIVE

Kalee.

I froze. Not from the flurries or mounds of powdery flakes consuming the land, but from shock and horror mingling with one another, ripping through my body. All I could do was stare as Kalee, *Kalee*, peeled the prince's shirt over his head, revealing a surprisingly toned, muscular torso. He returned the favor by ripping apart her own. Thank the *gods* their tryst took them into another room obscured from view. Nothing would be able to wipe *that* image from my memory.

Even as shock dissipated and reality sank in its cruel claws, my feet made no move to retreat. How could Kalee, of all people, betray me like this?

Whether the prince assisted the osnádúrtha or not, he remained the son of my mother's murderer. Not only did Kalee understand what my mother meant to me, she knew how I felt toward the Crown. She herself had ranted about how they were nothing more than bigoted brutes. She knew my Bond was a delayed death sentence. There was no escape from it. Once the king grew tired of me or deemed me useless, he would kill me like the others. How could she associate with, much less bed, someone whose father dangled my life in his meaty hands?

How did she even garner the prince's interest? She was beautiful, but Kalee? A handmaiden?

Both parties reappeared half an hour later with disheveled hair and skewed clothing. Kalee brewed a pot of tea, Ronan assisting her as they went through the motions of grabbing the kettle and cups. Mundane tasks otherwise otherworldly for a prince. Their faces turned severe, deep in conversation, any previous joy replaced by hard lines and tense muscles. I should have left while I still had the chance. And yet, years of spying propelled my feet forward from the safety of the grove. With the Midwinter ceremony a mere two hours away, there wouldn't be time for the snowfall to cover my tracks. I grabbed a fallen tree branch, using it to wipe away any evidence of my trek across the lawn.

Snow consumed my hands and knees, crunching as I crawled next to the cottage—the sound deafening in the stillness of the land. I winced. Under the kitchen window, I tucked in my legs, careful not to attract any attention. Kalee's blood always ran hot. Even in the dead of winter, the window was cracked open. I ignored the burning sensation in my extremities, snow soaking its way through layers of clothing, and leaned in as close as I dared until their voices drifted out the window.

"It's time, Ronan," Kalee said. I wasn't sure why, especially after what occurred, but I was surprised to hear her call the prince by his given name. I doubted many people used it so casually. "The attacks have become more frequent. She could be the one to help us uncover the culprit."

To avoid being discovered, I refrained from peeking through the window. I couldn't see her from where I sat, but I could hear the fear in her voice, the slight tremble in it.

"You're right," the prince sighed, his voice rich and almost soothing, "If Byrne couldn't find any information considering how wide his contacts spread, I fear we have no choice. Are you sure she'll be able to keep this information from my father?"

Kalee sighed softly. "With how many near-escapes the network has been facing lately...I'm beginning to suspect Saoirse's the reason behind it."

My brows shot up to my hairline. *What?* A bird fluttered from the windowsill, stirring up snow, and before I could give another thought to Kalee's declaration, icy clumps slid down the back of my tunic. My hand clamped over my mouth, but not before a small squeal escaped.

Voices ceased and heavy footsteps advanced to the window. The glass pane rose higher with a groan. I squeezed my eyes shut and prayed to the Mother the shadows swathed around me held.

"We are taking a risk, but it is a necessary one," Kalee continued while

Prince Ronan surveyed the area. I tamped down the urge to throw a rock at the abhorrent feathered creature.

"After what he did to my mother, Kalee, I have no doubt he is involved in it somehow."

My mind raced, trying to recall what I remembered of the late queen. She died before I came to the castle. My mother met her once by chance when Centra was still peaceful. She had said the queen was kind and smart and cunning. Other than that, I knew little of the prince's late mother or his sister. The princess was a child when the queen died. Younger than I, the princess was but a phantom to Centra. Rarely seen and always sickly—too unwell to leave her tower. The queen's death drove her daughter into sickness…and the king against magic.

"I agree," Kalee said, "but we must be sure. People will continue to die unless we seek help."

Prince Ronan slammed the window down, shutting me out of their conversation. I chanced a glimpse into the cottage. It was precisely how I pictured Kalee's home would be—tidy, but lived in with stacks of books scattered throughout. Kalee didn't talk much about her late father's cottage. I hadn't known where it was until now. I suppose there were many things I didn't know about her.

When I was satisfied neither of them would be leaving soon, I ran.

My thoughts were chaotic and confused, fragmented like broken glass, each sharp enough to cut. When I secured myself in my bedchambers, I leaned against the door, chest heaving, not caring about my bruised back as I slid to the floor. The stone was old and comforting, but it did nothing to soothe the fiery thoughts racing through my head.

I cradled my head in my hands. What had Kalee gotten herself into? She wouldn't bed the son of my mother's murderer—my abuser—unless she had an ulterior motive. It must be linked to the attacks they spoke of. But what attacks? It was as if they were a dream, elusive and forgotten. There was no word, not even a whisper, of such events. Nothing but the usual disagreements between the upper and lower classes. And why, for the love of the Nine, would Kalee serve *me* up to the prince?

The bell chimed, signaling the imminent start of the Midwinter ceremony, pulling me from my thoughts. Hastily, I donned the only dress in my possession. It might have been simple and well-worn, but it was cherished—a Midwinter gift from Kalee two years ago. The blue fabric flowed like liquid satin. *To complement your eyes*, she had said. It was the only garment I possessed that wasn't black; it shone like a beacon in a sea of darkness. And when I wore it, it was the only time I felt beautiful. Oversized tunics and trousers weren't exactly complementary to curves.

While most faie were tall and lean, I hadn't been gifted with such looks thanks to my mother's human genes. Short, even by human standards, and bulkier than most faie, I didn't fit in with my faie kin. But in this dress, none of that mattered. It hugged me in the right areas, complementing my waist instead of criticizing it. The long sleeves came to a point, small bands hooked over my middle fingers, perfect for concealing my silver swirls from prying eyes.

It was hard to look at the dress now after what I'd witnessed. Despite my anger, it was difficult to believe someone who gave me such a precious gift harbored malicious intentions.

I stuffed twin daggers into sheaths wrapped around my ankles. Weapons on display weren't exactly welcome at a religious ceremony. Forged with steel, iron, and lead, they weren't designed for killing humans. I suspected the king gave them to me for this reason—in case he ever commanded me to draw them across my throat. More than once, I contemplated how the blade might feel against my flesh. But even if I wanted to escape this life, I couldn't. The king forbade me from doing so when he thrust the daggers in my hand. He'd given me tools to end it all, yet it was still out of reach. A cruel, vicious gift.

The small hole along the seam of my forearm snagged, and I made a mental note to fix it. I threw my hair into a braid before scurrying down the hall. Another chime echoed through the halls. It grew louder as attendants approached the temple doors. People filed in, keeping their distance when they took notice of my ears, or more likely, the silver tendrils peeking from the bodice.

Lit candles lined the temple's walls and aisles. The new addition to the castle was constructed after the original in Rothcek had been destroyed, giving the monarchy further control over our lives. The Conqueror King demolished all the first temples and built new, grander ones, insinuating our devotion was to him and not to the gods. Images of the king, either carved into marble or woven into tapestries, lorded over us as we found our places. A single depiction of the Nine—the first gods—was tucked away in the back.

The king used old holidays and gods whenever he could to assert control and emphasize his power. The people were required to pay homage to the man who considered himself a god in the form of coin on top of the rising taxes. The Bonded were reminded we weren't at the mercy of the gods, but of the king. I hated him all the more for it. He referred to us as the gods' mistakes, but there was no denying the magic flowing through our veins. It was difficult, however, to feel connected to the gods when my prayers and pleas remained unanswered. I couldn't outright deny their existence, as my very magic derived from one of the many who used to walk this earth, but it was apparent that they had left us long ago to allow someone like the king to rule and control us as he did.

The royal family sat in the first row, the nobles behind them in order of their ranking. Small and frail, the princess perched between her father and brother, her sunken eyes wide as she surveyed the crowd. She was only a few years younger than I, yet she resembled a child. Prince Ronan's gaze stayed trained on his sister as if he feared she might disintegrate before him.

The Bonded squeezed together in the back behind Rothcek's poorest residents. Not even they dared to come close. A young girl with stained, tattered clothes looked me up and down. I offered her a small smile, only to be met with her scrunched nose before burying herself in her mother's skirts.

Typical.

Samhain was the last time I saw all the Bonded together. I counted them as I always did. Fifty Bonded were here today. Eleven short of only a couple of months ago, but there were a few new faces in the crowd. They all packed together, doing their best not to acknowledge one another.

"It's nice to see you so soon, little shadow," the Hunter preened next to me, his voice low among the murmurs of the growing crowd.

"Must you always call me that?" I hissed, thrumming my fingers against the wooden pew in search of Kalee. There. Several rows ahead with the other servants. She didn't look frazzled, however. Her appearance was polished and pristine, as expected of all castle staff, not a wrinkle on her yellow dress nor a chestnut curl gone amiss. Unchanged, she exuded her typical calmness, concealing any trace of a major secret.

"Don't tell me you prefer Informer?" he chided, a stupid half-grin plastered on his face.

"Well, I know you prefer your title. How many of our brethren did you deliver to the king this week, *Hunter*? How many were forced to take Bonds or die because of you?"

Two of the Bonded shifted uncomfortably behind us, either because of my statement or concerned we might catch the attention of the wrong eyes. Either could lead to punishment.

The Hunter straightened next to me.

More chimes cut him off at a chance of a reply, silencing everyone in the temple until the High Priest held everyone's attention.

"Today marks the longest night of the year. We give thanks to the Nine, to the many lesser gods, and to the Mother for their sacrifices and pray to them to lead us into another successful year," the High Priest said, his words rising and falling for dramatic effect. My fists clenched into my skirt. Successful was an overstatement. Crops declined year by year, and once curable illnesses ran rampant through the poorer classes since the osnádúrtha were taken.

"I am Bound, just as you are. I have no control over it," the Hunter whispered low enough so only I could hear.

I bristled at his nearness, the tips of my ears growing hot. "Ah, yes. But I was forced into this life. *You* chose it." I wasn't sure why I bothered to reply to him. He was arrogant. Vile. Malicious. No one could get through to someone like that. The Hunter was as horrible, if not more, than the king himself.

"To the Mother," the High Priest continued, "we express our gratitude for creating the world from a kernel of yourself, forming the land we know —the grass, the trees, the plants, and all the animals who inhabit it." The priest didn't mention the magic the Mother used to create it.

The last one died after saying such a thing.

"The Mother's sole purpose was to bear children, and she eventually birthed the gods we required. To the Nine who shaped the world." The High Priest raised his hands toward the sky. The oversized ivory fabric of his robes fell below his knobby elbows, exposing thin, frail arms.

I scoffed under my breath. The goddess who created it all was too easily cast aside. Nameless. Forgotten. Known for nothing more than her children. While everyone spoke their mumbled gratitudes to the Nine, I thanked the Mother for her sacrifice instead.

"We express gratitude to the gods who possessed the strength to bring forth sentient life. Even though the osnádúrtha have plagued our land with their cruel magic," he paused, his gaze alone could have lit us on fire, "we give thanks to our king, our true savior of this land, so we may one day correct this oversight. For it has been our king, our liberator, who has balanced the scales of power by ridding this land of excess cruel magic. We pray that all of Rúndaiaithe may one day experience the same salvation."

The Bonded remained silent while everyone else murmured their thanks. My gaze narrowed on the king. How could one man bring a land filled with osnádúrtha to its knees? Humans and osnádúrtha once worked together until the Reckoning—the beginning and the end to the one-sided war when the king's soldiers hunted the osnádúrtha and anyone who stood in their way. Without warning, the king's guard tore osnádúrthas from their homes, either killing or capturing them to bring before the king, burning entire villages in their wake. Their hunt started in Rothcek and branched outward. With Centra's borders closed, my mother and I made it a year before our village was ransacked.

I was the reason we had to go into hiding. Blessedly human, my mother possessed no magic or pointed ears, only a daughter who made her a target. She would have been safe if not for me. I wanted to be angry at the father I never knew for passing on his faie genes, but he died before I was born, a merchant lost at sea. For a time, I didn't think my magic would ever come in, and I was happier for it. I thought it a blessing. We were happy in our secluded village surrounded by friends who'd become family. Security checks had grown sparse, making it ideal for the osnádúrtha who dwelled there. It wasn't until my shadows appeared in front of a guard that it all came crashing down. Dozens of lives lost. Our village no longer a marker on a map.

I waited for the dismissal chime, ready to seek shelter under my bed sheets, but none came. Instead, the High Priest signaled to the temple entrance. Murmurs scattered over the crowd like dead leaves caught in a restless wind. Another priest dressed in a white robe guided Lord Byrne by the chains shackled to his wrists, his Bonded, the water-wielding faie who performed party tricks, chained behind him. The priest led them down the aisle and up to the dais, putting them on display before the crowd.

My stomach sank.

"It is an affront not only to the gods to not correct their mistakes, but to the king himself, who works so tirelessly to make our kingdom a better, safer place," the High Priest said. Shouts of agreement echoed along the walls. "Do you wish to live with the faie in Arundell or the witches in Ilythia? Captive and enslaved, forced to do their bidding? Or perhaps you want to witness your children being dragged into the ocean by the merrows? Never to be seen again?"

The crowd answered in angry shouts, some leering at us as if the Bonded before them were solely responsible for these crimes. I wanted to scream at the lies spilling from the High Priest's mouth. The other kingdoms may be ruthless, but the osnádúrtha who came to Centra had sought peace. They viewed humans as their equals, but history was rarely written by the conquered. The crimes of the other kingdoms might have held some truth, yet it was osnádúrtha in Centra who were forced to face the king's vengeance.

"Defenders of these mistakes are no different from the osnádúrtha they seek to preserve. Trust the gods will bring those people out into the light and punish them."

Lord Byrne trembled as the High Priest pushed him to his knees. He was still in his nightshift, his appearance suggesting he was plucked from his bed before spending some time in the castle dungeons. However, the faie male held his head high and grasped Lord Byrne's hand in his, the two sharing a meaningful look.

The faie's face showed no fear as he scanned the crowd. His gaze landed on the Bonded and gave a slight dip of his chin. The gesture was meant to show solidarity among the Bonded. It felt like a brand instead. I should have burned on the spot. I should be the one on my knees before the crowd. The faie turned back to the lord, his frantic whispers inaudible amidst the commotion.

Tears welled behind my eyes and threatened to spill over. *My fault.* They were going to die because of me. I knew the king would kill Lord Byrne for treason, but I hadn't thought about the lord's Bonded. I'd assumed he'd be gifted to another. I didn't even know his name. While I've seen this scene play out again and again, it never got easier. Not when I was the reason.

"This kingdom has no place for traitors or osnádúrtha sympathizers. The gods will not stand for it." The High Priest waited for the king's confirming nod and sliced open their throats.

"Tell me, Informer," the Hunter said, his voice solemn and low under the cheers of the crowd. "Are we really so different?"

Maybe we weren't.

Chapter Six

The resounding *thump, thump, thump* of my heart pounded in my chest as I distanced myself from the temple doors. I tried to forget Lord Byrne and his Bonded, but images of their open necks clung to my vision, refusing to let me unsee what I had done to them.

The Hunter was right. *I* killed them. I was as awful and cruel and vile as he was.

Breathe, I reminded myself. The hot pang of guilt pierced the back of my eyelids, my already hollowed chest bordering on collapse. Shadows swirled beneath my skin like angry vines as I stumbled out of the castle and into open air.

My feet carried me with no particular aim. I didn't care where I went; I just needed to get *away*. Cool air brushed against my cheeks, tender as gentle hands, drying the trickling tears. I wandered aimlessly and hadn't realized how far I'd gone until I found myself back in the market. Lanterns flickered overhead, some of their flames burning out. Several of the shops remained open for the longest night of the year, and vendors shouted out their wares to those who passed.

No one paid any attention to me with the heavy hood obscuring my face. Drunk patrons stumbled their way down the cobbled street, singing as they went. I paused, stopping in front of a bookshop. It was my favorite vendor. The lights were out, no signs of life inside, but I could still see books of every size, shape, and color on different displays through the windowpane. An older woman, Aoife, ran the shop. She'd taken a liking to Kalee and then to me. Aoife was kind enough to let me go inside if there weren't any customers. Sometimes, she would give me a copy of her favorite reads.

It was what I wanted—to own a simple bookshop. To share my favorite books with those who might appreciate them. To live life free and as I choose.

It was a dream holding me together.

It was nothing more than a delusion.

I stared at my reflection in the glass, the sapphire eyes of my mother staring back at me, and I removed the hood of my cloak to complete the image of her—my long, wavy silver hair identical to hers. It was the closest I would ever come to seeing her again. The locket, which hung around my neck, warmed in my hand.

I wasn't sure how long I stood there before the shout at my back.

"Oi, Bonded!" A uniformed guard called, his golden lapels glimmering under the light of the lanterns. I bristled but said nothing as he walked toward me.

I pulled my hood back over my head. It was foolish to remove it in the first place.

"Where do you think you're going, Bonded?" the guard sneered, his face nearing mine. The smell of his greased hair and mead on his breath permeated my senses.

"I was just returning to my assigned quarters at the castle," I answered, keeping my head low, hoping the guard would catch the hint I belonged to the king and not loaned out to appease some noble. At least then, he wouldn't kill me for the fun of it.

No one killed the king's Bonded. At least no one the king didn't allow.

I turned to leave before he could say anything else, but he caught my wrist and clamped down, yanking me backwards.

"Let go!" I fought to loosen his hold. His grip tightened, and his other hand framed my jaw, forcing me to stare into his dead eyes.

"Keep fighting," he whispered. "I like it when they do that."

Any warmth I held fled as the cruel, cold realization of what this man might do sank in. The shadows thickened, but they couldn't fight him off. Instincts took over, and my knee connected with his groin. The guard doubled over, but his recovery was fast as he drew his sword.

"You'll pay for that one, Bonded." The wicked gleam in his eyes strengthened my resolve. Faster than his puny human brain could comprehend, I grabbed my daggers from their sheaths at my ankles.

"Fuck you," I spat. Consequences be damned, I'd sooner meet the king's blade for killing a guard than let this man lay another finger on me.

"Is everything alright here?" another asked from behind. I froze. His tone commanded authority. I looked from my daggers and back to the guard, his smirk conveying everything I feared. If I hadn't been before, I was in for it then.

The guard straightened, saluting the intruder. "Yes, Lieutenant Olcéad. This bitch tried to attack me after I'd informed her she was out after curfew."

I turned with my head down, clasping the daggers behind my back, and tried to catch my breath, praying I might get lucky and the lieutenant didn't see them. Gods, I needed to get out of here. When they were distracted with one another, I would run, and once I was out of sight, I could hide. They wouldn't find me. I just needed a head start.

"Did he harm you?" the lieutenant asked. It took me a minute to realize he addressed me and not his brother-in-arms.

"I'm fine. I was about to return to my quarters. I'm sorry, I didn't realize it was past curfew," I said, eyes downcast. I fixated on his boots, waiting until they turned so I might flee. They were thicker than mine and far nicer, shielding him from the snow-blanketed ground. Perhaps they were heavy enough to slow him down.

"Look at me," he commanded, as if sensing my thoughts. I obeyed by snaking my gaze up his legs and torso. The gold and crimson uniform barely contained his muscular figure. His broad shoulders evident even under the thick fur of his cloak. When I reached his face, I recognized him immediately: Prince Ronan's personal guard.

Mother save me.

His dark eyes held me in a stark silence, their color impossible to discern in the dim glow of the fading lanterns.

"Did he hurt you?" he asked again.

I shook my head. There was no point in saying what the guard would have done if given the chance. It didn't matter. He wouldn't be reprimanded or discharged from his position.

"Good," the lieutenant said before turning his attention back toward the guard. "You're dismissed."

Shock marred the guard's features, his mouth hanging open. In truth, I probably bore a similar expression. Violence was encouraged by the other guards, especially by their superiors. The dismissal left me uncertain of Lieutenant Olcéad's intentions.

"Touch her again, and you'll regret it. Say anything about this encounter and you'll never so much as step another foot inside Rothcek," the lieutenant warned. The guard glanced between us, his eyes molten fire, before saluting and stalking off.

"Now," Lieutenant Olcéad said, "shall I escort you back to the castle?" He offered his arm. I ignored it. Staying out after curfew wasn't an option, but I didn't want to chance pissing him off either—most of them enjoyed showing off their power. My legs shook from the aftershock as I began the journey back, unspent adrenaline pulsing through every nerve ending. To my dismay, the lieutenant followed.

"I hope he didn't give you too much trouble," he said, breaking the silence as we walked. He glanced sidelong at me, eyeing the silver patterns moving beneath my exposed skin. I held back a reply. All men were cruel creatures, especially those employed by the king. He might have saved me from the guard, but it didn't mean he harbored no ulterior motive. My pace quickened.

"Are you not freezing out here?" he continued, keeping up with me and unbothered by my silence. I ignored the chill seeping into my bones— the unforgiving ache in my lungs. I hadn't thought to change out of my dress in my haste, and the sharp sting of winter had long since crept through my cloak.

"What is your name?" Lieutenant Olcéad asked yet another question. Was this man so afraid of silence?

"The King's Informer," I replied finally, tasting bile.

"No," he chuckled. "What's your real name?"

I stopped to assess the lieutenant under furrowed brows, craning my neck to really look at him. He was clean-shaven, as were most of the castle guards. The lieutenant kept his hair sheared short to his scalp, the color only a few shades darker than the reddish-brown ochre of his skin. Every- thing about him screamed duty and discipline, from his immaculate attire to his perfect posture. Despite my natural aversion to the guards, he was handsome, I realized, and not for the first time. His jaw was well-defined, his lips full, and his deep brown eyes held a light behind them that was absent in many of the other guards. It had been too dark to notice earlier, but now we were closer, and there was no hiding the rich, warm hues. The lieutenant's hand rested on the open ring pommel of his sword, though I suspected more so out of habit than warning if his relaxed gait was any indication.

"What do you care?" I blurted before I could think better, my annoyance taking over. Only Kalee ever called me by my name. To everyone else, I was the Informer—reduced to a title.

The lieutenant's brows furrowed. "I'd prefer to address you by a name other than the one bestowed by the king. If you like, you may call me Eoin."

"What do you want from me?" It couldn't be a coincidence that he happened upon me mere hours after I discovered Prince Ronan's and Kalee's secret affair. It's possible he was also kept in the dark, but something told me that wasn't true.

"Only to see you returned safely to your chambers," he said in earnest, resting a hand over his heart—a playful gesture.

"Why?"

"Does it matter? Would you have preferred to come to blows with that loathsome buffoon? What would have happened after you killed him, hmm? Let one of the king's hunters trace his murder back to you? Because you would have killed him. Even if he wasn't stumbling from drink, I have no doubt."

I shuddered to think what might have happened. I couldn't flee Centra, not with the Bond. I might have been able to hide in plain sight for a time, but the king's hunters always got their answers. Still, I couldn't help but feel his interest was a carefully laid trap.

"Because I am a bloodthirsty faie seeking to steal as many human hearts as I can?" I quipped.

"Because you are a survivor."

I scoffed. Rats survived. Cockroaches survived. Just because I'd made it this long didn't mean I was worthy of any praise.

I couldn't look at Eoin the rest of the walk back. He stared at me in a way that made my pulse jump, like he was looking at me as someone of substance with thoughts and feelings. Any other guard would have hauled me straight to the king for pulling daggers out against one of his own, regardless of the reason. Any other guard wouldn't try to get to know me, much less speak to me. Eoin wasn't like the others. It was terrifying.

Festivities were still well underway as we approached the castle. Revelers danced around bonfires erected throughout Rothcek. They would eat, drink, and dance until dawn, using the holiday as an excuse to gorge themselves until morning. The Bonded weren't afforded such luxuries with the curfew in place.

The formidable castle was made entirely of gleaming ebony stone. Despite the full moon, the rock's darkness consumed all the light. All happiness. Several stories high, it overshadowed all other buildings in Rothcek. I readjusted my hood, securing loose silver strands. Six wide, round guard towers encircled the castle, but they did nothing to hide the monster of the main building—its points piercing the sky like arrows aimed at the gods. Crude windows were scattered throughout the protective walls. Pointed arrowheads caught the moonlight every so often, their iron tips glittering like stars. Guards stood sentry in front of the towering iron gate. The only way in or out.

I hated looking at it. My prison for the rest of my meaningless life.

Eoin escorted me all the way to my bedchamber door, nodding to the guards we passed as he did so. They never looked twice at us. Never questioned why he might be escorting me, but my blood pounded all the same.

"This is it," I murmured. "In case you were wondering, it locks from the inside."

Eoin's brows furrowed before pity seeped into his eyes, understanding dawning on him. I wanted to hate him for it, but I was too exhausted.

"It was nice to meet you..." He paused, giving me a curt nod, waiting for my name.

I slammed the door in his face and locked it.

CHAPTER SEVEN

I was picking at my afternoon meal when the Bond yanked on my gut. *Come immediately,* the king's will rang in my head as if he spoke next to me. His thoughts couldn't invade my mind, but his commands could. He didn't need to summon me to give a command, though it was far stronger if he issued it in person. I haven't been able to test the limits of the Bond, never having a reason to travel outside of Rothcek. Though I suppose this was by design. The Bonded were never far from those who commanded them.

The roast turned sour in my stomach.

I looked up from my plate to Kalee flipping through the pages of her book as she ate. At least the summons served to save me from an awkward lunch.

"I'm being called upon," I said, breaking the silence, my chair scraping across the stone floor.

Her brows knit together. "You barely ate anything, Sersh. Everything alright?"

"Fine. Still shaken from the Midwinter ceremony, I guess. What happened to the lord and his Bonded...it was horrible," I probed. Prince Ronan had mentioned Lord Byrne to Kalee, acting as if she might have known him, too.

Kalee closed her book, marking her page with the present I'd given her. "It was terrible. Those poor men didn't deserve their fate. Did you…I mean, did the king–"

"Kalee," I warned.

She held up a placating hand. "That's not what I meant. I only wanted to say that whatever happened, whatever you might have been forced to do, it wasn't your fault. Those who embark on dangerous dealings understand the risk that comes with it. And while what happened to them was horrible, it wasn't your fault, Saoirse. I'm sure you did everything you could."

We stared at each other for a moment. We didn't talk about what I did for the king. More importantly, I never discussed what I *didn't* do. My guilt wouldn't let me consider the former, and the fear of anyone finding out my indiscretions kept me from talking about the latter. Kalee had voiced her suspicions to the prince on Midwinter, and she all but declared them to me now. I refused to be the first to break, to reveal what secrets I kept if she couldn't do the same.

I wanted to keep her as far away from my crimes as possible, whereas she was more than willing to bring me in without so much as an explanation. She'd convinced the prince of that last night. I stared at her, waiting for her to reveal her motivations. For her to come clean. Her eyes swam as if trying to read my thoughts. I didn't have time to confront her now, not with the king waiting on me. Already, it was too late; the Bond tugged at my feet, beckoning me to the throne room.

I just needed *something*—some type of reassurance or omission of guilt. I held out a moment longer.

"Be well, Saoirse," she said, noting the way my legs carried on.

A curt nod was my only form of goodbye. She acted as though everything was fine, like nothing had changed. But after what I saw last night, everything changed.

I left with more questions than answers. Was she ever my friend? Or was I merely a job assignment? A means to an end. A tool to be used to suit her own purposes. I thought we shared something special. We were all each other had. I considered her a sister. Kalee never treated me differently because of my faie heritage. But I couldn't help but wonder if our friendship was a facade.

My heart ached as I walked the halls. I would confront her about the situation after my meeting with the king.

The great, oak doors opened as I approached. It didn't matter how many times I entered the throne room; it was as if I was nine years old again. Stares from the sentries pierced my back as I walked. The large painting of the king hung high above the marble throne. His portrait peered down at me from the edge of his nose—identical to the expression he wore now. The chancellor was blessedly absent, but another man stood in his place.

Eoin.

Blood drained from my face. Had he told the king I was out after curfew? That I drew a weapon on another guard? My gait held steady as I walked, even though internal alarm bells blared. Eoin didn't flash his handsome grin as I approached. His expression gave nothing away as he stood at the bottom of the dais. There was nothing I could do but bow before the Conqueror King.

"Rise, Informer," he boomed at last after my knees had begun to ache.

The throne room was silent save for the occasional shifting of armor from sentries trying their hardest not to move. I waited on bated breath as the king eyed me—assessing the shadows running in nervous squiggles under my skin. His sinister smirk threatened to make my knees wobble.

"It appears my son has a use for you. For now, you will obey Prince Ronan of Centra as you do me. But remember who your true master is," the king commanded. I clasped my hands tightly behind my back in an effort to conceal their shaking. The prince had never requested my skills before. The idea of discovering his true intentions made me want to run, to hide, to never return. I had to believe Kalee did not wish to see me dead. My fear twisted into anger, curling into a serpent, ready to strike at the next person who came too close. She gave me no warning before I took my leave during our meal, nothing to indicate why I was being summoned. Either she didn't know…or she didn't care.

The Bond Mark burned at the king's command. Tingles pricked down my spine and along every nerve ending as the magic between the king and I sealed itself. Lights flashed behind my eyes, making me dizzy, playing tricks on my surroundings. Even the king's golden medallion seemed to flash with it.

There was a tiny part of my inner self still fighting, protesting against the king's will as magic shoved itself down the Bond. A small resistance dwindling away with each command and picked at my resolve until there would be no fight left.

"Yes, Your Majesty," I bit out through clenched teeth, flexing my hands as I adjusted to the magic.

"Lieutenant Olcéad, you may take her now." The king flicked his wrist. The golden rings adorned on each of his tanned, slender fingers glinted in the light.

"Thank you, Your Majesty." Eoin bowed. "Informer," he said, dipping his chin, signaling me to follow. His movements were stiff as we left the throne room. Part of me was relieved Eoin kept what happened last night between us, but at what cost?

I had never been lent out before. Ever. Only the king possessed the power to create the Bonds, so it wasn't uncommon for the Bonded to be leased to other members of nobility or for Crown officials to borrow us from time to time for our unique skill sets. But I was different—I belonged solely to the king.

The Conqueror King liked the faie for our elemental magic. Some could control crops or level a building with the wave of a hand. Others could set fire to the king's enemies or flood an entire village. To my knowledge, there were no witches under the king's control, though I suspected he wouldn't mind having one for their knowledge of potions, especially poisons. The faie primarily made up the Bonded, but there were a few merrows who had been captured during the burning of Sóngnahánn's islands. The king stationed them in his navy because of their distinctive control over the ocean tides.

Eoin and I walked in silence beyond the castle gates and toward the heart of Rothcek. My shadows spiraled more out of control the further we went. Eoin revealed nothing, and it only served to make my heart pound to the point of pain.

The market was alive under the afternoon sun. Patrons crowded the busy streets, leaving little room for carriages. Children spooked the horses as they ran between them. I jumped when one reared back, its disgruntled whinny shaking me to my core. Despite myself, I closed the distance between me and Eoin. If I were to be run down by a horse, maybe it would trample him first.

Before we stepped onto the main road, Eoin yanked me by the elbow, veering us through the large crowd, and slipped into an alley.

"Excuse you!" I tugged my arm out of his grip.

"Quiet," he hushed, scanning our surroundings. Everyone around us was too preoccupied with their shopping to notice the two cloaked figures slipping out of sight.

"What is going on?" I hissed.

"I'll explain everything in a moment."

Nothing save for discarded crates and stray cats prowled the area. The cats, it seemed, were wary of us, their eyes tracking our every movement.

We continued until we reached a dead end—only a brick wall in front of us. The cats were unnervingly still, observant as we stood in front of the wall.

"What are you—" I flinched when Eoin took out his dagger. Surely, he didn't bring me all this way to kill me. He had plenty of time between the castle and now to do it with fewer people to come across my lifeless body. There was some satisfaction, however, knowing the king would be livid if I died by the hand of another.

"Turn around," Eoin instructed.

"To make it easier to stab me?"

"I am not going to stab you, Informer," he sighed, "but I need you to trust me and turn around. I will explain everything in a moment."

"Why should I trust you?"

"Have I not earned even a small semblance of trust from the other night?"

"He brought it upon himself."

Eoin chuckled. "Never said he didn't. But either way, we don't really have another option at this moment."

"Fine, but I don't trust you," I grumbled and turned my back to him against my better judgment, folding my arms across my chest.

"Keep watch."

A retort formed and died on my tongue when a deep, guttural groan sounded—as if the bricks ground against one another. I turned around to find the bricks had moved, parting themselves into a doorway big enough for us to squeeze through. I stared at the gaping space, unblinking.

"Holy Nine."

"Aren't you more impressed I didn't kill you?" He winked and grabbed my wrist, pulling me with him through the doorway. I stumbled after Eoin into the dark, grappling for footing. The bricks returned to their original position on their own accord as soon as we crossed the threshold, smothering out the last bit of light as they fell into place.

I yanked my arm back and drew my daggers out of instinct, uncertain of Eoin lurking in the darkness. "Eoin—" I warned.

"It's called the Underground," he supplied, lighting a sconce. His sharp cheekbones came into view, highlighted by the flickering flame. It took a moment for my eyes to adjust. We weren't in a room, but some kind of tunnel.

"You're taking me to the fighting rings? Or are we going to gamble?" I asked with feigned amusement, my unease dissipating a fraction as I sheathed my daggers. The Underground was notorious for its excess of illegal activities. I've never been, only heard whispers of the place. I hadn't realized the name was so literal.

"Not that Underground. They bear the same name to create confusion for anyone who might come looking too closely. This Underground is different, but still *very* illegal." Eoin beckoned me to follow, and with no other option, I took a tentative step forward. Our footsteps echoed as we continued down the stone tunnel, the air damp and reeking of mildew.

"What illegal things are we to do? More magic?" That's how the bricks parted—magic—and not the type any aes sídhe could produce. No, a witch lived in our midst for this type of magic. Like all osnádúrtha, the witches' magic came from the natural world, but they were connected differently. Whereas aes sídhe and merrows could channel their magic freely and innately, witches relied on spells and herbs. However, their spells were much more potent in trained hands and could last lifetimes. Eoin wasn't a witch, but he would be sentenced to death if anyone reported him being in contact with any unauthorized magic.

"Something like that," Eoin hedged. He led us on, passing entrances to offshoots of the main tunnel. Either he was too trusting, or there was leverage he was about to hold over my head. No one in their right mind would openly perform magic if they weren't Bonded, and certainly not before the king's Informer. If the king found out a lieutenant in his royal guard was using witch magic, he was sure to meet a brutal end. I eyed Eoin. At least I had something over him.

"This place couldn't have been made since the Reckoning. How has it escaped the king's notice for so long? And how do *you* know how to open it?"

"The Underground was created before you or I walked this earth. People have died to keep it hidden from those who would use it for malicious purposes, so you can imagine your discretion is appreciated. As far as the bricks go, well, they were spelled. Think of it like a magical lock; anyone can open it as long as they know how."

Eoin's steps were sure and even as we traveled down the long tunnel. We turned down one of the many offshoots until we reached a door. He pushed it open to reveal a dimly lit room with the outline of someone sitting on a settee at the far end.

"Hello, watchdog," a rich, male voice drawled.

CHAPTER EIGHT

Prince Ronan of Centra sprawled across the settee, looking as though there was no other place he'd rather be. He took up most of the space; his broad frame overpowering the small nature of the settee, fingers thrumming against the plush, floral print cushion as we stared at one another in stagnant silence, waiting to see who might break first.

I'd be damned if it was going to be me. My brow arched in indignation, holding out for the prince's explanation. By now, I knew well enough when it was time for silence and when it was time to speak. The silver shadows under my skin thickened, pulling from the dark corners of the room, their need to conceal me almost overwhelming. Eoin placed a casual hand on the hilt of the sword at his belt. My hands rested on the daggers strapped to my hips.

"Do you know why I called you here?" Prince Ronan asked, crossing a leg over his knee.

"You're the one who summoned me." My fingers trembled, but my voice remained steady. Part of me worried the prince would lash out for speaking to him in such a way, gods knew his father would. The other part, however, was emboldened. The prince needed me to find information about the attacks he and Kalee spoke of. He must be desperate. Why else would he go through such great lengths to speak to me directly? I wasn't going to show my hand first. Let him think I'm oblivious.

I surveyed my surroundings with a feigned boredom. The room didn't appear to lead anywhere else aside from the door where Eoin guarded. It was an odd space. The air held a comfortable warmth, despite the cold dampness of the tunnel and the lack of a heat source. Steam emitted from untouched teacups as if they were prepared moments before our arrival. Where he brought the tea in from, I didn't know. Prince Ronan gestured for me to sit across from him. I remained where I stood.

"This is the kind of meeting where I *ask* you for your services and give you something in return." He shifted in his seat, the muscle in his jaw ticking—the only sign of his irritation.

"Ask me?" I scoffed. These types of people did not *ask* me for anything. "Why ask me when you could command me to do whatever you wish." I flicked my gaze to Eoin, trapping me in the room.

"That may be true," the prince answered, "but you will find my father and I are two very different people. I want to offer you a choice first."

"What do you want?" I asked, despite knowing the answer.

"A bit of information." He adjusted the cuffs of his gold-trimmed tunic. His demeanor was calm despite the anticipation licking at my spine. Why bring me all the way here? Surely Kalee trusted me enough to ask me herself. Though the more I thought about it, perhaps the prince wanted to offer a bit of trust. And leverage. If either of us were found in a place shrouded in magic, our heads would be the cost.

I chewed the inside of my cheek.

"I have reason to believe you have been aiding the smugglers."

I started to protest. If he thought I would openly tell him I was committing treason, he was daft. The prince held up a hand as if sensing my thoughts. "I have reason to suspect this because I have been doing the same."

I could have choked on his openness. He outright confirmed my suspicions, but there was still a chance this was all a giant ruse.

"Why are you telling this?" I asked.

"Because power is in your hands now. You could end everything I've accomplished with a single word. I'm not immune to my father's wrath. Tell him what I've divulged, and he'll kill me all the same. This should bring you a bit of comfort and an idea of where my allegiances lie." His gaze hardened, staring into the very depths of my soul. If there was any hint of doubt before, I believed him now.

"What you suspect of me is true," I said quietly.

"Good. Now, we'll get to what I need from you. There have been attacks scattered throughout Centra. No one has been able to pinpoint the source. The only thing we know for sure is all the victims have one thing in common—they are all descendants of the osnádúrtha."

"Attacks like during the Reckoning?"

"No, these are different. The victims are of osnádúrthan descent, but they aren't being taken to the king for Bondings or killed by my father's soldiers. Their magic is so faint, I doubt the average person would have known it existed. Whatever is out there is capable of sensing their magic. Based on the remains we've found, I believe this creature might be draining the magic of the individuals, however little they might have. I can only guess it's amassing more power for personal gain."

"When you say this thing drains them of their magic…"

He hesitated, looking toward Eoin, hoping his friend might lend him the words.

"They are nothing more than a shell of what they once were—only a dried-up, shriveled husk. As if they are one gust of wind away from turning to dust," Eoin supplied.

"Does the king know?" Not that he would care if any trace of osnádúrtha were dying out.

"Yes, several citizens have held court hearings about the attacks. He's completely unconcerned, and no concrete action has been taken. With the attacks growing more frequent and closer to densely populated areas—"

"You need me to see if I can gather any information the king is withholding?" I finished for him.

"Yes," the prince sighed. "We have tried on our own, but no one has your skill set."

"What do you expect me to do? It's not like I can go gallivanting around the castle. The king might find it suspicious if his son has me watching his every move."

"You have your shadows, don't you? It's rumored you can become invisible with them. Plus, now you have Eoin at your disposal to escort you wherever you need to go."

Eoin's face betrayed nothing as he stood sentry, one hand atop his golden, open ring pommel. It wasn't standard issue—the other guards' swords bore the kingdom's golden color, but they were plain in every other way. Eoin's swirled in an intricate pattern achieved by skilled craftsman-ship—a gift perhaps?

"Say I agreed and did what you asked." I crossed my arms over my chest. "Will you kill me after you're through with me? I may be on loan to you now, but I will eventually return to your father. You are a fool to believe neither he nor his chancellor won't ask me every detail of our time together."

The prince tilted his head. "I'm well aware, and as a solution, I will break your Bond with my father."

My breath caught. For a moment, I thought I was trapped in a dream. I pinched myself to be sure. "How?" I laughed. "No one knows how the king is Bonding to the osnádúrtha, much less how to break them. You're lying."

"I swear to you there is someone in Centra who is capable of breaking the Bonds. The moment you find the answers I seek, I will take you to them, and you will be free to do as you wish."

It was almost too good to be true. I didn't want to trust the prince, yet he gave me no reason not to. He cared for the osnádúrtha; that much was obvious. He wasn't holding his power over me. I had plenty of information to betray him. Everything I thought I knew about him told me to run away while I still could, but the hope flickering to life in my chest was hard to ignore, however. This chance may never come again.

Once the Bond was broken, the king would know. He'd sooner believe my death before thinking a Bond could be broken, but a man like him needed proof. When there was none, he would learn of my deception. This man would hunt me down and kill me himself rather than risk letting me go. I had no family, no money, no one who cared if I lived or died. There was Kalee, but I didn't know what to feel about her now. This was a big risk. I needed assurance.

"If I agree," I said shakily, "I require safe passage as soon as the Bond is broken and coin before I leave. Enough to set up a life elsewhere."

"Bartering with a prince?" Prince Ronan smirked. "I will agree to your terms. There's a ship that sails frequently to Arundell. Find the person responsible for the attacks, and there'll be a ticket and a bag of coin with your name on it."

My pulse raced. Arundell was the only known continent allowing refugees. I couldn't have hoped to try and stow away on a boat before. My shoulders relaxed a fraction.

"Can I ask one thing?"

"Ask away," the prince said, clasping his hands in his lap.

"Why bother with the attacks at all if your father doesn't care? Why risk your life and those close to you to help those your father hates most? Why go against the king at all?"

"Innocent people are dying, and they will continue to do so unless something is done. My father may be comfortable sitting back, watching his citizens perish, but I am not."

"You aren't worried I'll divulge your schemes to your father?" It would boost my standing with the king. Maybe make my punishments cease altogether if I proved my allegiance outside of the Bond commands.

"You've shown yourself capable of keeping information from the king in times of stress. I understand the sacrifices you've made to protect your people and keep my *schemes*, as you call them, under wraps. I trust you are clever enough to keep doing so."

A lump formed in my throat. There was no going back now. All of our secrets lay out on the table. All but one.

"I know you and Kalee are together."

Prince Ronan stiffened.

"Are you using Kalee to get to me?" I asked when the silence stretched too long, my voice low. Threatening a prince was not on my agenda today, and I was still mad at Kalee, but if he was using her…

"I am not using your handmaid to get to you, Informer, but the how and why is her story to tell."

"Fair enough." I sighed, letting the information sink in. The prince's offer was more than anything I could have hoped for. This was the moment I quietly dreamt of in the darkest of times. This was the chance I'd been praying for although I'd never thought it would come true. This was *everything* if I dared to take it. The hairs on the back of my neck rose in warning as if refusing his offer might be the biggest mistake of my life.

I took a deep breath and said, "I will agree to help you uncover whoever is responsible for the attacks in exchange for my freedom."

"Excellent." Ronan's eyes lit up. There was so much hope there—something I hadn't dared to feel in a very long time. "We'll get started right away. Before I let you go, there is something we must do."

"What?" I asked, worried I would already come to regret my decision. Had I traded one monster for another?

"I must command you to never repeat what was said here or about what you've seen in the Underground."

"So much for choices and my clever maneuvering, then?"

He grimaced. "This is bigger than both of us, Informer. Surely you understand."

"Saoirse," I corrected. There was power in a name, and the king had been determined to strip mine from me. Perhaps his arrogance would be his downfall. Perhaps this level of trust in the prince, in hope, would be mine.

Eoin straightened by the door when I uttered my name. I refrained from telling him last night, but if we were working together, he would learn it eventually, if he hadn't already.

"Very well," Prince Ronan nodded. "Saoirse, I forbid you to utter a single word to anyone other than myself, Eoin, or Kalee about what you saw or heard today in the Underground. What occurred during your time here shall stay between the four of us and no one else unless I give you permission otherwise."

I didn't revel in the prince commanding me, but I understood. And in truth, I might have suggested it as a small level of assurance. How his command would hold up against the king was unknown, but it didn't hurt to try. I prayed I would never have to test this theory. The familiar tingle of magic coursed through my system as the command sealed itself within my very being. It didn't hurt as much as it normally did.

"You are much better at that than your father," I murmured. The prince was careful and precise with his wording. Unlike the king, who used vague commands. At least this way, it would be more difficult for the king to bypass.

"My father has grown lazy over the years. We can use it to our advantage."

I prayed he was right.

CHAPTER NINE

We didn't stay long after swearing my life away. Prince Ronan watched Eoin and me leave, promising Eoin he'd be fine returning on his own. Anticipation itched at my skin as I followed Eoin through the tunnels. The faster I could fulfill our bargain, the better, but the thought of spying on the king left my insides quivering. The prince at least gave me plenty of reasons to trust him, or rather, enough evidence to betray him if he went back on his word. Eoin, however, did no such thing.

I eyed the lieutenant sidelong, biting the inside of my cheek. This man held enough information to ruin my only chance at freedom. Either the prince was a fool to blindly trust Eoin, or they made their own bargain.

"So what's in it for you?" I asked, curiosity taking over.

Eoin's brows furrowed. "What do you mean?"

"You can't tell me you're doing all of this," I gestured to myself and the Underground, "out of the kindness of your heart?"

"And if I was?"

"I wouldn't believe you. You have a good life, do you not? Why risk it all?"

"Ronan has a good life, yet you believe him. Why can't it be the same for me?"

"Because he, at least, gave me ammunition to use against him."

"Can you not use the same evidence against me? I'm just as involved as he is."

"Well, yes, I suppose." I frowned. My apprehension eased a fraction, but I couldn't help but suspect there was something more going on. I'd expected some declaration of how the king scorned him or some kind of connection to the osnádúrtha. Prince Ronan clearly despised his father, believing the king had a hand in his mother's death.

"What?" I asked. Eoin openly stared; the shadows swam under his scrutiny.

"You have something in your hair," he said, the torch illuminating his face, displaying a grim twist to his mouth.

"What?"

"There's something in your hair." He reached out to grab it, but I swatted his hand away.

"I think I'm perfectly able to pick it out myself, thank you." I sifted through the thick braided strand, feeling for whatever it might be to no avail.

"Please, allow me. Watching you struggle is killing me," he groaned, placing his hand over his heart.

"Fine."

Eoin's touch was feather-light as he pulled the object free, lingering only a hair longer than necessary. "Pesky twig," he muttered and flicked it away.

"Thanks."

"It was of no consequence. No twig has bested me before."

"No," I sighed, "I mean to thank you for last night. When you stopped the guard." I hadn't forgotten what he'd done, even if it had been a ploy to earn his trust. The king would have loaned me out to the prince whether Eoin stopped the guard or not.

"Oh. That, too, was of no consequence. It was the right thing to do," he said, his brows furrowing. We stared at each other for a moment longer before continuing down the tunnel. He contradicted everything I knew about castle guards. As difficult as it was to believe, Eoin didn't appear to find pleasure in the cruelty toward the Bonded, but rather viewed them as real people.

When we finally left the Underground's tunnels, we emerged from the floorboards of what appeared to be a stockroom. Eoin offered a hand to help me from the ladder, but I disregarded it. Around us were jewels of every color, shape, and size. The shopkeeper of Precious Emblems greeted us, as if somehow alerted by our presence.

"Eoin. Isn't this a nice surprise? Who's your friend?"

"Ralph, this is Saoirse. Saoirse, this is Ralph."

I met the shopkeeper with a slight nod. He pushed his circular glasses onto the bridge of his nose as he studied me. The shadows kept themselves at bay; only my silver hair stood out.

"Any more of your friends coming through?" Ralph gestured to the trapdoor we appeared from.

"Not today, Ralph," Eoin replied, shutting the door with a thud. The outline disappeared when it was flushed with the floor, making it undetectable. I wouldn't have known anything was there if I hadn't experienced it with my own eyes.

Ralph grunted his reply, parting the woolen curtains separating the back and front rooms. "Come quick." He waved us in with a meaty hand. "The shop is empty for now."

The jewelry store's showroom was even more impressive up close. Glass cases displayed a variety of jewels, all glittering under the deliberately placed lighting. Amazing how so much wealth was contained in such a small space. It was hard to look at. People purchased these at their leisure. Even if I were freed from my Bond, I would never know this type of luxury.

Eoin grabbed me by the elbow, halting my departure.

"Ralph, there is one other thing I need before we leave."

"Oh yes! I almost forgot." The shopkeeper returned to the back room and came back with a small, gray sack, barely the size of my palm.

"Here ye are," he said, handing it to Eoin. Eoin pocketed the sack and thanked the shopkeeper, signaling our leave.

"What is that?" I nodded to the area of his cloak concealing the sack.

"None of your concern." Eoin's dazzling smile popped against the ochre of his skin. I rolled my eyes and followed Eoin down the main market street. To anyone patrolling the area or any of the chancellor's many spies—primarily poor, unsuspecting children with whom he bartered coins—it would have appeared we'd been in the market all day.

I started to ask another question, but Eoin cut me off.

"Later," he said with an imperceptible nod, signaling to the man leaning against one of the shop buildings on the other side of the street.

The Hunter.

My muscles tightened, begging to run far away from here—from him.

Eoin rested a reassuring hand on the small of my back when my steps stuttered. The touch alone almost made me stop completely.

"Keep moving, Saoirse, don't pay him any attention," he murmured.

The Hunter didn't move from where he stood, but his eyes followed us as we passed. His glare was like a brand. A snarl emitted from him—too quiet for Eoin to hear—a low, guttural sound. A warning. As if he could sense every treasonous thing I've committed. I shuddered to think of the machinations forming in his wicked mind. The encounter stayed with me long after it was over.

CHAPTER TEN

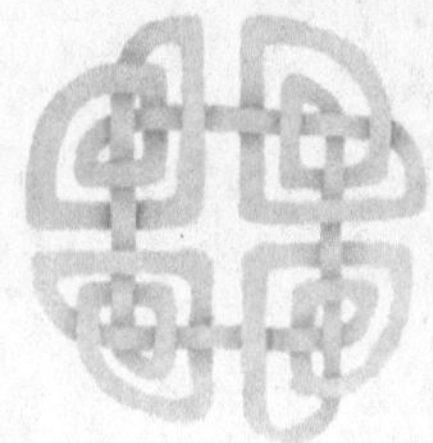

Anger and nerves fought for dominance when my bedchamber door appeared. There was a good chance that Kalee waited inside. Then again, she could be avoiding me. I couldn't decide which was worse: confronting her now or her purposely staying away. She couldn't evade me forever. At some point, she would have to own up to her secrets.

Eoin might have said goodbye, but I couldn't hear it over the blood rushing to my ears as I turned the door handle.

"Saoirse," Kalee called from the dining table, standing when I walked in. My stomach churned.

"You owe me an explanation," I said calmly, crossing my arms over my chest. I wanted to yell, to ask a million questions, to throw up my hands and pace around the room, but I refrained for once.

"I know," she said, smoothing her apron. Her braided chestnut hair lay neatly over her shoulder, delicate stray ringlets framing her face. "Frankly, I'm not sure where to start," she laughed nervously.

"The beginning would be nice."

She sighed, taking her seat at the table and gesturing to me to do the same. I complied, and she pushed a plate of fresh scones toward me. A peace offering. A soft, buttery aroma enveloped me like a warm hug, the tangy hint of cranberry making my mouth water. Damn her apology scones. I took one despite myself.

"Three years ago, after you had a particularly bad bout with the chancellor, when you were unconscious for four days, I sought a way to free you."

I nodded, remembering the time both vividly and hardly at all. The chancellor had suspected the shoemaker at the end of the market row was aiding the osnádúrtha. His spies had been right, of course; the shoemaker housed them on the upper level until they could be moved. My magic wavered in front of them, and I'd been caught.

It was the first time I looked directly into the eyes I was set to betray.

Instead of begging for his life in the presence of the king's Bonded or offering the lives of the osnádúrtha in place of his own, the shoemaker begged me to let them go and take him instead. It would have garnered me favor with the king to do so and would have been enough of a boon that I wouldn't have had to admit my failure at being seen.

It would have been an easy out, but I couldn't do it.

I should have taken the shoemaker to the king. He was one human to the seven osnádúrtha hiding in his shop. Instead, I let them all go. Helped them gather their things and ushered them out the door, making them hit me on their way out. My memory turned fuzzy after I confessed to the king that not only had I been caught by the shoemaker, but he and the osnádúrtha subdued me before they escaped.

My memory went blank after the chancellor put his hands on me.

"I was so scared I was going to lose you, Saoirse. I couldn't stand to sit here any longer while your life was constantly at risk. Once you were stable, I sought to find someone who could help. There were whispers of those aiding the osnádúrtha before, and I followed those trails until one of them was true."

She paused, taking a sip of her tea, and gathered her thoughts. I wiped my hands on my pants, trying to rid myself of the sweat collecting there. Some memories were better left untouched—especially those concerning the chancellor.

"There was nothing we could do, of course, not with your Bond. But by then, I couldn't turn my back on those I could help. So, I stayed in contact with the smugglers, helping whenever I could, hoping one day I would find a way to get you out."

My throat tightened. "Why risk your life for me? Especially when they told you there wasn't a way?"

Kalee cocked her head to the side, her brows wrinkling in confusion. "Because I love you, Sersh," she said simply. Kalee reached across the table and grasped my hand. "We are family. I would do anything for you."

Tears welled up behind my eyes, and guilt gnawed at me for being so angry toward her. There were too many words. Too many emotions threatening to spill over if I spoke my thoughts out loud. I hugged her over the table instead, not caring as scones tumbled to the ground.

"What about the prince?" I asked.

"Ronan was one of my contacts. I didn't know who he was, of course. Not at first. As a handmaiden, I have more access to the castle than most. Plus, I have the advantage of blending in, learning the latest gossip, and garnering any information from you." She bit her lip. "I'm sorry, I hope you aren't mad. I wanted to tell you, but I couldn't—not without putting you at risk."

"I was upset at first, but I was wrong. I'm sorry. If anything, I should be thanking you. But the *prince*?"

Kalee tucked a stray hair behind her ear, her bronze cheeks reddening. "I was apprehensive toward him at first. You can understand my shock when his true identity was revealed. But I swear, he's not a bad man. There are things about his past which have shaped him." She cut me off before I could even open my mouth. "No, I will not divulge Ronan's secrets. He can tell you himself. And he will, once you both gain each other's trust."

I nodded. "How long have you known there was someone breaking Bonds?"

"Not long. Ronan discovered the information a few days ago. When he told me, I proposed your involvement as a win-win. I know you've been helping the smugglers where you can, even after the shoemaker. There have been too many coincidences and close calls. I thought you would like the opportunity to help the osnádúrtha in this way, too. But, you don't have to, you know. Ronan seeks to destroy the Bonds altogether. He would probably do it if you decided not to aid us."

I took a deep breath, letting the weight of Kalee's words sink in. Would it be wrong to demand freedom and ignore those in need of help? The guilt would eat me alive. I would also run the risk of the prince revoking my passage to Arundell, along with the coin he promised. "Are the attacks as bad as he says?"

"Probably worse than he described, knowing Ronan. I will not lie to you or sugarcoat the situation. Innocents are dying, and the king is ignoring their pleas."

I nodded, steeling myself. When I freed the shoemaker and the osnádúrtha he harbored, I'd suffered for it. But even though Death had waited nearby, I did not regret my decision. I would still make the same choice today.

"What I said to Ronan remains true. I will help."

Kalee beamed at me, embracing me once more. The last of my anger and frustration toward her dissolved. Even though I'd been blinded momentarily, I trusted Kalee's judgment. She didn't betray me, not truly. If she believed in the prince and Eoin, then I could try to do the same, at least until they proved themselves otherwise.

"So is he any good in bed?" I asked, half-joking.

"Saoirse!" she laughed, swatting my arm. I grinned, any remnants of tension between us shattered, not like glass, but like chains undone.

Chapter Eleven

"What do you think you're doing?" I asked from the dining table later that evening, a bite of roast moments from my mouth. I was so preoccupied with Kalee's and my earlier conversation that I hadn't heard Eoin knock. Hadn't even noticed him come in until the door clicked behind him.

"I wanted to check on you and see how everything went."

"I'm fine. Everything is fine. You can leave now." I set the fork down with a clang. Eoin was still dressed in his guard's uniform, the golden breastplate polished to perfection. His hands rested on the pommel of his sword as he surveyed my chambers.

"This is…cozy." Eoin gestured to the bare walls, the stack of worn books in the corner, and the single settee by the window.

"My sincerest apologies that my decor isn't up to your standards. You may leave now to rid your eyes of the appalling sight," I deadpanned, returning to my roast. I wished Kalee were here, but she was busy with her evening duties within the castle. She would know how to make him leave—or at least distract him enough so I might slip away. The shadows from the corner of the room migrated toward me, wanting to shield me from the lieutenant's assessing gaze.

"Alas, I haven't come here to judge the layout of your chambers. You have agreed to help, yes? Or are you going back on your bargain?" Eoin's mouth crooked up in the corner, his brown eyes twinkling from the light of the hearth.

I narrowed my gaze. "I don't remember us dining together being part of the bargain."

"One of the many perks, fortunately. Just think—the faster we solve the attacks, the faster you can rid yourself of me." Eoin's smirk turned into a full-on grin, showcasing his white teeth.

"Fine." I gestured to the seat in front of me and pushed Kalee's place setting toward him.

Eoin took his seat, helping himself to the roast, the vegetables, and the scones left over from earlier. I looked at the clock above the hearth, praying Kalee would be back soon.

"How do they work? Your shadows, I mean," he asked once he made himself comfortable.

I lifted a brow. "Excuse you?"

"I'll need to know how your magic works if we are to use it to our advantage."

"Oh, right. It's hard to explain the feeling. If I want to be hidden, they make it so." I held out my hand, showcasing the silver swirls, and watched Eoin's fascination as the shadows of the room seeped into me until it looked as if I was no longer there.

"Truly remarkable." He reached his hand out until it collided with mine. Eoin held me there, rapt fascination glazed over his brown eyes as he twisted my hand this way and that, testing the shadows. They didn't make me wholly invisible, but more so blurred the lines of reality. The outline of my hand was clear, but the dimness of the room made it easy for the magic to obscure me. Eoin's touch was warm and feather-light. Gooseflesh crawled across my skin.

I let the shadows go, materializing once more. I cleared my throat and pulled my hand from his grasp. It was hard not to squirm under his gaze, not used to such blatant fascination. He was interested in what I could do for him, yes, but it was as if we were awed by my magic itself. I loved my magic. I, too, thought it was beautiful. It was easy to forget, though, when my kingdom hated me because of it.

"What do you plan to have me do?" I asked, needing to change the subject.

"I am devising a way to gain access to the king's private study. If all goes well, you can slip in undetected and glean the information we need on the attacks."

A knot formed in my throat. I reached for my water, but the feeling remained no matter how much I drank. "Is starting with the king's private study really such a good idea? What if we're caught?"

"We've already exhausted all other options. No one has been able to break into his study. Not even Ronan is allowed in unattended."

"What, exactly, do you propose I do?" My heartbeat quickened and threatened to jump out of my chest altogether. I knew accepting the prince's offer would be dangerous, but I hadn't had time to prepare myself for the reality of what was expected of me. I twirled my locket between my forefinger and thumb.

"The king will be in council tomorrow at noon in the throne room. We will have approximately one hour to get in and out. While the king is distracted, you will slip in and have about an hour to conduct your search."

"If it's that easy, how come no one has been able to do it before?"

"Guards are stationed at the doors at all times, not to mention the lock. I can create a diversion to distract the guards, but we will need to find the key to the study before we ever hope to enter. And quickly, if we are to execute our plan tomorrow, or we must wait another month until the next council meeting," he said, thrumming his long fingers on the table.

"I can pick the lock," I said without thinking, instantly regretting it. What if this lock was more complex than any I'd come across? The thought of the king's guards catching me mid-act turned the roast sitting in my stomach. I pushed my plate away.

Eoin sat up straighter, a mischievous grin splayed across his face. "Cunning creature. Then it's a date."

My cheeks were still warm from Eoin's words the following day as he and I walked through the castle. Guards, servants, and noblemen alike hadn't given us a second glance on our way to the king's private study. It wasn't unusual for the Bonded to be escorted about the castle, and no one questioned the intentions of a high-ranking lieutenant. My heart thudded painfully with each step.

"If you keep acting guilty, then they'll start to think you're up to something," Eoin muttered after I looked over my shoulder yet again.

"I'm Bonded. They always think I'm up to something."

"Remember the plan?"

I nodded and fell back in the guise of lacing my boots. Eoin continued on as if nothing happened. I slipped into the alcove, pulling the shadows around me as I did so. The king's study wasn't far ahead, and I waited for the signal. My hands fumbled for my pins in the pouch fastened at my waist, my breaths coming in rapid succession.

Something clattered and broke against the stone. A scream pierced the air. I hurried toward the study on silent footsteps, keeping the shadows wrapped around me. Kalee lay on the floor, clutching her leg into her chest, sobbing hysterically.

"I think it's broken," she cried, and I swore I could see real tears streaming down her face.

"Don't just stand there, men," Eoin yelled, and the two men guarding the king's study came running, huddling around her.

I seized the opportunity and knelt at the door, not giving my friend another glance. My fingers made quick work of the lock, its simplicity almost laughable—my earlier worries deemed useless. It was insulting, really. The smuggler's locks had been far more complex though their secrets were exponentially more dangerous.

Kalee's muffled sobs ceased as I closed the door behind me and clicked the lock back in place. A sigh of relief escaped my lips, and my shoulders relaxed a fraction. Getting in was the hardest part. Now, all I needed was the information itself.

My shadows dropped in favor of conserving energy. The king's study was as ornate as I expected. A wide oak desk owned the majority of the space by the window, and two iron spiral staircases framed the room, leading to the loft above. Overstuffed bookcases kissed the ceiling, and a map of Centra had been pinned to the drawing table on my right, another door next to it. Eoin prepared me for the possibility of scribes working on the other side of it, though it was unlikely without the king's presence. According to the prince, no one was allowed in the king's study when he was out. Not even the servants. I held my ear against the wooden door, but there was nothing save for silence.

My fingers trailed over the documents laid on the desk, careful not to disturb their placement. Some men were particularly organized. The king struck me as one of them. Most of the papers were correspondence letters with those stationed along Centra's borders. Others were scrolls or sealed reports. Nothing pointed to any sinister creatures under his command.

In truth, I hadn't the slightest idea of what I was looking for. With smugglers, it was easy. There were always coded documents in a secret drawer or panel behind a painting—something to indicate a shipment of sorts. But this? I didn't know what I would find. I checked behind tapestries and paintings, inside vases, and under the area rug. There was nothing to designate the source of the attacks Eoin and the prince spoke of.

Minutes passed too quickly, and my search became frantic, to no avail. Then, the wall clock chimed. My hour was up, and it was time to go. The hot pang of tears swelled at my frustration. This had all been for nothing, and I wasn't any closer to achieving my freedom.

Defeated, I went to the scribe's closet. The servant's stairwell would be through the door, and I could only pray no one was on their way to attend to the king. My hand wrapped around the door handle and my eyes traveled to the loft. I'd been so focused on the king's desk, I'd forgotten about the upper level.

Before I could think better of it, I ran up the stairs, taking them two at a time. Another, smaller bookcase ran across the length of the wall. A reading chair and a table had been tucked away in the corner. I cursed myself for wasting valuable time. I started to make my escape, but the map lying across the table caught my attention. It was the exact replica of the one in the chancellor's office. I peered over the railing, studying the map on the drawing board below, comparing it to its sibling. While the map below held figurines of his men stationed throughout Centra, this map, however, displayed the same black flags pinned to the different kingdoms of Rúndaiaithe. The only discrepancy between his and the chancellor's was the red 'X' marked over a section of the Barrens.

I picked it up, studying the markings up close. Strange patterns came to life at my touch, inking themselves across the parchment in intricate patterns. An unknown language etched itself all over the map. I gasped, dropping the map back onto the table. The markings disappeared in an instant; only the black flags and the single red 'X' remained.

A deep voice boomed behind the study doors. I'd recognize it anywhere. The king approached. With no time to flee, I ducked. The king barrelled into his study a heartbeat later, Ronan trailing in after him. Our eyes locked before the shadows wrapped around me. To his credit, Ronan showed no signs of panic as the doors groaned shut, trapping the three of us in the study. Sweat pooled at my back.

"Have you had any luck with your task?" the Conqueror King asked.

"Not yet, father. The Informer is still searching."

The king huffed. "She will find what you need. My training has suited her well enough."

"Of that, I have no doubt. There is something I would like to ask, however."

The air stilled as if it, too, was holding its breath. A crash sounded, and the king yelped. I took it for the diversion I hoped it was. With the shadows still firmly around me, I crept down the spiral staircase closest to the scribe's closet.

The king cursed. "Clumsy boy. Don't let them get wet," he ordered.

Ronan crouched next to his father, the king's back to me, as he murmured his apologies. Broken glass and papers were laid out on the floor, and the pitcher of water was toppled on its side. The two of them worked to save the papers from a watery grave.

Without another glance, I shoved myself into the scribe's closet and flew down the servant's stairwell. Even though no trouble came in the servant's tunnels, my heart threatened to punch out of my chest well after I was secured behind my own doors again.

Chapter Twelve

"Rise, Informer," the king demanded the following day.

My hands shook as I came to my feet. It wasn't unusual for the king to call upon me often, but something was wrong. He didn't wear his normal, satisfied smirk. No, this one was malicious. Venomous like a predator ready to go in for the kill. His dark eyes narrowed on me, searching for signs of weakness. Did he know his son and I conspired together? I hadn't taken anything from his study, and I was careful to put everything back in its place. My palms perspired nonetheless.

The chancellor stood next to the king; a horrific smirk turned his lips. A Bonded I recognized from Midwinter stood off to the side. Like the other Bonded, he was dressed in all-black, unassuming clothes. His cropped hair glowed redder than any fire.

"My men searched Lord Byrne's desk and found something rather intriguing," the king said, twirling his beard into a sharp point. "Any idea what it might be?"

"If I recall correctly, there were names of other osnádúrtha the lord smuggled out of Centra as well as the supplies he acquired to do so." I tried to steady my racing heart—its relentless pounding made it difficult to breathe—reminding myself I burned the evidence of the smugglers. The king had nothing on me.

"And what else?"

"I–I don't know," I stammered, sweat beading down my back.

"What then, do you suppose this is?" The king handed over a piece of parchment. Evidence of more smugglers filled its page. Evidence I missed in my haste.

"When asked for proof of co-conspirators, you said there were none," the king continued. "Explain your deceit, now."

The magic of the Bond sparked to life, twisting my insides into knots. "Your Majesty, I must have overlooked it in my initial search. Lord Byrne had come into the office, and I had to hurry and—"

"Very well," the king interrupted, satisfied with what the Bond made me say.

I prayed he would dismiss me. I prayed he wouldn't ask more questions, have the chancellor beat me for my negligence, and be done with it. But this was far from over.

The king read the names off the list as guards escorted men in chains into the throne room. "Look at all the traitors you left behind. Imagine the damage they could have inflicted to this kingdom if they weren't caught in time."

Ten in total. Some of them were shaking. Others wore steeled expressions. We all knew their fate. There was no room for traitors in Centra.

"Enforcer," the king called. The red-haired Bonded stepped forward. His lankiness sparked doubt about any pain he could inflict. Expressionless, he stood before the men, his arms relaxed at his sides.

"End them."

The air grew stale, hanging heavy in the air as if everyone held a collective breath. Brittle silence filled the room while time stretched, turning sluggish—every second bleeding into the next, dying a slow, painful death. Then, they gasped for breath, clawing at their necks. The Bonded clenched his fists as he stole the very air from their lungs. A wind wielder. There was nothing I could do but watch in horror as their faces turned from red to blue to a ghastly gray.

No. I bit the inside of my cheek, trying to remain expressionless. Because of me, because of my carelessness, these men—who'd done nothing but help the osnádúrtha—struggled to breathe, strangled before my eyes. I deserved this, though. *I* failed them, and I earned the memory of their horrific deaths seared into my mind forever.

"Look what happens to those who dare defy me."

Once the last of them fell, the king whistled, signaling to his guards. The doors to the throne room opened once again. My legs buckled, threatening to send me to my knees at the sight of twenty faie, all clasped in iron chains, being shoved into the room. At the head of their death march was the Hunter.

The Hunter guided them to the center of the throne room, and the permanent scowl on his face burned me where I stood. His tall, broad frame towered over the others, and the afternoon sun filtering in through the stained glass created an ominous glow around him, accentuating his bronze complexion—an angel of death ferrying souls to the Otherworld.

Bile burned at the back of my throat. It was bad enough that the smugglers were dead because of me. But the faie? The Hunter may have been the one to bring them to this death castle, but my carelessness led the king directly to them. I couldn't look them in the eyes—couldn't face what I'd done.

"Slower this time," the king directed the Enforcer. The Bonded's freckled face remained blank as he looked upon our kind and clenched his fists, coaxing their lives from them.

My shadows swirled in wild squiggles, trying to pull from the dark corners of the throne room before the king commanded me to stop. Agony yanked at my gut, and I strained against the Bond, my magic desperate to conceal me from this horror.

"You cannot hide from what you've done, Informer."

Everything went numb as I was forced to watch the osnádúrtha die. My blood ran cold, the aching pluck of a sharp string rang in my ears. Something inside of me shifted and cracked, toggling between the present and past as flashes of memories stole my vision. Flowers my mother and I picked in the garden, once bright, then burned to ash. My friends, laughing, their smiles wide before their faces grew slack. My home. Razed to the ground. My mother, dead. Eiric. Dead.

A faie bearing similar features to him stared at me with pleading hazel eyes like Eiric once did. He was the only Bonded I'd ever known by name. We'd shared many things, including our hearts. Eiric was executed in front of all the Bonded half a decade ago, caught for treason. No one had ever known we were lovers, save for Kalee. A piece of me died with my mother. Another piece, with him. Soon, there wouldn't be any pieces left.

For the first time in fifteen years, I couldn't hold back my tears in front of the king as the faie dropped one by one. The satisfied smirk of the king and his chancellor sent me reeling. I was consumed by an overwhelming need to lash out. I didn't just want to hurt them. I wanted to *destroy* them.

"Let this be a warning, Informer. The next time you disappoint me, you will be the one to end them."

All I saw was red as I walked past the slew of bodies when the king dismissed me, my limbs shaking. My stomach threatened to spill its contents for everyone to see. Neither the Enforcer nor the Hunter appeared disturbed about their actions. Was I the only one who still cared about the osnádúrtha? Or maybe, they knew caring was futile—fighting back was futile. The nausea didn't stop until I returned to my room, heaving until there was nothing left. The king's warning rang in my head well into the night. Defy him again, miss anything again, and it would be my life he ended.

I had to get out. I couldn't take this anymore—this helpless, useless feeling gnawing at my very soul. I needed to leave before I was devoid of feeling completely. Before I turned into the Enforcer or the Hunter. A soulless monster. Ronan's bargain couldn't have come sooner. I'd already agreed to help. Before, I was hesitant about the risks. Now, hardened determination settled low in my aching belly. I would find the source of the attacks. I would free myself. And then, I would run far, far away. I would never see the king again, never be subjected to another act of cruelty.

I would leave before it was too late.

Chapter Thirteen

"I want to go to the site of an attack," I said to Eoin the next morning. The king's private study produced no real results. The more I thought about it, the more useless the information became. It wouldn't be unusual for the king and his chancellor to have maps of Rúndaiaithe, no matter how strange it might be. While Ronan was intrigued by a magical map, he, too, believed it wasn't connected to the attacks. Plus, it wasn't as if we could steal the map. My frustrations grew stronger with every passing minute as we drew further away from having the answers we needed.

"I was thinking the same thing," he said. "Lucky for us, there were reports this morning of an attack last night not far from here." Eoin bit into his toast, sitting across the dining table from Kalee and me.

"Do you think it's wise to put yourself at risk again so soon? Between yesterday and the king almost catching you in his study, I fear you are beginning to press your luck, Sersh," Kalee said, her hands clutched around a mug of tea.

"Every day I spend Bonded to the king is another day we risk him uncovering this whole operation. I am tired of waiting." I pushed my plate away. My appetite disappeared after what happened in the throne room.

Kalee nodded and patted my leg under the table.

"Exploring the site of an attack could reveal new discoveries. Ronan and I both have examined them before, but you might be able to give us a new insight." Eoin scratched his clean-shaven chin.

"Why do you put so much faith in me?"

Eoin shrugged a shoulder. "You're observational… Don't give me that look. It's a compliment."

I didn't know how to interpret the approval. Instead of accepting or acknowledging the praise, I asked, "When do we leave?"

WE DEPARTED AFTER WE BROKE OUR FASTS. SUNSHINE WARMED MY CHEEKS by the time we entered the compact village—a brief reprieve from winter's harsh chill. Despite the pleasant day, the village remained empty. People were undoubtedly scared of the creature from the recent attack.

"How is it that news of these killings hasn't spread?" I asked. The village was only half a day's ride from Rothcek. It didn't neighbor the city, but it wasn't on the outskirts of Centra either.

"We suspect the king is burying the information. A few people from an array of villages throughout Centra have traveled to the capital to voice their concerns. They are told the crown will look into it and then handed stock or gold before shooing them off."

"The king is buying their silence?"

Eoin glanced sidelong. "They somehow forget to bring up the matter again. My only guess as to how news hasn't spread is because the attacks are happening far enough away from the city, no one is talking about them."

"Surely someone must have an aunt. A cousin. Some relative or friend they write to in the city."

"I, a kingsguard, am strolling about after an attack just last night, and no one has come to give a report or point us in a single direction. They're afraid, Saoirse." A chill shuddered down my spine, hearing him say my name aloud. It was still so foreign coming from anyone but Kalee.

Eoin was right. All the windows had been boarded up. Anyone walking about did so fast-paced and head-down, scurrying to their destinations.

"Do the attacks only happen at night?" I asked as a scraggly dog raced toward us, carrying something in its mouth.

A girl shrieked, chasing after the dog. Eoin stiffened beside me. Tears covered her cheeks, and her tattered clothes were too big for her frame.

Understanding what she was chasing after, I stopped the dog. Even though his game was over, he didn't seem to mind the attention. I pried the rag doll from the mutt. He sat patiently, wagging his tail, and waited for me to throw it so the game could resume.

I held it up to the girl. "I take it this is yours?"

The child nodded, her lip quivering.

"It's okay," I reassured her. "Look, good as new." I wiped the slobber off on my cloak. It was nowhere close to new. The doll's condition matched her dress, but she smiled as I handed it over, hugging it tight against her chest. The pallor of her skin and the hollowness of her cheeks were difficult to ignore. She was so thin it looked as though she hadn't eaten in days.

"Are you hungry?" I asked, crouching down.

Her eyes grew wide, and she nodded, her tattered braids coming loose. I had little but… "Here," I offered, unwrapping a spare piece of bread from my cloak pocket. Since the night I followed Ronan, I made it a habit to bring something to eat when I left for my missions.

She grabbed the bread with caution, as if afraid it was a trick, then ran.

"Wait! Is this your dog?" I called after her, but she paid me no mind.

The dog sat there, waiting, tail wagging.

He, too, was thin, his ribcage painfully visible under his matted black fur. Despite his haggard appearance, his eyes were bright, and he looked as if he were smiling as he panted.

"Fine," I sighed and handed over the last of the bread I saved for the trip back. He snatched it out of my hand and took off back toward the girl.

"What?" I asked when Eoin eyed me.

"That was nice of you."

"Sometimes I like to be nice."

"How come you're not nice to me?" he teased, the hint of a smile giving him away, but I bristled all the same.

"I don't know you. Nor do I trust you." Eoin might be aiding Prince Ronan in his smuggling endeavors, but I still didn't know his motives.

"Have no fear, Saoirse, I will change your mind eventually."

His smile was big and true now, the crinkles around his eyes disturbingly cute. Eoin rested his hand on my shoulder in what was supposed to be a comforting gesture. My pulse jumped.

"We shall see," I said, removing his hand with disdain. "Can we focus on the task at hand?"

Eoin cleared his throat. "It's difficult to determine the exact timing of the attacks because of the condition of the bodies. All of our known victims have been discovered the morning after they were last seen, so we've concluded they were either killed late at night or in the early hours of the morning."

"What kind of creature sucks the life out of a person?" A chill cascaded down my spine as I recalled the horrifying tale my mother used to get me to behave. The description of leathered wings and fangs came to mind—creatures snatching misbehaving children in the middle of the night.

"If we knew that, we wouldn't need you."

I gave Eoin a hard glare. He smiled.

We approached a humble home on the outskirts of the village. The body was gone, their ashes having already blown away, but the large gashes in the stone home remained—this horror forever imprinted on the building. I trailed gloved fingers along the mark. My fingers sank to the second knuckle of the deepest gash. Four thick claws dug clean cuts into the building as if stone were nothing more than butter.

Despite my search, I found no additional signs of the beast. There were no tufts of fur. No tracks or blood trails to follow. The only evidence left behind was the claw marks plucked straight from a nightmare as if the creature vanished into thin air.

We stayed in the village until nightfall, searching for clues that may have escaped someone else's notice. After interviewing several reluctant villagers, we returned to the carriage defeated and no closer to discovering the truth behind the attacks than we were hours ago.

In silence, we sat across from each other on the cushioned bench during our journey back to the castle. The landscape passed in pigmentless blurs as we advanced. Though we rode with haste, a strange stillness hung in the air. No life scurried about; only the endless snow shrouding the earth in its icy embrace, as if all life faded with the sun.

"What?" I asked, breaking the silence after I caught Eoin's gaze on me again. He was always staring. I shifted in my seat.

"Nothing. It's hard not to look at you. Better than the view outside, at least."

"Thanks," I deadpanned, rolling my eyes. At least he wasn't sneering at me.

"No—I only meant—"

"I know what you meant." I turned to look out the window, warmth spreading to my cheeks.

"What will you do once your Bond is broken?" Eoin asked, changing the subject. Ever since our bargain was struck, I consciously avoided giving too much thought to this question.

"How do I know what the prince said was true?"

"It's true. I know the person he speaks of. Ronan has helped many osnádúrtha escape before. Now that there's a way to end the Bonds, he'll work to free them all. Above all else, Ronan is a man of his word and won't stop until he fulfills his end of the deal."

I chewed on the inside of my cheek. Since our meeting, the prince conflicted with my perception of him and everything I thought I knew about him. How had he become so different from his father?

"If you could do anything, what would you do?" Eoin probed, pulling me out of my thoughts.

"I am Bonded. It doesn't do well to have delusions of another life," I said. I did have such delusions, though. I've clung to a dream during the late nights to keep myself from shattering. One where I have my own bookshop, spending my days reading or in discussions with others. I've never told Kalee this dream—I had never spoken of it out loud, too afraid of giving too much power to it. I could never be disappointed in something if I didn't believe it would come true.

"You are Bonded now. What about after it's broken?"

"You can ask me then."

Hope was a dangerous, fickle thing. Too much of it, and the despair from sheer disappointment would be crushing. I wouldn't voice my wants. Not yet. Not when the prospect of breaking my Bond was still so far away.

"If I could, I would also go somewhere far away," Eoin offered, his brown eyes fixed on the distant view outside the carriage window.

"Do you not like working for the Crown Prince?" I inquired, praying that what I'd seen of Ronan wasn't just another mask he wore.

"He is one reason I stay." He turned to me this time, meeting my gaze. "But I was destined for greater things."

"Like what?"

"Maybe it's farcical, but I cannot live my life in the shadow of another forever. My goal is to become someone worthy of admiration. I want to help others. I love Ronan, but I want to be my own person, not the Prince of Centra's glorified sitter. Taking orders for the rest of my life is not what I imagined for myself." Eoin gave a weak, pensive smile, his posture softening.

"It's not preposterous." I shook my head, sitting up straighter. "I understand what living for another is like." For the last fifteen years, my purpose was the king's purpose. I held no authority over my choices or the way I lived. There was no autonomy in my life. Perhaps Eoin and I were more similar than I imagined.

We held each other's gaze for a moment longer than necessary. His eyes flicked toward my lips, and my mouth went dry. I had the strongest urge to lick my lips. It had been a long time since I'd been in the arms of another. I shook the thought out. Fucking Nine, what was the matter with me? Just because a good-looking man kept staring at my mouth and giving me compliments did not mean I needed to jump into bed with him. Gods, especially not Eoin. The thought of bedding a castle guard, spy or not, made my skin crawl.

"Don't get me wrong," Eoin said, dropping the tension to a much more manageable level. "I love Ronan like a brother. I'm choosing to stay and help him find his way, but it is not something I can see myself doing forever."

I nodded, wondering if Kalee felt the same. Would she feel like she was finally free of me and move on to bigger and better things, or would we travel together? She and I fantasized about life beyond Centra before. About sailing to Arundell to see how the aes sídhe live, or traveling even further to discover unknown lands.

"Have you always liked reading? I can't help but notice the only things you accumulate are books," Eoin asked when the quiet stretched too long.

I gave him a wry stare, never having come across someone so uncomfortable with silence. "Yes, Kalee taught me how, and I haven't stopped since."

"You didn't know how to read?" Eoin's brows furrowed.

"Well, nobody's born knowing how to read, are they? I knew my letters and rudimentary words," I clarified at his assessing stare. "I was taken before I could move on to more complex teachings for gods' sakes." I refrained from mentioning how my mother had to scavenge for scraps of parchment, writing utensils, or books themselves. At nine, I should have known more, but learning supplies were scarce before the Reckoning, much less after.

"Your education didn't continue when you arrived at the castle?"

"Do you really believe the king cared about my education? He was more interested in honing my magic instead."

"How were you able to garner the information the king required of you?"

"I told you, I knew basic words." I shrugged. Those days felt like a lifetime ago. "Besides, you know something is important if it's locked away. I was able to get by most years by overhearing the right information. It wasn't until my missions became more important to the king, more dangerous to myself, that I finally asked Kalee for help."

"I can see why you are so fond of her," Eoin said, crossing his ankle over his knee.

I nodded. I'd been wary of Kalee at first. I didn't know if she reported my every move to the king. She worked for him, after all. After I told her I was unlettered, Kalee became more than my handmaid, more than a tutor. She became my friend and eventually my sister.

Part of my yearning to own a bookstore was because of her. I'd like to do for others what Kalee did for me by providing access to information. After Kalee taught me to read, I spent any spare moment with my nose in a book. Immersed in captivating stories and vibrant characters, I could escape the confinement of the stone castle. I would be transported to faraway lands where good triumphed, love flourished, and families were happy and whole.

Eoin's stare bore into me before he returned his gaze to the window.

This time, it was my turn to stare. Moonlight cast softly upon him, highlighting his face's sharp, masculine planes beatifically. His crimson uniform brought out the russet undertones of his rich complexion. Gold pins indicating his rank glinted every so often. He stroked something idly between his thumb and forefinger.

Eoin turned back toward me to ask another question, but his words were stifled by the screeching halt of the carriage and a piercing cry.

"Stay here!" he demanded before dashing out of the carriage.

Heart racing, my eyes shot to the window, but it was too dark to see anything with dense clouds occluding the moon in thick tendrils. The shrieking ceased soon after Eoin stepped out of the carriage, but he had yet to return. I counted a minute. Two. With a curse, I gripped the door frame, checking the daggers strapped to my hips before stepping out into the unknown.

Chapter Fourteen

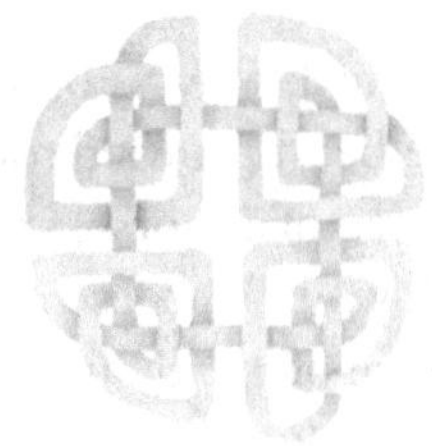

A single lantern flickered from its hook on the coach box, its small flame threatening to shroud me in total darkness. Eoin and the driver were nowhere to be seen. Milky white fog eddied around my ankles and the floor of the muddy path carved out by carriage tracks. The stench of decay was so prevalent in the air, I had to tug my cloak over my nose to keep from gagging. Internal warning bells blared as the hairs on the back of my neck stood on end.

"This is a bad idea," I muttered, unsheathing a dagger.

My shaking fingers fumbled to retrieve the remaining lantern, its twin missing. As I clutched the lantern in my right hand, dagger in my left, I glimpsed a pool of blood in the driver's seat. It dripped onto the road and beyond. I cursed Eoin for leaving me. Stupid man. Staying together was better than this.

Because venturing out on my own wasn't a good idea. Nor was staying here.

The horse still attached to the carriage grunted, pulling violently at the reins. I checked for the other horse, but Eoin must have taken it.

"Promise you won't kill me if I free you?" I asked the animal. It bucked, frightened by whatever had come. I cursed. Would it be wrong of me to leave it here? Temptation was heavy on my mind, but what if whatever took the driver came back? I thought of the claw marks from the village. As much as I disliked the horse, I didn't want to see it dead. And I would sooner walk back to the castle than ride the thing. "Don't make me regret this," I sighed and cut the horse free of its reins. It reared back and dashed away.

I followed the smattering of blood leading into the forest and edged further into the woods, stopping when the morbid trail ended. Lantern outstretched, I scanned my surroundings to no avail. Even with my faie eyesight, the fog made it nearly impossible to see beyond more than a few inches.

I took a tentative step forward, only to be stopped by a deep, rumbling growl. To my right, a massive beast prowled toward me, the fog dissipating in its wake. A gray wolf the size of a horse, shrouded in shadows reminiscent of my own, crouched low, its hackles raised. The wolf's appearance was akin to the billowing smoke of heady fire, thick and suffocating as if it had one foot in this world, one foot in another. My mouth went dry. Its eyes, glowing kernels of embers, were trained on me. Blood dripped from its maw, and an earth-shaking snarl revealed large, yellow, jagged teeth.

This wolf was a nightmare come to life. It shouldn't exist. And yet, I've seen it before. I've stared at it more times than I could count. It was one of the monsters from the chancellor's tapestry.

We stared at one another for a few heartbeats, sizing each other up. Compared to the giant beast, my daggers might as well have been toothpicks. Despite my skills, they wouldn't be much use against something so massive. Not to mention, I'd have to get close to the damned thing. I was faster than most, but judging by the sheer muscle of it, I wouldn't be fast enough. If Eoin, trained guard to the royal family, was already dead, then there was no chance I would survive. I pulled from the shadows anyway.

Thunder boomed in the sky and sleet fell in violent sheets. To make matters worse, the half-formed ice stung against my exposed skin. The gods had been no help to me before—now it was as if they sought to make matters worse.

The wolf howled, the sound deafening, before it launched itself. When its front paws were off the forest floor, I flung the still-lit lantern toward it with all my might and rolled out of the way.

The wolf landed mere paces away. Instead of a distraction, my lantern provided nothing more than an annoyance, bouncing off its snout. The shadows were around me now, but they were useless. The wolf snarled at me as if scenting me through the shadows and stalked forward.

I cursed and clutched daggers in both hands. We locked eyes, circling one another in a dance orchestrated by thunder and sleet. I made to throw one of my daggers, but white lightning cracked the air, halting its release.

Too late.

The wolf leapt, pinning me to the ground. Despite being made almost entirely of shadows, the sheer weight of the animal was excruciating. My bones threatened to snap at any moment. The wolf hovered over me, its breath hot against my face, our shadows swirling around us. A heartbeat until I felt it. As if the wolf was sucking my magic into its very being. I gasped, my shadows fighting to stay attached to my body as they were pulled toward the wolf.

I panicked and yanked at the darkness faster than I ever had before, despite how useless my magic had proved moments ago. The wolf yelped as if startled. For a second, I thought I pulled from the very shadows it was made of. There was no time to dwell on the odd occurrence, however. A noise sounded from behind, distracting the wolf, causing it to shift its weight. I pulled hard, freeing an arm, and somehow managed to keep hold of my dagger. I didn't wait for the wolf to notice before I stabbed it in the leg, startling it enough to loosen its hold on my other arm.

I scrambled backwards, praying it didn't follow. It couldn't see me with the shadows, but they wouldn't stop the wolf from scenting me again. It remained, distracted with whatever caught its attention.

Eoin.

My breath caught as Eoin yelled at the wolf, throwing rocks at it. They were nothing more than pebbles bouncing off its head. The image itself might have been funny if it wasn't for the gigantic wolf stalking toward him, its hackles raised in warning. Eoin drew his sword. The audible sharpness of the double-edged blade rang out in the night. Its sound promised death. The wolf's answering growl pledged pain.

They leapt at one another, steel clashing against teeth and claws. Eoin was fast for a human. His years of training in the royal guard gave him a fighting chance, but the wolf was not of this world—that I knew for sure. Its movements were unnatural as it cut through the air, nothing more than the very shadows it was made of. Eoin was too slow, however, to avoid the beast before it flung him against a nearby tree with a sickening thud.

"Eoin!"

Eoin groaned, sword somehow still in hand, and slumped against the tree trunk. His eyes were closed in pain, but at least he wasn't dead. Yet.

The wolf stalked toward its prey, its teeth on full display. *Oh gods.* It was going to tear Eoin limb from limb.

I rushed the wolf, daggers in hand. Before I could think better of it, I leapt onto its back, sinking the small blades into its shoulders. Its fur scratched my skin. The tissue squelched as it gave way. Hot, black liquid bubbled to the surface and coated my hands. My last meal threatened to reappear. Gods, the smell.

The wolf bucked and thrashed underneath my daggers. I stabbed it again and again, fighting to hold on, to do something other than fling about at the wolf's mercy. I wished more than ever my shadows could lash out at the beast.

I thudded against the ground and rolled to a stop, the shadows falling from me as I did so. I grappled for purchase, but I was too slow compared to the wolf. I braced myself to meet the gods who neglected this earth. With my blades still embedded in its back, I had nothing but my hands to protect myself as the wolf pounced. It wouldn't hesitate before it ripped out my throat. The rancid stench of carrion invaded my senses as it leaned into me, its weight stealing my breath.

I braced for pain. For death. But neither came.

The weight of the wolf grew lighter until it was pushed off of me. Eoin's sword protruded from its throat until Eoin freed the wolf of its head. I shuddered. Eoin stood over me, soaked and haggard. A shaky laugh sounded from him, relief evident on his face.

"You're alive," he breathed, extending a hand to help me from the ground.

Laughter left me as he hauled me to my feet. Eoin bled from a small cut to his temple, but otherwise appeared fine despite the ribs he was sure to have cracked.

"So are you," I said after I managed to compose myself. My thighs still shook from the sheer shock of the situation. Eoin wiped the long blade on the wolf's coat to cleanse it. He sheathed his sword, repeated the action with my daggers, and handed them back to me.

"Are you alright?" His hand cupped my face, his eyes searching for more than physical wounds. The caress of his thumb against my cheek was surprisingly comforting. I was reluctant to step out of his grasp.

"I think so. Thank you." I gestured to the fallen beast. The close proximity of the wolf only made it more terrifying. Its glowing red eyes dulled to the darkest black. Wine-red blood from its last kill dripped from its maw and covered its enormous paws. A shiver ran down my spine as the wolf's shadows splayed out—its body dissipating with it.

Nothing remained of the creature aside from the black stain of its blood.

"That is…unusual, to say the least," Eoin remarked.

"I've seen it before," I admitted. The resemblance was uncanny

Eoin's eyebrows shot up. "Animals disappearing after they've died?"

"No," I scoffed. "That's a first for me. The wolf. There's one like it depicted in a tapestry hanging in the chancellor's office behind his desk."

He frowned. "I'll see if I can get a look at it after we get back."

I nodded, every bone in my body suddenly aching.

"What happened to waiting in the carriage?" Eoin groaned; any sign of relief he felt before at the sight of my still-breathing body was now replaced with anger. "I thought you were dead."

"I thought *you* were dead! How could you expect anyone to sit there and wait for their demise?"

Eoin opened his mouth but swallowed whatever he wanted to say. Instead, he turned and walked further into the forest.

"The road is back this way." I pointed behind us.

"I know," he said, but continued in the opposite direction. I started to follow but stopped when he reappeared from behind a large tree with one of the horses that had been pulling the carriage. I gave them a wide berth as Eoin strolled past with the mare in tow. Her nostrils flared at the sight of the black residue of where the wolf once lay. I took another step back, letting them lead. If she was to rear back and run, I wouldn't block her path.

I followed them past the forest's edge and back to the road. The sleet ceased, and the fog dissipated. Even though the gods had a tendency to ignore my pleas, favoring chaos instead, I still sent a silent thank you to them for allowing us to walk out of the clearing alive.

When we reached the carriage, all that remained of it were fragmented pieces of glass and wood.

"Too bad I didn't stay in the carriage," I quipped, walking stiffly past the mare and the brooding man, shooting him a scathing glance.

The carriage was beyond repair, and the driver's absence was audible. I looked at Eoin, silently pleading for him to understand my unspoken question. The lieutenant shook his head solemnly, and I sent up another prayer for the nameless driver. As much as I disliked horses, I was glad I freed it when I did.

"Come." Eoin swung onto the horse's back and offered a hand. "We're right outside the city, but it will be faster if we ride back to the castle. Safer too." We were both drenched from the heavy sleet. My clothes were well on their way to crystallization. It would be foolish to walk back instead of riding the horse because of a silly fear, but the castle wasn't *that* far...

"I'll walk instead."

Eoin snorted. "Don't be stupid. You'll freeze before you get halfway there."

"I'll be fine," I said, starting toward the castle.

"Saoirse, get on the horse. We need to go," Eoin commanded, trotting beside me.

"I...I can't." A familiar shake started in my hands, and the shadows wiggled wildly.

"You can't, or you won't?"

I threw up my hands. "I can't, alright? They terrify me. One trampled me once, broke my arm, and I haven't been able to get close to them since."

Eoin dismounted and grabbed my shoulders, squeezing them slightly. "I will be right there with you. Nothing will happen as long as I'm with you. I promise."

His words did something strange to my stomach. Reluctantly, I nodded and took his hand as he helped me onto the tall mare. Eoin's body slid behind mine. His massive arms encased me when he gripped the reins.

"Alright?" he asked.

"Alright."

Tears welled in my eyes while we rode, the events of the night sinking in. Against my will, the numbing cold threatened to take over; my eyelids became leaden with sleep.

When we arrived at the castle, just beyond a secluded entrance near the garden, Eoin shook me.

"Saoirse," he said sharply. Was that panic in his voice? Despite his persistent calls, I couldn't bring myself to respond and let him know I was fine.

"What?" I finally managed.

"Are you alright?"

"Fine. Get me off this horse." I'd almost forgotten about the mare.

Eoin hopped down and grabbed for me, but a slicing pain cut through my middle when he tried to help me down from the horse's back. Dark, gruesome liquid coated my front and covered my hands. Where had all this come from? Panic seeped in. The thickness of my clothing, shock, and perhaps a touch of hypothermia masked any sign of the injury after the bout with the wolf. Looking at my abdomen now...there was so much blood. Too much.

A curse was all I could manage before my vision tunneled and the world went black.

CHAPTER FIFTEEN

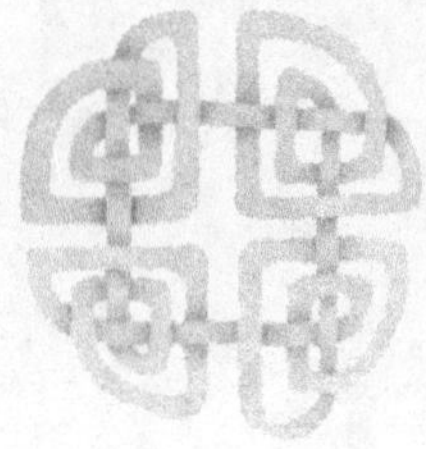

My mother held me in her lap, stroking my hair as a calm darkness wrapped around us, caressing me in its warmth. She held me this way often when I was a girl. Terrified from nightmares of horrifying monsters, she would coax me back to sleep with stories of gallant warriors and brave princesses. It was nice here—the burdens of the living world no longer present. Here, I was no longer Bonded. Here, I hadn't been responsible for the deaths of countless osnádúrtha.

Here, I was safe.

For a moment, I thought I was dead until the darkness flitted away, thoughts tugging on the edge of awareness as reality dealt its brutal blow. My mother couldn't be with me now because she no longer belonged to this world. I wouldn't have minded if I had died, if only to be held by her one last time before our souls moved onto the Otherworld.

Voices became recognizable as I blinked my eyes against the light. Familiar crimson sheets wrapped around me. No light from the window broke through the heavy drapes. Instead, lanterns cast a soft glow over my bedchamber. I was indeed being held, not by my mother, but by Kalee; her comforting hands smoothed my hair. Her lips were moving, but I couldn't make out the words.

Prince Ronan sat in the corner—weary-eyed and still wearing the same clothes from our meeting in the Underground. Honeyed strands broke free of his hair tie, framing the prince's face. He spoke, but the world was still too muddled. Eoin sat at the foot of my bed. He stood, almost knocking over his chair, eyes wide when they made contact with mine.

"What?" I croaked. Gods, my mouth was dry. I tried to sit up, but Kalee's hands pressed down on my shoulders. Pain laced across my abdomen. Another groan left me at the movement.

"Glad to see your bluntness is still intact after almost dying," Eoin joked, but concern still shone through his features. Without having to ask, he grabbed a glass of water and held it to my lips. I drank in greedy gulps as the cool liquid relieved my aching throat.

"What happened?" I asked, feeling as though I swallowed a handful of rocks.

"It seems our shadowed friend did more damage than we thought." Eoin set the glass down and looked me over as if he couldn't believe I was okay. It was then that I noticed crusty black blood covering his uniform. His sleeves were rolled up to his elbows, revealing corded forearms. Some of the blood was still streaked there, as well as on his face and neck, but it was clean for the most part. Almost as if he had scrubbed it off in a rush and missed a few areas.

"Are you—"

Eoin cut me off with a simple wave of his hand. "Fine, none of it is mine." Tension in my shoulders eased some.

"At least we killed it," I sighed, gaining more strength by the minute. I lifted the coverlet to peer at the damage. It was worse than I thought. A bandage wrapped around my lower abdomen and stopped just above my breasts. Warmth ignited across my cheeks. Aside from the coverlet, I was practically bare in front of the two men. Thank the gods somebody— Kalee, if I were to guess—had dressed the rest of me. Flowing lilac night pants replaced my tattered and bloodied trousers.

Everyone stared at me. The wince on Kalee's face made me uneasy.

"What is it?"

Finally, Ronan sighed, deep purple lining his under eyes. "There's been another attack. Another village, closer to the Eastern Coast. Another person of osnádúrthan descent drained into nothing.

I shuddered. "There was a moment when my magic felt like it slipped. Like the wolf was taking it away from me."

Ronan and Eoin exchanged a glance.

"By Eoin's account, whatever it was cannot be of this world. At least nothing we're familiar with."

"The chancellor, he has—"

Eoin placed a hand on my ankle. The coverlet remained between us. Still, the weight of his hand was so stunning that my words died on my tongue. My gaze dropped to his hand. Neither he nor I pulled away.

"I told Ronan about the tapestry you mentioned. You were right. The wolf was the same."

"And other animals and creatures I don't want to even think about." Ronan shuddered. "The problem is we still don't know *what* it is."

"At least we know who is behind it."

Ronan's gaze darkened. "I'm not counting my father out of this. The chancellor is his closest advisor. Whatever this is, it's likely they're in it together."

I nodded. I wouldn't have excluded the king either. Both of the men were equally horrifying. I looked up at Kalee; tears lined her warm amber eyes, making them almost glow. I couldn't recall seeing her so sad before.

"Are you alright?"

"I thought I'd lost you. I thought you were dead when Eoin carried you in. It's all my fault," she cried, her tears no longer restrained as they spilled out from her lids and streaked down her face. She wiped them from my forehead as they fell.

"It was my fault. I should have left you out of this," Ronan sighed. "Even tonight, it attacked you not far from the castle and shredded one of my men into ribbons. If Kalee had been with you, I—" He cleared his throat. To think other people have had to face those monstrous creatures was abhorrent enough. But if Kalee had been there as the prince suggested, I would have never forgiven myself.

"We need to figure out how to stop them," I said.

"First, I want to figure out exactly what manner of creature we are dealing with. Saoirse, thank you for helping us find the person behind this. We haven't made this much progress in months. As far as I'm concerned, you've fulfilled our bargain. You've nearly died doing so. The least I can do is get in touch with my contact to break your Bond."

Eoin gave Ronan an odd glance, but I was too stunned to think about what it meant. Break my Bond. Freedom. Which also meant leaving Kalee to deal with whatever these things were because something told me she wouldn't leave.

"I'd like to break my Bond more than anything, but let me also help where I can. At least while I heal." I bit the inside of my cheek. Guilt tugged at my insides. The thought of leaving Kalee behind was unsettling. But there was no place for me here in Centra once my Bond was broken.

"I would like that very much," Ronan smiled. "It will take a couple of weeks to reach my contact about the Bond. I'll see if I can find someone to help with this issue as well."

"Would the person breaking my Bond not be able to help?"

"No, I'm afraid not. This goes beyond their knowledge."

"Ronan—" Eoin warned, but the prince silenced him with a look.

"Where do we begin?" I asked. The sigh that left me was audible, and to my dismay, Ronan's smile only grew.

It began with bed rest. And reading, lots and lots of reading to try to discover what manner of creature we encountered. Dusty tomes, at Ronan's behest, which Kalee managed to get her hands on and smuggle back to my rooms. I picked through the pages Ronan marked for us, searching for any signs of the wolf from the forest.

Thanks to a well-trusted healer, I recovered quite nicely. The healers at the castle were rumored to carry magical remedies. How they were able to get their hands on some, I didn't know. But, looking down at the angry, red scar sliced from my navel to sternum only days after the attack, I believed it to be true. Whatever she applied to the wound worked.

The healer, Reana, went before the king and prince, informing them I was ill and required to remain in my chambers until the end of the week. Ronan knew the true reason, of course, but he played his part nonetheless. To my surprise, the king had only sent one of his servants to verify what Reana claimed. Unfortunately for the man, a stern Kalee met him at the door and threatened him with catching his death if he took a step inside. I could only imagine his shock before the door slammed in his face.

Eoin, however, managed to charm his way past Reana's sternness. He sat in the chair closest to my bedside, an ankle crossed over his knee as he flipped through frail pages. We exchanged fleeting glances, my cheeks growing warm every time our eyes locked. Any downtime Eoin had from his duties, he spent with me. There was something so familiar about him now that every time he was called away, I ached for his company.

Eoin shut his book, laying it carefully on the small table in front of him before coming to sit by my side. The mattress sank beneath his weight, his warmth radiating through the thick blankets.

"Are you alright, truly?"

I nodded. "Reana keeps saying my wound is healing nicely."

Eoin gave me a soft smile. "Reana is the best Centra has to offer. She's stitched me up more times than I can recall. But are *you* alright, Saoirse?"

I thought for a moment. The image of the wolf flashed in my mind. I'd been so scared. So sure it was going to kill me—to kill us. "I am alright," I said carefully. "I still see it sometimes in my dreams. Can still smell its breath or feel the weight of it on me."

Eoin grabbed my hand, and I let him hold it, his grip warm, rough, and comforting.

"What about you? You're the one who killed the thing," I said, squeezing his hand. I hadn't hesitated in attacking the wolf. Would have killed it myself if I needed to, but the cost of taking a life—even an otherworldly life—could have its toll.

"Have you ever felt like some choices burn themselves into you, yet you would make them over and over again despite knowing the cost? They create scars on your soul, but still, you choose it."

"Yes," I breathed. My memory flashed on osnádúrtha and smugglers alike.

"Then you know what it means to do what is necessary." Eoin's gaze locked onto mine. "I don't make choices I'll regret, Saoirse. I did what had to be done, and we're alive because of it."

I nodded. I didn't mourn the horrid beast, I was happy it was dead. Any concern I had for Eoin vanished. He was right. I shouldn't dwell on the life of a murder wolf. Especially not when it would have easily killed us and done the same to others. We shared a long look, searching for something I didn't know.

"Saoirse—" Eoin leaned in, only a hair's breadth away, and my pulse jumped. Eiric's face flashed in my mind. What we'd shared wasn't a soul connection, but I loved him nonetheless. He was one bright light in the darkness. We had bared ourselves to each other in every possible way. Would he feel betrayed or happy if my heart made room for another?

"Time to shoo, Eoin," Reana called from the main door, carrying a basket of supplies into the room. "My patient needs her bandages removed." Whatever connection between us dropped when Reana strolled in, and part of me was thankful for it.

Eoin checked the timepiece affixed to the wall. "I've got to get going anyway. I'll come by later?" He said it like he would a question. I nodded, receiving a kiss to my knuckles and a broad smile before he was gone, my thoughts lingering on him—my knuckles burned by his touch.

Reana, a slender woman in the middle of her life marked only by the wrinkles at the corners of her eyes and mouth, removed my bandages and applied another layer of a sickly sweet-smelling salve with deft hands.

"No need for any more bandages, lovey." Her accent was thick and rich. I couldn't place where it originated; I'd never heard anything like it before. "Use the rest of this salve twice daily to help with the scarring. It won't disappear completely, but the redness should dull some. You're lucky to be faie. If you were human, not even I could have healed you."

Reana's comment struck a nerve.

"Thank you for all your help—and your confidentiality." If the king ever discovered the truth behind my absence, it wouldn't be just my head on the chopping block.

Reana grabbed my hand and patted it gently, shooting me a grin of wicked delight. "Anytime, but try not to make a habit of it." She winked. I couldn't help but return her smile as she took her leave. I would miss her company.

I walked to the full-length mirror by the window and lifted my free-flowing shirt to reveal the misshapen scar. The afternoon light highlighted the worst parts of it. At least two finger widths in size at the widest part, it was jagged and horrid looking. I sustained more minor marks on my fore-arms, but those had already faded. No, this one would not disappear like the others, but it could be easily covered.

Lost in thought, I didn't hear Kalee come in until she gave a slight cough. Embarrassed, I shoved my shirt back down and offered an awkward smile.

"It doesn't look too bad," she tried. Bless her for her sweetness because it did look gruesome. My only answer was a slow blink.

"Okay, fine, it's not great, but it will fade more. And compared to what it was… it's not so bad."

"It'll be fine. It's not like anyone will see it anyway." I tried to shrug off how much it bothered me, but the ugliness of the scar was forever imprinted on my flesh, a reminder of the horror I'd faced. It didn't help that I wasn't too keen on my figure before an ugly scar sliced down my abdomen. Looking at the stack of books she carried in her arms, I changed the subject. "More dusty books from Ronan?"

She nodded with a sigh. "He has a knack for finding the truly dull ones, even for me." We scoured several books in the last few days over different types of wolves, dogs, and the like in search of something in resemblance to the beast Eoin and I faced in the forest. Much to our dismay, we found nothing. All books pertaining to magic were burned during the Reckoning. It was unlikely one of these would have anything on the creature, but it didn't hurt to look.

"Did you and Eoin have any luck today?" she asked. My cheeks warmed at the mention of his name.

"No, only the usual useless information."

I strolled over to her and took the one off the top of the stack she still held in her arms. It was a well-worn, thick tome, the title barely legible. Cobwebs still stretched over the cover and spine, entangling themselves in the fore-edge and text block. I blew out a swift breath of air onto the cover and wiped away the remaining grime, careful of its frail nature. *A History of the Gods* was scrawled out in faded, gilded cursive on the front. I turned it toward Kalee and raised a brow in silent question.

"He must be getting desperate." She shrugged, holding up a book titled *Children's Folklore and Legends*.

"Do you think it's from his personal collection?" I laughed, picturing the prince as a rambunctious toddler.

"It certainly looks well-loved," Kalee remarked, a smile tugging at her lips as she flipped through the worn pages.

Unsurprisingly, the *History of the Gods* was long and didn't supply any information I hadn't already known. It discussed the Mother and how she plucked a small kernel of magic from her own heart, forming the land around us—eventually creating other gods and goddesses to help tend to and enjoy the land she loved so dearly. But instead of crucifying the gods for their creations, it revered them.

Where had Ronan found this? Books speaking highly of all the gods' creations, including the osnádúrtha, were also burned in the Reckoning.

I studied the cover, looking for the author or any date for which the tome was scribed, but there was nothing. It was worn and ragged, but damn, how old could it be?

I skimmed over the illustrations positioned beside the texts. The Mother, her face long forgotten with her name, was pictured in an elegant cloak of various flowers and greenery, obscuring her face. Only her saccharine smile was visible underneath her hood. The Mother's nine most powerful children, who created humans and osnádúrtha alike, were depicted with ethereal beauty exuding grace and power. *The* Nine. I flipped through a few more pages before I paused on a familiar scene.

A perfect replication of the chancellor's tapestry.

Beside the image read, *The King of Shadows and his army of fomorii demons waged war against the gods as punishment for his years of neglect and abuse. With the humans and the osnádúrtha coming to their aid, the gods defeated them. Unable to be obliterated, the false king and his creations were banished to a realm of their making—a realm of shadows.*

I shuddered when I beheld the other illustrations, armies of shadow demons—fomorii as it referred to them. The creator of the demons who led the forces was a giant of a man. The army behind him was little more than a mass of swirling shadows taking various shapes. Most were humanoid, but others took on animalistic forms, resembling boars, goats, crows, and wolves. The glowing red eyes and the long, jagged, flesh-slicing teeth of the monster I met in the forest stared back at me. There it was. The monster from my nightmares. I looked between the illustration and my hands, at the shadows that always lingered there. My throat worked. I was different. My shadows were merely a coincidence. The wolf had been shadows given a physical form. I was *real*. My blood ran red, not black. My shadows were an accessory of me, not my entire being.

"Kalee…." I trailed off. I was at a loss for words as I brought the illustration to her on the settee with stacks of books surrounding her.

"Is that it?" she asked, eyes wide. She shuddered when I nodded. "Gods, that's terrifying," she said, flipping through the pages.

"What does this mean?" I asked. The book referred to creatures who prowled our world centuries ago before they were banished into another realm. How had they returned? The ember eyes of the illustration bore into my soul. I could almost feel the weight of the wolf on top of me—smell the carrion on its breath.

Kalee shook her head. "I'm not sure. Maybe Ronan will know how we proceed from here."

I barely escaped with my life against one. Two more attacks occurred since I'd been injured at opposite ends of Centra. They told us there was more than one more of those things prowling around. I shuddered to think what facing an entire pack would be like. And if there were other types of fomorii like the illustrations depicted…

"We know the chancellor and the king are involved. We'll find a way to stop them." Her back was straight, and her gaze leveled with mine—

not an ounce of uncertainty shown on her face. Fear? Yes, as there should have been, considering the information we uncovered. But there was no doubt about the need to find the source and protect innocent lives.

Chapter Sixteen

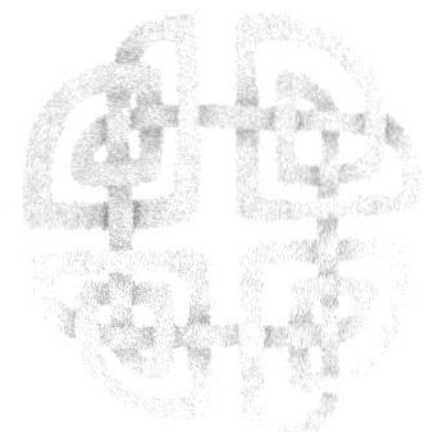

The tug on the Bond wasn't unexpected once my official bed rest period ended. I knew I would be punished for being out of commission in the week it took me to heal. I was, however, relieved the king had bought Reana's story of my illness. The nature of my injury would have been too suspicious for the king or chancellor to overlook.

To my surprise, Prince Ronan had burst into the throne room shortly after the king agreed to the chancellor's choice of punishment. Ronan argued he needed me in good health, and injuring me after I'd recovered would only serve to delay his use of me further. It hadn't been enough to stop my punishment, but the chancellor agreed to go *easy* on me.

I followed the chancellor to his office. Punishment was never easy, but at least we hadn't been compromised. That thought alone helped me stomach what would come next. The chancellor glanced back at me as we walked. Perhaps I looked too relieved. I wobbled my lower lip.

"Don't worry, Informer, I know how to not break you. I'll have you well enough to do as the prince wishes, but never fear, you will learn from your mistakes," the chancellor crooned.

My back straightened. Not at the chancellor's words, but at the sight of the Hunter walking toward us. His stride was quick and powerful, a murderous gleam in his eyes. I bit the inside of my cheek, refusing to meet his gaze as he passed, continuing on to the throne room.

Did the chancellor punish the Hunter as he did me? The Hunter was a hulking brute of a man. I couldn't picture him having to submit to anyone, much less the chancellor.

I'd learned from my mistake after my last lesson by dressing in an undergarment so low, it nearly reached the base of my spine. As I had many times before, I drifted out of my body while the chancellor took his favored cane to me, staring at the tapestry I now knew depicted the fomorii demons. The king hadn't had anything like this in his study, and I wondered how much the chancellor knew of the creatures woven behind his desk. It couldn't be a coincidence.

"Are you listening to me?" The chancellor asked. I grunted from the whack to my lower back, my knees buckling under the force. I'd lost track of how many times he hit me with the cane. My mind and body connected once more, and the throb in my aching back told me it was more than a few.

"Hasn't anyone taught you how rude it is to ignore your superior?" He sneered. His hot breath crawled across my neck.

"Sorry," I muttered in a voice I didn't recognize.

The chancellor pulled away, throwing his cane to the ground. I relaxed a fraction at the sound of its clatter. I didn't move, however. That was a mistake I wouldn't make again.

"This should remind you." The chancellor gave me no warning before pressing a hot iron poker against my shoulder. Agony ripped through every nerve ending, my scream nearly animalistic. The skin of my back split and sizzled. Burning flesh permeated the air, filling my nostrils until I was sick. I couldn't hold it back. Vomit rose and spilled onto the chancellor's desk.

"You little bitch," the chancellor spat as I shook in my own retch. "You will either hold yourself together, or I'll keep going until you're unconscious." The chancellor pulled the poker from the fire again, and it took everything in me not to beg for mercy.

A knock at the door interrupted him. The heat of the poker whispered at my back.

The chancellor set the poker in the fire and flung the door open, sweat dripping down his face. "What?"

I remained where I was over his desk, hiding my face in my trembling arms.

"His Majesty requests your presence," the Hunter said from the doorway.

I peered at him, our eyes locking for a moment before I turned away, embarrassed. His gaze still held a murderous gleam about them, but I wasn't sure it ever left. It wasn't the first time the Hunter found me in the chancellor's office, but he'd never seen me in such a state before. At least I hadn't pissed myself. Once, I'd overheard the guards talking about how the chancellor had made another Bonded do that before.

"Tell him I'll be a moment."

"He requested you immediately."

"Very well," he ground out. "Get out of my sight, Informer."

I gathered my things as quickly as I could and pulled my cloak around me, everything aching. I didn't look at either of them on the way out, though the Hunter's scrutinizing gaze burned into the back of my head as I left. Let him think whatever he wished. It's not like he cared for anyone but himself.

My steps were stiff as Eoin, Kalee, and I traveled through the labyrinth of the Underground the following day. Kalee suggested we postpone our investigations another day or two to let me rest, but I was tired of doing nothing, and I desperately needed to get out of the castle. If I were gone, the chancellor couldn't pick up where he was forced to leave off.

We walked down the main tunnel. Each extension off the carved path displayed a small symbol above the entrances I hadn't noticed before. The markings were iridescent glimmers in the torchlight. They appeared to be an indicator of where the tunnel led. One of the symbols was a singular diamond—perhaps it carried on toward Ralph at Precious Emblems.

"Where are we going?" I asked as we passed the diamond symbol. Eoin hadn't given us much information when he found Kalee and me in the garden, and hadn't said much since we descended through the secret alley entrance.

"To meet with Ronan. He believes he found someone who can tell us more about the fomorii," Eoin replied, keeping his gaze forward as he led us on.

"Who?" I asked as a rat scurried across the tunnel floor. Kalee jumped toward me, her shriek drowning out my question.

Nonetheless, Eoin replied, unfazed by the rodent and the echo of Kalee's scream, "A seer."

His disgruntled voice told me everything the back of his head didn't. Seers were notorious for either withholding vital information or telling entirely too much. Even when magic flourished throughout the land, most avoided seers at all costs—too afraid of meeting an untimely demise or going mad. Only the desperate sought them out. I never thought I'd be one of them. Ronan must be out of options.

"Is there no one else?" I asked anyway, Kalee's hand gripping my elbow.

"Apparently not." The muscles in Eoin's jaw tightened.

"I thought they all fled before the Reckoning?" *Without warning anyone else* is what I didn't add.

"Most of them did. This one remained here. How the seer's gone unnoticed by the king, I don't know." Eoin paused at one of the tunnels, a strange symbol reminiscent of a tree above the entrance.

"Why do we have to go? Ronan is the one desperate enough to get guidance from a seer."

Kalee nudged me in the ribs with her elbow.

"There is a better chance of the Crown Prince leaving with his sanity if the seer has more than one person to focus on." Eoin turned toward us. "For the record, I was against this inane plan, but unfortunately, I was outranked, and my opinion, apparently, means nothing."

I glanced sidelong at Kalee. She only shrugged in response, though the tension in Eoin's voice was unmistakable.

"Did you know about this?" I whispered.

"No," she said. "Even for Ronan, this is a bit extreme."

"Kalee, perhaps you should stay behind. Surely Eoin and I can handle this."

"Don't even try, Sersh. I already told Ronan I would do whatever I needed to help you. Neither you nor he can convince me otherwise."

I grumbled but said nothing more about her decision.

When we arrived at the end of the tunnel, the stone path became dirt once more as we ascended. There was no ladder this time, but a gradual incline as we approached a wooden door. When Eoin was satisfied we wouldn't run into unwanted company, he held it open for Kalee and me.

We emerged from what appeared to be the inside of a tree. Passing through the trunk, a strong, woodsy scent filled my nostrils, reminding me of the village I used to live in with my mother. I shielded my eyes with my hand, the sunlight nearly blinding me after being underground for so long. Like the trapdoor in the jewelry shop, the door disappeared when Eoin shut it into the trunk behind us—nothing more than an unassuming tree.

"How—?" I started.

"Witch magic," Ronan answered, waiting for us along with two horses. Instead of his usual, glittering gold attire, he wore a nondescript gray tunic and black trousers.

"Yes, but this is…intricate." It must have been around for centuries before witches secluded themselves in Ilythia because no single witch could accomplish this alone. The tunnels of the Underground seemed to branch out throughout Rothcek and beyond. It would have taken decades of skilled work.

Ronan only shrugged as he handed one of the horse's reins to Eoin and lifted Kalee up on their horse. Without her skirts, she might have made it on her own, her height working to her advantage. But the women of Centra were expected to dress as if they had nothing better to do than sit and look pretty all day—even the servants fought the frills of their petticoats. I, however, didn't have to worry about such problems with my trousers. As a Bonded, I wasn't regarded as anything but a tool to be used. The king didn't need me to look beautiful when I was meant to stay out of sight.

Eoin held out a hand, waiting for me expectantly.

"I guess the seer couldn't have lived within walking distance?" I quipped with a bravado I didn't feel, avoiding the horse's gaze.

Ronan smirked. "It's odd, really, for someone who would become imprisoned to be so secluded."

Clenching my fists, I moved toward the animal—if it wasn't so deadly, it might have been beautiful with all its speckled spots.

"My promise still stands, Saoirse, you are safe with me," Eoin murmured so only I would hear.

I nodded and accepted Eoin's offer of help. Even if I could mount the horse myself, I didn't trust it not to move just to watch me fall. Not that I minded the excuse for us to be so close. I tried not to think about where Eoin's hands gripped my waist as he lifted me with ease, my heart racing so fast I worried he would notice. His touch burned through my winter clothing long after he released me. Embarrassment threatened to take over.

Instead, I focused on the forest coming alive around us. Definitely not on Eoin's body heat at my back or the way his muscular arms surrounded me. Not on the way his legs, astride mine, lingered against me every so often. Much less how *safe* I felt with him at my back.

No, definitely not that.

I focused on the small animals scurrying about the forest floor and on the back of Ronan's blonde head, where he and Kalee rode ahead of us. I focused anywhere except the man who sat behind me and the beast of an animal under me.

"I'm sorry I was so terse earlier," Eoin said, so close his breath tickled the back of my neck exposed by my braided coronet. I barely managed to repress a shiver. "Ronan makes me so frustrated when he refuses to listen or see reason."

"I can understand. You care for him and don't want to see him get hurt."

"I'm very protective of the people I care for."

Either I was imagining it, or his arms tightened around me. My breath caught. Was I now someone he deemed worthy of protection? He saved me from the fomorii wolf. Granted, he needed me and my skill set. I was only useful to Ronan alive, and yet…he sat with me every spare moment he had while I healed. Read with me. Laughed with me. Distracted me from the pain and entertained me when Kalee had other duties to attend to. I found myself wanting to be part of those deemed worthy of his protection. I thought of Eiric and the way I somehow found safety with him. I wanted it again.

"We're nearly there," Ronan called, pulling me from my thoughts.

The forest changed; the liveliness was no longer present. Only the crunch of hooves on dead leaves and crusted snow sounded. Encircled in a grove of trees was a small, dilapidated cottage. Wind chimes tinkled on an eerie breeze as we grew nearer. The prince's horse halted at the tree line.

"Looks like we're on foot from here," Ronan said, dismounting, then helping Kalee out of the saddle. Eoin did the same, and I found comfort in his touch—entranced and disturbed by our surroundings. "You all can stay here if you want. I can take this risk by myself."

"No," Eoin cut in. "I already told you the only way we're doing this is if we go with you."

"Speak for yourself," I muttered, and Eoin shot me a look.

"I'm going with you, Ronan," Kalee said, grabbing his hand.

"Fine," I sighed. "Yes, yes, I am with you, too. Let's rally around the prince who dares to dance with the unknown."

Ronan grinned, and I found myself smiling back at him despite the uncertainty before us.

"Prepare yourselves," Ronan warned. "A seer does not give information freely. It all comes at a price, and rarely is it coin. Whatever bargain we strike, we must adhere to it, or the consequences could be devastating."

"What would happen?" Kalee asked, looking more intrigued than nervous.

"I don't know. Seers are…complicated beings." Ronan's brow furrowed. "They were once witches whose power grew too great. Some can contain it. Others, like this one, reached a point where the magic consumed their soul. They are nothing more than a vessel through which the gods speak in the form of visions from the past, present, and future. Sometimes, seers are prone to benevolence; other times, they have more malicious intentions, depending on which gods speak with them. Repercussions of breaking or unfulfilling a bargain could be as simple as having bad luck until the bargain is complete, or it could be more catastrophic."

"Like?" Kalee's eyes grew wide with anticipation.

"Death," I answered. "Any bargain made in magic could end in demise if anyone involved leaves it unfulfilled."

"Which is why I'll be doing the bargaining. Be careful what you say." Ronan paused to look us all in the eye. "Or better yet, don't say anything at all." He flashed a princely smile and led us toward the cottage.

Kalee held Ronan's hand as we walked up the path. It felt wrong to disturb the loose stones—every inch of my body begged to turn around and never come back. Eoin stepped closer, one hand on the hilt of his sword, the other on my back. Mine found my daggers, their leather grips cool to the touch. Without having to knock, the door opened on a long creak.

"Royalty enters my home," a voice, somehow both young and old, male and female, sounded from inside the room when we entered.

Chapter Seventeen

The cottage was in disarray. Baubles of every size, shape, and color hung from the rafters like the bursting buds of catkins drooping from branches. Decanters and vials of strange liquids occupied every available counter space—something moldy with an underlying sweetness tinged the air. The seer sat cross-legged on the only furniture in the room, a straw mattress covered in a multitude of furs.

"Curious," the seer said, tilting its head. Exposed by the woolen cloak, the seer's skin was white as ash, excluding their fingers and lips, which were the deepest ebony. Inky veins crept from their fingers and up to their forearms. Their eyes were mismatched—one black, the other white.

Ronan walked toward the seer, careful not to disturb the odd artifacts scattered about the room.

A mischievous smile spread across the seer's face, revealing sable teeth. "What do you seek, prince? Come to find out how to save your sister from her prison? Or do you seek the truth behind your mother's death?"

The seer's heterochromatic eyes bore into me. "Or you, shadow? Do you wish to learn about from whom your magic derives?"

No aes sídhe or merrow could pinpoint which god their magic came from, only that it was from one of the many. After the Nine, there were dozens of gods, all with similar or varying magic, their names lost to the centuries. It never bothered me not knowing where my magic stemmed from because it was impossible to know without a doubt. But now, I found myself desperately needing to know the answer, no matter the cost. Something in my gut tugged as if trying to pull me to my knees and beg. Words formed on my tongue to offer up whatever the seer wanted. Eoin stepped in front of me, and the feeling vanished. I blinked, the haze of whatever magic the seer wielded dissipating.

"Enough," Ronan cut the seer off, "I wish to know about the fomorii attacking throughout Centra."

The seer laughed—a horrible, maniacal sound. "If what you seek is answers, then you must give me answers in return."

"A question for a question?" Ronan asked.

"It's as simple as that."

"Then we have a deal." They shook hands, sealing their bargain with a twisted smile from the seer. "How are the fomorii here in this realm?" Ronan asked.

"Shadow demons derived from the banished one are slipping through the cracks of the realm through stolen magic."

My heart raced, my thoughts drifting to the petrified remains of the fomorii victims Eoin had described. Eoin's shoulders tensed, and I wondered if he'd come to the same conclusion.

"Why are they back?"

"The answer is the same now as it was centuries ago. To deliver a vengeful king's wrath against the gods. Their goal today remains the same—to free their master." The seer looked between us, his gaze narrowing on Eoin, then Kalee, and finally, me as I peered around Eoin's broad form. Again, the need to ask the seer bubbled on my tongue.

"You mean the King of Shadows?" Ronan asked, catching the seer's attention.

"Yes. Tenebris, King of Shadows. God of Darkness. He bears many names," the seer clarified. I shifted from one foot to the other, tucking my hands behind my back to hide the shadows swimming along my fingertips.

"But he was banished to the Shadow Realm," Ronan countered, his brows furrowing, my need for answers gone.

The seer spoke to Ronan but turned his eyes to Kalee. "Banished does not mean dead, prince. The Shadow King seeks to return to this world once more to finish what he started."

"Is the Shadow Realm real?" Kalee asked, and I elbowed her in the ribs, hoping to pull her out of whatever trance the seer held her in. Ronan's fair skin lost what little color it had, looking sidelong at Kalee.

The stipulations of the bargain were unnamed, and now, with Kalee asking her own question, she could be dragged into it as well.

"Do not act surprised, girl. For you know there are other realms coexisting with our own—we coined the term Otherworld, but it is one of many. Unless one knows how to walk between realms, our souls are bound here until our mortal bodies fail us and we move on to the next, born anew. There is one realm the gods favored and another they built for Tenebris. His prison for all eternity."

"And if he manages to free himself?" Ronan challenged.

"He will seek to enact his revenge against the gods by destroying that which they created and taking the realms for himself," the seer replied evenly as if they hadn't just mentioned the ending of everything.

The air grew stagnant. If Tenebris wanted to overrun this world and the other realms, then this was a much bigger conflict than we initially thought. The look on Ronan's face told me he was not prepared for this answer. Eoin's brow furrowed. Ever the soldier, calculating ways to deal with a new threat.

"How do we stop him?" Ronan asked, his voice soft.

The seer ignored him and turned to me once more, eyeing the steady swirls of silver crawling up my neck and twisting on my hands. "What an unusual gift you have. How unfortunate it is suppressed—and will die if time runs out."

"What do you mean?" I stuttered, unable to prevent myself from asking the question.

"You're on borrowed time, girl," the seer warned.

"How much time?" I nearly choked on a bitter laugh. The gods were cruel. My freedom was closer than ever, yet I was destined to die an early death.

"That is entirely up to you. You will not see past your next name day if things continue as they are. But, if you break your bonds and accept your Fate, your time could be insurmountable."

Kalee and I shared a look; my twenty-fifth name day was less than two months away.

"My Fate?" I choked. My only Fate was to serve the king through the Bond until he killed me. And if by some miracle Ronan managed to break my Bond, all I wanted was to live a quiet life. The image of my imaginary bookshop flashed through my mind.

"The magical bond is not the only thing binding you, girl," the seer warned as if reading my thoughts. A chill ran across my skin.

"We're already trying to break her Bond," Ronan interjected.

"You will fail, prince," the seer said matter-of-factly.

"How so?" Ronan eyed me curiously. Eoin stared at me, unblinking, as Kalee grabbed my hand and squeezed.

"Your father's Bonded are bound through unnatural circumstances. Have you ever heard of a human's soul connected to another like osnádúrtha are to their mates?" The seer smiled, and when Ronan shook his head, they continued, "I didn't think so. The Bonds are created through dark magic—an imitation of a mating bond. Only the Cauldron of Power will be enough to release anyone who is Bound to the Conqueror King. No witch, no matter how powerful, can do it alone. The cauldron is your answer."

"Cauldron?" I asked, but the seer only smiled at Ronan, their rotten teeth on full display.

"Impossible," Ronan scoffed. "It is a child's tale."

"Impossible, like a sole-surviving witch in a kingdom where magic-wielders are constantly hunted? How have they managed to escape their sisters in the West all this time? Or the Conqueror King, for that matter?" the seer mused. My ears perked up. This must have been the person Ronan had planned to break my Bond. But a witch hiding in Centra? The idea was almost unheard of. Witches were notorious for keeping with their covens.

"Answer what I asked of you. How do we stop him?" Ronan's voice was little more than a quiet anger. Kalee shifted next to me.

"You play a game that started long ago. One in which its players had been removed from this plane. Now, one of those players is looking to get back on the board. Tell me, have you heard the tale of The Serpent and the Sparrow?"

All of us exchanged glances. "No," I answered, shaking my head.

The seer looked horrifically gleeful. "There once was a cunning, ambitious serpent who held grand delusions of reshaping the world and balancing the scales of power. But over time, its good intentions turned sour. For you see, the serpent's strength and magic came at a cost, having to shed its skin over and over again, until it started to become the thing it hated most. Then one day, a sparrow flew into the serpent's den. Despite the warnings, the sparrow still took a chance, and for a time, the serpent's story was written in another pen. That is, until the serpent's true nature overshadowed its heart. Too entwined in the throes of power, the serpent risked everything it once loved to which it did depart. In retaliation, the sparrow aided the very forces he attempted to defeat and cursed the serpent for its wickedness against them. For you see, the serpent sacrificed its own children to create its name. It sought revenge against the gods and so, a god it became."

"What was the curse?" I whispered.

"His immortality would fail him at the hands of his children."

"But if he killed them all, then he cannot be killed." Ronan frowned.

The seer gave a gleeful laugh. "It would seem that way, yes. And even still, it takes a weapon forged by a god to kill another god."

"Enough with the fairytales. Can you give us any useful information?" Eoin demanded.

The seer flashed their sable teeth again, delighting in our frustrations. "Come closer, girl, let me touch you," the seer beckoned.

Eoin put a hand on my shoulder to stop me, but I wrenched free from his grip. My feet had a mind of their own—compelled either by magic or my own curiosity. The seer placed a cracked, blackened hand on my forehead, their hand chilling me to the bone. Nothing happened at first, but then, a second later, a bright light flashed. I tried to turn and shield myself, but I couldn't move. I stood frozen until my sight adjusted.

I blinked away the vestiges of the haze, and I was no longer in the seer's cottage. Instead, I stood in a home. A fire crackled in the hearth—a small cauldron bubbled over it, its contents sweet in my nostrils. Colorful quilts draped over a rocking chair occupied by a woman with raven hair.

"Hello? Where am I?" I asked, but the words went unanswered. Maybe she couldn't hear. I put a hand on her shoulder so as not to startle her, but it went right through her. I reared back. Was I some sort of specter? I examined my hands, which were whole but held a faint glow about them. The woman's gaze remained fixed on the hearth, stirring the contents of the cauldron every so often. Still, she did not acknowledge me when I stood before her. It was as if I didn't exist. Panic started to creep its way in.

A soft knock rapped at the door, and the woman rose to answer it. Her visitor wore a thick cloak of a purple so deep it was almost black. Neither of them noticed my presence. I thought I'd finally lost my mind until the guest removed her hood.

It was me. But not. The woman appeared to be years older than me, but we shared the same silver hair and sapphire eyes. My chest ached, and my vision blurred as I beheld my mother for the first time in fifteen years. I hated myself for not recognizing her immediately. The cruel curse of time blurred those little details like the crinkles around her eyes when she smiled or the vibrance of her demeanor. Those lovely things were not on display for long, however. They were quickly replaced by concern and desperation.

"Racenda, you made it," the middle-aged woman said, holding out her arms.

My mother handed her the bundle of cloth. "It was not easy, Aislinn, but we managed."

The cloth cooed as she transferred it to Aislinn. Silver hair peeked from the uncovered head. A baby. *Me.*

"Aislinn, may I present my daughter, Saoirse Aíne Órlaith."

A lump formed in my throat. I hadn't heard my full name in so long I'd nearly forgotten it.

"She looks like you. Her poor father must be so disappointed," Aislinn joked.

My breath caught. I loved that I looked like my mother, but now, my heart ached learning I didn't resemble the father I'd never known.

"He'll recover. Bran is practically his replica. At least now, I can say one of my children finally resembles me." The crinkles around her eyes became visible once more—tears blurred my vision.

A brother. *Bran.* My mother told me of my father's fate but had never said anything about a brother. The shaking in my hands grew uncontrollable as did my shadows, though I doubted they could do anything for me in this place. Why had she not told me about my brother? Was he still alive? If she lied about Bran, did she lie about my father as well? There were so many questions, but those who had the answers couldn't hear me.

The two women stood next to the simmering cauldron, the sickly sweet smell almost overwhelming now. "Is the potion ready?" my mother asked, holding me tighter.

"Nearly." Aislinn—a witch—stirred the contents of the cauldron clockwise. "Are you sure you want to do this? You know better than anyone, magic is not given freely."

"I am aware and prepared to give it, no matter the cost."

Aislinn's lips thinned. "For what you are asking, the price will be steep. To ensure her safety for the first twenty-five years of her life, to make sure death will not come early for her, it will cost twenty-five years of your own."

My mother looked down at me, still cradled in her arms, and stroked my head. A single tear fell from her, but her voice did not waver when she said, "I know."

Twenty-five years would have been nothing to my faie father, as our lifespans are much longer than a human's. But a human? What if *I* was the reason she died before her time? Not only was I unable to save her, but I was also the catalyst. Breathing became difficult.

My mother drank the yellow potion before feeding me mine. Her face contorted at the taste, but there were no other signs that anything had happened. She turned with me in her arms, taking her leave, when Aislinn grabbed her shoulder.

"Please, Racenda. Stay with me. I am sure I can find a place for you and your daughter in the coven. Petra may be unhappy about it at first. But she will understand when she realizes yours and the baby's safety is at risk."

My mother shook her head. "I appreciate the offer, Aislinn, but you know how she is. Besides, Zephyr and I made a plan. I will remain in Centra until the trouble in Arundell settles down. Zephyr doesn't foresee it lasting long. Centra is a peaceful territory, and Tara will be close by to look after us." She patted the witch's arm. "We will be fine. The Louths will be there with me. I will try to send word once we are there."

The Louths were our neighbors. I remembered their blonde-headed boy who loved to chase me. He was one of the many friends I had in the village. His broken body was so small next to his parents' when the king's soldier cut them down.

"Be safe, sister." Aislinn embraced my mother, hugging the two of us tightly.

Chapter Eighteen

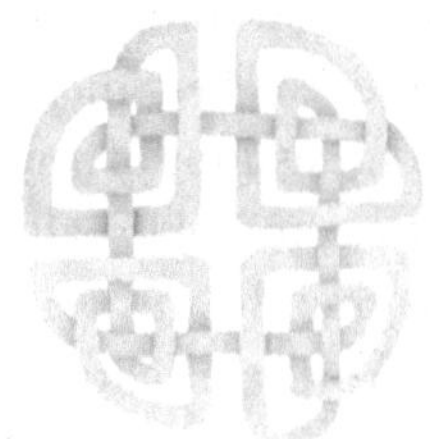

The memory ended, and I was once again back in the seer's cottage, collapsing to the floor. Kalee and Eoin rushed toward me, helping me back to my feet, but standing was too difficult. My limbs were heavy as the images of reality crinkled in, and I struggled to stand on my own while fighting against the wave of nausea. Eoin pulled me closer, letting me lean against him for support. To my surprise, the hardness of his uniform—the golden chest plate of the king's symbol I despised so much—was something I wasn't immediately repulsed by.

The seer still sat before us, their wild eyes full of mischief, glee, and something I couldn't quite place. Was that hope mingled in or something else?

"Did you see?" the seer asked expectedly.

"Yes," I panted.

"But did you *see?*"

"Yes, for gods' sakes, I saw," I snapped. Everything I'd ever known was a carefully crafted lie. I had an aunt. A brother. A father who could still live. My mother wasn't a human but a witch. My brows furrowed. I couldn't have been born of both witch and faie bloodlines. The idea was unheard of. I shook out the thought. Perhaps my mother hadn't inherited the witch gene. Of course, the witch gene not passing down the female line was practically impossible, but I chose to live in my delusion for a little while longer.

Whatever the case, it didn't change the fact that my mother deceived me into thinking my father died on a merchant vessel, lost at sea—that we originated from Centra and not Arundell. Who he was, why she left him, and why my brother still remained, were a mystery. As was the reason behind the protection spell. My mother had been my everything, and now, I wasn't sure if I knew who she was anymore.

"We're done here," Eoin said, shuffling me to the door.

"Ah—not so fast. Would you dare go back on a bargain with a seer?"

"No, we wouldn't," Ronan answered, shooting Eoin a glare.

"I didn't think so," the seer sucked their teeth. "By my recollection, you owe me fifteen answers to questions of my choosing."

My head swam trying to remember all we had asked. For an all-knowing being, I couldn't imagine the answers the seer sought.

"Six," Ronan corrected, "You've already asked questions of your own, and four of ours went unanswered."

The seer smiled, a horrible, wicked sight I didn't think I would ever get used to. "Eight questions. What you refer to has already been answered. It isn't my fault you weren't paying attention and three of mine were left unresolved, unless you would like to settle them now?"

"No, I wouldn't. One down, seven to go." Ronan smirked.

"Does your father know what you are?"

"No," he ground out, though, in my opinion, the answer was obvious. Ronan wouldn't be standing before us if he did. The Conqueror King would kill Ronan if he'd ever uncovered his smuggling operations.

"How have you been able to hide it for so long? I suspect your father would have noticed a traitor in his own house."

"My mother taught me how to keep things from him, to control my emotions long ago." Ronan's jaw muscles flickered—the only sign of his irritation. I imagined Ronan had plenty of practice keeping his composure at court if their views were so polarizing. It was easy to understand why the prince kept his true thoughts to himself, but part of me wondered if he'd ever try to reason with his father. Of course, that meant the Conqueror King would have to be a reasonable man.

"How does it feel to walk freely while Ceana remains caged?"

Ronan's fists clenched at his sides. "Guilt hangs heavy in my heart every second of every day since my sister has been condemned to her tower."

"Why?"

"Because I couldn't protect her from him."

Ronan never talked about his sister before. However, she was easy to forget. The princess never made an appearance, always too sickly to venture out of her room. Why would a princess need protection?

"Do you intend to free her from her confines?" The seer asked.

"Yes."

"If you succeed, prince, I want you to bring her to me."

Ronan's jaw ticked again. I could tell he itched to ask the seer why, but doing so would only prolong our visit. Instead, he said, "Not a chance."

"Deny me all you like, but you'll see. And when you do, you'll need help. Ceana will need help. I am prepared to give it freely." The seer splayed out their hands.

"Nothing is given freely," Ronan spat bitterly.

"Live in your disbelief, Prince Ronan. One day, you will remember this moment and wish you'd taken my offer sooner. As a show of good faith, I will forgo my remaining questions if you agree to consider bringing her to me when the time is right."

My brows lifted, but I kept my gaze trained on Ronan.

"I will not take my sister from one captor to another," he said softly.

"I said nothing about being a captor. I merely ask that you *consider* the notion. You are not obligated to bring her, but you will appreciate my offer when the time comes. Deal?" The seer's voice grew irritated. Whatever they wanted with Ceana couldn't be good if they were this desperate to get their hands on her. But why would a seer want anything to do with the princess?

Kalee and Ronan shared a look, communicating in silence. I knew that look; I'd seen it on her many times before. Sheer resolve and determination.

"Deal."

"Now, we're leaving," Eoin ground out, applying pressure to my back.

The seer hissed at him and grabbed my arm with a firm hand.

"Remember, girl, there is no life without death and no death without life. You must get to the cauldron first if there is a hope to defeat Tenebs," the seer said before releasing me.

"You shouldn't have done that," Eoin said as we followed Ronan and Kalee back to the Underground. Our pace was slower than before, the weight of what we learned heavier than our innocence.

"What?" I asked, my brows knitting together. "Letting the seer touch me?"

"You don't know what it could have done to you, Saoirse. You need to be more careful."

"I am not a child, Eoin. I'm perfectly capable of handling myself."

Eoin gave me a disapproving frown but said nothing else on the matter.

Ronan didn't wear his usual lopsided smile as we traveled down the road, our horses trotting along side-by-side, happy to put distance between us and the seer's cottage. It was odd to see the prince slip from his usual casual demeanor.

"Ronan," I called. Kalee raised a brow. I'd yet to address the prince by his first name. Prince Ronan ignored me.

"Ronan," I called again, louder, this time pulling him from his thoughts. "I'm sorry about your sister." I didn't know the extent of her entrapment, but the look on Ronan's face told me it couldn't be good.

We stared at one another. Ronan looked so tired and...scared. Was this the true face of the prince? Living in constant fear of his father and terrified of the fate of his sister?

"Thank you." Composing himself, the prince's mask slid on once more, again the calm royal everyone expected him to be.

"What do you know about the cauldron the seer referred to?" I asked. Prince Ronan was a man of many secrets. I could sympathize with him about his sister, but he was still withholding information about the cauldron. When the seer mentioned it, something had sparked in him, though he did his best to hide it.

"What is there to know? It's a myth—a children's tale. It doesn't exist. Or so I thought," Ronan sighed. "Supposedly, it belonged to the Nine and was gifted to the witches. It would be impossible to find."

It was unlikely the cauldron in the memory was the same. Since Aislinn was a witch, she might know where to find it. Assuming she'd be willing to assist us—she was my aunt after all. She acted as if she cared for my mother and me when I was a babe.

"Do you know of a witch named Aislinn?" I asked when no one offered any other solutions. I hadn't mentioned what the seer had shown me, and I didn't want to share all the details. But if this brought us closer to finding the cauldron, I had no choice but to hand over this pebble of information.

"I don't know anyone by that name," Ronan replied. Kalee and Eoin both shook their heads.

"Why do you ask?" Eoin questioned.

"When the seer touched me, I was shown a memory...of a witch named Aislinn helping my mother."

"Helping her with what?"

"The details are still unclear," I answered truthfully, "but the seer had to have shown me this for a reason."

"Can you ask your mother instead?" Eoin asked.

"No." My jaw twitched reflexively.

"We don't have to get her involved in any of this, we can—"

"We cannot ask her because she is dead." I cut Eoin off. I turned my head so they couldn't read my pained expression.

"I'm sorry," Ronan murmured.

And just like that, the guilt and anger always sitting below the surface rose once more. It broke free of its confines, threatening to take me out altogether, holding me in its grasp until I suffocated. All sympathy I'd harbored toward Ronan withered away. I was working with the man whose father practically killed my mother.

"Are you?" I couldn't help but snap.

"Yes. And I am working daily to ensure nothing like that ever happens again. The information the seer divulged is...complicated at best. But I will not break my promise to you, Saoirse." Ronan's eyes bore into my soul. The guilt lessened its hold on me by a fraction. I had to believe him. For my sake, I had to trust what he said was true and that he would end the Bondings altogether.

"Saoirse, all we want is for you to be free of your Bond and live," Kalee added, her voice soft as if she spoke to a wounded animal.

"We need to track down Aislinn. As of now, she is our only link to the cauldron itself," I said firmly, confident this was the direction the seer wanted us to take. "Unless your witch friend in Centra can help us?"

"No," Ronan answered a little too quickly.

"Why not?"

"I assure you, they know little about Ilythia. There is a reason they reside in Centra."

I frowned. What type of witch didn't know anything about their homeland?

"How are we supposed to track down someone we know nothing about?" Kalee asked, turning the subject back to Aislinn.

"I have an idea." Ronan winced. "I'm not sure any of you will like it."

Everyone grew quiet. Even the horses silenced themselves, waiting to hear what the prince would say next.

"Just tell us," I sighed. I was beginning to realize I wasn't too fond of most of the prince's ideas.

"The Hunter."

"No," Eoin and I said in unison.

"We have a place to start. This Aislinn likely resides in Ilythia," Kalee added.

"We have a general direction, yes. But the witch kingdom is unknown territory. Not even my father has a map of Ilythia. If anyone can track down someone we know nothing about in a *place* we know nothing about, it would be him."

"The Hunter sought your father out to become one of his Bonded. He knew he would be forced to find the osnádúrtha and bring them to slaughter. He is a sadist and cannot be trusted," I ground out, my teeth aching.

The Hunter was the last person who needed information on what might be my only living family. He excelled at getting under my skin. Not to mention the damage he could inflict with such knowledge.

"I have to agree with Saoirse," Eoin chimed in.

"We can't be certain the Hunter won't run back to the king and get us killed or use it against us for his own purposes," Kalee said. "He has the potential to ruin everything we've been working toward."

Ronan rubbed his jaw. "The Hunter doesn't *have* to know anything. As the prince, I am entitled to use the Bonded as I see fit. All we need is her location. He wouldn't have to know our true purposes for seeking her."

"It's not worth the risk," Eoin said. "There are more than our lives at stake. What if your father learns about this cauldron?"

"Which is precisely why we must find it first. If the cauldron does exist, then it is powerful enough to remove my father from his seat and put an end to the Bondings altogether. We mustn't dally. The Hunter is the only one with the capabilities to do what we need."

"How do you expect to use him without your father being suspicious of our intentions?" Eoin raised a brow. "It was not difficult to do so with Saoirse, but the Hunter is a different story. There is no way your father would allow you to use both of his prized Bonded, especially when you have never asked to use them before."

"Logistics, dear Eoin. You let me handle my father." Ronan waved him off.

Eoin gave me an exasperated look as if to say, *See? This is what I have to deal with.*

"Alright," Eoin finally conceded, crossing his arms. "But I don't want the Hunter out of my sight."

"Then it is done." Ronan grinned from ear to ear. "Eoin, you and I will accompany the Hunter as he tracks down Aislinn. When we receive the information we need, we'll send him back to the castle. Once the Hunter is out of our hair, we'll bring Saoirse to the cauldron and break her Bond. As for the threat of the Shadow King...the cauldron should help us with that, too, since it was crafted by the gods. Perhaps this Aislinn might be able to shed more light on the situation. For now, we pretend as if nothing has happened." Ronan looked toward me. "I'll retrieve you when this whole Hunter fiasco is over."

My mind whirled as we halted before the entrance to the Underground where we would part ways. Eoin, Kalee, and I would go to Precious Emblems like before. Ronan would take another route. If we left now, I knew what lay ahead. I would continue on as the king's Informer. Continue to let the fate of my life depend on others while I would be forced to work against my people.

I was done letting others dictate what I do. My mother risked her life so I might *live*. My life now was far from it. Besides, if I had this so-called protection spell, I might as well take advantage of it.

"Wait," I said before I could contemplate my following words. "I want to go, too."

"No," Eoin ordered, but Ronan furrowed his brows, waiting for an explanation.

"Aislinn is my aunt," I confessed. "If we are to find her, I want to meet her." The words were heavy on my tongue as if speaking of her, acknowledging her, and she would slip away. I'd already lost so much, but maybe this was my chance to gain more than my freedom.

Kalee gasped at my words but did not object to my request. She knew how much this would mean to me.

"We can find her without you, and I will take you to her later," Eoin suggested.

I forced myself not to scoff. "No. There might not be enough time. We can't be certain she knows where the cauldron is, much less what we need to do to use it. Besides, you heard the seer. My death quickly approaches. I won't waste an opportunity to meet the only family I have left."

I tried not to think about my alleged brother, Bran, or the possibility of my father being alive. I couldn't allow myself to get my hopes up. Not yet.

"Alright. You may accompany us. I will ensure your presence will not be suspicious to my father… We can make it work," Ronan said, more so to himself—a plan hatching behind his ocean eyes.

This was it, then. This was the moment I'd been waiting fifteen years for. For countless nights, I prayed to gods who didn't listen or care that I might one day step foot outside of Centra. That I might be free and have a family again. I didn't believe in Fate or destiny or the graciousness of the gods. But I believed in Kalee. In the determination swirling behind those eyes of liquid honey. I believed in the trust she had in her prince. And, oddly enough, I believed in his word.

And maybe, by some miracle, I'd live to see past my next name day.

Chapter Nineteen

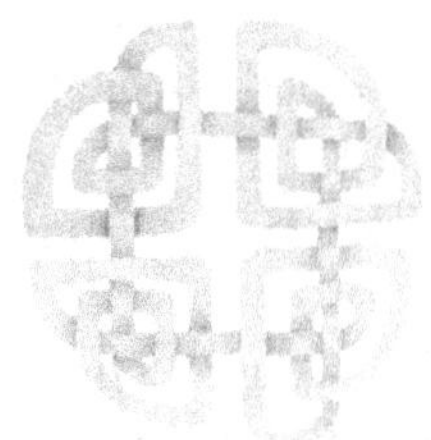

"You want to take both my Informer and my Hunter?" the Conqueror King growled. His stare bore into the back of my neck as I knelt before him, my head hanging low. The Hunter bowed beside me. It was difficult enough to be in the presence of the king, but to also be so near the Hunter…the contents of my stomach swirled with unease, threatening to send my head spinning.

I expected the summons through the Bond this morning. Kalee filled me in on Ronan's plan after dawn's first light. I'd been confident after we'd gone over it, but now, positioned before the king, my hands threatened to shake—nervous he might see through our ruse.

Eoin stood sentry next to Ronan. His expression remained stoic as always, his freshly polished breastplate glittering in the light streaming from the arched windows, not a nerve in sight.

"Have you not had my pet for long enough?" the king asked. "And now you wish to take my second most prized Bonded?" His words grated against my skin. To be reduced to nothing more than one's plaything was humiliating at best.

"Not take, father, merely borrow. Your Informer has managed to uncover one of the people responsible for a sizable smuggling operation. All we have is a name and a general location. I need your Hunter to track her down."

"Very well. Take my Hunter and leave the Informer. You have your culprit."

"We have but one piece of a larger puzzle," Ronan argued. "I have reason to believe this person can lead us to the others, and we could, quite possibly, take down the entire ring. Only your Informer's abilities can uncover this information."

I resisted the urge to look at the king for his reaction.

"You have proof?"

Ronan stepped forward, forged documents in hand of reports corroborating his story. The king flipped through him, my heart thundering harder with each passing second.

"My Hunter is skilled at torture. Use him to ferret out the rest of the information you seek."

I glanced sidelong at the Hunter. His gaze remained fixed on the polished floor like the obedient Bonded he was. Did he revel in his work? Rumors of the Hunter's *abilities* were well known throughout Rothcek. I knew he was responsible for tracking down the king's targets, but to have the king confirm he tortured them as well… I feared Ronan was biting off more than he could chew.

"My king, this is no ordinary person, but a witch smuggling osnádúrtha into Ilythia. We have the opportunity not only to destroy a larger operation, but to glean information across Ilythia's borders. You know how the osnádúrtha can be. They are a slippery bunch. I'm afraid we will be missing a great opportunity if we don't go after them now."

The seat of the throne groaned.

"Very well, prince. You've made a compelling argument, and I trust you will not humiliate me with your efforts. I would like an extensive report when you return, especially regarding Ilythia's defenses. And, I ask you to bring this witch to me. She must be made an example of. I expect you to return a victor."

"Yes, Your Majesty."

"Informer. Hunter. Rise."

The king's command tingled through my bones, compelling me to stand. My knee ached from leaning on it for so long, but I held in my wince as I got to my feet. The glare from the chancellor was difficult to ignore even as the king sneered down upon us.

"You will both obey Prince Ronan as you do me. But should I call for you, you will return."

The familiar burn of the Bond Mark scorched my neck at the king's command, the lights behind my lids churned what little food I ate that morning. The Hunter appeared unfazed as he stood stoic, waiting for his next command.

"Bonded, follow me," Eoin ordered after the king dismissed us.

Eoin's steps were sharp as we followed him out of the throne room, the muscles in his jaw working with every click of his heel. He must be nervous about the prince's plan. I knew Eoin was upset we needed to involve the Hunter at all. Or perhaps he also noticed the chancellor's questioning gaze.

When we exited the castle, two carriages waited for us along with Kalee holding two brown, leather duffels. Prince Ronan had made his feelings about Kalee coming known, but I knew he would lose that battle. Despite the uncertainty of what lay before us, a smile tugged at my lips.

Ronan spoke to one of the drivers as footmen loaded our luggage. Two soldiers readied themselves and their horses alongside the carriage. Prince Ronan hadn't mentioned accompanying guards as part of our plan, but it might have been suspicious for the Crown Prince of Centra to travel without extra protection. At least it was only two soldiers and not an entire company.

"Hunter. A moment," Ronan called, pulling the Hunter to the side.

"I must warn you," Eoin said, keeping a respectable distance away, his voice low enough so only I would hear. I waited, my pulse hammering. "Ronan and I will need to keep up appearances in front of the other guards and the Hunter. We can't have them going back to the king." I nodded, figuring as much. "And," he continued, "the carriages only seat four."

I raised a brow, questioning why he was divulging this bit of trivial information.

"As Bonded, you're not allowed to share a carriage with the Crown Prince. Plus, it would turn heads if I were not with the prince."

"And where is the Hunter sitting?" I asked, though I knew the answer. There were only two carriages stationed outside. Eoin's only reply was an apologetic look.

Off to the side, Ronan and the Hunter were deep in conversation. Ronan would be making him swear to whatever happened on our journey between us before we set foot off of castle property. As much as it pained me for the Bond to be used against any osnádúrtha, the Hunter was different. He couldn't be trusted. It was the only way to ensure our safety.

Kalee and I glanced sidelong at one another.

"Informer," Ronan called, walking toward us, not sparing Kalee a glance. She gave nothing away, but the action had to have pained her somewhere deep down. How she'd been able to keep this part of her life a secret for so long, I had no idea.

"Your Highness." I dipped my head, nearly forgetting my manners, so used to the informality of the last few weeks.

"Prepare yourselves in the carriage. We will depart shortly."

I cracked the door open when a hand, seemingly out of nowhere, halted its progress.

"Not so fast, little shadow," the Hunter whispered, "I'll take the front bench."

I stiffened against the caress of his breath along my neck, prickling every nerve ending. His hand engulfed mine, and heat crawled up my neck, remembering how he led the aes sídhe into the throne room like cows for slaughter. My fists clenched, aching to collide with some part of him. I stepped out of his way despite the need to wipe the smirk off his face, but he only held the door open.

"It's a door, little shadow, not a marriage proposal. But I can make one of those, too, if you'd like," he said when I didn't move.

"I pity the poor soul who'd ever vow their life to yours."

His smirk split into a wide, feral grin.

Kalee and I huddled together on the back bench. I kept the Hunter in my sights as he took his seat before us. The carriage sagged under his weight. It was a miracle it fit him at all—the top of his head grazed the roof.

"You're welcome to sit with me, little shadow, if that bench is too crowded for you," the Hunter teased.

"I am quite comfortable, thank you."

"That's fine, I quite like my view from here." He smiled slyly. I shot him a murderous glare. The heat blossoming in my cheeks threatened to betray me. Kalee glanced at me. I told her of the Hunter's brashness before, but experiencing it in person didn't do my tales justice. The Hunter laughed and held his hands up in mock surrender.

The rumbling wheels turned into white noise as silence filled the carriage, its thrum threatening to soothe me into sleep if not for the jarring motions. We aimed to get as close to Ilythia's border as possible, starting our search in the border town of Willowmere. If all went well, the Hunter would gain information about Aislinn there and then, and we could rid ourselves of him soon after.

Kalee's head fell against my shoulder. Her mouth parted in sleep, snoring softly. Somehow, even then, she still managed to look beautiful.

The Hunter's eyes were closed, and I might have believed him to be asleep if I didn't feel his gaze on me like a stain when I wasn't looking. He sat with his arms crossed over his broad chest, his back stiff and too big for the space. The light of the setting sun filtered through the window, casting its soft glow over his features, bringing out the bronze of his copper skin. I'd never looked at him for so long with such little distance between us.

The wild look he had was tamed in this light. He was beautiful like a forest untainted by the hands of men. His black hair, which had always seemed so plain, was streaked with varying shades, making it far more interesting. It was a shame someone with his good looks was wasted on such a malicious heart.

I didn't want to fall asleep in the same space as him and relinquish my guard, but the carriage's lull, however, was too strong to fight as I drifted into nothing.

I JOLTED WHEN THE CARRIAGE HALTED, THE IMAGE OF THE CHANCELLOR chasing after me plaguing my vision. I lunged forward in a half-awaken state, reaching for help that wasn't there. My lungs squeezed, the air too heavy to breathe. I gasped, forcing it down because I refused to lose myself in such a small space. The familiar shake in my hands started, and I squeezed whatever I held onto.

My wide eyes met the Hunter's, his gaze drifting to where my hand gripped his knee. I reared back, wiping off the feel of him onto my trousers.

"Looks like we're here," he said blandly, not acknowledging my near-panicked state or the fact that I clung to him like my life depended on it. I forced my muscles to relax and assessed our new surroundings. The sun had disappeared altogether, replaced by the moon hanging overhead, lighting the forest around us. Aside from the pines, the leaves of the trees had long fallen. What remained were the dried, weathered branches weighed down by winter's touch.

Eoin pounded on the carriage door, startling Kalee into consciousness. "We're stopping here for the night," he said, leaving without another word.

"Is he always so pleasant?" the Hunter asked, sarcasm dripping from his mouth.

"What do you know about being pleasant?" I hissed and moved to open the door. But before I could do so, the Hunter stopped me, his large hand splayed over mine on the door handle.

"I know a great many things, little shadow," he said, exiting first to open the door for us once again.

The air was crisp when we quit the warm confines of the carriage. Only the pine trees held any life to them, and I savored their sweet scents. Compared to the bustling city of Rothcek, the forest was fresh and inviting despite the frigid weather.

"Where are we?" I asked no one in particular.

"We're just over halfway there. We will make camp for the night and head out at first light. We should reach Willowmere by dark tomorrow." Eoin tossed the tent supplies to me.

I sighed. Once again, nothing more than a Bonded—Kalee, a handmaiden. We tried as best we could to put the tent together, but the poor construction threatened to topple over with one strong gust of wind. I'd all but given up when the Hunter came across our haphazard attempt.

"Here," he said. "Do it like this instead."

The Hunter demonstrated how to adjust the supports to make them more evenly spaced. We stretched the hide together, creating enough space for Kalee and me. He placed the final stake in the ground and walked away before I could thank him. Eoin watched with his arms crossed. He said nothing, but I could feel his disdain coming off in waves. Was he worried the Hunter would hurt us?

When we settled for the night in our prospective tents, I couldn't sleep. Kalee dozed soundly next to me. But my nightmare from earlier still lingered, as did the looming threat of Tenebris. Not to mention the protective spell my mother instilled. How many times have I escaped death because of it? I would do anything if only to speak to her one last time.

I couldn't stop thinking about the recent events that have changed the course of my life. About Aislinn. About being one step closer to breaking my Bond. And about the Hunter who threatened to topple it all.

I let out a shaky breath. I didn't want to get my hopes up about any of it, but the possibilities were more tangible now than ever. My thoughts were too clouded to allow me to attempt sleep. Kalee stirred but didn't wake when I opened the tent flap.

The lingering scent of an extinguished campfire carried on the rattling wind. Dying embers of dark orange flickered from the ashes. No one stirred behind the other five tents. The prince's tent was across from ours. Kalee hadn't seemed bothered by their limited interaction, but still, I worried for her.

Eoin's tent sat between Ronan's and the Hunter's, no doubt wanting to be a barrier between the two. The carriage drivers shared a tent next to mine. They were both quiet and unmemorable, as expected by the king. The two guards accompanying us were on the other side of the Hunter. While they were wary of the Bonded in their presence, they hadn't sought to torment me. Perhaps I had the Hunter to thank for that.

The guard on watch dozed softly by the campfire. I suppressed a snort. I should have woken him, but I didn't want to chance him ordering me back into my tent. The shadows concealed me as I crept further into the forest on silent feet. It was quiet, save for the occasional flapping of wings —a snowy owl perched on a branch, cleaning its feathers.

The calm of the forest was enough to quell the lingering nightmare. I let the pull of the wind carry me in whichever direction it wished to go, not caring how far I walked. I was still in Centra, but I'd never been so far from the king. Each step felt a little more like what freedom might be.

A branch snapped.

I whirled around. Nothing but the dark and no other sound save for the pounding of my own heart. Relief was temporary, however, when a firm body pulled me into them. A hand covering nearly half my face clamped over my mouth. I tried to scream, but a low voice silenced my attempt.

"If you want to live, you will stay very, very quiet," the Hunter whispered, his lips brushing against my ear.

CHAPTER TWENTY

H*e knew.* The king had seen through Ronan's excuses and allowed us to leave, only to command the Hunter to kill us all. My breath turned quick and shallow, every muscle begging to run. I squirmed against him only for his arms to squeeze me tighter, my body pinned against his solid chest. Was I the first to die, or had he gotten to the others already? My eyes squeezed shut to the point of pain. Would he torture me for more information or kill me quickly? If I could escape, I could warn the others if I wasn't too late.

I wrenched a hand free, grabbing for one of my daggers. Trembling fingers brushed against its soft leather hilt. Before I could draw it, the Hunter, his words little more than a whisper, said, "If we are to return to camp alive, you will do exactly as I say."

We? Against better judgment, I stilled.

"Something lurks in this forest," the Hunter murmured. "I heard it on my walk and was in the middle of tracking it before you stumbled along. I believe it's headed toward our camp. If I'm correct, which I nearly always am, it will be upon us shortly. Camouflage us with your shadows."

My magic didn't work like that. At least, I didn't think it did. Before I could object, the Hunter commanded, "Do it. *Now.*"

Fear pulled the shadows from the darkest parts of the forest, enshrouding me at a rapid pace. I strained as I concentrated on extending those shadows to the Hunter until we were wrapped in a cocoon of darkness. Sweat broke along my brow despite the cold. I could still see the Hunter through my shadows, but we were invisible to the outside world. I couldn't believe it worked. I would have been overjoyed, had it not been for our scents... I started to tell the Hunter about the limitations of my magic, but another topic overpowered it.

"Why haven't you woken the others?" I hissed, horrified that the Hunter might have been stalking me despite his claims.

"I wanted to be sure it was real before I raised any alarm. Don't tell me you were worried about me, little shadow? I assure you, I'm quite capable of handling myself."

Every inch of me sizzled where my body and the Hunter's collided, his warmth suffocating. I wrenched myself free of his grasp. "I assure you *that* was not my concern."

The Hunter chuckled, a low, captivating sound. "Now, do you know how to use those daggers, or are they just for show?"

"Want to find out?" I threatened, the faint smirk showcasing his stupid dimples.

"So violent," he crooned. "I like it." His dimples disappeared when a low, guttural growl emitted to our right. I stilled. Thoughts of the fomorii from the woods a few weeks ago worked themselves to the forefront of my mind. My scar tingled at the thought, my hand resting against my abdomen on instinct.

It was not a massive shadowed wolf prowling toward the campsite, but a man. Or a twisted idea of one. His skin was sunken and wan—a sickly glisten clung to him under the light of the moon as if he'd never known any nourishment. Tattered clothes were little more than rags as he walked, his right foot lagging behind the left. Black tendrils of smoke twisted around twitching muscles, moving beneath his skin like my silver shadows, but composed of the purest darkness akin to the fomorii wolf. I'd never known anyone to possess magic like mine. He wasn't faie, not with the roundness of his ears. I wasn't sure if he was even human. No. This was another fomorii.

"Follow my lead," the Hunter breathed into my ear. His voice was so quiet that not even the fomorii mere paces from us heard. A bright light flashed in the distance, turning into a blazing fire. Halting his steps, the shadow demon cocked his head in question before he lurched toward the source.

The king had always been so careful about keeping the Bonded apart from one another. None of us really knew what the others could do. I've never seen the Hunter's magic before—this fire magic. The Hunter was a skilled tracker by his name alone, but I'd never considered the type of magic he possessed. His flames burned as bright as any celebration pyre, its heat licking toward us.

We followed the fomorii, creeping through the forest. I unsheathed my daggers, preparing to strike while we still held the advantage of surprise. The Hunter grabbed my arm and shook his head. I furrowed my brow, but we were in the Hunter's element, and I had no choice but to trust his plan…whatever it may be.

Mother help me.

The flames grew hotter with each step, their luster threatening to extinguish my shadows. Already, they quivered in what little hold I had on them.

"The light," I warned. Each breath became more labored as I worked to keep the shadows in my grasp. The Hunter understood what I meant because he steered us behind a copse of trees. My shoulders relaxed a fraction.

The fomorii circled the bonfire, sniffing the air akin to a predator hunting its prey. The Hunter's magic burned brightly of its own accord. Its flames waved back and forth, beckoning the fomorii, yet, careful not to catch the surrounding trees. Despite the light of the fire, the fomorii's long black hair dripped with darkness, giving it a wet appearance. The fomorii's gaze turned toward us and took a step in our direction. Another. Blood rushed to my ears. I tried to steady my breathing to slow my heart rate and the adrenaline coursing through my veins. The fomorii inched ever closer.

The Hunter pinched me.

"*Asshole*," I hissed, rubbing the inside of my arm. "What was that for?"

"You need a distraction," he said smugly, "You reek of fear. It's overwhelming."

"Maybe I wouldn't need a distraction if we had attacked him earlier when we had the chance."

"Yes, but then his friends would have gotten away, or worse, to the camp."

Twigs snapped on the other side of the bonfire, and three other figures stepped into the light. They, too, looked human but not. Two females and a male approached the fomorii, and we crept closer to the clearing, mindful of the light. Like the other fomorii, their skin was pallid and waxen, with dark tendrils snaking beneath the surface. And their eyes, so bright against the light of the fire, burned red with the same intensity of the Hunter's flames. Same as the fomorii wolf.

The formorii congregated together, hissing every so often.

"What are you three doing here?" the original fomorii asked, his voice a grating gravel.

"Master wanted to ensure you gathered all the necessary information," the woman with the long, thin hair answered.

"I don't need your assistance."

"Tenebris disagrees," the other woman cackled.

I bit the inside of my cheek, and the Hunter nudged me. His expression asked me for answers I didn't know how to explain without giving everything away. I shook my head as if to say, *Later*.

"I am more than capable of relaying a simple report."

The fomorii bickered and hissed at one another, their tones hushed and difficult to make out. They were not here by chance, that much was clear, but what, exactly, did they seek?

"Who goes there?" Eoin called out, approaching the clearing. The fomorii all turned at once and hissed, baring razor-sharp teeth. The Hunter cursed and stepped away from my shadows. Before the fomorii could attack Eoin, the Hunter flared his fire, nearly blinding everyone present.

The Hunter unsheathed the long blade strapped to his back without sound. "I have dealt with a creature like this once before," he said as I followed after him. "Do not let their slow gaits deceive you. They are quick and sure-footed as they are strong. You can inflict mortal damage on them like any other man, but they do not fall easily. They heal fast, like us. Faster even. It's best to aim for the heart or the head because, despite slicing them to bits, I have reason to believe they don't register pain the same way we do."

I nodded and drew out my daggers, the softness of the hilt a comfort to my shaking hands. I knew how to defend myself, but I rarely had to. The fomorii wolf was one thing, but they looked more like people. Evil people, I reminded myself, with long-pointed nails perfect for gouging eyes. I shuddered, swallowing any hesitancy for violence. Reana wasn't here to heal us now. It was either them or us.

Chaos ensued as the fomorii descended upon us. One of the fomorii females raced toward me, and there was no time to see if Eoin was surprised by either mine or the Hunter's presence. Her movements were fast and frantic. Yellowed nails struck me across my face, slicing my cheek open as she cursed at me and clawed for my throat.

Blood dripping down my cheeks, I deflected and stabbed both daggers into her frail neck, shoving her back with a heavy kick that nearly knocked me on my ass. Black blood sprayed. Bile rose to the back of my throat. She didn't cry out in pain as her wounds gushed, or when her head thudded against the ground. Clots formed, and her skin worked to stitch itself together. She shrieked loud enough to make my ears ring, my hands itching to cover them. Rage and frustration twisted her already horrifying features.

She lunged, ready to rip out my throat, but my daggers found her heart first. My stomach churned as her flesh squelched under my blade. The embers in her eyes flickered out and died as she slumped against me. The weight of her was nothing compared to the wolf, hardly more than a flesh-covered skeleton. It took only a moment before her shadows evaporated—her body with it, just like the fomorii wolf had done in the clearing.

Two pools of black blood lay at the Hunter's feet—the fomoriis' bodies long gone. There wasn't a scratch on the faie. I shuddered to think what it would be like to stand at the wrong end of his blade. Poor Eoin had lost his sword at one point, his face marred with small incisions from the remaining female. He'd been able to recover, however, as he regained his weapon and shoved his sword through her chest. She was gone before the blade was pulled from her heart.

Eoin panted, glancing between us until his gaze settled on me. "What were you thinking Saoirse? You could have been killed for gods' sakes."

Gods. He was right. If the fomorii had found me instead of the Hunter, protection spell or not, I wouldn't have been able to fight off all three of them by myself.

"Do either of you want to tell me what the Nine is going on and what, exactly, you two are doing out here?"

"I was going to ask you the same thing." The Hunter stood with his arms crossed, glowering at Eoin.

"I don't have to explain myself to the likes of *you*," Eoin spat.

"Can you two stop arguing?" The two looked moments away from coming to blows, and I needed silence to think. "We need to tell the prince what happened and ensure there aren't more. They were here to meet someone. We can't secure the area if you two insist on squabbling."

The color of Eoin's cheeks deepened, and the Hunter smirked, but both men held their tongues. Satisfaction hummed through me. I wasn't used to using my voice like this, much less having any sway.

"You." I pointed at Eoin. "Let's go back to camp to make sure everyone is alright."

Eoin's brows rose. I didn't know if he was angry that I was barking orders to a commanding officer, but someone had to.

"And you." I gestured to the Hunter. "Search the perimeter. Make sure there aren't any more of those things. And put this fire out. We don't want to add a conflagration to the list of things that have gone wrong tonight."

"For you? Anything." The Hunter smiled in wicked delight, holding out his hand and making a fist—extinguishing the fire with practiced ease —before vanishing off into the night.

CHAPTER TWENTY-ONE

When the two palace guards and the carriage driver were either occupied or out of earshot, Eoin relayed the events in the woods to the others. Both Kalee and Ronan were rightfully disturbed by the fomorii's nearness. The Hunter recounted his experience with one not far from Rothcek a few weeks ago. He'd come to blows with the fomorii while on duty for the king, not realizing what it was, but his account was the same: glowing red eyes and black shadows moving under their sallow skin. He, like so many others, had mentioned this encounter to the king and never heard anything of it again.

The Hunter stared at me from across the carriage, the brazenness of his gaze unapologetic. This faie was no fool; he knew there was more to the fomorii we weren't telling him. I could see it in the way his brows knit together, how he watched us with careful, contemplative eyes. My shadows caught his attention, running like ribbons along my hands and crawling up my neck. I wondered if he saw what I did. And so, with a feigned boldness, I stared back, daring him to address the dragon in the room.

The shadows of the fomorii were disturbing. We were still different, the fomorii and I, but our shadows behaved much the same. The likeness between my magic and theirs gripped me by the neck, refusing to let me turn a blind eye. I didn't want to learn what it meant if I was linked to them. Didn't want the others thinking I was like them. Kalee had caught my unease and assured me it was only a coincidence. It did little to settle me.

I pushed these thoughts somewhere deep down. There were bigger, more pressing matters demanding my attention. My worries drifted to Aislinn—my aunt. If we would find her. If she would even remember me. If she knew why my mother threw away twenty-five years of her life. Part of me assumed Aislinn had put us out of her mind long ago. My mother certainly never mentioned a sister before. What I might say to Aislinn sprouted and died like the first fickle spring bloom before another frost took it out—too many thoughts colliding with one another, until there was only the horrible truth left.

Hi, I'm your long-lost niece. Did you know I've been held captive for fifteen years? Oh, your sister is dead by the way, and it's all my fault.

Despite the anxiety picking at my cuticles and gnawing the inside of my bottom lip into a bloody pulp, there was a tiny kernel of hope I dared to acknowledge. Even if Aislinn didn't claim me as her kin, she might know of my father and brother. Maybe one day, we would be reunited. I didn't dare contemplate why they never tried to find us or why my mother never spoke of them.

My throat squeezed as the carriage came to a halt. Night greeted us like a familiar friend. We were a day behind due to the worsening weather, but Willowmere was finally in our sights. Time and neglect crept over the inn outside my window, the roof's wooden slats desperate for repair—its door crooked on its hinges. Gods, what was the state of the inside? For as much as I despised Centra's castle, my bed, at least, was warm. Its sheets, clean. My room, quiet. Not to mention the private bathing chamber I'd grown accustomed to. Eoin banged on the door without a word, signalling us to exit.

"Does it not meet your standards, little shadow?" The Hunter said, his voice dripping with sarcasm.

"This will be fine," I said sweetly. "I'm more worried about how you're faring. You must be exhausted from carrying around your ego."

The Hunter's lips split into a grin.

My initial assessment of the inn didn't improve when we walked through the broken door. Patrons either filled the circular tables or sat on rotting wooden stools at the bar top stained with drink, food, and something I didn't want to ponder too hard about. Glasses clinked together, spilling their contents, from where cheers and shouts sounded around a game of cards. Cobwebs stretched from beam to beam of the dropped ceiling and all the way up the stairs.

"What can I do ya for?" the innkeeper asked, cleaning a glass with a stained rag. His beady eyes narrowed on Ronan, taking in the fineness of his dress—the Centran red and gold he bore, before sweeping his gaze to Eoin's and the two other guards' armor. Something clicked behind his eyes as he beheld the golden boar carved into their breastplates—the armor of the king's royal guard. Even if the man didn't know Ronan's status, it didn't take an intellect to assume his importance. The innkeeper's meaty hands fumbled, dropping his glass. Broken shards splayed across the floor. Every patron turned their head at the crash as if time itself stilled for the prince.

"I need rooms, hot food, and some of your finest ale," Ronan said, not bothering to introduce himself, letting the innkeeper form his own speculations of his true identity.

"How many rooms do you require? I have the best in all of Centra. Our bed sheets are washed after *every* guest."

I tried not to grimace and must have failed miserably because the corner of the Hunter's mouth twitched.

"Six will be fine," Ronan answered. "Three of them will need to accommodate two to a room." He surveyed the area and offered the innkeeper a nod, satisfied with the conditions of his inn. It wasn't much, but it was better than the hard, cold ground we've had to deal with thus far. I didn't care how bad it was, I decided, as long as I got a bath out of it. After two days of travel, I was ready to peel out of my skin.

The innkeeper beamed. "Of course, sir. But, uh, we don't serve their kind." His head dipped toward the Hunter and me. Between my shadows and our pointed ears, we couldn't be anything but faie.

"Surely you can make an exception. These Bonded are with me on official palace business. I want to keep my eye on them." Ronan leaned in as if confiding in the innkeeper.

"Oh, I understand," he chuckled. "But I am forbidden by decree of the king. Plus, the other patrons wouldn't be too pleased. I'd hate to run them off."

Gone were the smiles and laughs from the patrons. They, too, had taken note of the Hunter and me. Some of their hands twitched by their sides, their fingertips dancing at the hilts of their iron daggers. The Hunter looked bored by their reaction, but their glares alone were enough to make my shadows writhe and reach out toward the safety of the darkness.

"Of course," Ronan deadpanned. "Then we will find another inn."

"Wait!" The innkeeper scrambled, halting Ronan from his intended departure. "The closest inn is two towns over, and he won't take them either, but I have another option."

Ronan raised a brow.

"The stables are only half full. I cleaned them myself this morning," the innkeeper boasted.

Ronan looked at me, almost apologetically. "Fine. I'll need *four* rooms and dinner sent to them all, including the stables."

Kalee tugged on my arm.

"Where do you think you're going?" I asked.

"To the stables." Her brows bunched together as if I'd asked the most preposterous question.

"You're not sleeping in the stables, Kalee. Don't deny that your back is aching. Besides, one of us should get to enjoy a warm bed. I'll be fine, promise."

"I'm not going to convince you, am I?"

I smiled, shaking my head.

She sighed and squeezed my hand before turning a glare on to the Hunter. "Behave yourself, Hunter."

"It is not me my little shadow needs to watch out for."

"I'm not *yours*," I hissed.

"We'll see."

I huffed out a breath and stomped toward the stables. I paused at the threshold, my heart sinking to my stomach. Horses stood restlessly in the stalls, swishing their tails, staring at me with their wide, lightless eyes. Of course there were horses. I loosed a curse as one of them huffed at me. Incorrigible beast. The Hunter arched a brow, our stew in hand, but I ignored him as I settled in the furthest corner from the animals.

The innkeeper exaggerated the pristine conditions of the stables. Flies swarmed us, attracted to the stench of the animals. I stared, unblinking, at the stew and pushed it around with the rusty spoon. The musky smell of dust, feed, and animal droppings wasn't exactly conducive to an appetite, nor was the nearness of the horses themselves, but exhaustion still weighed heavily on me from the other night. I needed to replenish my strength.

One of the horses whinnied, and I nearly jumped out of my skin.

"That's it," I announced, hopping up from where I sat, my stew untouched. "I'm sleeping outside."

I rummaged through the carriage rack, my hand blindly reaching for the tents. Even on the ledge, I was still too short to see over the top.

"I believe you're looking for this," the Hunter said, holding up the canvas and poles. I jumped down and snatched the supplies from his outstretched hand. He pulled away at the last minute, shoving my untouched bowl of stew in my face.

"Eat. I'll pitch the tent."

"I am capable of doing both." I crossed my arms over my chest, though any tent I slung together was sure to be lopsided.

"It's going to go cold. Either you eat it or I will."

I glared at him, taking the bowl out of spite. His answering smirk was enough to make my teeth grind. Though I'd be lying if I said I didn't take some enjoyment from watching the Hunter work as I savored my meal— even if it was freezing out in the open.

The Hunter nailed the stakes into the ground with ease, finding a soft spot under a few trees and out of the way of the townsfolk but still close enough to the inn. I pulled my bedding in, thanking the Hunter, and left him to the cold.

He followed in after me.

"What do you think you're doing?" I asked, stopping him at the threshold.

"Making sure you don't freeze to death or aren't murdered by someone who holds a grudge against the Bonded. Do you truly wish to sleep alone, little shadow?"

I glared at him for a moment. My lips parted to argue against him— that he was the last thing I needed—when a chilled breeze blew into the tent, wracking shivers along my body.

"Get in," I groaned.

We didn't speak as we lay there, the sounds of his breathing filling the space, a siren in my ears. The Hunter wasn't close enough to touch me, but I still sensed the feel of him, the warmth that begged me to cling to. I put my back to him, my gaze trained on the sidewall. I'd been around the Hunter more times than I cared to count, but this was the first time, I realized, we were alone for more than five minutes. He'd corner me whenever he'd gotten the chance, but our exchanges had always been clipped.

My thoughts drifted to every time he'd found me bent over the chancellor's desk. We never talked about it before. There was nothing to say. I didn't owe him any thank yous for a coincidence, even if it did make the chancellor stop. Yet, as our silence stretched on, these memories were louder than any yell.

I curved inward, wrapping the blanket tighter around me. The temperature dropped, and chills wracked my body, my teeth chattering.

"You know," the Hunter called in the darkness, "we would both be warmer if we slept next to one another."

"You would like that, wouldn't you?"

"Yes, I would like to sleep," the Hunter said mildly. "It's hard to do if I have to listen to your chattering all night."

I sighed into the darkness and prayed for the Mother to give me patience. "Fine."

The heat of the Hunter's body was immediate when he scooted closer. He doubled our blankets and put his back against mine. I expected my skin to crawl—for his nearness to disgust me. He'd always been so vile and arrogant and a general nuisance to my mental stability. Instead, I savored his heat. I couldn't help it. The Hunter burned hotter than most as if the fire magic he possessed flickered just below his skin. Gods, it was nice. Not that I'd ever admit it to him.

"You would be warmer if I turned over," he suggested when my shivering didn't subside.

"Absolutely not," I protested through chattering teeth. The Hunter's nearness had helped, but a storm rolled in, and the wind picked up.

"Please. At least until you stop shaking. You're going to wake the whole village." Was that genuine concern in his voice?

"For warmth," I warned, agreeing to his inane idea, convinced this cold was starting to make me lose my mind.

"For warmth," he murmured and rotated toward me, curling his arm around my middle. His fingers splayed over my abdomen in a near possessive hold. My muscles went taut. His hand was like a brand, burning through the travel-worn clothing, and I was painfully aware of the bath I'd been robbed of. My breath hitched under his touch, unused to being held in such a way, not even by Eiric. Our trysts were quick, covert— something to take the edge off. We'd never lay together longer than necessary out of fear of being caught. And never had I fallen asleep in his arms.

Eiric was my friend. The Hunter was my enemy. A traitor to our kind. He would sell my life to the king the moment he got a chance.

But he was warm, and I was desperate.

"Is this alright?" he asked, his voice a heady whisper. I nodded, and he relaxed behind me as if he were relieved I didn't deny him. His warmth encased me. And damn him, even after days of travel, he still smelled good. The salty scent of dried sweat lurked behind notes of juniper and spice, the winter aroma overpowering everything else.

"We live in a world filled with lies and deception," the Hunter said, and my very blood chilled. He must know then—what we sought wasn't what Ronan declared to the king. "Tell me one true thing," he asked, almost pleading.

I could have ignored him, pretended I was asleep, but my breath hitched enough for him to notice. Was he probing for information to relay to the king? Did he think in a moment of kindness I would share my deepest darkest thoughts with someone I didn't know?

"Why should I tell you anything?" I asked instead.

"Because, little shadow, in a world full of people who will turn on you the moment it benefits them, it helps to know who your true allies are."

"I should consider you my ally?" I nearly laughed.

"You should consider me your closest ally," he corrected.

I snorted. "I hate you, remember?"

"And yet, you don't really know me."

"Do I have to?"

"A tarnished coin is still silver, little shadow."

I opened my mouth and shut it, swallowing my retort. It wasn't long ago when Prince Ronan contradicted everything I'd believed of him. This was different, though. Ronan actively sought to help the osnádúrtha. The Hunter chose to work against them. And no matter how pretty the words, actions always spoke louder.

"I hate being forced to sleep outside," he offered after the silence stretched too thin. "But I am glad I'm not alone." The last of his words skittered across my skin in a breathy whisper. He wasn't searching for closely guarded secrets, but connection. A truth for a truth. The life of a Bonded was cruel. Lonely. Isolating. I was lucky enough to have Kalee. The Hunter had…no one.

"I hate being despised for something I have no control over," I whispered, offering up a small truth. It wasn't life-altering information or something the Hunter could use against us, but it was honest, nonetheless. "And—," I found myself saying before I could think better of it. "I'm also glad I don't have to sleep here by myself." As much as I disliked the

Hunter, the thought of being forced to sleep out here alone was borderline depressing.

"Thank you," he whispered and dared to hold me tighter, pulling me into him. I should have revolted, but the gesture was…nice. The paltry truth was an odd thing to thank me for. I didn't know what to make of his words. This side of the Hunter was someone I'd never known. Perhaps I should have given more thought to our conversation, but then, there was only the thrum of his heart beating steady against my back, its rhythm a lullaby singing me to sleep.

CHAPTER TWENTY-TWO

"What are you doing?" Eoin demanded, looming over me. I blinked the blurriness away until his figure cleared. His face contorted in a way I'd never seen before. Anger furrowed his brows and thrust out his hands, gesturing wildly. I turned to where he pointed.

Straight into the Hunter's broad chest.

We had moved closer during the night. He held me in a tight embrace, his arms wrapped around me, and to my dismay, mine draped over his muscular torso. I yanked my arm away as if seared by his touch, the low simmer finally hot enough to burn. My cheeks ignited. Instinct pushed the Hunter away, yet guilt tangled with my conscience. He hadn't done anything wrong. The opposite, in fact. There'd been nothing stopping him from letting me freeze to death. Before last night, I would've thought he'd prefer it.

Eoin hauled me to my feet, dragging me out of the tent.

"Do you have any idea how long I have been looking for you? Gods, I thought you were dead." Eoin gripped my upper arms to the point of pain, brown eyes searching my figure as if looking for any damage the Hunter might have inflicted. Yet, I didn't see Eoin. His golden armor blinded me; his face melted and blurred, reshaping into the countless guards who gripped me in such a way, hauling me by my arm and pushing me to the ground.

I didn't know what was wrong with me. I'd endured far worse. But something inside me fissured. Perhaps it was my lungs because it hurt to breathe, my breaths coming in quick, shallow successions.

The Hunter stalked toward us, his figure but a flash, and tore Eoin's grip from me, knocking him into a tree.

"Touch her like that again and you will lose your hands, Lieutenant."

"I should be the one threatening you, *Hunter*. How dare you take advantage of her."

The Hunter looked down at Eoin so they were nose to nose, his tone a low growl, as he said, "Try sleeping in the stables and see how you like it."

Something flashed over Eoin's face as if a thought clicked into place. His gaze flicked to me before returning to the Hunter. "Ready yourself and meet me by the stables. Prince Ronan has a task for you. That's an order, Hunter."

The Hunter tore himself from Eoin and collected his swords from the tent. He strapped the two blades to his back, one longer than the other. Gentle fingers touched my elbow, his grip feather-light. "Are you alright?"

"Fine," I rasped, my lungs expanding again. My fingers curled around my locket, finding comfort in familiarity. His lips pursed like he didn't believe me, then he nodded before stalking off.

"Saoirse—"

I met Eoin's gaze, the hot pang of tears threatening to blur my vision. I pushed it down. Eoin would not see me cry. "I'm fine, Eoin."

He frowned. "I hadn't thought about what staying in the stables would mean for you. I'm sorry, truly."

"Are you off to find Aislinn?"

"We'll return once we pick up a trail."

I nodded and started to walk off, needing space to breathe. Eoin caught me by the arm, his touch far more kind than before.

"Be careful around the Hunter. I do not trust him or his intentions, no matter what he says."

KALEE, RONAN, AND I WANDERED ABOUT THE TOWN, MY MIND preoccupied. Gone were the drivers and extra guards, busy with gods knew what Ronan set for them. I followed Ronan and Kalee past the cobbler, the hatter, and the blacksmith pounding his hammer. Away from loose lips, they were less cautious about interacting with one another. They talked freely, their hands brushing together every so often—the touch of a breathy whisper. Something louder stirred in the quiet contact, sweet and aching.

An odd sense of sadness struck me. I'd never been able to love so freely. My time with Eiric was short and clandestine, only lasting a few months before he was killed. When he was gone, well, I never tried to find another. My thoughts returned to this morning. Eoin had been fraught with worry. It wasn't his fault that my mind played tricks on me. He wasn't like the other guards. He'd proven it to me time and time again.

Maybe I was afraid.

I could see myself being with Eoin. He was loyal to a fault. Protective. I would have much rather woken in his arms this morning instead of the Hunter's.

"Sersh, look at this one." Kalee grabbed my hand, leading me to the bakery window, her wide smile dispelling my worries. "Doesn't it look delicious?" She pointed to an almond cake dusted with delicate sugar. Saliva pooled in my mouth.

"You two will ruin your afternoon meals if you go straight to dessert," Ronan chided.

Kalee and I glanced at one another before she replied, "I don't think we care."

Ronan laughed and purchased three slices.

We ate our cakes, and my thoughts stopped dwelling, forcing myself to focus on the present. I couldn't remember a more carefree time since before I was taken from my village. Merchants were so eager to attend a well-dressed man, they hadn't taken note of the cloaked faie in their midst. We perused different vendors and their wares: chimes tinkling in the wind, tapestries woven with skilled hands, iron charms promising protection against the faie. My shoulders slumped. Even on the outskirts of Centra, the king's reach still gripped his subjects by the throat. The taste of their bitterness burned like acid on my tongue.

When the sun hung high overhead, Eoin and the Hunter returned.

The five of us sat around a table in a tavern too busy for the barmaid to offer more than a glance. She slammed a bowl of stew and a mug of mead down in front of me, their contents sloshing. Cloying honey invaded my senses. The Hunter watched me, amusement dancing behind his green eyes.

"It's not going to bite, little shadow."

I shot the Hunter a look and drank deeply from the tin cup, a hint of metal prickling my tongue. Warmth ignited down my flesh, heat crawling up my cheeks, the effect of the mead almost immediate.

"I found her," Eoin said, his eyes wild. My heart skipped, and I took another long pull from my cup. I hadn't expected our efforts to succeed, especially not so soon.

"*We* found her," the Hunter amended, adjusting the hood of his cloak. "Her cottage is located a few miles beyond the border. Three of the villagers confirmed she sends errand boys to and from Ilythia."

"And?" Ronan asked, hanging on the edge of his seat.

"Well, we found one and have the precise location." The Hunter smiled. It wasn't the kind that showcased his dimples. No, this one appeared false in comparison.

"Perfect. If we leave soon, we might be able to get back before dark."

"Are you sure it's such a good idea?" the Hunter asked, glancing toward me. "Ilythia is unknown territory. The tensions between them and Centra are often taught. Surely, whatever you want from this woman isn't worth the risk."

"Like I told my father, we're after smugglers, Hunter. We cannot risk her getting away."

The Hunter leaned forward, his voice low. "You and I both know this isn't about smugglers, prince. Your father may be an idiot, but I am not. Clearly, you were desperate enough to ask me. If you want my help, don't lie to me."

"What we seek is knowledge, and it is worth every risk. You can wait here while we obtain what we desire," Ronan stated, but his fingers drummed nervously against the table.

The Hunter pressed his lips in a thin line. "With all due respect, *Your Highness*, we don't know what lies beyond the border. You may need my magic."

He made a compelling argument. Even I would feel better if the Hunter accompanied us to Ilythia. The prince also seemed to think so because he said, "Very well, Hunter, but I shall remind you of the terms of our agreement."

"No," Eoin interjected. He and Ronan eyed one another.

"You will accompany us, Hunter. My word is final."

Eoin's jaw ticked, but he said nothing else.

The Hunter dipped his chin, and I wondered what the prince's terms entailed. Aside from being an asshole, the Hunter didn't appear as malicious as his reputation made him out to be. I was growing used to the Hunter and his antics after being in such close proximity the last few days. He wasn't as horrible as I expected. Even this morning, when he thought Eoin was hurting me, he tried to help in his own way. The Hunter was arrogant and egotistical, yes. But there was something, just below the surface, that seemed genuine and, dare I say, even kind.

The prince fooled me with who I thought he was. I didn't try to look past the behavior he wanted everyone to see until I was forced to acknowledge his true self. Perhaps the Hunter was doing the same. Or maybe I was naive, and it was all a facade. After all, he still volunteered to be Bonded with the king.

But I couldn't fault Ronan for his cautiousness, especially if my aunt was involved. I didn't want to chance the king learning of her despite being relatively safe across the border of the witch kingdom. The Conqueror King knew no limits, and I wouldn't put it past him to try to kill her to spite me.

"We will make haste," Ronan said, and slammed back his mead.

Chapter Twenty-Three

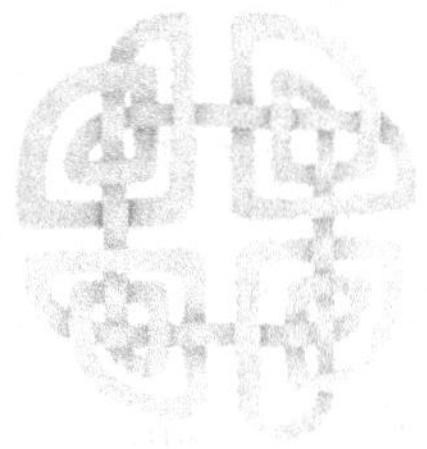

Mead churned in my stomach. My head was light, my thoughts fuzzy enough to dilute my worries. We quit the tavern as soon as we devoured our meals, marching toward the stables. I'd hoped we would leave the guards behind with the carriage drivers, but they remained insistent that they accompany Ronan. When the Hunter offered me the reins to the brown mare, any courage I'd gained from the alcohol withered away.

In a rare moment of understanding, the Hunter did not ridicule me but offered to be my riding partner instead.

"The Informer will be riding with me," Eoin said, making me jump. I'd been too stunned by the Hunter's offer, and I hadn't noticed Eoin from behind. Hearing him refer to me as my title and not my name felt wrong —like I was reduced to nothing more than what I was to the king.

Eoin held out an expectant hand. Familiarity twitched at my fingertips, but I didn't reach for him. His tone, his words, weren't a request but a command. I'd already planned on riding with Eoin to discuss the events of the morning and would have chosen him over the Hunter in a heartbeat, but his order gave me pause. I'd known more freedom in the last three days than I had in fifteen years. Wandering the forest or loitering about the town without being imposed on by the king were paltry freedoms, but the little taste I had was crumbs to a starving man. Now, I was greedy for it—willing to do anything to get more. Accepting orders wasn't on my agenda anymore.

Caught in the middle, I stood between the two men, each of their gazes glued to me as if they could will me into making a choice. I took Eoin's outstretched hand, and satisfaction turned the corners of his lips. Something flickered over the Hunter's face.

The Hunter's expression crawled underneath my clothes, burrowing into my skin. *I* made the choice. It wasn't my fault ,that he didn't like the outcome of my decisions. Taking Eoin's hand didn't mean he was commanding me when I would have chosen him regardless. Eoin glared at the Hunter, the muscles in his arms around me tensing.

"What you saw this morning—it's not what you think," I said to Eoin once we fell to the back of the group, my voice low. Up ahead, in front of Kalee, Ronan, and the two guards, the Hunter stiffened, though he continued to ride the same, easy gait. "It was a misunderstanding. I couldn't stay in the stables. I couldn't. And when—"

Eoin's chest heaved behind me as he took a deep breath. "I know, and I'm sorry. When I couldn't find you in the stables, I was so worried something bad had happened. I thought…"

"What?" I asked when Eoin didn't finish.

"This world is cruel, Saoirse. My father was a useless drunk. He cared more about emptying his cups than he did for his family. I was away when my mother and sister were taken. When I came home, they'd been gone for two days, my father oblivious—too lost in a haze. When I found them… No one should ever have to endure what they did. When I couldn't find you. I thought the worst."

I put my hand on Eoin's.

"I made a vow that day. To do whatever it takes to protect those I care about. No matter the cost."

"Oh, Eoin. That's horrible. I'm so sorry."

"It's been a long time, but I hope you understand why I acted the way I did."

I nodded, shoving the concerns of my panic from the morning somewhere deep down. Eoin had acted out of fear born of good intentions. He didn't mean to frighten me; it wasn't his fault that my mind reacted the way it did.

"And when I discovered you in the arms of the Hunter…well, my jealousy might have gotten the best of me," he chuckled, the heaviness of the conversation lifting.

"So you were jealous?" I teased.

Eoin huffed a laugh. "You have no idea." His voice grew husky, and it did something to my insides, my worries nothing but a forgotten dream. My gaze drifted back to the Hunter's easy stride. I knew he could overhear our conversation, just like I could hear the leaves rustle under his horse's hoof steps. My cheeks heated. Eoin's arm came around my middle, squeezing me in a hug.

"It's difficult not to be jealous when I find you in the arms of another man."

My pulse raced, trying to sort through Eoin's words. Maybe my earlier daydreaming was not so far-fetched. Though Eoin held no official claim to me, maybe he wanted to. Maybe *I* wanted him to.

"And if I were in yours?"

Eoin shifted in his seat, leaning forward, his breath skating across my neck in a seductive whisper. "I'd never let you go."

Gooseflesh prickled across my skin. The Hunter turned in his saddle to speak to Ronan, but his gaze narrowed on me. I held his stare, refusing to break.

Up ahead, Prince Ronan signaled everyone to stop.

"For those who wish to not find out why Ilythia is so exceptional at keeping out intruders, I suggest waiting here or, better yet, turning around." Ronan's blue gaze darkened, and we all exchanged nervous glances.

"What waits for us at the border?" I asked, biting the inside of my cheek. Whatever it was, I couldn't turn my back on meeting Aislinn now.

"The Song of the Willows. An enchantment with a knack for sending people into an early grave. Not much is known about the defense mechanism, but we suspect it targets those who harbor strong negative emotions, presumably toward the witches themselves."

"Is there a way to prepare ourselves?" Kalee asked.

Ronan shook his head. "You can be woken from the enchantment, but it will require at least one of us to not fall into the willow's grasp. I believe I'll be fine, but there's no guarantee, and I am but one of seven. I fear I won't be enough to protect you all. If you decide to proceed, you must do so at your own risk."

"And if all of us are entranced?" one of the guards asked.

"Then today may very well be our last."

Chapter Twenty-Four

Nervous tension spiked the air, but no one turned around, not even the guards who held their swords at the ready. A hush fell over the landscape when we approached the border, twisting the atmosphere into something sharp and predatory. Melodic voices carried on a cool breeze, kissing my cheeks and dancing through my hair, loosening my braid.

The sound grew and grew until we reached a broad river: the divider between Centra and Ilythia. Weeping willows lined the river, their leaves long since fallen. Their bare, frost-coated branches swayed in the wind as if beckoning me to the river itself.

I wasn't prepared for the enchantment to sweep me away as I held no ill will toward the witches. But there was nothing I could do. The music permeating my senses, seemingly flowing through me, guided me to salvation. I was consumed, unable to focus on anything but the song, which spoke to my innermost convictions.

The melody was one of despair—its harmony full of sorrow. A steady thrum of misery pulsated, calling to me, vocalizing my grief. The only thought in my head was that of my mother. The willows understood the weight of her death and the deaths of the other osnádúrtha at my hands. They wanted to comfort me. To hold me. To punish me for it all the same.

I moved closer.

My mother's blood spattered on the grass.

I deserve this, I thought, and took another step.

Lord Byrne and his Bonded's throats hung open.

I deserve this. Another step.

Twenty purple faces peered at me with lifeless eyes.

I deserve this. Another.

What *this* was, I couldn't say, but I needed it like I needed air. Ronan's warning was long forgotten. Something pricked at the back of my mind, and I pushed it away. Gone were the others. Where they went, I didn't know, and even though I knew I should have cared, I didn't. There was no one but me as I approached the glittering veil up ahead. I didn't question it. Whatever was behind the veil, I had to have it. It was the only way I could be happy again.

"Don't," the Hunter commanded—his voice like a tether, pulling me back to reality. I blinked away the sparkling vision. The Hunter stood in front of the horse, preventing it from going any further than we already had. I hadn't noticed the reins I gripped with white knuckles. The leather, broken and worn, cracked under my tight grasp. Behind me, Eoin's eyes were glazed over, his blank face fixated on the rushing river. He leaned forward, pressing into my back, and forced me to bend underneath his weight.

"Eoin," I gritted, but he pressed further, reaching blindly for the reins.

The Hunter held the horse in place, keeping him from fleeing. Off to the side, Ronan tried to catch Kalee's attention by shaking her shoulders. Up ahead, the two guards ambled to the rushing river. The same river, I realized, the enchantment had beckoned me toward. Both Eoin and I would have fallen in if it hadn't been for the Hunter. The sheer volume of the river's roar was enough to indicate we wouldn't have swam free.

"The guards," I grunted to the Hunter, noting how quickly they approached the river's edge. Ronan was still too preoccupied with Kalee, and Eoin was incapable of doing anything but crushing me under his weight.

"Let them fall." The Hunter's voice was deadly, his gaze murderous. "They knew the risks of crossing into Ilythia. They'd sooner watch us die than lift a finger if the roles were reversed."

Every face of every osnádúrtha I'd come to know flashed through my mind, and I knew the Hunter was right. They would probably cheer as we fell into the river. Two fewer osnádúrtha plaguing this earth. Yet...

"If we let them die because of who they are, it doesn't make us any better than them," I said.

We held each other's gazes, his forest green and my sapphire blue. Something shifted in the light brown specks hiding amongst the meadow, and he gave me a curt nod.

"If you get too close to the river, I'm letting them fall and coming for you instead."

The horse whinnied and pawed at the ground. The Hunter shushed the horse with a gentleness I hadn't expected of him. He seemed like the type to remain calm in high-stress environments, but *gentle* was not a word I associated with him.

"I'll handle Eoin, you grab them."

The Hunter didn't question me again before rushing after the guards. I pushed myself against Eoin to no avail. No matter how loud I screamed his name or how hard I pounded his thigh, he pressed further, grappling for the reins. The guards dismounted their horses and were dangerously close to the river's edge. There wouldn't be enough time for the Hunter to reach them. I threw my head back, colliding with Eoin's, pain blooming on the back of my skull.

"FOR NINE'S SAKE," HE SWORE AND GRABBED HIS NOW BLEEDING NOSE, snapping out of the enchantment.

The body of the first guard disappeared over the river's edge. The Hunter's fingertips brushed the back of the second's before he, too, fell in. Eoin cursed again. A pang of guilt passed through me, but at least Eoin was safe. And Kalee finally returned to her senses.

Tears stained my cheeks. I wiped them away with my cloak, unsure when I started crying. Embarrassment shuddered through me. For so long, I'd been able to hide my vulnerability, to push it down until I was alone. I studied my boots, not trusting myself to not cry again. The strange music might have abated, but the feeling of utter despair and guilt still weighed heavily on my heart.

Ronan's brows furrowed as he looked in the direction where his men once stood. He held Kalee against him as if she too was struggling to forget the stain the willow's song left on her.

"I don't harbor any ill will or hate toward the witches. Why did it enchant me?" I asked, troubled.

"The workings of the willows are mostly unknown," Ronan reiterated. "Anger and hatred are a driving factor, but there are also others like guilt or jealousy that can make the willows call to you." He frowned. "It must not be limited to the witches if you three were also enchanted."

The Hunter eyed me in a way that threatened to see through the walls I put up, to peel back the emotions I didn't want anyone to see.

"Does everyone hear the same song?" I asked. It had been so powerful, so grief-driven and all-consuming, that it was as if I'd been crying for hours. No one else's face was stained with tears. Did they experience different emotions, or was I too far gone in mine?

"It is unlikely, considering we all share different experiences, different sentiments. The willows have a tendency to exploit our innermost thoughts."

"Let's move on before one of us gets trapped in the willow's clutches again," the Hunter interrupted and pressed forward. If he was bothered by the willows, he didn't show it. In fact, he acted as if the willow's song didn't faze him in the slightest. I scrunched my nose. If the rumors of wickedness were true, how could he not harbor any hate in his heart? That also meant he didn't harbor any guilt for what he'd done either.

I wanted him to be the person who offered me his warmth in the tent, but it was hard to ignore the way the willows hadn't affected him. I'd felt the guilt from hurting the osnádúrtha in my bones. Had nearly died from it. Any hope I had for the Hunter's compassion was shattered. He wasn't remorseful for those of our kind he betrayed by handing them over to the king.

Perhaps he wasn't capable of feeling anything.

The river's rushing water roared in my ears—its channel width too wide and current too strong for us to cross.

"Up ahead," the Hunter said, pointing to a decaying bridge several footspans from where we stood. Several planks were either broken or missing altogether. What was left of the bridge was rotten and unstable. Kalee and I looked at each other, questioning our life decisions up to this point.

"We'll have to leave the horses," Ronan said, dismounting before assisting Kalee. She was more than capable of doing it herself, especially with the trousers she now wore, but I had a feeling Ronan used any excuse to be close to her.

"Let's fasten them," Eoin said, guiding our horse to a nearby tree.

"No, we don't know how long we'll be. It would be cruel to leave them when there are no guarantees."

"So you would rather us walk back?" Eoin asked Ronan in disbelief.

"It's really not that far, Eoin. We'll manage."

Eoin started to argue, but he must have thought better of it because he snapped his mouth shut, the muscles in his jaw working.

We neared the bridge, its rickety state taunting us.

"The best way—"

"We will go one at a time," Eoin instructed, cutting the Hunter off. "You first, Hunter." Eoin smiled, and I shot him a look, bristling at his command. Soulless or not, the Hunter still kept us both from meeting the same fate as the guards.

The Hunter replied with a vicious smile of his own and gave Eoin a mockery of a bow. As he approached the bridge, he didn't seem concerned by the fraying rope or decayed wood. Instead, he walked across it with ease and didn't hesitate when a piece of the wooden plank broke, falling into the river.

"I'll go next, unless you wish to order more of us around." I shot Eoin a glance. Just because the Hunter was an ass didn't mean Eoin had to be one too.

"Sersh," Kalee started, but I held up a hand. There was no room for argument.

"Out of all of us, I'm the only one with a protective spell to keep me from death," I reassured her, though the spell sure as Nine didn't keep me from feeling fear. Or pain.

Water sprayed my face as I approached the rickety bridge. It might have been frozen if the current hadn't been moving so fast. Each step was slow and deliberate. The Hunter made it look easy when he crossed. Water sprayed, and my vision clouded, but I managed to make it near the end before the snap.

Without warning, my back foot pierced through the plank. The broken wood tore through my trousers, ripping my skin. I yelped and fought to regain my balance.

"Saoirse!" Kalee cried out, rushing toward the bridge, but Ronan halted her before she could run across.

"I'm fine," I ground out.

"Do you need help?" The Hunter asked, only paces from me at the end of the bridge.

"I can handle myself." My leg pulsated against the jagged wood. Warmth from my blood trickled into my boots. I tried pulling my way out to freedom, but the broken edges lodged firmly in my skin.

Groaning, I smashed the rest of the plank with my fist. The rotten wood dropped into the river before the current whisked it away. My injury was worse than I thought. Blood gushed from the wound when I pulled out the wooden stake embedded into my thigh. I stood with shaking legs, but I managed to make it the rest of the way. Sweat dripped across my brow and down my back by the time I reached the end.

"If you had let me help, you wouldn't be so exhausted now," the Hunter commented.

"I. Don't. Need. You," I panted and rolled onto my back, savoring the coolness of the ground.

"You don't," he agreed, "but one day, I'll have you begging for me."

"Saoirse, are you alright?" Kalee ran to me, quashing my chance at a comeback. By the time Ronan and Eoin had crossed the bridge, my leg stopped bleeding, but the gash remained. Eoin bent down, taking my leg in his grip, and tore my trousers to better access the wound. Cool water from his canteen cleansed the area. I gasped, not ready for the sudden assault on my senses.

"May I?" the Hunter asked, pulling out a small tin from his pack.

"Get on with it," Eoin ordered, but the Hunter didn't move. Instead, his gaze held mine, waiting for permission.

"What is it?" I asked.

"A healing poultice. It will sting, but it will help you heal faster than what you're capable of on your own."

I nodded, and the Hunter knelt next to me. "I'm going to hold the wound closed before I apply the paste, okay?"

"O-okay."

With a surprising tenderness, the Hunter laid his calloused hand on my leg and applied the earthy, yellowed paste with deft fingers. Fuck, it stung, though it worked nonetheless.

"Well, that's useful," Ronan remarked, studying the way my flesh stitched itself together.

Eoin helped me to my feet, my leg still too weak to bear all of my weight, but his concern didn't stop him from pressing the group further to find Aislinn. Kalee tried to support me, but her human strength lasted only a short time before we lagged too far behind the group. Despite helping me earlier, Eoin hardly took notice as he continued on. I fidgeted with the trim of my cloak, my annoyance lingering at the frayed edges. Ronan offered to carry me, but I refused his help. My pride wouldn't allow the Prince of Centra to aid me, even if I was starting to like the man. The Hunter, however, heard none of my protests as he hauled me over his shoulder as if I were nothing more than a sack of grain.

"Put me down," I demanded, smacking his back, his earlier words returning to me. *I'll have you begging for me.* Gods, what an infuriating faie. One moment, he was kind; the next, he was *this*.

"Are you always so stubborn?" He asked.

"Yes," Kalee and I answered.

I shot Kalee a look, but she only shrugged. "What? It's true."

"You're not supposed to agree, Kalee."

"You'd rather I lie?"

"Yes, actually. Now let me go, Hunter."

"Not if you want to make it before nightfall."

I grumbled my annoyance but didn't protest further.

Like the willows, the woods were alive with unusual sounds that I wasn't convinced came from animals. The air smelled different here—fresh and untamed. The unmistakable energy of magic tinged the atmosphere as if the land itself pulsed with it.

I hadn't noticed the chalet until the Hunter lowered me to the ground. Icicles dangled from the overhanging wooden eaves in varying sizes. Winterberries and snowdrops bloomed in the front planters. Evergreens were plentiful, and the crisp pine scent was a welcoming one.

Magic cleared the walkway free of snow if the pristine lines were any indication. We approached the blood-red door—a beacon signaling us in the crisp landscape. I imagined my mother climbing up these very steps with me in her arms nearly twenty-five years ago and wondered what had changed since she was here. Four sets of curious eyes looked to me either for permission or to make the first move; I wasn't sure. I knocked. Quick and loud, yet not so loud as to startle. The door swung on its hinges, revealing a middle-aged woman with raven hair and arctic eyes.

Chapter Twenty-Five

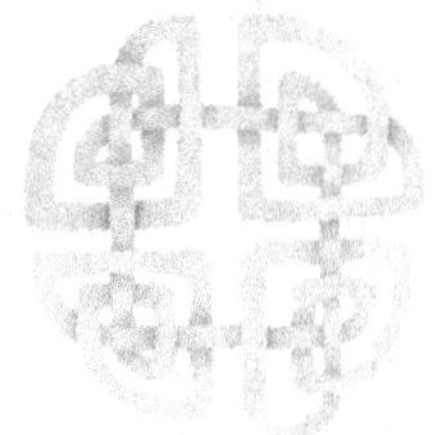

The hard lines of Aislinn's face split and reformed before they softened. Surprise. Doubt. Sorrow. Relief. All etched themselves into her as if she couldn't believe I was standing before her. Like I'd crossed over from the Otherworld, and I was but a specter.

Maybe she saw my mother.

"Saoirse," she whispered after a heartbeat and an eternity passed all at once, gripping me into the kind of hug that was long overdue. Though Aislinn had aged over two decades since the memory the seer showed me, she didn't look it—not that I'd expected her to. Witches lived about as long as the faie. As they aged, their features remained untouched for far longer than humans. Time was merely a word to the osnádúrtha, not a consequence.

In Centra, witches were known to sport vicious personalities, their ruthlessness unmatched when it came to protecting their own. Their hatred toward humans unparalleled. Surveying Aislinn, she didn't look soulless or gruesome as the king often claimed. She appeared anything but.

The few, thin lines Aislinn possessed outlined her lips and sprouted at the outer corners of her eyes, the kinds that formed after repeated years of smiling. Aislinn's broad grin faded as she inspected the rest of the group, her gaze lingered on the Hunter, then narrowed on Eoin and Ronan, their attire a dead giveaway from where they hailed.

"Aislinn, I—" The words died on my tongue. I'd been so afraid of disappointment, of failure, I hadn't let myself believe this was a viable possibility, much less prepared a decent explanation.

If she was surprised I knew her by name, she didn't show it. Instead, she took me by the hand. "It's alright. Come in, all of you. You all must be exhausted."

We all bore the haggardness of a long day's travel. Ronan's hair, for once, was out of place, the blonde strands breaking free from their leather strap. Eoin and Kalee both reflected how I felt. Exhaustion burned, burrowing beneath skin and muscle and bone—the effects of the willows still splintered on my soul. My leg was fully healed now, but smears of dried blood remained. My pants were more strips of cloth than trousers, my thigh almost wholly exposed.

Fresh sage, warm and inviting, filled the space. Not much had changed from the memory the seer showed me aside from new plants hanging from the rafters and a single silver streak in Aislinn's hair.

Like the memory, a crackling fire blazed in the hearth—the now finished, patchwork quilt draped over the rocking chair. I almost expected to see my mother walk through the door next. A pang of guilt stabbed deep in my chest.

"Let's sit," Aislinn said, ushering us into the dining area. "The best stories are ones told over a meal."

I examined the two-person dining table and the notable lack of chairs. Before I could question her, Aislinn dug into the leather pouch strapped to her waist and sprinkled its contents over the table. At the last of her mumbled words, a plume of smoke shot out, quadrupling the table's size. She repeated the action, and six plates stacked with food lined the table.

"There, that's better," she hummed.

"Incredible," Kalee gasped, and I mirrored her awe. It was a wonder the king hated magic when even the simplest things were nothing short of magnificent. "How does it work?" Kalee asked, gliding her fingers over the wooden table. We sat, the others wasting no time tucking into their food, but the knots in my stomach suppressed any appetite.

"There's magic all around us; one only needs to know how to manipulate it. The earth provides us with the tools." Aislinn pointed to her leather waist belt. "I just have to say a spell to make it happen."

"Does using your magic make you tired?" I asked. "Using mine for too long makes me feel like I'm walking through mud."

"When I was young, it did. But after a few hundred years or so, a witch learns a thing or two. Including how to increase her tolerance." She winked. "Now, as long as I have herbs available—which a good witch always does—I can cast several spells. Of course, those meant to last indefinitely require much more of me. Magic always comes at a price. Whether it's me who pays for it or another."

"So, niece," she continued, "are you going to tell me what brings you and your companions to my home? Or are you all to eat my food without so much as a word for why you're here?" Despite her words, she smiled.

My gaze met Ronan's, and he nodded. I prayed whatever he made the Hunter swear to would hold against the king's Bond, and I wondered, for the first time, if Ronan also promised the Hunter freedom to ensure our secrets remained safe.

Instinct demanded I share only what was necessary to get us to the cauldron. Information was a double-edged blade—sharp and brilliant. Useful yet lethal. I'd witness how it shaped or destroyed lives. I'd grown used to keeping as much as I could to myself. And yet, I was desperate to find answers of my own. The only person who had them sat before me. I hadn't noticed how much she resembled my mother when the seer showed me the memory. Her hair was pitch black, opposing my mother's silver. But they had the same eyes—the same high cheekbones and soft lilt to their lips.

So, I told her everything.

All the words I'd ached to tell my mother poured out of me like water bursting through a dam. I told Aislinn of the seer and about the memory —why I needed the cauldron. I told her about the Shadow King and the fomorii. About my mother's fate and how I'd become one of the king's Bonded. I couldn't bring myself to explain the things the Conqueror King commanded of me or about the osnádúrtha I betrayed.

"Your Bond Mark, let me see it," she said in a deadly whisper.

I turned and lifted my braid off my neck. Aislinn sucked in a breath, her hand cool against my Mark. The serpent with a knot in its middle pulsated under her touch. She cursed.

"Your seer is right. This magic is…old. Formidable. Only the cauldron is powerful enough to unravel it."

"Then you know where it is?" I asked, an embarrassing amount of hope in my voice.

"Yes," she sighed. "But it will not be an easy task to retrieve it."

"Where is it?" Eoin asked.

"With my sister, the queen."

I nearly choked. Another sister. A queen at that. I'd been without family for so long, the thought of reuniting with not one, but two aunts sent my heart soaring.

"Don't look so hopeful, human," Aislinn said to Eoin. "Just because she is my sister doesn't mean she'll help us. The Queen of Ilythia doesn't often bother herself with the plights of others."

"And what about Tenebris?" Ronan asked. "Will she lend any aid to him?"

"My sister knows of the False God. It's a bit of a complicated history in Ilythia. His history has turned into a cautionary tale—a bedtime story for the witchlings. To convince her of his return, she'll want more than a seer's word. She'll want proof."

"The seer's word isn't enough?"

She laughed. "You met one. Do you believe it had your best interest in mind?"

Ronan didn't answer. My heart sank. How were we supposed to gather evidence when the fomorii were only in Centra? Not to mention, any time we killed one, its body disappeared.

"I'm more worried about your Bond, Saoirse. Once we rid you of it, then we'll worry about Tenebris."

"Do you know why my mother wanted to place a protection spell?"

Aislinn's expression softened. "She was worried. Arundell was going through another one of its squabbles between the courts, and there'd been an assassination attempt on your family. Your brother was older, but you were a babe. Your father sent you and your mother to Centra until tensions calmed. It was a peaceful territory then. The protection spell was a last-minute precaution. I tried to get you both to stay here, but she and our eldest sister never got along. Her mind was made up."

"Why would someone try to assassinate my family?" Since I could remember, my mother had always been careful, always looking over her shoulder. I assumed it was because I was faie, but perhaps she was fearful for another reason.

"Did she not tell you who she and your father were? What *you* are?"

I shook my head. "My father was a merchant who died at sea. I only just found out about my brother."

Aislinn frowned. "Your father was a faierie king, child. Your mother, his queen."

I choked on a piece of bread. "Come again?"

I found Kalee's wide eyes across the table. It couldn't be true. It was the most preposterous thing anyone could have said to me, never mind the family I'd gained or the fact that my brother and father could still be alive. My insides turned to lead.

"I suppose once she learned of your father's and brother's deaths, she would have wanted to keep you as far away from Arundell as possible, even if it meant erasing your history."

The lead inside my gut sank deeper, dragging my heart with it. The hope of meeting my brother and father flickered out and died once more.

"So my mother knew they were dead and she still didn't tell me anything?" Anger bubbled and frothed at my lips. "She never once mentioned I had a brother, you know. Much less anything about you or your sister." I stood, my chair scraping along the floor. Eoin grabbed my wrist, his touch intended to comfort me. I pulled away from his grip.

"It's laughable, really. How much she kept from me. She especially didn't mention anything about a throne," I scoffed. I couldn't care less about any claim to the aes sídhe, but she had hidden my entire life from me. I'd hoped to find answers with Aislinn, not more questions.

I turned on Aislinn. "Why didn't you come for us—for me?" My voice broke. Put my back to the others. Aislinn came up behind me, her hand on my shoulder.

"I'm so sorry. When the borders were shut down, I couldn't go to you, and it was not for lack of trying. My sister forbade any witch from leaving Ilythia. It wasn't an order I could disobey, no matter how much I wanted to. I'd prayed your mother would find her way here with you, but she never did."

"Surely she would have known her sister was in danger. Why would she do such a thing?"

"What's good for one isn't always good for the many," Aislinn said solemnly. "Once Tara and her coven were killed, she fortified our borders. She couldn't risk any more witches, even if it meant sacrificing her sister."

My brows furrowed. "Who's Tara?"

"My mother," Ronan said. I whirled around. Kalee and Eoin hadn't so much as flinched. Only the Hunter appeared as taken off guard as I had.

"Let me get this straight," I said slowly as if tasting the words for the first time. "Your mother, the wife of the king who despises magic—kills people because of it—was a witch?"

"Yes."

I laughed, hard and cruel, not missing the irony of the situation.

"It also means," Ronan continued, "I'm a witch."

Again, I looked to Kalee and Eoin to find the shock marred on their faces, but none was there. They'd known and hadn't said a word. I wanted to be angry at this, too, but I had no right. If the roles were reversed, I would have taken it to my grave.

"The witch gene in the male line is so rare, but my sister had always been so powerful," Aislinn said, examining Ronan with a sort of awe in her eyes.

"*Your* sister?" Ronan and I said in unison. I coughed, choking on my water. Ronan's eyes were wider than I'd ever seen them. It might have been comical if my entire world wasn't shattering around me.

"You two didn't know?" Aislinn asked, looking between us. "I assumed you did since you were travelling together. Tara was my youngest sister."

"I assure you, us being cousins was the last thing I expected you to say tonight," Ronan said. "No offense, Saoirse."

"None taken," I deadpanned, deciding *this* was the most preposterous thing anyone could have told me. "I can confirm my mother conveniently left this out as well. How many sisters do you have exactly?"

Aislinn stood to retrieve something from the next room, explaining as she did so. "I have many sisters within the covens and fewer brothers. But I have three sisters by blood." Aislinn handed me a portrait of Aislinn and her sisters. "Saoirse—your mother, Racenda. Ronan—your mother, Tara. And Petranella, the Witch Queen. Petra sent Tara to Centra and Racenda to Arundell to *build alliances*." Her voice thickened at the last two words.

The silence was audible as Ronan and I examined the likeness and then each other. I studied his face, his hair, his eyes. He never looked anything like his father, but I didn't realize how similar we truly were. We had the same blue eyes, fair skin, and high cheekbones. My cousin had been close to me for almost half my life, and I had never known.

A horrible, dreadful thought dawned on me. "Oh gods. If you're my cousin, then your father..." I was going to be sick. The air grew too warm, the fire in the hearth suddenly ablaze.

Ronan rubbed the back of his neck, a half-attempt at a smile tugged at his lips. "You know what they say, the blood of the covenant is thicker than the water of the womb, right?"

"Does he know?" I asked.

"No. He doesn't know what I am either."

Would the king care if he knew I was his niece? Would he care if he knew the truth about his son? All those years, my cousin and my uncle were within reach. My uncle, who sanctioned my abuse. Who forced me to bow to him. Forced me to go against those with magic running through their veins. No. That box was too full to unpack right now. I shoved it deep, *deep*, down.

"How have you managed to hide it all this time?" Aislinn asked.

"The witch gene is so rare in males, he didn't think twice about it. My mother, however, caught the signs early on. She taught me how to hide it from my father before she passed."

"What is there to hide?" I asked. Witches weren't like the aes sídhe or the merrows. They bore no fangs or pointed ears or scales, for that matter. They looked utterly human.

Ronan's eyes flashed black, lightless and gruesome. I gasped, taken aback at the sudden change.

"What happened to your eyes?"

"It's a defense mechanism," Aislinn answered for him. "The lid protects our eyes during flight or battle as well as enhances our vision and focus, which is why it can appear when a witch is angered or stressed. It takes formidable will to control it in a high-stakes environment."

Ronan drank deeply from his cup. I reached for my own, wishing it were something stronger.

"What of your sister, Ronan?" Aislinn asked when the silence stretched a little too thin.

"Ceana was not so lucky. Her prophetic abilities were too powerful to control or hide," he said, explaining why the seer had been so interested in her.

Aislinn's face blanched. "Is she—?"

"Alive," Ronan confirmed. "But locked away. Forbidden from leaving her tower." Ronan scrubbed a hand over his face. I understood now why he risked so much to help the other osnádúrtha escape Centra. He didn't just want vengeance for his mother's death; he sought to help his sister if he had the chance.

"The witch the seer spoke of hiding in Centra—were they referring to you?" I knew the answer, but I couldn't help but ask.

Ronan nodded. "I was studying how to break your Bond. Until the seer said otherwise, I thought I could."

Raw emotion flared in my chest. "Thank you," I choked.

Ronan pressed his lips together. "Saoirse, I didn't—"

"Thank you for trying. For helping the others." When Kalee told me she'd been searching for a way for me to escape, my heart felt full.

Hearing how Ronan sought to free me himself threatened to burst my heart with gratitude. Even though their plan kept falling apart, I was thankful to have people who cared enough to try. I was alone for so long. It had only ever been myself and Kalee. Perhaps there was now room for others.

My cousin nodded once again, accepting my gratitude.

The table had gone completely silent. Food remained untouched after Aislinn revealed the impossible. But there was one more question on my mind ever since I learned of Aislinn's existence.

"So, if my mother was a witch, am I a witch too?"

"It's hard to say," Aislinn answered after what seemed like an eternity. "It's more common for the witch gene to appear in females. But your father was faie—the magic may have been conflicting within you until one took over."

"The witch's mark is one indication of a witch," she continued, tapping the space outside of her eye. I suspected our similar colors were due to genetics, but I was wrong. "There is also the protective lid." Her eyes flashed black like Ronan's, transforming into a vicious, ethereal creature.

Nope. Definitely not capable of that.

"The biggest difference between faie and witch, as you know, is the magic between us. Both originate from the Mother—from what she seeded into existence. The aes sídhe—the faie—their magic comes from the gods, whereas witches pull magic from the earth and require spells to manipulate it. I suspect you do not need spells or the earth to channel your magic?" Aislinn studied me and the shadows eddying around my hands.

I shook my head.

"Do you know if my father's or brother's magic was like mine?"

"No, I believe they were both wind wielders."

I held in a sigh. It would have been nice to inherit one thing from my father. I had nothing to connect me to him.

Under the table, Kalee grabbed my hand and squeezed it. Grateful, I squeezed it back.

"What can you tell us about the cauldron?" Eoin asked.

"The cauldron, *boy*, is nothing to trifle with," Aislinn chided. "The First God gifted it to his beloved sister, who made the witches. It is the origin of our existence. The cauldron of knowledge, power, and death must never leave the witch kingdom. Do you all understand?" Everyone nodded their agreement except Eoin, who eyed her suspiciously.

"We can use it to break your Bond, but then we must return it without anyone knowing," Aislinn said.

"Can we not ask your sister if we can use it?" I questioned. Even if they didn't get along, surely it wouldn't be an issue if we were to borrow it once.

"No. She would never agree to let another wield its power, especially someone who potentially has a claim to her throne. My sister does not share her power willingly or without a great cost. We will have to steal it if you want to use it."

I should have been concerned that Aislinn's first thought was thievery, but she was more familiar with her sister and this kingdom than any of us were. I had no other choice but to trust her judgment. "Where is it?"

"Assuming she still possesses it, and it's not locked in a tomb somewhere, it will be at the Mountain Castle."

"How long would it take to travel there?" Eoin asked.

"Four, maybe five days on foot. Or, we can fly and get there in two." A mischievous smile spread over Aislinn's face, eerily similar to the ones Ronan got when he concocted wild plans.

Mother save me.

CHAPTER TWENTY-SIX

We stayed up well into the night, hatching a plan to steal and use the cauldron before the Witch Queen noticed its absence. Aislinn was confident she knew how to break the Bond but wanted Ronan's assistance. He, of course, agreed. The two were thick as thieves, inventing one preposterous idea after another. When Aislinn's wife, Alice, came home, she wasn't surprised to find five strangers sitting at her table.

"Alice is a healer. She's used to taking in the strays," Aislinn joked, greeting her wife with a kiss.

By appearance, Alice was Aislinn's opposite. Where Aislinn was fair-skinned with jet-black hair, Alice had a deep brown complexion with hair as white as winter's first snow. Their eyes, however, their witch's mark, were the same crystal blue. Their minds, it seemed, were also the same. Without having to ask, one knew what the other wanted, as if they could communicate with thoughts alone.

"We are anamcharas," Alice said simply when I commented on their connection.

"Anamcharas? Are you not married then?" Kalee asked.

"Like what you humans call soulmates. It's the Triple Goddess calling two souls together. Witches may marry, but when an anamchara bond is accepted between two people, it's not a wedding; it's a mating. Sadly, it doesn't happen for everyone, but when it does, well, it's magical. So no, Aislinn is not my wife, she's my mate."

Alice and Aislinn reached for one another at the same moment, a wordless conversation passing between them.

A weight settled on my chest. I blinked back the burn behind my eyelids, the ache that bloomed in my heart, weighing heavily on my limbs. I'd been alone and without love for so long it hurt. I had Kalee, of course, but the kind of love radiating from Aislinn and Alice? I feared I'd never find it. To be cherished. To be wanted, not for what I could do, but for who I was—a soul connection.

"I believe the aes sídhe use the same term," Alice added, looking to me for confirmation, catching me off guard. My cheeks heated. I knew so little of my culture, having grown up in a predominantly human world.

"Yes, but the aes sídhe have only one anamchara," the Hunter answered, and I envied him for knowing more about our people.

My thoughts returned to the seer—on the king performing his own bastardized version of the anamchara bonds. The unknown clawed at me like a wild animal trapped in a cage, thoughts pacing, slamming into the same unanswered questions over and over again. *How? Why?* Next to Kalee, Ronan's brow furrowed, and I wondered if the same questions prowled his thoughts.

"You can have more than one soul mate?" Kalee asked. If Alice let her, Kalee would interrogate her all night. She'd already requested to view their collection of books. When it came time to leave Ilythia, I had no doubt that Kalee would know more about the witches and their history than Ronan.

"Yes...and no," Alice answered. "We can indeed have two anamcharas, one line is reserved for our life partners, the other for our familiars. While the line to our familiars is not romantic in nature, it is still just as powerful. Centuries ago, it was common to have a soul connection with the dragons."

"Now they're primarily cats or nosey owls ever since the dragons died out," Aislinn added, setting down tea for everyone. An owl hooted in the distance, and Alice slapped Aislinn lightly on her wrist at the jest.

"Can you talk to your familiars?" Eoin asked.

"Of course. Our bonds allow us to communicate no matter the barrier." Alice gave Aislinn another loving look, her blue eyes shimmering like light bouncing off water in the wake of a sunrise.

"My mother used to tell me stories of dragons," I said, the memory resurfacing out of nowhere.

"She was obsessed with them." Aislinn smiled, her eyes distant. "If she could have raised them from the dead, she would have."

The weight of my mother's absence hung heavy in the air. I would have given anything to hear the truth from her lips. Lies tainted her memory, and I found myself questioning everything I'd ever known. Another thought struck me. "Is Alice the reason why you weren't sent off to another kingdom like mine or Ronan's mother?"

Aislinn's smile was almost sorrowful. "Sometimes Petranella is capable of kindness."

"She has a funny way of showing it," Alice scoffed, taking our empty teacups. "Stationing you all the way out here. She wanted you out of her hair."

"She wanted someone she could trust to protect the border."

Alice shot her an incredulous glare. "Here, you're not a threat to her crown."

"Come now, my sweet. She knows I'd never touch it."

Alice sighed but didn't argue. "The hour is late. If you all are going to commit treason in two days time, you need to stock up on your rest."

Ronan stood. "I don't want to intrude, we—"

"I'll have none of that," Alice said. "You're staying. All of you. Follow me, I'll show you to your rooms. You'll have fresh clothes and baths. You can't go sneaking around a kingdom looking like that." Alice gave us a once-over. Between my torn clothes, Kalee's dress, Ronan's Centran patch, and Eoin's armor, we were far from blending in. Only the Hunter appeared ready for espionage.

She gave Aislinn a knowing look over her shoulder before she led the others down the hall. I remained, twirling my half-drunk teacup.

"Are you sure there's plenty of space?" I asked.

"Magic, darling Saoirse. We always have room for as long as anyone needs."

Something in my heart squeezed at Aislinn's words, the way she looked at me—like she loved me. I didn't even know the witch, not really, but I wanted to so desperately it hurt.

"You can stay with us, you know—when this is all over," Aislinn said, her voice soft. "I know I'm not your mother, I'd never dare to try to be, but Alice and I…well, we'd treat you as our own. Not that you need mothering, you're grown for Goddess' sakes, I only meant—"

I wrapped Aislinn in a hug, tears threatening to spill over. My heart ached so much it nearly imploded. Once my Bond was broken, I knew I could never return to Centra. In truth, I didn't know what I was going to do when it happened, but being here with Aislinn, this was the most obvious choice.

"Unless you'd like to try to reclaim the throne in Arundell," she added when I didn't reply.

"Gods, no," I laughed, wiping at my eyes before she saw. "There's no one for me there. I would like to stay with you very much." I smiled, big and true, for the first time in over a decade. Since Ronan offered to break my Bond, I hadn't let hope grow. I'd given it no water, no sunlight. I kept it locked away, dark and secluded, too afraid to let it be seen—afraid someone would snatch it away at first glance. Now, there was no hiding it. It bloomed in my chest, wild and free. Aislinn's offer emboldened me, and for the first time in fifteen years, I allowed myself to dream. To hope.

To live.

"I was the one who suggested we go west in the first place. I might be *just a human*, Ronan Toirdelbach, but I'm an asset. I'm going, and that's final." Kalee stood with her arms crossed over her chest, her honeyed eyes hardened with defiance. The leathers Alice had given her hugged every hard line. A sword I hadn't known Kalee knew how to wield was strapped to her back. Despite Kalee's badass appearance, Ronan was insistent that she remain at the chalet with Alice. I had to agree with him. I didn't want her anywhere near conflict if our plan went south, but I also understood what it meant to make your own decisions, so I remained silent on the matter.

I looked down at my own leathers; the thin underlayer of fabric was soft and flexible, hugging my legs, back, and torso, fitting like a glove—the leather was stretched and warm. They caressed every curve, unlike my usual oversized attire. The men had also been outfitted in flying leathers, hugging the Hunter's and Eoin's backside in a sinful manner. Something curled low in my stomach. Nope. Not looking.

"You've lost, nephew." Aislinn smiled and handed Kalee flying goggles before Ronan could dig his grave any further. "Here," she said, handing goggles to Eoin and me. "Human, you're with me. Kalee, with Ronan.

Follow my lead and trust yourself. Your instincts will kick in once you hit the air," Aislinn commanded. "And you, Aodhán, are you going to use what you've got, or do I need to tie you to the broom and drag you the whole way there?"

I jolted at the Hunter's surname. How did she…?

The Hunter gave Aislinn a wry smile before conjuring massive, mottled gray, feathered wings. My jaw fell open as did the others. The Hunter stretched his wings out wide as if it was the first time they'd seen daylight in a long while. They gleamed in the morning sun. Breathtaking.

"Ready?" He smirked, holding out his arms.

This, it seemed, was my mind's breaking point. It was no longer accepting surprises, so the shock at his wings wasn't allowed to take hold. "No, thanks. I'll take my chances with Aislinn or Ronan."

"Oh no, you won't," Aislinn stated. "We can't carry more than one person at a time. You will have to suck it up and fly in the arms of a pretty faie male. Horrible, I know."

The Hunter laughed, but I failed to see the humor in it.

Eoin rolled his eyes, stepping before me, leaning down until his lips were a hair's breadth away from my ear. "Fly safe, Saoirse." He kissed my temple. A flush crept up my neck. I guess since everyone's secrets were laid out on the table last night, Eoin no longer felt the need to keep up with appearances. I sighed in relief. We could all relax a little. Eoin wouldn't have to treat me like a Bonded anymore.

The Hunter cleared his throat. My flush deepened.

"Come, human. We need to move soon if you want to retrieve the cauldron by tomorrow night." Aislinn kissed her wife goodbye, and her eyes flashed, turning into two dark abysses. She readied herself on her broomstick, Eoin following her lead. It looked rather uncomfortable, but neither she nor Eoin complained. Ronan's face turned green when he mounted his. Kalee, on the other hand, grinned from ear to ear.

The Hunter's hulking arms grasped me against him, hooking an arm under my knees, the other wrapping around my middle. He didn't wear goggles, nor did his eyes darken like Aislinn's and Ronan's, but he didn't flinch at the rush of air as we climbed *up, up, up.*

My heart fell into my stomach, and I clung to the Hunter, my arms wrapped tightly around his neck. Breakfast threatened to return to the ground before we leveled out. To our left, Aislinn's cackle carried on the wind. Eoin's face paled while the sickly green color of Ronan's complexion was replaced with a grin. He was a natural in the air. Ronan weaved and bobbed, getting a feel for the broom's handle. The prince belonged in the sky.

Ilythia was cold and vast, with trees so thick it was hard to discern what was on the ground. No maps of Ilythia existed in Centra, and no clear markers stood out. Now and then, plumes of smoke would clear through the trees, signaling life amongst the pines.

"What's with the wings? Does the king know?" I asked the Hunter, needing to satiate my curiosity and give me an excuse for staring at him. Looking up at his face was unavoidable in this position.

"Gods no. I glamour them for obvious reasons. The people of Centra aren't exactly welcoming of our kind, and the less the king knows about me, the better. I didn't want my wings to become something he could use against me. As for why, well, it's not uncommon for the people of my court to have wings."

"Glamour?"

"Do you truly know nothing of our kind?" The question wasn't mean-spirited, but an honest one. "The aes sídhe use glamours to alter their appearance or the appearance of the things around them. What may appear to be a quill could truly be a dagger."

"Is it difficult to do so?" I asked, wondering how much energy he'd been expending to disguise himself all this time.

"It can be challenging to master, but once you get the hang of it, it becomes second nature. I can teach you if you like."

My brows scrunched, giving the Hunter a wary gaze. He'd been suspiciously kind to me since we'd left Rothcek, and now he was offering to teach me. It was difficult to discern truth from lies—earnest intentions from carefully crafted masks of deceit. The truth was, I *would* like to take the Hunter up on his offer. Maybe then, and once I was free of my Bond, I could become someone new. Change my appearance. My life. Disguise my shadows and the skin of Saoirse—a woman who had lost so much of herself, who had been used to carry out the horrible deeds of another. Yet something told me it didn't matter whose skin I wore, that guilt would always be beneath, right under the surface.

Instead, I asked, "How does Aislinn know who you are?"

He paused as if considering his words, weighing them with the clench of his jaw. "We've met before in Arundell. Aislinn, along with a few other witches, escorted the new queen—your mother—to the castle. All the courts were there for her coronation." His grip on me tightened. "I didn't realize who Aislinn was until I saw her. She looked familiar, but I couldn't place where I knew her until she said your mother's name. It had been so long, I'd nearly forgotten. And when I remembered, I didn't want to interfere with your conversation. Had I known we were looking for your aunt, I'd have said something sooner."

I eyed the Hunter. I took Aislinn not slamming the door in his face as a good sign. Aislinn didn't act like she hated him, but she might not know what he'd done for the Conqueror King.

"You knew my parents?" I asked, taken aback. "You've known who I was—what I was? And you've never said anything?"

"Would you have believed me if I did?"

I didn't answer. There was no need, because I wouldn't have. If Aislinn hadn't addressed the Hunter by his surname, I might not have believed him now. Even still, suspicion wrapped around his words.

"How old are you?" I asked. He looked to be around my age, if not a few years ahead of me. But, like any osnádúrtha, faie aged differently. It was impossible to tell. If he'd known my parents, had met Aislinn, he would have been much older than I thought.

"I'm approaching my hundred and tenth name day."

"Practically ancient." I'd been around humans for so long, the number was staggering, though it was considered paltry for the faie.

"Yet still young enough to try to seduce you." He winked. I would have smacked him if he didn't quite literally hold my life in his hands.

The wind tugged at my braid to the point of pain. "I still don't understand why you would leave Arundell," I said, changing the subject. "Most osnádúrtha are desperate to get out of Centra, not in."

"To look for you." The emerald of his green eyes cut sharper than any jewel.

I choked on my saliva.

"Excuse you?" I finally managed after my hacking. "I must be stuck in a fever dream because I couldn't have heard you right. Why would anyone do such a thing? Why would *you*, the biggest bastard of the Bonded—and I mean that when I say it—want to save me? You don't even know me. You've never been nice to me. Not until recently, anyway." My cheeks heated, and I hated him all the more for it. If his embrace didn't keep me from falling several thousand paces, protection spell or not, I might have hit him. Never mind the wings or the Hunter knowing Aislinn, or my family's secrets. *This* was the most shocking revelation of all.

"After your father was killed and his throne usurped...well, Arundell changed. I'd heard the queen and the princess escaped. I was glad, relieved even. But years later, when I learned their daughter was forced to Bond with the king, I felt responsible for getting you out of that shithole. Your father was my idol. He did so much for me than he ever knew. I didn't have a chance to repay him for his kindness before he passed. The least I could do is honor his death."

"So you needed to be a gigantic asshole to me because?"

He laughed, and some of the tension between us eased.

"I couldn't have anyone grow suspicious. No one could know I had any kind of connection with you. You know how they don't like the Bonded befriending one another."

I nodded. He was right. We were kept separate from one another to keep from banding together. I didn't even know his true name, for gods' sakes.

The corner of his mouth kicked up. "Though I'm not all sorry for it. I do enjoy getting a rise out of you."

I pinched the space between his neck and shoulder without thinking. His eyes snapped to mine, and the air hummed around us. Just like that, the tension between us tightened, making my heart flutter so hard I was worried he could feel it wracking my body.

"How did you plan to rescue me if you were Bonded?" I asked, needing to change the subject. "Unless that is also a falsehood?"

"It's real, unfortunately," he sighed. "But necessary to get close to you. I intended to break mine, thinking I'd be able to learn how the human king was making Bonds and reverse it. I'll admit I underestimated the nature of the Bond until it was too late. The least I could do then was keep an eye on you and help keep you safe." He paused for a moment as if debating whether he should divulge the next bit.

"When the king found out about the smugglers Byrne colluded with, it wasn't the first time you'd left information behind. It was just the first time I wasn't there to catch it. I know I haven't always seemed to have the best intentions, but I needed to keep up the appearance that I wanted nothing to do with you, like I did with any other Bonded. I didn't want to chance anyone drawing a connection between us, at least not before I knew how to get you out of there."

I stared at him for a long moment, my mind trying to sort through everything I thought I knew about him—all of our previous interactions. I blinked. "So when you called the chancellor away?"

"I orchestrated it. And a few other times as well. Fuck, it took everything in me not to kill him where he stood." The Hunter's grip tightened around me. "I know you hate me, little shadow. I do not fault you for it. So many times I wanted to whisk you away. To put as much distance between you and the chancellor. I failed you. I'm sorry."

I thought back through the two years since the Hunter had been Bound to the king. Had I still been punished? Yes, but they'd been shorter. Most of the time because the chancellor was called away.

"You have helped me," I admitted. "My punishments have eased somewhat since you came to Rothcek." I didn't know what else to say. I wouldn't thank him. I wouldn't fall to his feet and forget his previous actions toward the osnádúrtha because he had occasionally been able to pull the chancellor away.

"But you've also hunted and killed other osnádúrtha for the king," I said, the words thick on my tongue. "Ronan said the Song of the Willows preyed on strong, negative emotions, and you made it through unscathed. If what you say is true, how do you not feel guilty for your actions?"

"I didn't enjoy what I had to do, but I will not feel guilty for protecting you. I'll never feel guilty for keeping you safe. I'd do it again if I had to." The heat from his gaze warmed my cheeks, but I forced myself to look away. He hadn't done this for me, but for my father. For gods' sakes, the Hunter didn't even know me. Not truly.

"So you risked your life for me because of my father? Because I cannot grasp why you would come to my aid when you do not *know* me." Something in my gut twisted. "How exactly did you know my family?"

"Your mother and father were my king and queen—the rulers of the Upperlands. I came to find you because I wanted to. No ulterior motive. I wanted to see you safe, little shadow. So no, I didn't know you when I came to Centra. Even still, I don't know you well enough now, not the way I want to. But I didn't have to get to know you first before risking my life. These last few days we've spent together have told me all I needed to know. I would do it again in a heartbeat."

My pulse thundered, and I was grateful for the screech of the wind, for I feared he would hear the way his words made me react.

"You're mad, Hunter. Has anyone ever told you that?" I huffed a laugh, shaking out the thoughts. There were too many conflicting feelings warring with one another. The most critical being suspicion for the male who risked his life, his freedom, for someone he'd never met.

"Cillian," he corrected.

"What?"

"My name is Cillian."

"Cillian," I repeated softly, my tongue working of its own volition, rolling off smoother than I would have liked. I could have sworn he shuddered when I said it as if it had been too long since someone spoke his name.

I crashed the moment Aislinn conjured a bed for me in her cabin, which acted as our halfway point. Morning came too swiftly, and our breakfast was quick before we departed at dawn. Aislinn was insistent we arrive at the Mountain Castle after sunset—*to let the night camouflage us.* Part of me wanted to stay in the cabin, secluded by the forest and unbothered by obstacles arising every step of the way. The threat of the Shadow King existed outside these doors. My freedom lay beyond this cabin, but so did the possible disappointment of failing to retrieve the cauldron. And then there was Cillian. Our conversation took hold of my dreams and replayed in my mind as soon as I woke.

"Tell me about Arundell," I said as soon as we were up in the air. Cillian appeared genuine enough, but I longed to uncover any deeper reason he had to break my Bond aside from the loyalty he held to my father.

My lack of knowledge of our homeland was no longer a shock to Cillian. He didn't hesitate when he explained, "Arundell is divided into four courts. Samhradh, the summer lands; Earrach, the spring lands; Fómhar, the fall lands; and Geimhreadh, the winter lands." He maneuvered his grip on me to demonstrate their location as he listed them, using a hand to stack them in the air to indicate the courts' locations. Samhradh being the most southern court and Geimhreadh the most northern.

"The aes sídhe lands are not only divided by the courts, but also by the Upper and Lowerlands," he continued. "Fómhar and Geimhreadh make up the Upperlands, and the Lowerlands consist of Samhradh and Earrach. The Upper and the Lowerlands are always squabbling, as are the courts within them, but the main conflict is typically between the two Upper courts and two Lower courts."

"And which court are you from?"

"Fómhar. Your family is from Geimhreadh," he offered.

Geimhreadh. I wondered what it looked like. Was it a land made of eternal ice and snow? It sounded cold. I repressed a shiver.

"What did you do in Arundell?" I asked, fishing for more information.

The wind whipped through his black hair, making it difficult not to get lost in the various shades. "I was a commanding officer in the Upperlands army," he said, shifting me in his arms. His brows furrowed at the mere mention of his past.

"Was?"

"The moment I left Arundell, I left that life behind, but I will help you break your Bond any way I can and, if you wish, bring you home to Arundell."

Home. "Aislinn…she offered…" Any home I had was with Aislinn now. I couldn't leave right after I'd found her. I didn't know Arundell. There was nothing there for me now that I knew my brother and father were dead.

The Hunter shook his head. "I will not force you to return to Arundell. It will be your choice. You will always have a choice."

"Why would you offer to take me back to Arundell if there was no life for you there? Not that we'd make one *together*," I amended. Oh gods. Why did I say that? My face grew hot as embarrassment crawled up my throat. I wanted to rip out my own tongue.

The green of his eyes twinkled, a million different retorts passing behind his gaze, but he didn't seize the opportunity to taunt me.

"It is your birthright," he finally answered.

I laughed. Actually laughed. In his face. Cillian didn't find it as amusing as I did, however, if his scowl was any indication.

"Just because it's my *birthright* doesn't mean it's the right decision. I know little about Arundell or its people. There isn't any chance I would ever make a good ruler." Besides, I'd seen what power did to someone. I wanted no part of it.

"Those who are reluctant to lead often make the best leaders."

I rolled my eyes and tore my gaze from him, letting the wind drown out our conversation.

The Mountain Castle was visible far before we could travel to it on foot. If you weren't paying attention, it would have been easy to miss. It didn't dominate the land like the one in Rothcek; it *was* the land. The castle conformed to the side of the mountain. A few turrets and bridges jutted out, but the body of the castle was carved out of the mountain itself.

Aislinn signaled for us to descend, and we landed in a small clearing a few miles from the castle.

"You five—follow this trail until you reach the door at the mountain's base." She pointed to a narrow footpath to her right. "It's rarely used, so there shouldn't be many guards, if any, aside from the watchtowers. Saoirse, when you get about a mile out, you will have to conceal the group." I blanched. When we crafted this plan, I knew what would be required of me, but it didn't make it any easier. It was hard enough to conceal Cillian when we came across the fomorii in Centra. Three more people? I feared I wasn't strong enough.

"Once inside, if the cauldron is there, Ronan should be able to sense it. The cauldron belongs to the witches. Its power calls to any witch of the royal line. It's possible you might be able to sense it too, Saoirse, but with your faie blood, I'm not sure. No one but Ronan is allowed to touch it, understand?"

"What happens if we do?" Kalee asked.

"Then my sister will know. You do not want to meet her under such circumstances." Aislinn's warning trembled through me.

"I will fly into the main entrance and occupy my sister while you all search for the cauldron. Meet me back here in two hours. That should give you plenty of time to get in and out. Do not linger in the castle longer than you have to. If you're caught, I will not be able to help any of you," she said solemnly. "My voice holds little sway. If I am not back within two hours, do not wait for me. Meet me at the cabin instead."

She grabbed Ronan and me, pulling us into a tight hug. "Be safe, be quick, be smart." She clasped Cillian and Kalee on the shoulder. "Look after my family. And you, human, don't do anything stupid," she said to Eoin, and then she took off on her broom. Aislinn's unbound raven hair whipped behind her, untamed as the wind itself, and soon she was nothing but a speck in the dusky sky.

CHAPTER TWENTY-SEVEN

"Let's move," Eoin ordered, stashing the last of the brooms behind a bush. The trek to the base of the Mountain Castle was swift. We jogged the first mile. Kalee lagged, struggling to keep pace with the rest of us, but she didn't complain or stop.

"You have this," I said, falling back to match her stride.

She grunted a nod, increasing her footsteps.

As Aislinn instructed, I used my shadows to conceal us a mile from the entrance. A headache bloomed behind my eyes at the effort, but I managed. Though I wasn't sure how long it would hold.

Hidden within the rock itself, the door to the Mountain Castle was difficult to find. But Cillian, ever observant, spotted it when the rest of us couldn't. There was no one at the entrance to the castle—no one along the trail at all. The only signs of any sentries were the guard towers and the occasional witches on patrol flying overhead.

Ronan approached the stone door and pulled from the pouch strapped to his waist. He pinched the herbs together before rubbing them between his palms and placing his hands on the door, muttering under his breath. The door snicked open, surprisingly soft for one made of stone.

"How did you know how to do that?" I asked.

"My mother taught me a thing or two before she passed. What mischief seeker doesn't want to know how to unlock doors?" He smirked.

"Either the witches are overconfident in their ability to defend themselves, or we are severely underestimating them," I whispered as Ronan inched the door open.

"Between the aerial patrols and the border protections, there is little risk of an attack. Besides, no one is foolish enough to attack Ilythia, not even my father," Ronan answered.

"We are, apparently," I grumbled. While we weren't attacking the witches with weapons and bloodshed, stealing their most precious heirloom was probably far worse. I grimaced.

"Patrol," Cillian warned. The trees were dense enough to provide sufficient coverage, but I still strengthened the shadows concealing us. Sweat broke out along my brow, and the leathers Alice lent me became too stuffy. Five witches flew overhead and looped in a circle before they veered off in another direction.

I loosed a breath, letting my grip on the shadows slacken. I would need all my strength once we were inside.

The natural, rough rock of the mountain transformed into a smooth, glittering, deep tawny stone when we crossed the threshold. Our footsteps were silent as we weaved down various hallways and up several flights of stairs.

"Are you sure you know where you're going?" I asked Ronan. It was only a matter of time before we encountered someone.

"Yes. It's here. I can feel it." Ronan pressed on. His concentration was focused solely on this task. We followed Ronan up a spiral staircase, his steps growing quick and careless.

I grabbed Ronan by the tunic and motioned everyone to get against the wall, pulling the shadows all around us as I did so.

Two stone-faced witches marched down the hallway, long blades and daggers strapped to their persons. Their footsteps were so quiet, I barely heard them in time. If I hadn't, Ronan would have run right into them.

Positive the witches were gone, I signaled everyone with a nod to continue. Ronan's steps halted before a gleaming black door with brass handles. It was then that I could feel it —the foreign heartbeat pulsating in my head.

The cauldron.

There might be more witch in me than I suspected.

Ronan's shoulders relaxed when the door clicked open.

"You'd think it would be locked or at least guarded," Kalee commented.

I warily nodded my agreement. It all seemed too easy.

Cillian shut the door behind us, and the sconces along the walls lit up. A single statue stood in the center of the room. The ancient, gray stone featured three women in different stages of life huddling around a stone cauldron. The first woman was young and beautiful—the second, matronly and plump with child. And the third was withered and hunched, moments from death—three moons etched beneath the women: waxing crescent, full, and waning crescent.

"The Triple Goddess," Ronan breathed, his eyes transfixed on the statue.

"Who?" I asked.

"The Triple Goddess, the patron goddess of Ilythia, represents the cycle of life and the need for change and transformation," Kalee supplied like a textbook when Ronan didn't answer. I raised an eyebrow in response.

Kalee shrugged. "I've already managed to flip through a few of Aislinn's books. The witches' magic may derive from the earth, but they solely worship the Triple Goddess."

"What do you think we should do then?" I asked. There was nothing else in the room. With no other door present than the one we came from, Cillian and Eoin searched the walls and floor to no avail. The only cauldron in the room was made of stone.

"We should ask her." Kalee pointed to the statue of the older woman huddled over the cauldron.

"I dunno, Kay. Something tells me she's not one for words," Eoin chuckled.

"She's right," Ronan said absentmindedly while he examined the depiction of the Triple Goddess. "Look how she's the only one clutching the cauldron, whereas the other two are standing over it."

"What does that have to do with anything?"

"Aislinn said the cauldron was full of knowledge. Wouldn't the oldest of the three be the wisest?" Kalee challenged.

"So we are supposed to ask the statue and assume it will give us what we want?" Eoin asked more seriously this time.

"No. We will ask the statue by giving it something first," Cillian said, coming to my side.

"Blood," Ronan confirmed.

"Why does it have to be blood?" I groaned.

"Because, as my light pointed out, the Triple Goddess represents the cycle of life. What better represents life than blood?" Ronan said, making Kalee blush.

Ridiculous as it was, Ronan was right. At the feet of the withered goddess was a small offering bowl. Ready to get it over with, I unsheathed my dagger and sliced my palm enough for the blood to swell. Everyone else did the same, giving our blood offerings to the cracked and shriveled goddess one by one.

"I knew blood was ridiculous," Eoin huffed, nudging Ronan in the ribs.

Ronan playfully pushed Eoin away. He crouched down, studying the statue from a different angle.

Just when I thought we wasted our time, fog poured from the stone cauldron until it eddied at our feet.

"Hah," Ronan said triumphantly, standing with his hands planted on his hips.

The ground shook, and the sconces rattled against the walls. Despite the noise, no one came rushing in to investigate. Rising from the fog came bodies in various stages of decay, resurfacing from whatever depths they came from. A few were mostly flesh, but others were nothing more than bones clad in armor and equipped with weapons. Ronan's smile faltered. Eoin unsheathed his sword, Cillian following suit. Those still with mouths didn't speak, save for strange grunting noises, but their intent was all the same as they drew their rusted weaponry.

"Kalee, what else did Aislinn say the cauldron had power over?" I asked as I unsheathed both daggers.

"Death," she whispered. Ronan kissed Kalee on the temple. She held her sword in a familiar grip, and I wondered if the prince had given her private lessons on wielding the thing.

A heartbeat, and then the soldiers attacked.

Out of the corner of my eyes, Cillian was death incarnate, wielding his two blades at once, knocking them back one by one. However, when one fell, another took its place. An undead soldier swung at me, his blade rusted but not dull. It hummed through the air, and I spun out of the way only to find myself in front of another. The second soldier struck me in the center of my chest with the eye of his axe, knocking the wind from my lungs and me straight to my ass. My daggers skidded across the room. He lifted his axe, ready to crack open my skull. I braced myself for pain. For death. But neither came.

Cillian blocked him moments before the axe came down on my head.

"I thought you said you knew how to fight?" Cillian smirked, towering over me.

I glared at Cillian and kicked the soldier back. "If I recall correctly, I told you I knew how to use my daggers. I can show you if you like."

"You'd have to hold them first, little shadow." Cillian laughed, slicing the soldier's skull clean from his vertebra. We shared a look before Eoin tossed a discarded long blade to me.

"That's too heavy for you." Cillian frowned and offered his short blade to me.

"I'll be fine," I gritted, drowning out Eoin's argument and heaved the blade up. Fuck, Cillian was right, not that I'd admit it. I needed more distance between myself and the soldiers surrounding us. Clearly, I wasn't as capable at defending myself as I thought. My newfound blade was meant to be a single-handed grip, but it was too heavy. With both hands, I wielded it while trying not to fall over in the process.

"They aren't dying!" Ronan called, soldiers closing in on him and Kalee. Those who fell against our blades did not stay down for long. Moments of reprieve were brief.

"How can something already dead die?" Kalee screamed in answer, reminding me of the seer's departing words.

There is no life without death and no death without life.

It didn't make sense when the seer said it, but it was a clue, just like the memory. It was stupid.

Really, *really*, stupid.

"We have to die," I huffed, deflecting a rotting soldier charging toward me. My arms burned in protest. I wouldn't be able to keep up for much longer.

"That is exactly what we do *not* want to do," Eoin gritted through his teeth.

"For once, I agree with him," Cillian called, pushing an opponent off him.

"The seer practically said as much when we left," I argued.

"You believe the word of a seer?" Eoin asked, his brows knitting together in concentration.

There were many times in Rothcek when I imagined my death. Reanimated soldiers from the Nine knew where was not what I had in mind. I wasn't sure what the Triple Goddess had in store for us, but my life either lay in the hands of the king I knew or the goddess I didn't.

It didn't matter because Death came for us all.

"Only one way to find out," I yelled, letting the sword clatter to the floor, surrendering before I could think twice about it.

Kalee screamed my name as a rusty blade split through my leathers and pierced my chest. The pain was sharp and searing and mimicked the fatal blow my mother received all those years ago. I wish it were her I saw and not the hollowed-out eye sockets of the soldier before I let out a shaky final breath.

CHAPTER TWENTY-EIGHT

I sucked in a gaping breath, clutching my chest. Cool stone pressed against my back, and my eyes skipped over the dimly lit room. It was the same, save for the absence of undead soldiers and my friends fighting for their lives. A woman with waist-length silver hair stood at the edge of the darkness where the statue of the Triple Goddess had stood. Her muted blue, gold-trimmed gown kissed the floor. Something about the dress's familiarity buzzed at the edges of my memory.

She stepped forward, her form shimmering.

"Mother?" I croaked. I'd always hoped it would be her who greeted me when I crossed over to the Otherworld. This, of course, meant my plan failed miserably, and I led all the others to their premature deaths. I would have sworn if my mother staring down at me hadn't stolen the very air from my lungs.

"I am not your mother, child. I merely borrowed her appearance." The woman looked like her, from her sapphire eyes to the small smattering of freckles sprinkled across her cheeks. Her voice, however, was different—ethereal.

"Then who—?"

"I am the Goddess of Transformation, Rebirth, and Inspiration, but you may call me Cerri. I am the keeper of what you seek."

"Then...I'm not dead?"

Cerri tilted her head. "You are very dead, and unless you want to stay that way, you must not remain here for long."

"And here is?"

"We are in the in-between."

It was then that I noticed the two archways on the opposite sides of the room. Mist swirled between the stones, akin to the sheerest of gossamer billowing in a soft breeze, yet I couldn't see anything beyond the archways—only smoke and fog.

My stomach clenched. "My friends?"

"They did as you instructed and are also in the in-between."

I looked around, but there was no one save for Cerri and me.

"You will not find them here," she said. "They are facing their own trials."

"What kind of trials?" I asked slowly.

"Did you think you could walk away with the Cauldron of Power so easily?"

"No, but I—" I stuttered, trying to find the words. "What do I need to do?"

Cerri circled me, gravity not a burden on her as she glided through the air. Her hard gaze assessed more than my physical form before meeting me face to face.

"To return to the land of the living with the gods' object you seek, something inside you must die so you can be born again." She must have sensed my confusion because she said, "You must give me your guilt, Saoirse."

I eyed the goddess. It seemed so easy, I almost laughed. Why would I want to continue to feel this constant ache? I would gladly give it up.

"It is yours."

"Silly child. It isn't as simple as you think. This guilt consumes more than your dreams. It drives every decision you make. You let it shame you, offering pieces of your soul like a penance." Cerri pressed her pointer finger against the center of my chest. "This guilt grips your heart like a vise, and it has festered like a poison seeping into your very blood for over a decade. It won't go easily."

My chest glowed sickly green where Cerri and I connected. It pulsed under her touch, tangling around my heart like overgrown weeds. I tried to pull it from the root and toss it her way, but it wouldn't let go; it was too thick, too ingrained. My heart sputtered. I couldn't relinquish the guilt because I deserved it. I was the reason my mother died. Why she took the potion that shortened her life. I was the one who couldn't save her. *I* deserved to bear this burden.

Cerri frowned as if sensing my thoughts. "It doesn't serve you any longer. If you don't let it go, it will consume you."

"I—I can't..." I gasped.

"Do you wish to give me something else, then?" Cerri circled me like a predator, switching her form into the King of Centra. She had every detail right from his polished boots to the scar in his brow. "What about your magic? You hated it when you were younger. I can sense your resentment for it now. Your life would be much easier without it."

Cerri switched forms again, this time turning into the chancellor. "Or perhaps you'd like to relinquish what little happiness you've found. You believe you don't deserve it. Give it to me instead."

My head spun, tears threatening to spill onto my cheeks. I pressed the heel of my palms to my eyes. I couldn't bear to look at her any longer. There were too many emotions warring within me.

"You must make a choice, Saoirse. You must leave part of you behind so you can return. What you leave is up to you."

I'd be a fool to give up my magic or my happiness to keep my guilt, but the goddess made a point. My life would be easier without magic. Everything that had gone wrong was because of it. I didn't deserve the happiness I've held onto, not when I'd been the cause of so much pain and suffering. There would be consequences no matter what I chose.

" I-I don't want to dishonor her memory," I said, knowing my guilt did me no service.

Cerri switched back into my mother's form. "You do not dishonor her by living a fulfilling life. You dishonor her by punishing yourself for something you had no control over. You waste your life, something she worked so hard to protect. You must choose to live, really live, if you want to return to the land of the living, or you will remain lost forever."

I thought of my mother and the days before she was slaughtered in the field behind our home. I thought of her smile and how deeply she loved me. Maybe Cerri was right. She wouldn't have wanted me to carry this guilt for so long. I could never forget or cease mourning her loss, but perhaps I didn't need to feel responsible for her sacrifice, nor should I continue to berate myself for it.

Cerri smiled and placed her palm on my chest. "Allow me to take it, and I will return you to your world."

I let out a shaky breath. "My guilt is yours, Cerri." The green light within me flared, growing brighter as Cerri absorbed it in her hand. It didn't fight like it had moments ago. It swelled, filling my chest until the pressure and the light disappeared altogether. Breathing came easier, my thoughts clearer.

"What about my friends?" I asked.

"Like you, they will need to give up something to return. They, too, have a choice. You will either meet them on the Otherside or they will travel to the Otherworld. Now, take my hand before it is too late."

The delicate hand of my mother reached out. A tingle vibrated through me, and we were encased in a bright, white light.

"Saoirse Órlaith, before you return, I will share one last thing. I've taken the guilt from your mother's death, but it doesn't make you immune from building it again. You must learn how to differentiate between grieving to heal and grieving to shame." Cerri blew cool, gentle air from parted lips that filled my lungs. As my inhale reached a crescendo, she faded from view. Instead of the darkness I came from, I was born anew into the light.

"Saoirse," Eoin said, shaking my shoulders.

I groaned. Grogginess lay over me like a wet blanket. My chest ached where I'd been stabbed, but there was no mark, not even a scar. Despite the soreness, I felt lighter than I had in years. The weight on my chest and the hunch of my shoulders no longer burdened me. I was…calm. Peaceful, even.

Ronan moaned to my left. My cheek kissed the floor when I turned to see him coming out of unconsciousness. Kalee leaned over him and tucked a stray strand of blonde hair behind his ear.

"Are you alright?" Eoin asked, caressing my cheek in his cool hand, turning me back toward him.

"I think so?" My encounter with Cerri was like a dream. The longer I stayed awake, the more the details blurred and disappeared altogether, leaving me with the feeling of her. "Are you alright? Did you die too?"

Eoin nodded. "We all did. I was the first to rise. Kalee regained consciousness shortly after me. Then you, and now Ronan." My heart swelled. They'd trusted me with their lives, and I hadn't cost them theirs.

"And Cillian?"

"Cillian?" Eoin frowned.

I shook my head, clearing the last of the grogginess. "The Hunter. Is he okay?"

"I know who you are referring to. I didn't realize you two were so close." He removed his hand from my cheek and stood. Something I didn't recognize passed over his expression. "He's still dead," he said flatly before checking on Ronan. My brows furrowed. What was wrong with him?

Cillian lay stagnant on the floor, a hole still gaping through his chest, blood pooling violently beneath him. The room spun as I stood on shaking legs. Cillian's olive complexion had turned pallid and cold to the touch. The usual pink color of his lips had now taken on a gray hue. He couldn't die. Not now. Not when I was beginning to like the bastard.

"Cillian." I shook his shoulder.

He didn't stir.

"Cillian," I hissed, shaking him harder. "Wake up, asshole." My vision started to blur. No matter how hard I shook, he did not wake. Did he fail the trial Cerri set for him? What part of him did he refuse to let go to return to the natural world?

Kalee rested her hand on my shoulder when I called his name again. There was no stopping the tears from falling. I didn't want him to die—no matter what Cerri took. I couldn't explain it, but part of me felt connected to him. Perhaps it was because we were both faie. Or because he was one of the few links to my past. Regardless, I needed him to wake the fuck up.

"Please, please, *please*, Cillian." I squeezed my eyes shut and prayed the Mother would grant me one small mercy.

"You do not need to beg, little shadow. I will do anything you say." His voice was strained, hardly more than a whisper. Muscle, sinew, and flesh stitched itself together faster than any faie, any poultice, could—his fatal wound gone. Color seeped back into his body, and warmth returned to the hand I held.

"If you weren't half dead, I'd smack you right now," I sniffled, dropping his hand.

"I would say I am mostly alive by now." He groaned, rubbing the spot on his chest where his wound once was.

"Took you long enough." Ronan smiled down on Cillian and extended his hand.

"Yeah, well, I'll try to be quicker next time," Cillian said, accepting

Ronan's help. "Does anyone have the cauldron, or did we all die for nothing?"

Somehow, I'd forgotten all about the cauldron. I scanned the room to find Eoin standing in front of the statue of the Triple Goddess. His gaze fixated on where the stone cauldron used to be. In its place was a simple copper pot, its belly worn and dented.

"Looks ordinary, doesn't it?" Kalee murmured, studying the gods' born object. The cauldron was plain, but the pull it had was anything but. Like before, it called to me—more potent this time. It begged me to take it, to touch it. Its plea thrummed in my temples, making it hard to concentrate.

"As long as we don't have to die again, I don't care what it looks like," Ronan said, and Cillian nodded his agreement.

Eoin remained silent as he gaped at the cauldron. His brown eyes danced in the light of the sconces, glowing brighter the longer he stared. I couldn't tell if he or the others felt its strange pull, but I didn't want to be around it any longer than necessary.

"Ronan, grab the thing so we can get out of here," I said, unease settling low in my belly. "We don't know how long we were gone. Aislinn could be waiting for us already."

Ronan reached for the cauldron, but Eoin grabbed it by the handle before anyone could stop him.

"No!" Kalee and I yelled. Aislinn's warning hung heavy in the air. It was too late, however.

Outside the room, signal horns bellowed.

CHAPTER TWENTY-NINE

Distant voices shouted as horns continued to blare. Their deep, full sounds promising death if they caught us. "We need to leave. *Now*," Ronan said, yanking the cauldron from Eoin, his cheeks flushing.

"I'm sorry, I forgot," Eoin sputtered.

"You forgot?" Cillian seethed, stalking toward him until Eoin was pressed against the wall, Cillian's hand wrapped around his throat. "You forgot the *one* rule we weren't supposed to break?" Cillian was nose to nose with Eoin, and for a moment, I thought he might snap his neck. I wedged my way between them.

"What's done is done. There's no use in killing him now."

Ronan placed a hand on Cillian's shoulder. "Saoirse's right. They'll be here soon. We need to go."

Cillian released his grip on Eoin's throat and prowled to the door.

"Wait—" I started. Something didn't feel right.

Before Cillian could grasp the handle, the doors flung open, revealing three fearsome witches.

I recognized two of them from before. Silent as wraiths, they flanked the witch in the center. They were dressed for combat. Their sleeveless, leather jerkins highlighted powerful biceps as their hands clenched around the swords sheathed at their hips. A wolf with brown speckled fur stood beside the one with tightly twisted braids. His growl shook the room. My gut tightened, remembering the fomorii wolf in the woods. This one wasn't as massive as the fomorii, nor was he made of shadows. But he was still large enough to reach the witch's waist.

The witch in the center was different. She bore no weapons, no fighting gear. Nothing to signify her as a guard. Her flowing black dress mimicked twilight itself, sparkling in ways that defied the natural world. A crown of moons sat atop her inky black hair, and a raven perched atop her shoulder.

All oxygen left my lungs.

The Witch Queen Petranella. Blood-painted lips curled into a cruel, cat-like smile. "Well, well, what do we have here?" she purred. She didn't bear as much of a resemblance to Aislinn as my mother, her features far harsher in comparison.

Blood rushed to my ears, and my knees threatened to collapse. Aislinn warned us she wouldn't be of use if we were caught. Would the witch queen recognize Ronan and me as her kin? If she did, was she more likely to kill us for it?

Ronan started to speak, but a hand silenced him.

"Do not bother with explanations quite yet." Her eyes narrowed on the cauldron. "I am surprised you all managed to retrieve it. No easy feat, but unfortunately, your efforts are useless. Escort them to the dungeon," she ordered the two witches. Queen Petranella snapped her fingers. The sharp sound silenced the room, and a metallic tinge filled the air. She didn't say a spell or sprinkle any herbs, but the magic obeyed the Queen of Ilythia nonetheless. The little I knew about witches' magic went out the window as my muscles tightened.

I tried to move toward the witch queen, to speak and plead our case, but I was frozen in place. I glanced sidelong at Kalee, her gaze catching mine as panic widened the whites of her eyes. None of us could do a thing as more witches filed into the room.

The witch with the unbound, coiled black hair moved to Eoin first. The springs of her curls danced across her shoulders with each movement. She tied Eoin's wrists together in front of him with little effort. Her companion did the same to Kalee, each action precise and deliberate. The wolf remained where he stood, but he didn't take his gaze off of us.

"The cauldron, Ahlani," called the witch with the braids. Ahlani took the cauldron with ease from Ronan's grip. His eyes strained, as if trying and failing to keep hold of the object my life depended on. Ahlani sneered at Ronan, her witch's mark contrasting with her skin's deep, rich brown, making her eyes stand out like two pools of seething waters.

Ahlani handed the cauldron to the witch queen while the other made quick work of restraining us before pressing her thumb against my forehead with surprising gentleness. She muttered words under her breath; its melodious, drawn-out sounds were almost soothing despite the situation. When she released me, my limbs became my own again, allowing me to move.

"Please," I tried. Queen Petranella was already gone, but maybe they would let us appeal to her, to hear our good intentions.

"Save it," Ahlani barked. "You'll face your trial at first light, and you will meet your fate." She had to be joking. Another fucking trial. "The cost of thievery to this degree is death."

Knots tangled and unraveled in my stomach. No one muttered another word as we were escorted to the dungeon, the wolf stalking alongside us. A sea of witches filled the halls, all of them sneering, some spitting at our feet, as we passed.

The stench of mold and death filled the air of the dungeons. Humidity slickened the time-worn steps so much that I nearly slipped. Ahlani shoved me into a cell without warning. I waited for the shadows to writhe and wiggle under my skin to express their dissatisfaction with such treatment, but nothing came.

My hands, typically laced in silver ribbons, were bare as if I were standing in broad sunlight, not the dimly lit cell. Ahlani smiled and tapped one of the bars with a sickening clink.

Iron.

"This entire dungeon is coated in it, so don't get any bright ideas."

My magic was useless here. I wouldn't have been able to get us out of this situation even if I did have it. But at least my shadows would have comforted me.

One by one, the witches locked us into our cells, separating us with at least one empty cell between us. They left without another word and snuffed out the lights, surrounding us in darkness. For the first time, I wasn't calmed by it.

WHEN AHLANI AND THE OTHER WITCH CAME TO CLAIM US, HER WOLF STILL in tow, my stomach was in knots. We hadn't been allowed to speak to one another, the guard posted in the dungeon silencing us each time we tried. I craned my neck to catch a glimpse of the others while Ahlani bound my wrists in chains before shoving me up the steps.

We walked for what seemed like forever, up and down, winding left and right until I didn't know which way was which. The walls here were bare, unlike the castle in Rothcek, which was adorned with paintings of the Conqueror King and depictions of his triumphs. Only torches lined our way as if the queen didn't want to take away from the natural makeup of the mountain. The floor had been smoothed out by either time or magic, but the rest remained a rough, glittering texture.

I couldn't tell if they were trying to confuse us or if the Mountain Castle was really this complicated. Everything looked the same. There were no differentiations between each level. How anyone knew where they were going was beyond me. We didn't stop until we reached two towering doors. Behind them, stacked benches filled with witches chattering amongst themselves. I scanned the crowd for the only face I knew. Aislinn wasn't here.

"Silence," a voice boomed. Then, the only sound in the great throne room was the pounding of my heart.

At the center of the dais on the lone throne sat Queen Petranella, the crown of moons atop her silky, black hair. The raven eyed us from atop its perch next to the stone throne. Alice said witches often had anamchara bonds with animals. The raven must have been the queen's familiar, the wolf belonging to either Ahlani or the witch with the twisted braids.

Our footsteps echoed along the polished rock as we approached the queen. Each sneer and glare from the witches looming over us threatened my knees to buckle with each step.

"Bow to the Witch Queen," the witch with the braided hair commanded and took her place by her queen's side, leaving Ahlani to guard us. It was useless to try to escape or attack. Any attempt would result in immediate death in a room full of witches. Not to mention the iron still clasped over my wrists, burning with each uncomfortable movement.

Ahlani pushed me down, my knee hit the stone with a sickening thud, and I threatened a curse. To my left, sweat gathered at Ronan's forehead —the only sign of the prince's nerves. To my right, Kalee's expression was stone, reserved for when she was deep in thought. I wished I could catch a glance at Eoin or Cillian. Were they as terrified as I was?

"Rise," Queen Petranella purred. Today, her lips were a deep plum, contrasting against her pale skin.

A sea of blue bore into the back of my skull as I felt a room full of witches' crystalline eyes on me. I fought the urge to shift and squirm. In the Conqueror King's court, he could detect weakness or fear by the slightest movements. I wouldn't give Queen Petranella the opportunity.

"You five are here today on the charges of theft to the highest degree. How do you plead to attempting to steal the sacred cauldron?"

Angry shouts and murmurs sounded throughout the benches.

"They are guilty, Your Highness. I witnessed it myself," the witch next to her answered before we could get a word out. The wolf growled in agreement. *Her* familiar then.

It would have been useless to lie. The queen herself saw the cauldron in Ronan's grasp, but she didn't know the reason behind it. Though Aislinn gave no indication, maybe the queen would be lenient if she knew why.

"I second it, Your Highness. I, too, bore witness to this atrocious crime," Ahlani said loud enough for the entire throne room to hear.

"Do you all deny these crimes?" Queen Petranella asked.

"No, but—" I started.

Queen Petranella held out a slender hand, silencing any protests. "Then you five are hereby found guilty and, as punishment, are sentenced to death. Immediately." The raven cawed. "Bring them to the courtyard," she said with a lazy wave of her hand as if ending our lives were nothing more than a chore for her—another thing to mark off her to-do list. My racing thoughts roared over the shouts and cheers from the crowd.

Death? My stomach clenched. This couldn't be happening. She didn't understand. I needed to talk to Aislinn to tell her to plead with her sister, but Aislinn was nowhere to be seen.

Ahlani shoved me forward toward the courtyard and to impending death. The wolf nipped at my heels, his teeth horribly long and pointed. Would my mother's spell hold against death's blow in the face of a crime I committed? Even if it did, the others didn't stand a chance, and I would rather die with them than live without them.

"Wait!" Kalee shouted, her words paralyzing my movement. "I invoke the Malartaím!"

The crowd hushed, and Queen Petranella's relaxed posture stiffened.

Ronan and I exchanged confused glances, though I wouldn't put it past Kalee to be familiar with witch customs and traditions when she had access to Aislinn's library.

"What did you say, girl?" the witch queen sneered, her voice strained as she ground them out. Her raven shifted, rocking side to side on its perch.

Kalee swallowed, the only sign of her distress. "I would like to invoke Malartaím for myself and my companions," she said again, her voice steadier.

Queen Petranella thrummed her fingers along the armrest of her throne, her glare pinning us to the spot. "Very well," she purred. "Are you aware of the rules for Malartaím?"

Kalee nodded confidently, but my insides twisted. What had she gotten us into?

"Then you know if you don't complete the Malartaím in its entirety, you will all die anyway?"

Kalee nodded once more. I tried to catch her attention so she could explain, but her focus never left the queen.

"Fine," the queen conceded. "Then, for your Malartaím, you five will retrieve something of mine. If you return with the item, you may leave with your life. And if you fail, your deaths will be more brutal than I intended." The queen smiled cruelly, any trace of Aislinn in her features long gone.

"What would you have us retrieve?" I asked, curiosity overpowering my fear.

The queen dug her gleaming red nails into the armrest, slicing into stone. "Something precious has been stolen from witch-kind. Hidden for centuries in cursed lands, Ilythians are forbidden from trying to retrieve it. Bring me the fire jewel and you shall walk away with your lives."

A collective gasp shuddered throughout the room. Excitement tinged the air as the witches shared eager glances. Either excited about our prospective deaths or the possibility of retrieving this jewel, I didn't know.

"We will retrieve the fire jewel in exchange for each of our lives, as well as the ability to walk out of this castle and leave this kingdom whenever we choose?" Kalee confirmed. I smiled despite the circumstances. If witches valued bargains as much as the aes sidhe, their wording could be detrimental—especially deals concerning life and death. We should have bartered to use the cauldron, but the queen was quick to speak.

She was only mildly put out when she agreed, no doubt annoyed at

Kalee's careful wording. "Ahlani, Niamh, Flore. You three escort them and ensure they do not conjure up any inadvisable ideas such as escape." The witch with the twisted braids, Niamh, placed a fist over her heart when the queen called her. Flore, a witch with short, straight black hair, stepped forward.

"They will escort you and monitor you. But they will not aid you in any way. Your fate is in your hands and yours only. Now, leave me," Queen Petranella demanded. Her raven preened, puffing out its black feathers.

The court of witches dispersed at her command. The three assigned to us released our shackles and led us out of the side of the throne room, Queen Petranella's stare burning into our backs.

We'd escaped death yet again, but I couldn't help but feel our worst fears were yet to come. It had been three weeks since we met with the seer, and my twenty-fifth name day was a mere month away. We were running out of time to get to the cauldron. Then, there would be no outrunning death.

Chapter Thirty

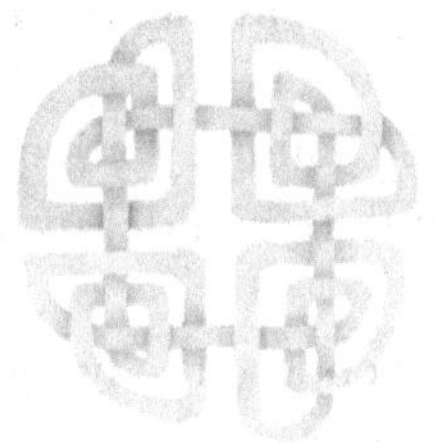

The forest was as wild as any witch. Free from the burdens society has on a land, Ilythia was ripe with sounds that called to some deep part of me. Perhaps it was the part I'd inherited from my mother, coming alive in her homeland. She once told me I received her looks, but the rest of my being was entirely my father. Being here now, I wasn't so sure.

The three witches revealed nothing about Aislinn. I hadn't dared to ask if they knew what happened to her. Whether she escaped her sister or had been caught in our scheme was unknown. The queen hadn't asked us how we infiltrated the castle or how we found the cauldron itself. My bones chilled knowing Aislinn would have to tell her. I knew in my soul Aislinn wouldn't outright betray us to save her own skin, but would she divulge to the queen who Ronan and I were or *what* we were to her? Would it matter either way?

Three days of trekking across Ilythia's rugged terrain sent my thoughts drifting further from Aislinn and closer to the task at hand.

"Is anyone going to tell us what the fire jewel is?" I asked the witches as I sat next to Kalee, finally resting for the night. Between the lack of food, improper sleep, and overall shock of the other day, no one had been much for words on our journey thus far.

"A myth," Niamh said. "A legend that died out centuries ago. The fire jewel is the supposed key to bring the dragons back." Her wolf rested his head in her lap, eyeing us with a careful gaze. Niamh stroked his head lazily as if he weren't a fearsome, flesh-tearing beast.

"Dragons?" I scoffed. "The dragons died out centuries ago. There's no bringing back what is already dead."

"So, any chance of completing this Malartaím is futile?" Ronan grimaced.

"Yes," Ahlani chirped as if she hadn't confirmed our demise. She scratched the wolf on the snout, and his tail thumped against the dirt, appearing more like a house pet and less like a wolf. I suppressed a smile.

"All myths and legends are borne of some truth," Kalee replied, unbothered by our inevitable failure. Perhaps we were never meant to complete the Malartaím, but it could buy us enough time to escape instead.

"Did you know she would choose the fire jewel?" I whispered to Kalee, not wanting to hear the witches' remarks.

"No, but I knew whatever she chose would be difficult," she sighed.

"You've only invoked her wrath further," Flore said lazily, ignoring our attempt at privacy.

"You did what you thought was right. Who knows? We may find this fire jewel. Stranger things have happened," Cillian said, and the muscles of Kalee's shoulders relaxed a little. Ronan nodded in support.

Dragons. I let the word sink in and thought back to the tapestry hanging in the chancellor's office. What if dragons were the key to defeating the Shadow King?

"If Ahlani and Niamh are part of the queen's guards, what are you to the queen?" Kalee asked Flore, watching her slice into her roasted rabbit with deft precision.

Flore bristled. "What makes you think I'm any different?"

"You carry yourself in a way the others do not."

Ahlani and Niamh didn't look offended as they tore into their food. Though they were all fitted with the same leathered armor and bore similar weapons, Flore was at odds with her sisters. As we journeyed through Ilythia, she would stop periodically, picking various plants to add to her leather belt. Ahlani and Niamh were also fitted with one, but theirs were poorly stocked in comparison. They certainly didn't bother to stop and pick flowers.

"Habits of a healer, I suppose," Flore replied.

"But you are still a warrior?"

Flore's blue eyes glinted in the campfire's light, the sleekness of her short black hair glimmering with it. "Yes. My magic is more profound at healing, but I am skilled enough to be considered one of the queen's top warriors."

"The queen allowed this?"

"Sometimes the lives people expect us to lead are not the ones we are destined for," Cillian cut in, sharing a nod of understanding with Flore.

Kalee squinted into the fire, her brows set in contemplation. I adjusted my seat on the fallen log, uncomfortable against my backside, but my legs and feet ached too much to care.

"Can I take another look at the map?" I asked. Ahlani and Niamh ignored me, but Flore, the nicer of the three, complied.

The thick parchment was yellowed with age and frayed along the edges. Gingerly, I splayed the soft material across my lap. This was the first map of Ilythia I'd ever seen. Willows were drawn along the country's border, save for a few, presumably, hidden areas. I trailed my finger along the river we followed to our destination: The Ennisi Mountains.

"How much longer do you think?" I turned to Cillian.

He frowned at the map. "At least a week."

I couldn't suppress a groan. Gods knew how many more fomorii plagued Centra in our absence. At least we didn't have to worry about them here. Assuming we retrieved this fire jewel immediately, it would take another week to return, giving us only two weeks to figure out how to use the cauldron and break my Bond. Not to mention, the king could tug on mine or Cillian's Bond at any moment, and we would have to obey. Or attempt to obey before the witches killed us. The Bond had been stretched thin in the witch kingdom, but I still felt its presence—my Mark burning on occasion. Did Cillian feel it, too?

Cillian rested his hand on my shoulder, the touch sending my stomach into somersaults.

"Do not worry, Saoirse, we will have enough time," Eoin said, squeezing himself between me and Kalee. His words of encouragement did nothing to settle my unease.

Flore's keen eyes looked between us—Ahlani and Niamh silenced their conversation. The wolf's ears stood alert as if waiting to catch any information we might spill. We hadn't told them why we sought the cauldron, and they hadn't asked. The witches hadn't bothered to pay any more attention to us than they were required to by their queen. They did, however, have the habit of eavesdropping.

"Hunter," Eoin continued, "why don't you make yourself useful and hunt down more water for our canteens?"

Cillian stared flatly at Eoin. "Do it yourself. We wouldn't be in this mess if it weren't for you."

"I'm turning in," I said, standing. They'd been at each other's throats since we left the Mountain Castle, and I couldn't take their bickering any longer. I had enough to worry about. Flore took the map back, her unasked questions hanging in the space between us.

I retired to my tent, pacing as I did every night. In a surprising display of mercy, we'd been given more than adequate travel packs, though the more I thought about it, the more I suspected it was to give us false hope.

A familiar metallic tang coated my tongue as I gnawed my cheek. We'd been so focused on getting to the Ennisi Mountains that we hadn't talked about what we would do when there was no fire jewel. The others hadn't appeared too worried, but I couldn't see any way all of us made it back alive. As each day passed, I felt more enthralled in death's grip—the gods arguing with one another over how I was to meet my end.

Tremors plagued my hands at the rising panic. It was all too much. We wouldn't succeed. My Bond would never break. I would die without ever living. The air grew hot, a slow, suffocating fog spilling into my lungs like I was drowning.

"Saoirse," Eoin's heavy hand rested on my shoulder, pulling me from my thoughts moments before they spiraled out of control.

"*Gods*, Eoin, you scared the Nine out of me." I let out a shaky breath, my lungs emptying again.

"Look," he said, oblivious to how close I'd been to breaking down. "I know you're worried about getting the cauldron again, as am I, but we will have it back in our possession soon."

"Eoin, we wouldn't be here if you hadn't touched it in the first place," I hissed, echoing Cillian's words. He had a point; this was Eoin's fault. If it weren't for Eoin's mishap, we would be back at Aislinn's, breaking our Bonds by now. "How do you know we will be able to get it back? The cauldron isn't part of the Malartaím. The queen will never let us use it after we tried to steal it."

Gods, I wanted to scream, but it wouldn't do us any favors.

"I know," he said solemnly, hanging his head. " I-I don't know what came over me. I was so anxious to get back, I forgot about Aislinn's warning. I've hated myself for it every day since." I remembered the pull I felt toward it. How it practically begged me to touch it. Maybe it possessed Eoin in a way.

Despite my frustrations, I grabbed his hand. He hadn't meant it. We had all died moments before the cauldron appeared. Maybe he deserved a bit of slack. "What's done is done. What matters is that we make the right choices going forward."

"I will make it up to you, to everyone. I promise."

"This also includes being nicer to Cillian. He's trying to help."

Eoin frowned. "He can't be trusted, Saoirse. I'm worried he's up to something."

"I know Cillian's reputation goes against him, but I have reason to believe he's not who we thought he was," I said for myself as much as I had for Eoin.

"Oh? Care to share this information?"

My throat worked. I wasn't ready to tell him I was the reason Cillian came to Centra. I shook my head. "It's not my story to tell. Ask him yourself if you must, but know I believe him. I–I trust him, Eoin, and maybe you should, too." The words surprised me, but when it came down to it, Cillian risked his life out of loyalty to my father—had helped me in Centra in his own way. He'd earned at least a semblance of trust.

Eoin sighed. "Fine. But my faith isn't in him, it's in *you*."

I smiled, relishing in this small victory. Eoin pulled me into him. My muscles tensed out of instinct, and I forced them to relax, letting him hold me. The last few days had been taxing to say the least. We all needed a bit of comfort where we could find it.

I pulled back, studying the stubble gracing the underside of his chin. His brown eyes met mine, and I searched for the solution to our problems in the different shades. My cheeks heated when I realized how close we'd become. Nearly nose to nose, our breaths intermingled.

"Sorry, I–" I hadn't meant to come so close, but the words were lost on my tongue as Eoin cupped the back of my head and threaded his fingers through my hair. He captured me in his grip, leaning in. I couldn't move if I wanted to.

"You must know I care for you, Saoirse," he whispered. I nodded, my heart thudding. "And you must know I will do whatever it takes to see you safe."

Something in me warmed at being welcomed into Eoin's inner circle. He would do anything for Ronan and, by extension, Kalee. And now me.

I could see it now. To be loved by Eoin would mean protection. Safety. And yet, something still felt like it was missing.

Before I could say anything, Eoin kissed me.

I froze. For a second, I thought of Eiric. He had been my first kiss and, until now, my last. A sadness threatened to overwhelm me, but I refused. Eiric would have wanted me to *live*. In that moment, just as I'd done with Cerri, I let the guilt of Eiric's death go.

Eoin's touch was firm. Unforgiving. I leaned into the hardness of it, the hardness of him. Gone was his guards' uniform—that wretched symbol of the Conqueror King left behind at Aislinn's. Nothing but thin, soft fabric between us, his muscles bulging beneath his linen tunic. He tasted warm and sweet. His hands cradled my face and roamed down my back, his fingers trailing the ends of my tunic.

My pulse jumped.

I broke our kiss, cool air kissing my overwarm skin instead. Eoin's brows knitted together. I wasn't ready for him to know about the scars littering my back. Wasn't ready for there to be nothing between us.

An explanation played on my tongue when Cillian cleared his throat outside the tent.

"Sorry to interrupt," Cillian said, peeking through the flap. My face somehow burned hotter than it already was. "Ronan is asking for you, Eoin."

My gaze met Cillian's, and something stirred in his forest eyes. Something sharp, deadly. Vicious. It fluttered low in my belly before they were gone, leaving me to stew in a flurry of feelings I didn't know how to name.

CHAPTER THIRTY-ONE

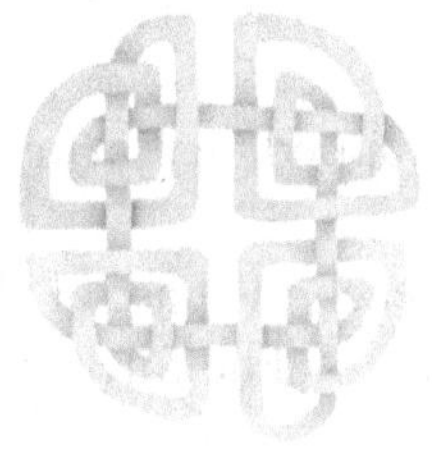

"He kissed me," I whispered to Kalee, clutching her arm. Her eyes went wide and searched for anyone who might overhear. Eoin's nose was shoved in the map for the hundredth time, Ronan next to him, and Cillian and the witches were far enough away.

"Who? Cillian?"

"What? Gods no, Kalee. *Eoin.* Eoin kissed me last night in my tent." The thought of kissing the Hunter? It was unfathomable. Laughable. It would never happen. Sure, he wasn't as evil as I thought he was, but he was still an arrogant asshole.

"How was it?" She leaned in closer, her honeyed eyes sparkling.

"I don't know. It was just a kiss. A regular, nice kiss."

Kalee's eyes knitted together, doubt creeping across her face. "Saoirse—"

"What do you want me to say? That it was the best kiss in the history of kisses? That he swept me off my feet and now we're madly in love? My life isn't a romance novel." It was closer to a horror story where they all die at the end.

"You don't have to be in love with the man, but there should be *something.*"

"There was something." I wasn't sure what it was, but Kalee didn't need to know that.

"Did you enjoy the kiss at least?"

"Yes," I said with certainty. The look on Kalee's face didn't indicate that she believed me.

"I know Eiric's death was hard on you and—"

"This isn't about Eiric. It's been five years, and I've let him go. Eoin is strong. Steady. Safe. I'd like to know him more."

Kalee hummed. "As long as you're happy. I want to make sure you are doing things because *you* want to, not because you feel like you have to or it's the most logical decision. It's time to start thinking with your heart, Sersh."

"I love you, Kay."

"And I, you." Kalee wrapped her arm around me and kissed my temple.

"Another day, and we'll reach the base of the Ennisi Mountains," Eoin called out. I suppressed a groan. The further we traveled into the forests, the more impatient I grew.

"You said that yesterday," Kalee chided as we caught up with them.

"It's not my fault that the weather is worsening. It doesn't help that these three are useless." Eoin jabbed a thumb toward the witches. Niamh picked at her teeth with her nails, unbothered by our frustrations. Her wolf's eyes narrowed into slits.

"Realistically, brother, will we reach the mountains by tomorrow?" Ronan asked. His expression had grown haggard over the days, and dark circles stained his under-eyes.

"Yes," Eoin answered without hesitation, but he was always confident in his answers. I didn't know if he was trying to make us feel better or if he was optimistic to the point of delusion. Eoin declared himself the sole navigator the morning after our kiss. I assumed to appease the guilt weighing on him. No one argued it at first, but now we were two days behind Cillian's initial week estimate.

Cillian said nothing. His usual teasing comments ceased, and I wondered if he, too, was troubled by the king or troubled by what transpired between Eoin and me. I shook out the thought. It was ridiculous. Why would Cillian care? Why would I care if he cared? No, Cillian was more concerned about the king. His freedom also depended on our success. He took the Bond on a gamble, and this was his last chance. That's it.

I slowed my gait, letting Eoin take the lead. Ronan was in the middle of one of his ridiculous stories, and even the witches seemed to listen in. Kalee's gaze followed me, but I didn't let the burn of it stop me. Cillian and I hadn't spoken since last night. At first, I avoided him out of embarrassment, but anytime I mustered up the courage, Eoin found an excuse to drag me away or engage me in conversation.

No. There was no reason to be embarrassed. I didn't owe anyone an explanation. Especially not Cillian. What transpired between Eoin and me was between us and no one else.

"Talking to me again, little shadow?" He asked, a smirk playing at the edges of his lips.

My mouth fell open and snapped shut, my ears hot. "Don't flatter yourself, my legs merely need a break from the quick pace."

"Tell me, what is on your mind?"

"Do you believe we will complete the Malartaím? Or would our efforts be better spent trying to escape Ilythia while we still have the chance?"

Cillian slowed his pace, putting more distance between us and the witches, and lowered his voice. "While I find your proclivity to violence admirable, we need the cauldron. You're as good as dead without it."

"The others—"

"If they want to try to escape, I will not stop them. But I'd sooner die from failure than leave you to fend for yourself."

My stomach fluttered despite knowing Cillian said these things because he needed the cauldron, too. His life was at just as much risk as mine.

"What if the king calls us back?" I asked, changing the subject.

"Then it is out of our hands. We will adapt."

Niamh, Ahlani, and Flore had been instructed to kill us if we tried to escape Ilythia before completing the Malartaím. How did Cillian plan to adapt to death?

"What if—"

"There is no sense in worrying about something we cannot control. Ronan's ruse was convincing enough. I've never known the king to turn down the chance to make an example of smugglers. It's easy to see the king trusts Ronan—otherwise, he would not have loaned us out to him. We will try our best and hope someone doesn't come looking for Ronan."

I bit my bottom lip. How long would the king wait until his son returned? Would he send men to search for Ronan if we were gone for too long? The drivers were back at the inn in Willowmere. Surely Ronan gave them instructions to wait for him, no matter how long it took.

"Please tell me there's an easy way to get up there," I asked the following day, standing at the base of the tallest peak of the Ennisi Mountains.

The witches were silent as usual while we examined the landmass towering over us. It was nothing like the Mountain Castle or any mountain I'd ever seen, which wasn't many. What wasn't occupied by bustling cities in Centra was filled with forests and plains. And while the Mountain Castle had been massive, it was nothing compared to the Ennisi Mountains. Queen Petranella told us the fire jewel would be at the top of the tallest peak. There was no question about which one it was. Assuming the jewel existed.

"Unless Cillian can fly us up one by one, I imagine we'll have to climb it," Ronan said.

"Would you be able to?" Kalee asked, studying Cillian's now wingless back.

Cillian looked toward the setting sun as it washed the sky in deep blues and purples. "I can, but it's getting dark, and we don't know what awaits us at the top of the mountain. It would be better to rest now and depart at first light."

A shrill, inhuman shriek cried in the distance, as if to prove Cillian's point.

"Hunter, find food," Eoin said after we'd finished setting up the campsite. "Ronan and I will collect firewood."

The coldness in Cillian's stare sent a chill over my body.

"I'll find food," I volunteered, needing a distraction from tomorrow.

"The Hunter is more than capable. You should stay. Rest your weary feet."

I crossed my arms over my chest. "I'm fine, and Cillian can decide for himself."

"No, little shadow, Eoin is right. I am far more capable than he is. Though I wouldn't dismiss your company."

"Why must you call her that?" Eoin snapped, halting me in my tracks. I used to bristle at the nickname, but now, I hardly notice it.

"You know my given name. Why must you call me Hunter?"

"Because it is the name I prefer," Eoin answered, his chest puffed out.

Cillian's lips twisted into a crooked smile. "Exactly."

Eoin huffed and stomped off. Ronan's brows knit together and followed after him.

"I don't know what you did to piss him off, but he really doesn't like you," I half-joked once we were far from the campsite. Cillian must have done something to warrant such disdain. I'd hoped after mine and Eoin's conversation, things would get better between them, but that was far from true.

"He doesn't like me because I don't take his orders like an obedient dog."

"Eoin doesn't—" I stopped. Eoin *did* order Cillian around even now, when we were no longer in the presence of the other guards. When there was no reason to pretend. Had I grown so used to hearing orders all my life that they no longer fazed me?

"He feels bad that he put us in this situation. He's probably stressed out and not realizing it," I said. Eoin was wrong, but he meant well. I would talk with him. He trusted me. Maybe he would listen this time.

"Eoin likes ordering those he deems inferior to him because it makes him feel like a man. He likes wielding whatever superiority he *thinks* he has, especially in front of you, because he wants to show off."

"No," I scoffed. No? No. He was wrong. "Eoin hates taking orders from others. Why would he do the very thing he despises?" This, at least, I knew for certain. From the conversation and the looks we've shared, there was no faking that. At his core, Eoin wanted to help others, which was why he was trying so hard to make up for his mistakes. Why he aided Ronan with his smuggling operations. Why he helped *me*. He saved me from the fomorii wolf and helped nurse me back to health. He cared for me.

"You look at Eoin like he understands you, but he doesn't. He never will."

"Oh, but you do?"

"Yes. I see you for who you are. He sees you for what you are."

I scoffed. "And what am I?"

"Something to keep for himself."

"You're wrong, Cillian."

He pressed his lips into a tight line."Whatever helps you sleep at night."

"I sleep just fine, thank you." I didn't. Not really. But he didn't need to know that, even if it had nothing to do with Eoin.

"And, yet, you could sleep better next to me"

"Please," I scoffed.

"You don't have to be so polite. You're always welcome."

"The last thing I want to do is crawl into your bed." Snow crunched under my boots as I stomped ahead of him, searching for any of the berries Kalee hadn't deemed poisonous.

"If you're afraid, don't worry, I can show you a few things."

I plucked a handful of the purple ones, shoving them into my sack. "Gods, Cillian, I'm not some inexperienced girl. Have you ever thought that maybe I don't want to sleep with you?"

"Funny, I've never had anyone complain before."

I let out a frustrated groan, quickening my stride, his chuckle nipping at my heels.

"If Eoin isn't satisfying you—"

"I haven't slept with Eoin, not that it's any of *your* business."

"Who, then, has had the fortune of stealing your heart?" Cillian asked.

His smile dropped when I turned to him. I busied myself with one of the bushes, dusting the frost from it. "I'm sorry," he said. "I shouldn't have intruded."

"His name was Eiric," I murmured before I could think better of it. "He was Bonded, like us. He died before you came to Centra. He was my friend. Or as close as one of us gets to having friends."

"Saoirse, I—"

"We should try the river," I said, changing the subject.

Cillian caught me by the elbow, turning me toward him—forcing me to face him. "I'm sorry for your loss. Truly."

I gave him a tight nod before freeing myself of his grasp. The river's bank was rocky and covered in ice, but there was enough flow to keep it from icing over. "It was a long time ago. I've made peace with his death. Eoin is not some wicked person, you know. Just as you are not a monster. You should give him a chance."

Silence.

I toed the rocks, edging closer to the river's edge. With any luck, we might actually catch something.

"Be careful," Cillian warned.

"Don't worry about me. You—" My foot slipped, throwing me off balance and sending me straight for the water. Cillian caught me by the waist before the river could catch me in its icy grasp.

"You were saying?" He chuckled, still gripping me by the waist, holding my front against his firm chest so I was forced to share his airspace.

"Arrogant bastard," I shoved both of my palms against him.

One moment, we were standing nearly chest to chest. The next—

Cillian's foot slipped on a patch of ice, sending us sprawling. I crashed down on him with a resounding *thud*. I winced, not for myself but for the sick thump of Cillian's skull against the ground.

"I'm so sorry, I—"

He laughed, softly at first, then deeper, the sound vibrating his chest. A chuckle bubbled out of me until it grew, resonating from my belly. The first true laugh I had in what felt like forever. The tension of our conversation fizzled, and Cillian held me to him until the laughter died out. Then, there was nothing more than the exchange of our breaths.

Heat bloomed from my face down to the tips of my toes, making every part of our bodies hypersensitive. Cillian tucked a stray hair behind my ear, brushing my temple. Eoin's face flashed in my mind, and all I could think of was how upset he would be if he caught us. Cillian must have seen it written across my face because he said, "Do not worry, little shadow, you may dabble with whoever you like. I know in the end, you'll be mine."

His words sent tingles down my spine. My mouth opened, searching for a retort or, at the very least, to deny him. But before anything could come out, another scream pierced the air—this one notably human.

Kalee.

CHAPTER THIRTY-TWO

Cillian and I scrambled to our feet, racing back to the campsite. I slipped on hidden blocks of ice, threatening to give way, but I didn't let it slow me down. The campsite was in disarray when we approached.

Fomorii were everywhere.

Ronan cried out as a fomorii wolf bit into his arm, shredding the skin beneath his tunic. Dark, red blood dripped from its maw, its growl rumbling the earth. Niamh's familiar answered with a growl of his own, grasping the demon in his sharp teeth. The fomorii didn't whimper. Didn't balk. It freed itself, snapping and snarling. Eoin and the witches did their best to fight off the fomorii men and women surrounding them. But there were too many.

We were outnumbered.

I palmed my daggers, though they wouldn't be enough against their claws and teeth when fighting in such close proximity.

"Saoirse," Cillian called, offering one of the swords he always carried.

I took it, relieved that the weapon was wonderfully light. It was shorter than most swords, which were always too heavy to wield. This one, however, could be maneuvered with a single hand. Its black blade sank into the fomorii with ease. The azuline veins and sapphire pommel gleamed against the polished black hilt in the moonlight.

Ronan lay prone on the ground, clutching his arm while Kalee and

Eoin fended off the fomorii around him. Niamh and Ahlani fought back-to-back, working their way through the demons circling them. Flore held her own, picking the demons off one by one. Cillian's wings appeared with a flash, and then he was gone, racing toward Ronan and moving him to safety before he was surrounded.

Either by accident or some rare show of mercy, Flore fought her way over to me. Swift as the wind itself, there was no denying why she was considered one of the queen's top warriors. In an unspoken agreement, we defended one another as the demons screeched, cursed, and clawed toward us.

Cillian wasted no time getting into the thick of it once Ronan was safe. *Faie warrior, indeed.* The muscles beneath his tunic bulged and rippled as he sliced and thrusted his sword into the fomorii again and again. The movements were like a dance, the fight a song in his blood.

My chest was heaving by the time Ahlani finished off the final demon. Niamh fussed over her, checking for injuries. Flore was inspecting herself when a dark shadow clouded behind her.

"Look out!" I flung a dagger at the fomorii as it took shape. Flore whirled around and sliced its head clean from its neck, giving me a nod of thanks.

Relief was only temporary as an awful squelching noise sounded, and Cillian released a guttural yell.

A straggler sunk its claws and teeth into one of Cillian's wings. His face drained itself of all color. He couldn't fling the fomorii off him, and I couldn't get a good shot with him moving so much. Eoin was closest, but he only stood there motionless—too stunned to react.

The fomorii's skin was heatless beneath my fingertips as I thrust my blade through its ribcage and yanked it off Cillian. Eoin sliced off its head before I could think about attempting to interrogate the demon.

Cillian groaned, his breath shallow and strained. My fingers trembled as I examined the wound. The left wing was untouched, but the right...

It was wrecked.

The once pristine, gray works of the gods themselves were now torn and tattered. Feathers bent in unnatural ways, soaked in Cillian's lifeblood. Some spots were bare where the fomorii had gotten hold of him. It wasn't a death wound. Not with Cillian's quick healing. But our chance at reaching the peak of the Ennisi Mountains tomorrow was ruined.

"I'm sorry," I warned, pouring the remainder of my canteen's contents over the wound. There was no telling what kinds of sickness might be trapped in their bites. Cillian sucked in a breath through clenched teeth. Water alone wouldn't be enough to disinfect it, but it was better than nothing. I rummaged through the bag in his tent, searching for the same brown, pungent paste he used on my leg after I injured it on the bridge crossing into Ilythia. There wasn't much left, but it was enough.

I held his face in my hands after I applied the rest of the paste. "You're alright."

It wasn't a question, but Cillian answered anyway.

"I'm alright. Go check on Ronan."

Tears glistened on Kalee's cheeks as she held a shirt to his injury. But there was too much blood. Ronan wouldn't heal quickly enough like Cillian. Images of my mother flashed through my mind. I cursed. I'd foolishly used all of Cillian's paste. Somehow, in my panic, I'd forgotten about Ronan. I should've known he would need it.

"I don't know what to do," Kalee cried. Fuck, she *always* knew what to do. Eoin ripped off his tunic, using it to replace the blood-soaked one.

"Is there an herb we can use?" I asked, my gaze skipping over the forest floor. The healers at the castle always used a crushed purple plant to help with my injuries. There was nothing here but dried grass caked in snow.

Ronan was ashen, a sheen of sweat coating his face. The witches crowded around us, watching with weary gazes and refusing to help.

"Please," I pleaded to Flore. She was a healer. She would know what to do. Her lips thinned. Ronan's protective lids flashed uncontrollably, switching between black and blue. If Ronan was losing control after so many years of hiding it from his father, the state of his injury must be life-threatening. Ahlani let out a small gasp, but Flore's face remained impassive.

"Please," I begged. Ronan couldn't die, and Kalee shouldn't be the one to witness it. Niamh's familiar whined, something solemn passing over his golden eyes.

"Only because you saved mine," was all Flore said before getting to work. Saving her life was an exaggeration, but I wasn't about to argue. If she needed an excuse to not go against her queen's orders, then so be it. I didn't mention that she probably wanted to save him since he was their kin—none of my business.

She pulled various herbs from the pouch belted around her hips. Crushing them in her hand, using Ronan's blood to mix them before applying the poultice to the area. Bile rose in my throat when she removed

Eoin's now-soaked tunic from Ronan's wound. The fomorii cut to the bone, taking a large chunk of flesh, muscle, and sinew with it. Kalee trembled against me. She shouldn't be here. She shouldn't see this. Flore packed the wound, filling it with mixed herbs. Both hands held them in place as she touched her forehead to the back of her hands, muttering swift words under her breath.

Smoke filled the space, but Ronan did not cry out. Instead, he sighed, slumping against Eoin as consciousness left him.

CHAPTER THIRTY-THREE

Eoin paced in front of Ronan's tent. Minutes turned into hours, and Ronan remained unconscious. Flore worked her healing magic on the prince, mending muscle and flesh back together.

"It takes time," she barked at Eoin before kicking everyone out of the tent aside from Kalee.

"Here." I handed Ahlani a water canteen. She nodded her thanks, taking a deep swig as if wishing its contents were far more potent. Something shifted between us and the witches. I didn't know if it was because they discovered their brethren among us or if we forged a bond from fighting the fomorii. They were friendly toward us. Or, friendly in their own way. Niamh didn't have as much of a murderous glint in her eye, and Ahlani smiled earlier. And not in a menacing way either. Progress.

Would it continue if they discovered Ronan was the Prince of Centra? Would they see Ronan for who he was? Someone who strived to do better —*be* better than his father, or would they take him at face value as I once did and destroy him for it? I didn't want to find out.

"Do you know what those things were?" Niamh asked, pulling me from my thoughts. She rubbed a gentle hand along Ahlani's back. She, too, sustained minor cuts and bruises. The wolf sat in front of them, but not before sweeping past me, letting his coarse fur brush against my side.

I looked to Eoin. Do we tell them all we know? If the fomorii made their way out here in the middle of the Ilythia, the Shadow King must be growing stronger. Would their queen stand against Tenebris if his shadow demons were in her kingdom? Perhaps the word of her queen's guard would be enough for Petranella.

Eoin dipped his stubble-lined chin. *What else did we have to lose?*

"Fomorii demons," I answered. "They are coming into our world to return power to their master."

Ahlani's brown skin lost its warmth. "The Shadow King?" she whispered.

"You know who he is?" My heart quickened. *Maybe they could lead us to the answers we needed.*

"He has many titles, but the one he is most famous for is God of the Darkworld."

"How do you know this, Ahlani?" Cillian asked, sharing my thoughts.

Niamh rolled her eyes. "He is a nightmare mothers tell their witch-lings, nothing more."

"And yet, you saw the fomorii. Fought them with your blades. You cannot deny their existence," I countered.

Niamh didn't answer.

"He lures witchlings into the murky depths of dark waters seeking revenge on the Triple Goddess who helped banish him to the Darkworld for all eternity," Ahlani clarified, shooting daggers at Niamh.

Cillian frowned. "How would witchlings help him achieve this goal?"

"Because he gets his revenge wherever he can. He knows witches cannot reproduce easily. It is by the Triple Goddess' grace the witch gene is passed on. He seeks to destroy all of the gods' creatures."

"Cillian, did you ever hear something similar about luring young ones?" I asked, something familiar about the tale tingeing the recesses of my mind.

"My father was never the storytelling type."

"It doesn't matter," Niamh cut in. "It is a *story* mothers tell their chil-dren so they don't wander off. These fomorii are one thing, but before today, we've never seen them in Ilythia."

"It isn't a *story*," Ahlani snapped. "I experienced it firsthand."

The wolf whined, soft and anxious, as it looked between the two witches. Niamh's eyes softened, and she reached for Ahlani. "Your mind was playing tricks on you, my love."

"I know what I saw." Ahlani pulled herself out of Niamh's grip, shaking her head as if she could no longer fight back the memories. "It was the end of our first year at the academy."

"The academy?" I asked, knowing full well Kalee would want to know about it when I filled her in later.

"Witchlings attend the academy once they reach a certain age so they may practice and hone their crafts. After graduation, we are given our assignments."

"Our assignments are the roles we must fulfill in our society until we age out—soldiers, healers, or potion makers," Niamh said, sensing my question. "Most witches perform their assignments until they physically can't anymore."

"At the end of our first year at the academy, the older students dared us to swim to the center and back of the Atrous Lake." Ahlani's throat bobbed. "The Atrous Lake is true to its name. The water is so black you cannot see your hands below the surface. No one knows what lurks beneath its waters, and students are forbidden from entering it."

"So naturally," Niamh cut in, "it is a right of passage for students who complete their first year to jump into the lake. It's been a ritual for centuries, and rarely does anyone not make it back."

"Clare didn't make it back," Ahlani snapped.

"Clare didn't know how to swim, and they forced her in anyway!" Niamh's voice rose as if she was tired of revisiting the subject.

"Yes, she did! I was right next to her. She was fine until something grabbed her."

"Nothing grabbed her, Ahlani. You are misremembering something that happened fifty years ago."

Ahlani shook her head. "I felt it. Something slithered across my legs and went for Clare instead. One moment, she was laughing, splashing those around her. The next, she was gone."

"It is possible," Niamh sighed, "some beast dragged her down. But it was no myth that killed our friend."

"She was never seen again. Her body was never recovered. The entire academy searched for her. Clare disappeared without a trace. I know she was taken to the Darkworld deep within my bones. Just like the stories said."

"I'm sorry for your friend," I murmured, breaking the silence.

Ahlani steeled her shoulders, not bothering to wipe away her tears. "If the Shadow King's soldiers are coming into our world, then the queen must know."

"We will tell the queen what we saw when we return, but we will not go to her with a child's cautionary tale," Niamh said, an order from a commanding officer to her soldier.

If Ahlani wanted to protest, she thought better of it by conceding with a nod.

Flore emerged from Ronan's tent, her hands covered in dark crimson.

I stood. "Tell me he's okay."

"He's stable and will fully recover with his arm intact, but he will need a few days to rest. I would advise against him climbing the peak of the Ennisi Mountains anytime soon unless you are healed enough to use your wings."

Cillian shook his head. "The wounds have closed, but they're still too fragile to risk flight, much less carry someone else. I will need at least a couple of weeks."

My heart sank to the pit of my stomach—*a few days* until Ronan recovered. We didn't have a few days to waste—not with my twenty-fifth name day fast approaching and not with the threat of vengeful kings constantly looming over my shoulder. It would be one thing if Cillian could fly us in a few days. But without him, who knows how long it would take to climb the mountain, much less retrieve the fire jewel?

"We can't afford to wait a few days." I looked at Cillian. He understood more than anyone the threat the Bond posed. "We must continue without Ronan."

Flore shook her head. "You have to complete the task together. Otherwise, the queen has grounds to invalidate the Malartaím."

I groaned, my shadows writhing in response. "Can nothing be simple?" I shouted, storming off to my tent, flinging open the flap.

The gods laughed at our pathetic attempts to survive. Anything we tried would be in vain. I fisted my hands in my hair, using pain to distract from the dreadful thoughts threatening to overrun my mind.

"Saoirse," Eoin called from the tent's entrance.

"What?" I asked hoarsely, biting back the panic threatening to seize my system.

He sat and pulled me down with him to my bedroll, warmth radiating through his thick clothing. His thumb stroked the back of my hand while I tried to breathe. His touch was kind. Almost calming.

"It may look glum now, but we will complete the Malartaím and return for the cauldron," he said once my breathing steadied.

"You keep saying the same things, but your baseless optimism is getting us nowhere," I snapped. Hurt flashed in Eoin's eyes, and I hung my head between my knees. "No matter how close we get, what we seek always slips between our fingers. We were *so close* to retrieving the cauldron, and then, in an instant, we've never been further from it," I said, softer now, tears threatening to fill my vision.

"Look at me." He grabbed my neck, his hand engulfing my Bond Mark. Could he feel it pulsing through my very being, taunting me with each heartbeat?

"We will get the cauldron and free your Bond." His amber-flecked eyes gazed into mine, but all I could think about was the green of Cillian's and how they seemed to see every part of me. I tried to push Cillian from my mind, but he was always there, lingering in the corners.

Eoin's hand held firm, refusing to let me turn away.

"How do you know? Every path we take is the wrong one. What makes you think we'll succeed?"

"I cannot say, but I know with every fiber of my being the cauldron will be ours. It has to be." His voice was steady, his expression leaving no room for doubt. Eoin truly believed we were capable. The odds were stacked against us, but his confidence was unwavering. Though it was unlikely, I clung to it and prayed to the Mother that it might be true.

CHAPTER THIRTY-FOUR

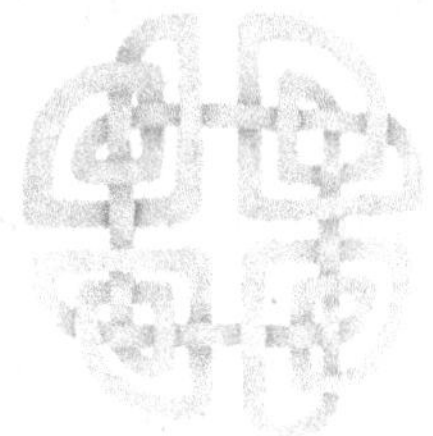

Two days passed before Ronan regained consciousness. I'd nearly bitten off my nails in the time it took him to wake. Another three, and he could raise his arm over his head. My nails were chewed to the nubs by then, so I shifted my attention to the inside of my cheek, gnawing it bloody. Two more days until Flore put a weight in his hand, working to rebuild his strength. His flesh healed thanks to her skillful hands, but not even she could repair the muscle fully.

"I think it looks striking. Makes you look courageous," Kalee said, running her fingers over the scarred and dented flesh.

The look on Ronan's face said otherwise, but he gave her an affectionate kiss on her forehead anyway. Kalee always had a way of turning someone's perceived flaws into something they should be proud of.

"Yes, yes, Ronan is very handsome, but can we please start discussing how we are to retrieve the fire jewel?" I paced back and forth, Niamh's familiar's keen eyes watching me. The wolf seemed to sense my unease and even approached me as if he, too, was annoyed with my anxious habits. I'd done nothing but pace and think and pace and think. But no matter how many plans about the trek up the mountain were formed, they all depended on Ronan.

"Will you be able to make the climb?" I held Ronan's azure gaze, praying he would give the answer I needed.

Ronan splayed his hand and flexed his arm. He wore an easy expression, but nothing could hide the tremor running through his upper arm.

My heart sank.

"Judging by the size of this mountain, it will take at least a few more days until we have to start the climb. By then, my arm should be good as new," Ronan said, studying the mountainside. "Besides, the land always provides for a witch in need."

Flore nodded her approval.

"We leave at first light," Ronan declared after a moment of silence.

The thrum of excitement and nerves vibrated through me. We were finally leaving. I couldn't stand another day at this campsite knowing we were running out of time. Each hour was a gamble. How long before the Conqueror King's patience wore too thin?

"Saoirse," Cillian said, regaining my attention.

"Hmm?" I looked up from the blaze of the campfire, the colors shifting from yellow to orange.

"Eat." He shoved a roasted rabbit in front of my face. My stomach growled in answer. Cillian had been doing that a lot lately, handing me food when I'd forgotten to eat, the unknown of Ronan's recovery stealing my appetite.

Cillian's lips pursed, giving me a wary look. He'd been doing *that* a lot, too.

I rolled my eyes but took the meat. Cillian hadn't fussed over me the way Eoin had—audibly and obnoxiously like a mother hen. No, Cillian saw what Eoin couldn't. He noticed when my faie instincts screamed from the lack of movement—the deficiency of progress toward resolving a threat. Cillian saw when my power begged to be used or when my body starved for food.

I see you for who you are. He sees you for what you are.

And what am I?

Something to keep for himself.

I pushed our conversation from my mind. It shouldn't be invading my thoughts at all.

"Come," he said after I devoured the food.

Eoin rested a hand on my arm. "Is it really necessary for the Hunter to continue to assault you day after day?"

I bristled. He'd nearly lost his mind the first day Cillian and I trained together when I returned with several bruises, not that they lasted long. The magic in my blood healed them fast enough. Besides, I welcomed the pain. It gave me something else to focus on. It kept my worries and the tremors at bay, making me exhausted enough to sleep at night.

"Cillian's not assaulting me. He's helping me. I need to know how to fight better if I'm going to survive without the protection spell."

"Why do you have so little faith in me? I can keep you from harm."

"I have to learn how to rely on myself, Eoin." I knew his concern stemmed from the loss of his sister and mother, but he needed to understand. For so long, I abided by the will of another. I was given clothes. Food. Shelter. I'd always felt so alone, but I knew nothing of what it took to be truly alone. Not when I had my mother's protection spell keeping me alive. With luck, I'd see the day it was no longer with me, but that thought was terrifying. I didn't just want to survive. I wanted to thrive. And that meant learning how to look after myself.

Eoin's nostrils flared, looking to Ronan and Kalee for help, but neither of them lent it. Niamh squared her shoulders as if daring Eoin to argue. He stomped off without another word.

For once, Cillian kept his mouth shut as I followed him deeper into the forests of Ilythia. We'd been doing this dance since we learned Ronan would live but needed time to recover.

I protested at first, not wanting to leave Ronan or Kalee in case he took a turn for the worse, but Cillian had reassured me Ronan wasn't going anywhere. Plus, Kalee and the witches were eager to not to watch me pace at all hours of the day.

Branches of densely packed trees brushed against my arms in greeting, welcoming us back to where we could let out our frustrations. As much as I needed it, Cillian needed it too. He, too, must have felt the shadow of the king's Bond around every corner, threatening to call him back before we completed the tasks we sought to achieve. He hadn't said it, but I knew his injury bothered him more than just the pain.

I caught Cillian's gaze across the small clearing, his hot stare making every nerve ending come alive.

"What?"

Cillian pressed his lips together as if trying to hide a smile. "Nothing," he said innocently. "Are you ready?"

I nodded, going into a defensive stance like he taught me.

As the Conqueror King's Informer, I never received formal training in fighting. I was meant to hide and observe, not fight. Knowing what I know now, dying wouldn't have been much of an issue with the protection spell, but it wouldn't last forever. Cillian insisted on teaching me because, according to him, the only thing I knew how to do correctly was use the right end of the blade.

As fast as the wind itself, Cillian threw himself at me, and I blocked and dodged as he had instructed on the first day we trained together. We moved throughout the clearing, taking turns between defense and offense. He didn't hold back, and neither did I. We soared across the clumped snow laced with grass, dirt, and rocks until I was panting. I let it all out. My frustrations with the Malartaím. With the Bond. With the Shadow King.

"You're catching on quick," he said, hardly a glisten at his temples.

"I'm a fast learner," I said with notably more effort, squeezing the words through clenched teeth. The cold did nothing to stop the sweat drenching from every pore, my hair sticking to my face.

Cillian swept out a leg, knocking me on my ass. "Not fast enough."

"Bastard."

"You'll learn," he laughed and extended his hand as a show of good faith.

I grasped it and yanked down as hard as I could, pulling him to the ground. Before he hit the snow, I pulled the shadows around me. For once, I'd teach *him* a lesson. We hadn't brought magic into our sessions yet. He had said I needed to know how to fight like a warrior and not like a *feral barn cat.*

"You may hide, little shadow, but I will always find you," he said in a low voice.

Our brawl from earlier masked my tracks as I backed away on silent footsteps. I held my breath in fear of being heard. Cillian stood gracefully, his muscles taut with anticipation. He turned and walked in the opposite direction.

It was too easy.

For all his arrogance and sureness, Cillian continued in the wrong direction. A giddy delight filled me. I crept behind him until I was inches away. He spun around and pinned me to a tree.

My shadows fell apart at his touch. His forearm braced above my heaving chest, pressing me into the bark enough to feel it, but not enough to hurt. Our eyes locked, and all I could see was green.

"Nice try," he smirked, that incorrigible dimple making its appearance. *Ass.* My chest heaved, struggling to catch my breath with him so close. And the way he was looking at me? It was as if he wanted to eat me alive and savor me as he did it. There wasn't enough space between us. His juniper and spice scent invaded my nostrils, his gaze so intent it was as if he could peer into my very soul, pursuing every fear. Every want. Every desire.

"Tell me one true thing," I sputtered, repeating the question he asked me that night in Willowmere. I needed something, anything, to distract myself from how damn close he was. Eoin was being overbearing, but after the kiss we shared—the trust we built with one another—I owed it to him to try to figure it out.

Cillian's eyes flicked to my lips, still holding me against the tree. Silence stretched before he answered as if he was warring with himself, deciding which truth to share. "I'm concerned the prince will not be ready for what lies ahead."

When he finally released me, I'd expected to be relieved, grateful he settled on an easier truth. Instead, I mourned his warmth.

"Do you think he can make the climb?"

"He's confident enough, but I worry it will only carry him so far," he said, offering a water canteen. "Your turn."

"I'm afraid I've doomed us all. Ronan wants the cauldron to stop Tenebris, but I can't ignore that I'm the reason we needed to find it so quickly. If it wasn't for me, he might have been able to negotiate with Queen Petranella or find another way."

"Do not confuse others' decisions for your own mistakes. Ronan, Eoin, and Kalee all agreed to seek out the cauldron. You did not force their hands. I chose to aid you in stealing it. Kalee invoked the Malartaím to buy us time. If the king were to summon us through the Bond tomorrow, not a single person here would fault you. We've all made our choices, we will deal with the consequences of our own actions as they come." Cillian placed a hand on my shoulder, solid and steady.

"But—"

"You don't need to hold the world on your shoulders, little shadow. You are not Fate weaving the misfortune of others. Blaming yourself for the choices of others doesn't change the outcome. You are only responsible for how you respond to it."

CHAPTER THIRTY-FIVE

I rose long before the glowing gold of first light broke through the horizon, unsure if I'd slept at all or if I merely closed my eyes for a few hours. A breeze played with my braid, my lungs burning from its crispness as I breathed the stillness in. My exhales rose in soft plumes, silver against the pale purple of dawn. A calmness settled over Ilythia as if the land held its breath. Watching. Waiting.

I prayed it was the Mother blanketing us in good fortune for our journey.

Eager to get on with the day, I broke down my tent while the others slept. Niamh, ever observant and always on guard, was the sole witness to my early rise. Well, she and her familiar who sat at her side. Niamh nodded as a way of greeting, acknowledging what the days ahead held. Either we'd earn our freedom or secure our deaths.

"Why?" Niamh asked after I finished packing a few essentials into the knapsack. Foraged food, extra clothes, and the flimsy blanket the witches gave us when we first embarked. Niamh hadn't been one for words since our paths crossed, but I knew what she meant all the same.

"Aside from the threat of the Shadow King?" Ronan still didn't have a concrete plan on how he was going to defeat Tenebris, but according to the seer, the cauldron was needed all the same.

She gave an answering smirk.

I sighed. What good would it do to hide my true intentions if we wanted to convince her queen to somehow let us use the cauldron?

"Because without the cauldron, I will die. A seer warned I must break my Bond to the King of Centra before I turn twenty-five, or I will be journeying into the Otherworld. No other witch can do it; the cauldron is the only way." I still wasn't sure if the seer had meant if I would die once I was twenty-five or if I was merely susceptible to death. Either way, I didn't want to risk it.

"How long is that?"

"Two weeks from now."

"Nines," Niamh swore, wincing. Something akin to pity wrinkled her nose. My throat went dry. The weight of how little time remained hung heavy in the air. It was suffocating. Like I was trapped in an hourglass, every second beating down on me, scraping my skin. Tremors twitched at my fingertips. Niamh all but confirmed how unlikely it was for Queen Petranella to allow us to use the cauldron.

"What a foul misrepresentation of a true bond. He is wicked for abusing such a sacred thing," she spat when the silence stretched too long.

"What is the true purpose of the anamchara bonds other than a declaration of love?"

"It is love, yes, but it is also a promise of devotion and protection. That one will always show up for the other, even in the darkest of times. By no means is it a way to control the other, and no osnádúrtha takes them lightly. I believe when the faie solidify their anamchara bonds, they can even share magic."

"But not the witches?"

"Our magic is different from yours. Each of us can perform simple everyday magic with our herbs as spells, but we also have specialties. Flore, for instance, is a profound healer. I can mend a small cut or bruise, but I would have never been able to fix Ronan's arm the way she did. If Flore were my anamchara, my healing capabilities would be as great as hers."

"What is your specialty?"

"Fighting, I suppose. The academy breaks us down to build us up again, stitching us into what Ilythia needs: either potion maker, healer, or soldier. There is no in between. Those whose specialties do not lie within herbalism or mending are trained as warriors."

"So do anamcharas choose one another, like when humans get married?" I asked. The humans at court often married one another out of political or financial advantage. What stopped the osnádúrtha from doing the same with magic?

"Yes…and no. You can't decide who your anamchara is. A soul connection is destined by the Triple Goddess and is not easily ignored. But you still have a choice to accept or deny the bond. Though most accept it when given the chance."

"And if they don't?"

"Then it will fizzle out, and it cannot be reclaimed once it is lost. The connection must not only be acknowledged but solidified by both parties."

"How does one do that?" I asked, hoping to understand how the king formed his. He'd somehow bypassed the willing participant portion of his Bonds.

"For both familiars and mates, it's similar to marriage vows, but it is more than a few empty promises. It is holding. Irrevocable. Those who marry may break their vows. Those who mate do so for life. The only way out is death."

Her eyes darkened, and my throat squeezed. I would have been shocked by Niamh not only indulging my questions but hearing so many words from her at once if it wasn't for the Mark pulsing against my neck as the king's Bond coiled around my soul, threatening to squeeze the life out of me. If this Bond was irrevocable, what if the seer was wrong and even the cauldron wasn't powerful enough to break mine? My Bond with the king wasn't the same as the anamchara bonds, but the rules of it were unknown.

"You said you have to solidify the bond. Does it leave you with a mark?" I asked, trying not to touch the knotted serpent on my neck.

"For Ahlani," she said, rolling up her sleeve, exposing her forearm and the two overlapping ovals with eight legs extending from the intersection, similar to a spider. "And for Airi." Niamh drew back the neck of her tunic, revealing the crescent moon etched below her clavicle. Niamh patted the wolf's head. Airi leaned into her touch.

"He likes you, by the way," Niamh said.

I smiled and held out a hand. Airi sniffed it and allowed me to scratch behind his ear. "I hoped he would. He looks fearsome, but I have a sneaking suspicion he's secretly cuddly."

Niamh barked a laugh, the first I'd ever heard from her, and Airi whipped his head back, but did nothing to halt my scratches. "Your suspicions are true. My deadly companion is rarely more than a spoiled dog."

Airi huffed at Niamh's comparison, but the witch smiled nonetheless.

"Did it hurt? The marks." I asked, thinking back to when my Bond formed. The pain had been excruciating when the king's soldiers held me down as I screamed until my throat turned raw.

Niamh tilted her head to the side, similar to how Airi would. "No. It was...tingly."

My experience was more than a mere *tingle*. It had been nearly unbearable. Perhaps this was because of the nature of the bonds. Niamh accepted hers with open arms, whereas mine was forced.

"I am sorry for your foul experience. Know a true anamchara bond is not like that." Niamh rubbed her thumb over the mark symbolizing her and Ahlani's mating.

The constricting feeling in my chest loosened some at the gesture. I noticed Niamh did it often. Ahlani always seemed to be Niamh's focus, and she was hers. They reminded me of Aislinn and Alice.

I missed them.

Any fondness in the witch's eyes disappeared when Eoin emerged from his tent, and she returned to the stone-faced expression of the hardened warrior. Airi did the same, resuming his position as Niamh's protector. Our conversation effectively over, I turned to help Eoin prepare breakfast when her low voice stopped me in my tracks.

"Be on your guard as you travel through the Ennisi Mountains. There is a reason why no witch has sought to retrieve the fire jewel and why my queen valued five of your lives for it," Niamh said.

"Are you not coming with us? Surely your queen would enjoy a reenactment of our deaths," I huffed a laugh.

Niamh shook her head, her blue eyes darkening. "We are to remain here and await your return. But do not think for one moment my anamchara cannot track you down. This nose of his is a gift. He doesn't forget a scent." Niamh glowered, making my knees want to shake.

Another threat—there was no way around the Malartaím. But there was something else there, too...a warning.

"What is in the mountains?"

The sun's orange rays painted across the sky, making her brown skin glow. If witches knew fear, I'd imagine something akin to it shadowed her striking face.

"The Ennisi Mountains may be in witch kingdom territory, but it is a cursed land—one not even Queen Petranella dares to cross. Here, take these." Niamh handed over four bows and three quivers of arrows I hadn't noticed sitting next to her. "No one knows what lurks in the mountains, but anyone who has dared to venture has never returned."

"Why do you have four bows?"

"It's always good to carry a spare."

"Thank you, this is very kind of you."

"No need to thank me, for you will find no kindness once you step on the Ennisi Mountains."

Though the sun brought warmth to us, I'd never felt colder than that moment. Ronan's ability to make it up the mountain was suddenly the least of my worries.

Chapter Thirty-Six

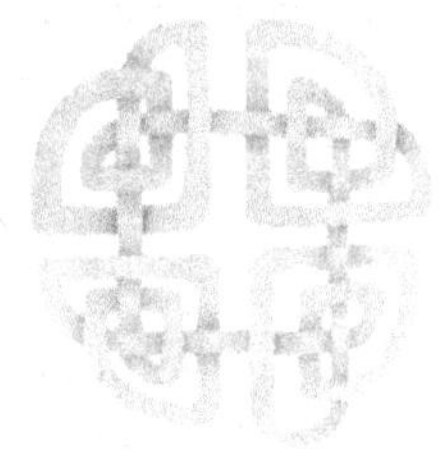

Niamh's warning clanged through me with every aching step. We said our farewells to the three witches hours ago, and still, my insides churned from her words. I passed her message on to the others and was met with grim faces. Only Ronan remained unbothered.

"Dramatics," he said, waving his right hand. His left, stiff at his side. The sleeves of his tunic covered the injury from where the fomorii gouged him. Even though he tried not to show how much it hurt, the slice of pain cutting through his eyes betrayed him anytime he was forced to use it.

Our trek up the mountain had been uneventful thus far, and I prayed Ronan's relaxed attitude was justified. Between the vibrant greenery and plants Ronan picked every so often without explanation, the mountain didn't appear cursed, other than the spiders littering it.

"Disgusting," Kalee screeched while trying to shake off the spider's web clinging to her hair.

"I would have to second that," Ronan said, helping Kalee pick off the near-invisible strands.

"They are more afraid of you than you are of them," Eoin cut in, moving ahead of the group.

"Doubtful," I murmured under my breath.

Cillian snorted, and Eoin shot us both a look of annoyance.

The further we traveled up the mountain, the denser the spider webs became, and the more my legs burned with each step. Sweat soaked my brow despite the chill clinging in the air. As the sky darkened, the mountainside came alive with hoots, howls, and other concerning sounds.

"We need to make camp for the night before it gets too dark," Cillian said, scanning our surroundings.

"The sun isn't down yet." Eoin scowled. "We've already lost too many days—we should press on. Visibility will not be an issue with the full moon."

Cillian sniffed the air and shook his head. "Something tells me we will not want to be exposed once night falls. We need to find shelter now."

"Where would you suggest, *faie*?" Eoin asked, mockingly splaying his hands.

"There."

I followed where Cillian's finger pointed through the dense trees, a cave partially occluded by a cluster of rocks.

"Where, exactly?" Eoin asked, his human eyesight failing him.

"There's a small cave up ahead," I supplied, not wanting to hear Cillian and Eoin get into it yet again. Since the Mountain Castle, Eoin's fuse was short, and Cillian was quick to ignite it.

Cillian's eyes danced with amusement, threatening to provoke Eoin further, but I gave him a look as if to say, *Can you not?*

Why not? It would be so much fun, he eyed back, his brow arching mischievously.

I shook my head, turning to hide the small smile that contradicted my annoyance.

The cave on the side of the mountain was large enough for the five of us and deep enough to keep us out of sight from predators. Our journey thus far hadn't been too exciting, but Niamh wouldn't have offered the information unless it was warranted.

An array of pink and gold streaked across the sky as we gathered supplies for the night.

"No fire," Cillian demanded when Eoin returned with an armful of kindling.

"It's freezing, and it will only get worse."

"We do not know what lurks around the mountain, but it cannot be good if Niamh thought it necessary to warn us. Let's not be an easy target."

When the sun set, we huddled next to one another, pressed against the deepest part of the cave. Cillian, a living flame, warmed me with his nearness, but my blood still ran cold. Shrieks unknown to any human or animal cried in the distance.

"What was that?" Kalee whispered, shaking between Ronan and Cillian. With Cillian's heat, I didn't suspect it was from the chill. The shriek, claws against my ears, was unlike anything I'd heard before. My pulse raced.

"I'm not sure, but it can't be good," Cillian muttered.

"Whatever it is, we will be safe here," Ronan said confidently.

"It's a good thing we're not attracting it with a fire." Sarcasm dripped from Cillian's mouth like spiced honey.

"Because freezing to death is the better option?" Eoin said through clacking teeth.

"Better than being eaten alive? Yes, I'd say so."

"Gentlemen, please, you're both pretty," Ronan interrupted. "There's no need to argue."

"Can you ever be serious, Ronan?" Eoin snapped.

"Eoin," Kalee hissed. "Don't project your bruised ego onto Ronan."

"Kalee!" Blood rushed to my cheeks. Thank the gods it was too dark for anyone to see the embarrassment staining them.

"What? It's clear he's jealous of Cillian and is only acting like this because he feels threatened."

Cillian chuckled, his chest vibrating. My teeth ground together so hard, I swore they cracked.

"I am not *jealous*. The Hunter's arrogance is merely so irritating that I—"

Another shriek. Closer this time.

Whatever Eoin was about to say was silenced by a ground-shaking roar. I pressed further against the cave wall, the stone a source of safety and terror. If that thing found us here, there would be nowhere to run, nowhere to hide.

Cillian's fingers found mine where they rested between us, and he gripped them tightly, not to show he was afraid, but to show solidarity— we were in this together. I clasped Eoin's hand in my other, hoping to send him the same message.

Screeches and guttural yells played throughout the night, making it difficult for sleep of any kind to come. Not even my nightmares dared to interrupt the monsters lurking beyond the cave. What seemed like no time and an eternity all at once, I awoke with my head in someone's lap.

Cillian's.

There was no mistaking his scent. Warmth and juniper and spice mingled together, wrapping around me—his cloak, heavy on my side. I breathed him in, not ready to open my eyes and ruin this sliver of peace. I woke up in the wrong man's lap, yet everything about this felt so right. His breath was calm. Stable. I would have thought he was asleep if it wasn't for the mindless strokes of his hand rubbing in idle circles down my back.

Gods.

The action almost made me forget about the horrors of last night. Almost. I shouldn't have wanted to stay in this quiet moment. Despite Eoin's rebuttal, I knew I was the reason he hated Cillian so much. There was no denying Cillian's feelings toward me. I felt it in his stares, in his touch. In the way he always had an excuse to be near. His comments about us being together were always teasing, but they held an underlying seriousness to them. Perhaps that's what scared me. Cillian always put me on the edge of something I couldn't name. If I fell, I wasn't sure I'd be able to come back.

His thumb circled over the tattoo on the back of my neck. Whenever I touched it or acknowledged it in any way, shame pulsed through me. But when he did it, there was something else in its place. Sorrow and something more lingered there, too…

A quiet moan escaped my lips when he scratched a hard-to-reach place.

His hand stilled only for a moment before continuing with his languid movements, as if waiting for me to bolt upright and scold him. But the moment was over. The quiet had been broken.

"Sorry," I murmured and attempted to straighten out what was sure to be a mess of my hair.

"You don't have to apologize to me, little shadow." Gone was his usual playful smirk, not a hint of a tease. "Stop shrinking yourself to appease others. You don't have to do that anymore. You're allowed to be yourself. To feel what you feel."

Gods, why did he have to talk to me like that? Like he knew me. Like he knew what I needed to hear. "Cillian, I—"

"You don't need to explain either. I told you before you may dabble with whoever you like. I'll be here, waiting. However you need me, I'll be there for you. Just say the word."

Nearly nose to nose, we shared the same airspace, yet I could hardly breathe. The heat of his gaze threatened to burn me on the spot. There it was again. That feeling of standing on the edge of a cliff, and I couldn't see the bottom. But I knew what it held. Either my damnation or salvation. Or somehow both.

I cleared my throat. "Where are the others?"

"They went to scout for food. I didn't want to wake you."

I could already picture the look on Eoin's face if he found me in Cillian's lap. The beginnings of a headache pulsed at my temples.

"Have they been gone long?"

"If you want to spend more time alone with me, all you have to do is ask," he quipped, his playfulness returning.

I shot him a look that said, *Really?*

He laughed, deep and hearty. The kind that shook his upper body and brought attention to his hand still on my waist. The touch seared my skin despite the thickness of my leathers. I wondered what, exactly, his hands would feel like with nothing between us. Would they be rough or gentle? Would I catch on fire like his magic?

Gods, I was losing my mind.

I stood abruptly, needing to clear my thoughts and stretch my legs. Cillian followed my lead, groaning at the movement.

"Did you sit like that all night?"

"You looked comfortable." He shrugged, the motion sending a flutter to my belly.

"Did you manage to catch any sleep?" I asked, noticing the purple under his eyes.

He frowned, and the light-heartedness of his expression fell. "I couldn't have slept if I wanted to. Not with what was lurking paces away from us."

My swallow got stuck in my throat. "Did you see what it was?" Had one of those things gotten that close?

"No, only the sounds it made."

"Then let's hope we never run into one."

"Agreed."

I shielded my eyes against the sunlight. Something grotesque and metallic hung in the air. Blood. A shiver snaked down my spine at the thought of whatever monster lingered being the cause of the sickly smell.

"Sleep well?" Kalee chirped as she approached, seemingly not bothered by the monsters we heard in the night and more interested in how she found me this morning.

"Fantastic, aside from the screeching beasts." I smiled sweetly, trying to give her my best *leave-it-alone* look. She laughed, and my smile faltered when Eoin's brooding form appeared shortly after her.

"Eoin—" I trailed after him.

His anguished face twisted my guts. Gods, he was so *infuriating*.

What did he want from me? I didn't owe him anything. I'd wanted to be his friend—had entertained the idea of more because I thought we understood one another. He was just so godsdamned difficult when he was like this.

"Save it, Saoirse."

Cillian took a step toward him, but I grabbed his wrist. He didn't need to fight my battles.

Eoin walked away, his anger hot enough to melt the snow. I was done chasing him—done apologizing for things out of my control. For fifteen years, I'd bowed to the wants of another. Had made myself small for someone else. It wasn't about Eoin *or* Cillian. It was about me, and I was choosing myself.

I squared my shoulders, standing tall.

CHAPTER THIRTY-SEVEN

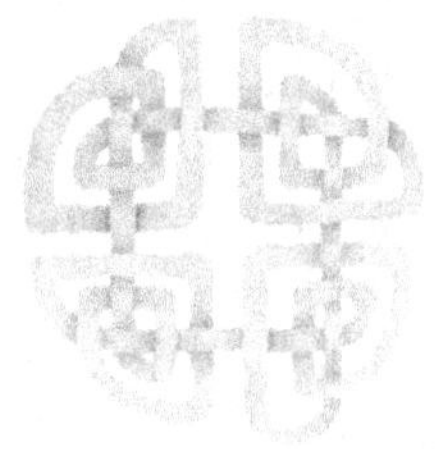

We traveled for days in a tense silence, Eoin too annoyed to even look at me, and everyone else on their guard after our first night on the mountain. The further we climbed, the thicker the air grew and the harder it was for Ronan to keep up.

"I'm fine," was all Ronan would say before applying more herbs to his injury, shoving sickly green ones in his mouth as some sort of pain management.

Cillian's wings were still too weak for flight, much less carting around four others. We had no other option but to make the climb. The mountain grew steeper as we went skyward, and we would have to grapple for purchase, but the terrain eventually leveled out.

"I don't see any signs of clear shelter," Cillian said, draining the color from Kalee's cheeks. We'd been fortunate thus far, always able to find safety before nightfall.

"Looks like our luck has finally run out," Ronan said, his tone morbidly light.

"Can you manage a little bit of seriousness, Ronan?" I asked, unsure whether I wanted to thank him for his light attitude in this terrifying situation or shove him off the mountain for it.

"What's the fun in that?" he said, giving Kalee a wink. A shaky laugh left her, bringing a bit of warmth back to her face as if she knew that if

Ronan could still joke, we still stood a chance. For that alone, I would deal with his cavalier ways.

"What are we going to do?" I whispered to Cillian, needing to hear a plan.

"We will figure something out, don't worry." He squeezed my shoulder.

"Yes, let *him* figure it out," Eoin thundered, throwing up his hands. Any tension Ronan released wound tight again.

"What is your problem?" I snapped. Eoin's constant bickering couldn't be about me alone. Cillian didn't hide his feelings toward me, but it wasn't as if I encouraged it. It wasn't as if I returned it. Whether Eoin was jealous of Cillian or not, he had no right to be.

"Do you not remember what a prick he was?" Eoin growled. "Did you forget you hated him before we left on this gods forsaken trip?" Birds flew away from the treetops at his words, the volume of his voice disturbing them.

"I hated Ronan, too, but it didn't stop me from befriending him. Not everyone is what they seem," I shouted right back. Despite the rage between us, Ronan chuckled at my words.

"Exactly," Eoin seethed. "Do you not find it strange we've run into more fomorii with him present than we ever had before?" The world turned silent at his accusation.

"You can't be serious." Cillian defended us against the fomorii more than anyone.

"Be careful of what you're implying," Cillian said with barely contained rage. The air warmed, an unnatural heat radiated from him—a warning of what he could do with the fire running through his veins.

Eoin did not concede. Instead, he pressed into Cillian, their chests touching. He had to look up to meet Cillian's eye line, but it was intimidating all the same.

"I know exactly what I'm implying. They all may have forgotten you chose to hunt down the osnádúrtha as the king's dog, but I haven't."

Cillian snarled, exposing his sharpened canines, more animalistic than I'd ever seen him. The two stared at each other, fighting for dominance. I knew Cillian would not back down. It was against his nature to do so. He'd sooner come to blows with Eoin than submit to him, and I wasn't sure how much restraint he had.

Finally, Eoin yielded, but not before flashing Cillian a wicked grin. He stalked past everyone, content with leaving it at that.

"Don't worry about him, he's just sulking." Ronan clapped Cillian on the back. "Now, can we discuss how we might live to see another day?"

Cillian burned a hole in the densely packed snow, forming a makeshift cave against the side of the mountain. Ronan secured the area with a fortification spell he learned from his mother to keep it from collapsing. It certainly wasn't as concealing as the natural caves we'd grown accustomed to, but it was the best we could come up with.

I blew hot air into my cupped hands, still numb from packing snow. Kalee and I huddled together, trying to preserve any remaining warmth. The sun hadn't set yet, and the others still searched for food. I doubted they would find anything of sustenance in this desolate, snowy landscape.

Cillian ducked into the snow cave with a pouch full of berries. "Kalee, do you mind looking at these to ensure I'm not going to poison us all?"

She laughed, taking the bag from his hand. "Of course," she said, looking between us. "But it is rather dark here, so I think I need to view these in whatever light we have left."

Cillian took her place by my side, not noticing the look Kalee gave me on her way out. It took everything in me not to hurl a ball of snow at her.

"I am sorry for what Eoin said earlier," I offered, wanting to break the awful silence between us. What Eoin suggested was horrible. There was no way Cillian could be working for Tenebris. Not if his reason for binding himself to the King of Centra was to help me.

"Why should you have to apologize for the words of another?"

"I don't. But you should hear it."

Cillian shrugged. "I have been called worse. It is no issue what other people think of me. I only care what you think of me."

"Why do you put so much stock in me?" His faith in me was unwavering, and I couldn't wrap my head around it. Couldn't understand what he saw. "I know you looked up to my father, but I am not him. I don't even know what he looks like, much less what his character was."

"You are more similar than what you give yourself credit for. His bravery shines through. His integrity. His fearlessness."

I huffed a laugh. "I am far from fearless. I'd spent most of my life cowering in front of the Conqueror King."

"Cowering and surviving are two different things. Even still, you didn't let it stop you from doing what was right."

I let his words sink in. Cillian always had a way about opening me up, pulling out the deepest parts, and forcing me to look at them, too.

"You want to know the biggest similarity between you two?"

"What?" I asked, breathless, hanging on his every word. Cillian was the only connection I had to my father, and I was desperate for any scrap he offered.

"Your bullheadedness."

I smacked his chest.

"What? It's true," he laughed, his grin wide, those incorrigible dimples making an appearance.

"I should have known you'd find a way to be an ass," I scolded, yet I was still grateful. His insight into my past meant more than he would know. I tucked the information away, guarding it close to my heart, feeling more connected to my father than I ever had.

Eoin barreled through the cave entrance, panting with his hands braced on his knees. Ronan and Kalee chased in after him. Their eyes widened at Eoin's haggardness. Bright red blood soaked the front of his tunic—his blood.

"What happened?"

"One of those things," he said, sucking in air between words, "went out early for a hunt. Barely killed it, but—there are others." He slid against the makeshift wall.

The sun was well on its way to setting, only minutes before it vanished. And a blood trail led straight toward us.

Chapter Thirty-Eight

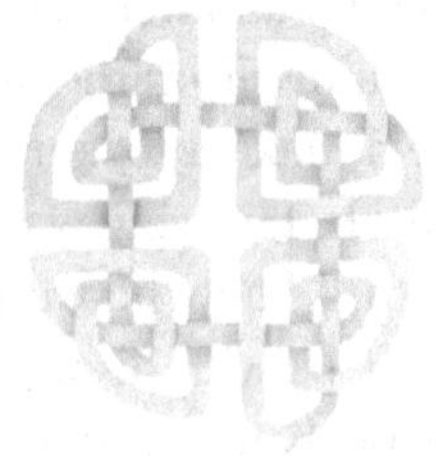

There was little we could do as the sun sank behind the mountain. The full moon hung high, but gave us little light through the densely packed trees as we scrambled to prepare for the monsters threatening to find us.

Ronan worked to staunch the bleeding from the claw mark across Eoin's chest, repeating the same movements and chants Flore had done on him days ago. Would Ronan have been a healer if he had been raised in Ilythia and not by his psychotic father?

Eoin's face drained itself of all warmth as the prince stitched his skin together faster than his human flesh had ever known. Sweat soaked both their brows. Ronan muttered repeated apologies between chants. The closure wasn't pretty. Eoin's tissue was crudely repaired, his scar tissue thick and jagged, similar to what I'd gotten from the fomorii wolf. Through it all, Ronan's hands held steady until he mended the last of the cuts.

Eoin's bloodied shirt was replaced by a fresh one from his pack. The torn and useless one was thrown to the center of the cave. Shrieks cried out in the distance.

"Did you remove your fortification spell?" Cillian asked, and Ronan nodded. "Good. Now, everyone, get to the trees."

"We could try to run," Ronan suggested.

Cillian shook his head. "Eoin may be healed, but he's lost too much blood." Another shriek. This one near enough to chill my blood. "We'll lure them into the cave and pick them off with arrows. At least we'll have the element of surprise. Go. *Now.*"

"Keep Kalee close," Ronan said.

Cillian and I both nodded. I scaled up the tree not far from our cave, years of climbing helping my speed. Kalee grabbed my outstretched hand, and I hoisted her up next to me. We were high enough in the trees to go undetected from the ground below, but not so high to be spotted from the sky. Ronan and Cillian helped Eoin up another tree on the other side of the cave entrance before Cillian hauled himself on the branch above me. I glanced at Kalee, praying to the gods we'd make it to sunrise. There was some comfort knowing Cillian was within reach. His wing was still sore from his injury, but if it came down to life or death, I knew he would risk flight. It was unlikely he'd be able to carry the two of us with his injury. But I, too, was willing to make sacrifices. If the need arose, Kalee would be the one in his arms.

Another shriek pierced through the trees, ringing in my ears.

"Do you know how to fire an arrow?" Cillian asked, shoving one of the bows Niamh had given us into my shaking arms, the other to Kalee, the quiver hanging between us. He'd already given the last of the weapons to Ronan and Eoin. The iron-tipped bolts were heavy in my hands.

Kalee took it confidently, her jaw set with determination.

"I've never shot an arrow before," I admitted, my fingers itching for my daggers instead.

"It will be easy," he reassured, "aim the pointy end at them." Cillian winked, his green eyes sparkling.

"Be careful, or I'll aim the pointy end at *you*," I threatened.

"Is that a promise?" He flashed a wicked grin. For a moment, I'd almost forgotten about the monsters stalking us. Almost.

The earth held its breath as we waited. Only the leaves dared to move as they rustled in the wind. How long would the three witches wait at the mountain's base before they presumed us dead? Our bodies would rot here with no one to retrieve them.

Assuming there would be anything left to retrieve.

"Steady," Cillian breathed, his voice barely louder than the breeze picking up. No, not wind. Wing beats.

I dared to crane my neck an inch, careful not to disturb the hood of my cloak that prevented any light from reflecting off my silver hair.

They landed with a thud, a puff of snow scattering underneath their black talons. Six of them, as tall as any man, prowled toward the cave, but that was where their similarities to man ended.

Leather wings folded against wiry backs as they approached on quiet steps. Their knees bent at unnatural angles. Short snouts glistened as the one at the front of the pack, the largest of them, sniffed the air. They congregated together, communicating with one another in violent clicks and growls through long, razor-sharp teeth. Something about them was distantly familiar.

"Liliachs," Kalee breathed. She fumbled for her arrows.

The name of the creature rang through my memories. My mother had told me about them—a cautionary tale intended to make children mind their parents. I could guess well enough that Kalee's knowledge came from one of the many books on Aislinn's shelves.

I shifted my focus to the cave and willed my shadows to conceal its interior. We'd guessed the nocturnal monsters were more than capable of detecting what lay in the dark. I counted on them being unable to see through an unnatural darkness.

One by one, the liliachs rushed into the makeshift cave, ready to feast on the blood they scented inside. When my shadows consumed the last of the liliachs, Cillian released fire from his palm and scorched the cave until it collapsed onto itself.

One moment. Then another.

No sign of the liliachs beneath the heaping mound of snow. Cillian must have incinerated them upon impact or suffocated them from the weight of the snow.

My sigh of relief was short-lived.

"Nines," Cillian cursed, shooting out another blast of fire with his outstretched hands. He summoned his mottled gray wings in an instant, a hint of pain tugging at his brows.

I barely had time to nock the arrow as a clawed, leathered hand punched through the snow. Then another and another. Six liliachs scrambled through the white powder, angry, ear-shattering screeches breaking through their lips.

Arrows and fire rained down on them, though our efforts appeared to be little more than annoyances, sticking to them like splinters. Irritating but not fatal.

"Iron is useless against them," Kalee said, fumbling with her arrows. The crack of wood splintered as if she snapped off their heads. I tried to remember what else my mother had said about them, but the memory was too distant.

"It's the best we have," I ground out.

Eoin cried out, and I watched in horror as he lost his seat, tumbling to the ground. A puff of snow clouded around him. Eoin was strong, but he was already injured as he drew his sword. There was no way he could outrun a liliach or climb back up by himself. One of my arrows embedded into the neck of a liliach, but its sight was locked on Eoin. Ronan let out a strangled cry as he let loose arrow after arrow into the liliachs inching toward him. There were too many. And they weren't dying. Even if Eoin had his full strength, he would be too slow for the liliachs.

Cillian whirled, wings out, as he fought to get to Eoin, two of the liliachs nipping after him. Seconds before they closed in on Eoin, Cillian grabbed onto him and flew him back to his perch in the tree.

The biggest shook out its wings, the others following suit. I swore and aimed a bolt at its outstretched wings, nearly doubling its height. Red veins tangled in the thin, leathery skin shone in the moonlight. My arrow nicked its wing, almost missing it entirely. It whipped its head toward me. Faster than what a beast that size should be capable of, it flew in our direction. Fangs bared and claws outstretched, I braced for impact.

I expected pain. But none came.

Cillian put himself in its path, the two landing with a sickening thud.

My shadows swirled, desperate to reach out.

I locked eyes with Cillian for a heartbeat. His were wide—not from fear, but perhaps surprise—as I leapt after him.

Chapter Thirty-Nine

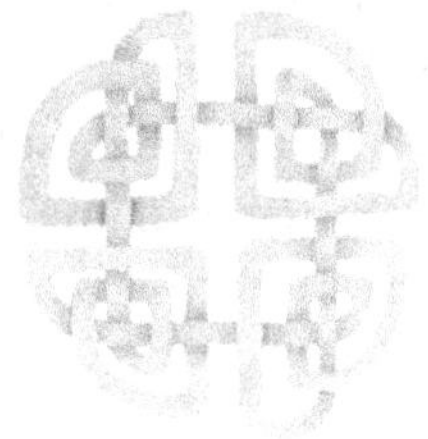

Instinct had a dagger in hand and poised at the liliach's back. Cillian let out an *oomph* beneath the hairy monster as we crashed to the ground, cushioning my fall.

Gods, the *smell.*

Bile rose in my throat. The liliach reeked of carrion. Its matted hair was coarse against my hands, its muscles taught with rage as it caged itself around Cillian. Cillian growled under the sheer strength it took to hold the liliach's snapping fangs away from his face.

I plunged my dagger into the monster's back, aiming for its heart, but resistance met my blade as if the organ was encased in steel.

"Push. Harder." Cillian's fire danced where his hands gripped the liliach's throat. The flames acted as nothing more than a source of warmth. Kalee yelled overhead, something like instructions to Eoin and Ronan, but I couldn't make out the words. All of my focus was glued to the liliach.

"I'm trying," I ground out, putting all my strength into the blade, my arms shaking. The dagger would sooner snap before it sank any deeper. I was nothing more than a nuisance as its maw snapped relentlessly, teeth inching closer to Cillian's neck. Cillian cried out as the liliach's claws tore into his flesh. The sleeves of his tunic fell away like scraps of fabric, exposing his straining muscles and veins pulsing under the monster's force.

"Saoirse!" Kalee called, grabbing my attention before tossing down an arrow. I caught the bolt, but the iron tip was missing. I glanced up at her.

"I think it's missing something!"

"Into the heart," she instructed. "Trust me." I didn't question her again as I drove the wooden shaft into the liliach, sinking into its flesh like a knife carving butter.

The liliach cried out before it slumped against Cillian, its lifeblood coated my fingers—red, hot, and sticky. The fomorii's blood was always black before their bodies disappeared. This…this was too similar to the blood spilled in front of me over the years. I couldn't look away. One moment, it was the liliach beneath me. The next, the many faces of the osnádúrtha. My shaking hands were still wrapped around the arrow's shaft, blood leaking from the wound, when Cillian called for me.

"Saoirse," he said, forgoing my nickname.

My eyes snapped to his. He rarely used my given name.

"The liliach, Saoirse. It's dead."

"I know that."

"You're still on top of it and me."

"I'm aware. I need a moment to catch my breath from saving your life." I stood too quickly to portray any semblance of being okay.

Cillian heaved the liliach off of him, and before I could turn away, he grabbed me by the wrist, his other hand cupping my cheek. Beneath the blood and grime and sweat, his scent still lingered. Juniper and spice. Earth and a wild wind.

"You're alright," he said, his thumb caressing my cheekbone. It wasn't a question but a statement, echoing what I'd said to him when the fomorii tore into his wing. When I'd said it, it had been to reassure myself. When he did, it was still meant to soothe my deceiving mind.

"I'm alright."

Kalee climbed down from the tree, landing next to us with a soft thud. "Eoin and Ronan killed off the others. You okay?"

"Yes, thanks to you two," Cillian said, his hand still clasped around my wrist as if he was afraid to let me go. Ronan ran toward us, Eoin's stiff gait close behind. Sweat beaded across their brows.

"How come the arrows didn't work before?" I asked, my pulse still racing.

"Only a wooden spike to the heart can kill a liliach; the iron tips prevented the arrows from penetrating," Kalee explained. "I read about them in one of Aislinn's books. Men turned monsters, their only drive is survival—for themselves and their kind. One bite from a liliach can cause the Turn if the person survives the bite itself." Her voice dropped, brown eyes searching Cillian for bite marks amongst the menagerie of cuts along his chest, face, and neck.

Any relief washed away at the sight of him. His tunic, along with his flesh, was torn and bloody. The liliach had gotten so close. What if Kalee hadn't helped me kill it in time?

"All fine," he reassured, holding his hands up. "Only claws, no fangs." Most of his wounds started to mend themselves, leaving behind trails of still-drying gore.

She looked him over warily and nodded once she was satisfied.

"We'll need to find shelter soon," Eoin interceded, his posture stiff.

As if on cue, a roar shook the mountain. Chills raced down my spine. We barely managed to subdue the six of them. If there were an entire horde of liliachs, or something worse, we might not make it until morning.

My fears of not surviving the night disappeared with the rising sun, and I'd never been more thankful to see the dawn of a new day even if the day was likely to end in certain doom.

"Are you ready?" Cillian asked from behind, making me jump.

"I think it would be easier if I knew what to expect." I peered up at the summit, craning my neck until it hurt. Snow coated the mountain caps, save for an odd gray smoke lingering around the tip, signaling the gods themselves.

"Eat," he said, handing over a sack filled with scavenged berries and nuts. My abdomen growled. "You will need all your strength today."

"And will you not need yours?"

"I have plenty." He winked.

I rolled my eyes but took the sack anyway, savoring the sweet flavor of the blue berries. My cheeks contorted against the tartness of the purple ones.

"That good?" Eoin asked, coming to stand next to us. He and Cillian shared a nod. Eoin's attitude toward Cillian finally shifted after last night.

"Here, you take them," I said, handing over the bag, now filled with mostly purple berries. Eoin chuckled, popping a few into his mouth.

"Delicious," he managed to get out, one of his brown eyes twitching. We laughed and for a moment, it was as if there'd been no animosity between us.

Eoin blew out a breath. "I am sorry for my behavior as of late. I've been so worried about completing the Malartaím and making sure we break your Bond, I've lost sight of my manners. And to you. Cillian. I've had my doubts about you, but I was wrong. I'm sorry."

Cillian held out his hand, and Eoin grasped his forearm. It wasn't a brotherhood, but it was civil and perhaps the start of something greater.

"Sometimes stress can get the better of us, and these last two weeks have been anything but relaxing."

Eoin chuckled, and a smile tugged at my lips. It faded when Ronan signaled us. We'd come as far as we could on foot. Now we had to make the climb.

"I'll see you at the top," Eoin said, surprising me with a kiss to my temple. Heat crept from my neck and into my cheeks, the shock of the action nearly knocking me on my feet. My feelings for Eoin were jumbled and confusing. Maybe once the Malartaím was over, we could finally figure it out.

"Are you sure you don't want to fly ahead and wait for us there?" I asked Cillian before he could say anything. He'd managed to use his wings last night without complaint. I took it as a good sign. Cillian adjusted my cloak, his fingers brushing against my neck with a gentleness that made my breath catch more than it should have.

"Where would the fun be in that?" He smirked, his hands lingering longer than necessary.

"Would you be able to carry Kalee?"

Years of being the king's Informer would help me make the climb. Ronan could handle himself if the way he could scale down the side of a building was any indication. Cillian and Eoin were both strong and capable. Even with Eoin's injury, I knew he could do it. But Kalee…Kalee was my handmaiden, her hands soft and unbroken.

Cillian's brows knitted together. "Your friend is not as fragile as you might think."

Next to Ronan, Kalee braided back her hair, her biceps flexing under the tight-fitted top. She'd always been thin to me, but under her dresses and frills, I'd never noticed how lean she was—how much strength she had. I hadn't expected her to wield a sword or handle a bow or hold her own against the liliachs. Perhaps it was time to stop doubting my longest friend and start seeing her for who she truly was: a survivor.

"But," he continued, "if it makes you feel any better, I will go last. If anyone starts to slip, I'll be there to catch them. After last night, my wing is still too sore to bear the weight of another, but I'll manage if need be."

Eoin coughed, calling out, "Unless you want to be easy pickings when night comes, I'd suggest we make haste."

Heat flooded my cheeks, but Cillian paid him no mind. Our eyes met. He searched for something I couldn't place.

"If I have to catch you, though, you lose," he teased, the look gone. A smirk pulled at the corner of his mouth instead, his dimple threatening to make an appearance.

My lips split into a grin. Our journey was far from over, yet our lives had been permanently altered. Once we reached the summit, nothing would ever be the same again. Regardless of what the outcome of today would be, I was proud of how far we'd come. I looked to my friends. To Ronan, pressing his forehead against Kalee's. To Eoin, checking the ties of his boots. To Cillian, staring down at me. For the first time in a long time, my heart was full. Even if the fire jewel were nothing more than a myth, even if this had been all for naught, I wouldn't have wanted to go through this with anyone else. We would face whatever was to come. Together.

CHAPTER FORTY

Despite the frigid temperatures, sweat beaded across my brow and dripped down my back. With gloved fingers, I clung to an open crack in the side of the cliff, using my lower half to hoist myself up further.

Kalee grunted below, her face skewed in concentration. Hair clung to her temples as she blindly searched for a place to grip.

"To your left," I instructed.

She mumbled her thanks, heaving herself up with strained arms.

"We're nearly there." I tried to sound positive despite my own trembling limbs. Though still several paces away, I could finally make out the top. My twenty-fifth name day was two weeks away, and the thought alone fueled me.

Cillian following us was my only comfort. He climbed with a practiced ease and hadn't even broken a sweat.

"Tired yet, little shadow?"

"Not a chance," I ground out, pulling up another inch.

As we approached the summit, the gray smoke grew darker and thicker until it turned black and coated my lungs.

"What is this?" I coughed.

Kalee examined the fog, but shook her head. I wasn't sure what concerned me more: the cloud swirling around the mountaintop or the fact that she didn't know what it was.

Up above, Eoin's foot slipped.

Gravel rained down on us. I turned in time to shield my eyes, but rocks pelted my head, pricking my fingers and shoulders.

"Sorry. You okay?"

"I'm fine." I spat out dust, debris, and the taste of ash.

Ronan heaved himself over the ledge, lending a hand to Eoin. They panted, arms resting on their knees as they caught their breath. When I was close enough, Eoin held his hand out. I grabbed onto him, solid and steady as ever, and he hauled me over the edge.

I rolled onto my back, my aching limbs savoring the rest. Ronan did the same for Kalee, and she collapsed next to me.

"You're hurt," Ronan said, inspecting a cut on her leg.

"It's just a scratch. I'll be fine."

I waited for Cillian—for the gloating that was sure to come. The teasing remarks that would somehow set my teeth on edge, yet also give me butterflies.

"You're taking your sweet time," I called down to him, peering over the edge.

I shouldn't have looked. We were impossibly high. A wave of nausea surged through me. The trees below—nothing more than blades of grass.

"Thought I'd savor the view."

Cillian took my outstretched hand despite not needing it. His grip was gentle yet firm. My pulse betrayed me when we collided. The warmth of his fire magic lingered beneath the surface and brought back the feeling in my fingertips. Once he reached the top, he grasped my other hand to do the same. I savored the warmth, wishing my entire body were encased with it.

"What happened here?" Ronan asked, his voice trailing off.

The summit was coated in debris, and in the center, a circular surface had been flattened out. Ash stirred with the whipping winds, and large craters littered the mountain top as if punched by the gods themselves.

"There's our smoke," Eoin said, pointing to a cave across the clearing where it billowed out.

Kalee crouched down, examining the crushed rock between her fingers. "The fire jewel must be in the cave."

"I suppose there's only one way to find out." Rock crunched beneath my boots, scuffing the black leather with gray soot. The smog was thicker near the mouth of the cave—the air warmer.

My eyes burned from the smoke. I missed Aislinn's flight goggles.

Breathing became laborious, my lungs squeezing to dispel the polluted air. I covered my nose with my shirt in an attempt to quell it, but the haze was too heavy.

The cave was large enough to hide an entire army. There were probably all sorts of tunnels and crevices within it, perhaps leading down to the core of the mountain itself. I braced my hand on the warm stone, leaning in to get a better look—a faint glow cut through the smoke.

It brightened, illuminating an object large enough to be a boulder.

The fire jewel.

Excitement buzzed through me. It was real and glittering and nearly as tall as I was. I didn't know how we were going to carry it down the mountain, but I didn't care. It was *real*—blood-red and smoldering, as if a burning ember was housed in its center.

I felt her before I saw her.

Two blazing orbs appeared through the miasma, with black slits down their middles. A growl shook the ground, all too familiar from our nights camping on the mountainside.

"Move!" Cillian yelled, but I was already in motion, lunging for Kalee and Eoin. We leaped out of the way before fire hot enough to melt our bones spilled out of the cave like a roaring river.

She emerged from the cave like a dream half-remembered. A gleaming black snout and sharpened horns tore through the smoke. Talons larger than Cillian slammed against the stone, shaking the earth with each thunderous step. She swiveled her serpentine neck, searching for whoever dared to disturb her.

Holy Nine, it's a fucking dragon.

"They're supposed to be dead," Kalee whispered, eyes wide in both shock and awe.

"*We're* going to be dead if we don't move!" I grabbed her wrist, dragging her back. But there was nowhere to hide. Nowhere to run unless we jumped over the side.

The dragon bellowed again and prowled out onto the mountaintop. Gorgeous and deadly, her hide glinted in the late afternoon glow. Scales of molten gold littered her coat, shining as bright as the sun itself. Flame-flecked serpentine eyes blew wide as she tipped her head back, flames sprouting past jagged teeth.

We crouched behind the largest boulder, but it would do little to protect us.

"Take Kalee and go," I pleaded to Cillian. His wing should be healed enough by now to at least clear the summit. As the hopeful heir to the hateful kingdom, Ronan would have been the more obvious choice, but at this moment, I was too selfish to care.

"I will not leave you."

The dragon roared once more, spitting out another blast of flames. I gritted my teeth against the heat.

"What do we do?" I asked Kalee. She always had the answers.

She shook her head fervently. "I don't… I don't know."

I peered around the boulder. We had weapons, but they were useless if we couldn't get close. Would they even be effective against her hide? The dragon pressed forward again, her tail still hidden within the cave. Something clanked behind it—a chain.

I frowned at the large shackles. Not one, but five cuffs attached to her legs and neck that tied the deadly beast to the earth.

I cursed Queen Petranella.

"The fire jewel is a godsdamned egg!" I half-cried, half-laughed. I would strangle the queen myself for sending us to retrieve a dragon's egg if I lived to see the day. The *last* dragon's egg. No wonder she'd wanted it so badly. This egg was worth more than any of our lives.

It was priceless.

"How come it hasn't hatched?" Eoin asked.

"Hatchlings can take centuries to emerge." Kalee's panicked breath had calmed, as if having the answer to something helped steady her again.

Rage and fear laced the dragon's cry, desperate to protect her offspring.

I couldn't blame her. Someone had chained her here—kept her hidden from the world for hundreds of years. Gods knew how long it had been since she'd come into contact with anyone.

A stupid, horrible, reckless idea formed.

"Stay here," I said to the group.

Cillian grabbed my wrist. Our eyes locked, and I tried to convey what I couldn't say. I should have wanted to run, but something—gods, I couldn't explain it—something deep within my soul pulled me toward her.

Maybe Cillian recognized it, because he let me go.

I followed the thread wrapped around my heart that drew me to her.

She paced before the cave entrance—a mother protecting her young. *The last of the dragons.*

The air cracked between us like a storm about to break.. My knees wobbled, nearly giving out, but not from fear.

No. This was deeper. Primal. Ancient. What little power I possessed surged to the surface, silver shadows running wildly under my skin like my magic recognized her—called to her.

I stepped forward. Slow and deliberate. The dragon stopped her huffing and eyed me carefully. Arching her neck to her full height, she towered over everyone, rivaling the cave entrance she'd crawled out of. She sniffed as if she could scent whether I was friend or foe. She didn't blast fire or take me between her teeth, as if she knew I wasn't a threat. As if she trusted me not to harm her.

And Mother help me, I kept walking because I felt the same.

I bowed on instinct, submitting to the ancient beast. Her massive head lowered and came so close, she blew back my fraying, braided hair. She was as majestic as she was terrifying.

The shadows danced beneath my skin, but were no threat. Behind me, I could practically feel the tension of the others while they waited.

Her molten eyes snapped to mine.

I couldn't move. Couldn't even breathe.

You smell like a witch, but you don't look like one, she huffed, nearly blowing me back.

"What?" I choked. She spoke as clearly in my mind as she would have aloud.

Yes, you can hear me. It has been that way between anamcharas for centuries.

I gasped. Alice had mentioned the anamchara bond between witches and dragons. She couldn't have meant she was *my* familiar.

Her head was level with my body. Instinctually, I reached out a hand and placed it on her snout.

I felt it then—the inexplicable pull between us. I grazed my hand along her black and gold scales. They were smooth like silk, but sharp as any blade around the edges. A comforting warmth bloomed beneath my fingertips, reminiscent of how Cillian's hand had felt in mine.

I didn't have the words, because how do you describe something that had always been yours before you knew it existed?

"I want to free you," I whispered. I couldn't think about the anamchara bond. Not right now. Not when so much was at stake—while I was Bound to the king, and he commanded me with only a thought.

And what else? She asked, sensing my hesitancy.

"And take you and your egg somewhere safe."

As cold as the witch queen appeared, she wouldn't harm this dragon or her egg. It would go against her nature to do so. She wanted the fire jewel because it had been stolen from the witches, and they were forbidden from setting foot on this cursed land.

"I know how it feels to be chained," I said, stroking her snout. "Let me see."

She complied by lying down, maneuvering around the chains. Nines, she was massive. My jaw slackened. The chains were nearly as thick as I was, and far heavier than I could lift alone. The shackle clasped around her leg came up to my chest. She moved, providing a closer look. Anger bubbled up in me at the raw flesh under the manacles. There was no keyhole. Not even a seam.

"Who did this to you?"

A monster.

"Ronan," I called. His white-blond head poked out from behind the boulder.

"You can't be serious," he said, eyeing the dragon.

Her nostrils flared, letting out a puff of steam. Could she scent the witch blood running through his veins, too?

"I need you to examine these chains," I said, recalling how he unlocked the door to the Mountain Castle. "Don't worry," I told the dragon. "He might be annoying, but he is a friend."

She eyed Ronan as he approached, mirroring my movements to present himself. Satisfied, she lowered her head once more.

He came to my side, not letting his eyes leave the curved teeth of her maw, as large as Ronan himself.

"Can you talk to him, too?" I asked her.

Ronan looked at me as if I'd gone mad.

No. Fate chose you, halfling.

"Why?"

It is not for me to question Fate's whims and reasonings.

I certainly wanted to question Fate, but that was for another day.

Ronan shifted his feet, looking between me and the dragon. I'd never seen him at such a loss for words. It would have been amusing if I weren't also in disbelief.

"Can you unlock them?" I asked. "They must be sealed with magic somehow."

"You're right," he said, running his hands over the iron. "It's tricky business due to its nature, but I think I can manage." He reached into the pouch at his waist, pulling out various herbs as well as a stone mortar and pestle. He pulled out a dagger and winced. "I'll need a bit of her blood. It's the only way, because of the iron."

"You're going to make *me* get it?" I growled.

"Clearly she favors you, and I quite like my body parts attached where they are."

I sighed and held the blade up to the dragon. "Do you mind?"

Go ahead.

I pressed harder than I would have liked to, piercing her hide, though she didn't squirm. He mixed the ingredients with the dragon's blood, smearing an odd symbol over the chain and muttering under his breath.

It unlocked with a loud *clunk* and crashed to the ground.

She gave an excited shrill, her spikes flaring behind her head as she reared up. He removed the other three chains around her legs before moving to the larger ones around her tail, then her neck.

She lowered her head, giving him easier access.

"If she is free—"

"No one deserves to be chained like this. Do it, Ronan."

He nodded, unlocking the last of the shackles. Before it even tumbled to the ground, the dragon was flapping her leather wings, nearly knocking us over.

She barreled for the mountain's edge and tumbled off the side, stretching wide and flying up, up, up and around the mountainside. Another excited shriek pierced the air.

"Now's our chance." Eoin moved from behind the boulder and toward the cave.

"Don't take another step," I warned. "If we betray her trust now, we will not survive."

She circled ever higher around the peak, but neither we nor her egg ever left her keen eyesight.

Gods knew how long it had been since she could feel the wind against her. Jealousy sank to the pit of my stomach. Freeing her was the right thing to do, but would it cost me my own freedom?

Once satisfied, she returned to the mountaintop. Loose rock and ash exploded under her weight as she landed.

She nudged Ronan and me with her snout. *Thank you.*

"Easy, big beasty," Ronan said, tentatively patting her.

Smoke billowed in his face, and his pale skin lost what little color it had.

My name is Órga.

"She said her name is Órga." I laughed at Ronan's stunned expression, his brows shooting past his hairline.

I would like to repay you for what you have done for me.

"I do not need payment for freeing someone who should have never been chained."

Eoin sputtered. I had all but given us a death sentence by failing the Malartaím. I couldn't free her only to take the one thing she'd been protecting for so long. It was wrong.

I likely wouldn't have much luck if I even tried.

Why did you come here?

"We were sent by the Witch Queen Petranella as part of a Malartaím," I explained. "In exchange for our lives, she asked us to bring back the fire jewel."

Órga's claws scraped against the stone. *To do what with?*

"She did not say. The queen only mentioned something precious had been stolen from them, and the witches were forbidden from trying to retrieve it."

Órga took a moment to weigh my words carefully. *Dragons and witches have long looked after one another. Our hatching grounds remained in Ilythia for centuries, until they were destroyed. Many witches died protecting them. I will agree to take my egg to the queen as long as she provides sanctuary for me and my offspring.*

My heart was a hummingbird in my chest. "I cannot speak for the queen, but I am sure she will be elated, and would do anything to protect you and your egg from harm."

I certainly hope so, Órga sniffed.

I wanted to ask about the anamchara bond, but I was afraid to know the answer.

Órga saved me from having to think more about it because she added, *Now, do you wish to stay on this mountaintop, or would you like to experience freedom?*

I sucked in a breath. That was what she was offering—freedom. If we delivered the egg to the queen, then we would complete the Malartaím. I didn't know the specifics of this bond between us, but regardless, I believed she would help me in any way she could, even against the queen. Maybe the cauldron wasn't out of reach after all.

"Freedom," I breathed, the words sweet on my tongue.

That's what I thought.

"What about my friends?" By now, Kalee, Eoin, and Cillian had emerged from behind the boulder, basking in her wonder.

If they are your friends, then they are mine.

Climbing onto the back of a dragon was no easy feat, and it took everyone except Cillian a couple of tries to mount her.

Órga surged, her first wingbeat slow and heavy. Ash clouded around us in a swirling wind. Órga climbed toward the sky, taking care not to send us tumbling to the earth—whatever magic she had kept us atop her back. By some miracle, we cleared the Ennisi Mountains as the sun sank below the horizon.

Órga swooped toward the ground, her talons skimming the treetops. Excited shouts and cackles carried on the wind as Flore, Ahlani, and Niamh rose to meet us on their brooms. Somewhere in the forest, Airi howled.

Finally, something had gone our way. And for once, the heavy feeling lifted in my chest. I raised my hands over my head—closer than ever to breaking my Bond.

CHAPTER FORTY-ONE

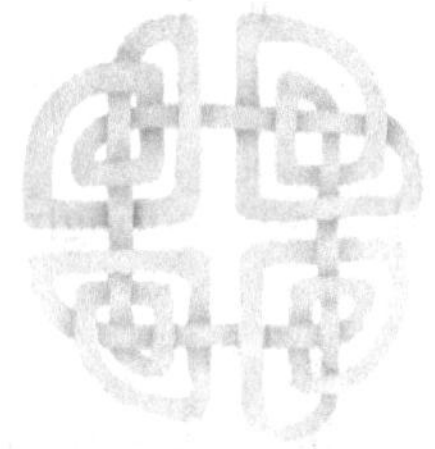

Gasps rang out amongst the crowd gathered around the clearing carved out of the Mountain Castle when we landed with a thundering *boom*. Flore, Niamh, and Ahlani landed close behind us, their expressions once again the hardened warriors they were trained to be as they took their positions next to their queen. There was no sign of Airi yet, no doubt still running through the Ilythian forests.

The Witch Queen Petranella was on the landing, away from the crowd, her raven swooping in. Petranella's black dress glittered in the moonlight as if the fabric had been plucked from the night sky itself. If she was surprised to see us or a dragon, she didn't show it. Aislinn, dressed in flying leathers, forced her way through. Purple and green bruises littered her face.

My fists clenched, and I contemplated asking Órga to flay the queen where she stood until Aislinn's eyes lit up. She was okay. Her eyes roamed over us, relief evident on her face.

"What have we here?" Queen Petranella's velvet voice silenced the crowd.

She is not the queen I remember, but her features are similar. I looked down at Queen Petranella, wondering how many queens before her Órga referred to. Órga lowered herself to the ground enough for us to dismount. She eyed the Witch Queen, her egg carefully hidden in her maw. I took comfort knowing even if our plan went to shambles, Órga could easily incinerate the queen.

"We have completed your Malartaím," I said loud enough for the gathered witches to hear. Hushed voices skittered across the crowd. None of the witches, save for the queen and her guards, dared to come near the dragon.

"The Malartaím was to bring the fire jewel. Not a dragon. No matter how impressive that may be." The queen eyed us, likely wondering how we managed to do so or how it was even possible that Órga existed. Her familiar cawed; its beady eyes made me want to take a step back, but I held my ground.

Órga opened her mouth wide enough to showcase what glowed inside.

I smirked. "Lucky for us, we did both."

The queen's eyes widened, the only show of surprise on her face. "So you did," she said, regaining her composure. "According to the terms of the Malartaím, you and your companions are free. Leave the dragon and the fire jewel in our care, where they belong, and rid yourselves of my kingdom."

"No." I crossed my arms over my chest. How quickly she was to rush us out now that not only had we done what she wanted, but we had also over-delivered.

"No? Do you wish to die, girl? If you do not give them to me, then the Malartaím will be invalid."

Órga's answering growl rumbled through the Mountain Castle, shaking everyone within reach. Her talons clicked impatiently as smoke plumed from her snout. *Dragons are not owned by anyone. The friendship between us is sacred, but not irrevocable. She will do well to remember that.*

"I will not *give* them to you as they are not mine to give nor yours to take. Instead, Órga has agreed to hatch her egg here as long as you grant them sanctuary. But they are free to come and go as they please," I said, relaying Órga's thoughts to the queen.

"You've spoken with her?" Petranella studied the silver shadows beneath my skin, my faie ears, my sapphire eyes—the only hint of witch blood running through my veins. I assumed the coloring was a mere coincidence as I favored my mother. But Alice had said only witches could have an anamchara bond with the dragons. If Órga and I were indeed connected, I shared more than a resemblance with my mother.

I nodded.

"Then what Aislinn said was true. You're Racenda's daughter," she breathed, her full lips parted. "And you…" Her eyes narrowed on Ronan.

Ronan straightened and dipped his chin. "I am Prince Ronan of Centra, son of Tara Toirdelbach and heir to Centra's throne."

Sneers and whispers of the Conqueror King spread throughout the crowd like wildfire. They assessed Ronan, sizing him up and perhaps wondering about his true intentions for coming to Ilythia. But he had foregone his father's name. His intentions were clear enough. Ronan did not consider himself the son of the Conqueror King.

"Will you follow in your father's footsteps?" The queen's scowl turned outright murderous. "Do you wish to not only extinguish the magic running through the land but to grow Centra's borders? To kill off our kind?"

"I'm not here to learn Ilythia's secrets. I've come to aid my cousin in breaking her Bond with my father. I do not share his thoughts or ideals. I have always been more of my mother's son." Ronan flashed his eyes black for show.

"I see. As a kindness to my late sisters, I will permit you and your companions to leave regardless of whether the dragon chooses to stay. By rescuing the fire jewel from the cursed mountain, you all have satisfied the requirements for the Malartaím and helped free something most precious to us." The Witch Queen craned her neck, looking up to speak directly to Órga. "Forgive me for my brashness; it has been an age since the witches have flown this earth with dragons. I would be both delighted and humbled if you chose to stay. We still consider the peace between our kinds sacred and will always help the dragons in any way we can."

Órga peered at me through a giant eye. *I will stay here with my egg—but only if you are freed, halfling.*

My breath caught. After years of oppression and weeks of worrying if I'd ever get this close, it hurt to breathe in hope that this was it. Everything I worked so hard toward relied on a queen's answer. I took a fortifying breath, letting hope fill me this one time, and steeled my shoulders.

"Órga has agreed to stay here with her egg, but only if you will let us use the cauldron."

It was a gamble that could turn Queen Petranella even more against us, but if my mother's stories about the bond between witches and dragons rang true, it was a one I was willing to make. There was no other way for us to use the cauldron. With Órga on our side, the queen could hardly deny us. She would do whatever it took to get Órga to stay.

A corner of Aislinn's mouth twitched.

The Witch Queen narrowed her cold, hardened stare, coating my veins with ice. "Do you have any idea what you ask of me?" But the sanctity between witches and dragons was as strong as I thought because after a huff of smoke from Órga, the queen said, "Fine. But you will tell me what you plan to do with the cauldron before I agree to let you use the sacred relic."

And so I told her of my mother and my time at the Conqueror King's castle. Of how I came to meet Ronan, Eoin, Kalee, and Cillian, and what the seer told us. Niamh butted in, giving her account of the fomorii we fought in the forest, Ahlani and Flore backing her. I told her what Cillian did to try to save me from the king's grasp, what all my friends did, and I asked the queen to allow us to use the cauldron to not only break my Bond, but Cillian's as well.

He tensed at my side, caught off guard by my request. Did he think I would let him continue as a Bonded after all he'd done? Not a fucking chance.

Queen Petranella's hard exterior cracked ever so slightly. She looked at her sister. Aislinn nodded, and something like regret flashed across the queen's face.

"You may use the cauldron, but I will be the one to break the Bonds," she said at last, satisfied my story was based on truth.

As she turned to walk away, the crowd of witches leaving with her, it was an effort to hold back my tears, to not fall to the floor from sheer shock. Relief flooded through me, washing away every worry plaguing my thoughts. I beheld the smiling faces of Eoin, Ronan, Kalee, and Cillian. All of them had tried to help me one way or the other. And, while their attempts had failed, I wouldn't be here without them. We had done it.

Breaking my Bond couldn't come fast enough. It had been over a week since we landed at the Mountain Castle. I felt an odd pull on my Bond now and then, as if the king was checking in to see if I was still alive. There would be no way for him to find out what we'd done through the Bond, nor could he sense my intentions. But I knew he grew impatient. Felt it within my bones. He'd never gone without me for so long., or

Cillian for that matter. I prayed Ronan's ruse would hold out a little longer.

While the queen agreed to break my Bond, she wanted to wait until the full moon. *The chance of the triple goddess' blessing is at its highest then,* she had explained. But that was three agonizing days away, falling on the night before my twenty-fifth name day. And so, between visits with Órga, I paced and trained and paced and trained until Kalee couldn't stand it anymore and took it upon herself to distract me.

"Again?" I groaned, sitting at the table across from her in our shared room. We played a game of cards, passing the time while we waited for the full moon. We'd already scoured the castle's library, searching for any signs of Tenebris, but other than the occasional folklore, we fell short.

Kalee's long, curly hair had been let loose of its confines, errant curls splaying down her back. I scratched at one of the many tight pins anchored against my scalp. She had begged to fix my hair, and I acquiesced by letting her curl and pin it to her desire for no other reason than we had little else to do. I couldn't deny her. Not if I didn't know when I'd see her again.

After our Bonds were broken, the others would return to Centra to resume their smuggling operations until they could figure out how to stop Tenebris. Cillian and I would be presumed dead: an unavoidable incident that Ronan himself barely escaped with his life. He had the scar from the fomorii and Eoin, a trusted guard, to corroborate his story.

"Are you ever going to take pity on me and lose for once?"

"Never," Kalee said with a sly smile. Mischief danced behind her eyes, likely planning my subsequent demise as she reshuffled the deck. The game required patience and skill, neither of which I had. She'd always been the superior player when we played back in Rothcek, and today was no different.

Cillian chuckled from the settee behind me, half paying attention to a book Niamh lent him, half focusing on the game.

"Keep laughing, and I'll make you play her next."

"Still at it?" Ronan asked when he and Eoin joined us, surveying our cards, sweat on his brow. Ronan usually spent his days conspiring with Queen Petranella, training with Aislinn, or searching the library for anything on Tenebris. Aislinn picked up on Ronan's magic education where his mother left off. They'd tried to get me to perform witch's magic. But when I'd ground the herbs and recited an unlocking spell, nothing happened. Not that I was surprised. The magic I possessed had never been strong to begin with.

"All these years and she's still losing," Kalee said, dealing my cards.

"You would think you'd be better at it, Saoirse," Ronan commented.

"You play against her and see what happens." I swatted him in jest. "It's not my fault that my only opponent doesn't make it easy on me."

Ronan's laughter died out, and the room grew quiet. "I am sorry you haven't been able to live a normal life. I know it hasn't been easy for you as one of my father's Bonded. Nor you, Cillian."

Cillian dipped his chin, his jaw set. He hadn't told the others why he was Bonded with the king. Hadn't divulged his past to anyone but me, and even then, I'd only received the scraps.

I grabbed Ronan's hand and squeezed. "No, it hasn't. But I am grateful to have gotten to know you, all of you, through this." Kalee's eyes glistened, and she clung to Ronan. "I can't imagine what the Conqueror King was like as a father. That couldn't have been easy, either."

"He wasn't always a villain. In my early years, I remember him as a kind and loving father. It wasn't until after my sister came into her magic that he changed. My mother had always been cautious around him. I used to think she was paranoid for wanting to hide my magic from him. But after he locked Ceana away…her fears became valid. Then, he killed my mother, and nothing was ever the same."

I'd always thought it was the queen's death that drove the king's hatred toward magic. It was hard enough being Bound to the king, but to imagine if my own father had been the one who killed my mother and imprisoned my sibling…I wouldn't have survived as well as Ronan had.

"I had Eoin to help me through it," he continued, nodding at Eoin— an unspoken understanding crossing between the two.

"Without Kalee, I would have lost myself long ago."

"I will be with you every step of the way and then some," she said, pulling me into her. My eyelids stung with unshed tears. I couldn't have asked for a better friend—someone who had fought with me through the impossible. Kalee deserved the world and so much more.

"My condolences for your mother, Ronan. I know what it's like to have a… complicated father. My own has never been easy to deal with." Cillian's eyes darkened into someone I didn't recognize. It sent shivers down my spine. He rarely talked about his past, and when he did, something about it haunted him. I could sense it in silence. In the words he didn't say. I knew that look all too well; I had borne it nearly every day.

"Does he still live?" Ronan asked.

"Unfortunately."

"Will you ever do something about it?"

Cillian looked at me but spoke to Ronan. "No. When we tried to steal the cauldron, I was met with the goddess Cerri. I gave up my vengeance toward him." There was more to his words, another meaning tangling beneath them. Something he wanted me to see, but I couldn't quite grasp it.

Ronan's brows furrowed. "She asked for my revenge toward my father as well."

"You're not going to kill him?" I almost stood. Something needed to be done about the Conqueror King.

"He will face justice for his crimes, but I'm no longer driven by what he did to my mother and sister. Everything I did was to spite him; now I can focus on what's right by serving the people and not be blinded by rage."

My shoulders loosened. I hadn't thought about what the others had to give to the goddess to return to our world. Kalee and Eoin stayed quiet. I wanted to prod, but I'd have to give up my own truth in return. I kept my mouth shut.

"Eoin, any tragic backstory you'd like to share with the group?" Ronan said when the silence settled like dust in an empty room.

"Aside from having to put up with your ass for a decade?" Eoin grumbled, though the corners of his mouth twitched.

"That, my friend, is tragic enough."

Kalee dealt the cards and demolished everyone who dared challenge her. I didn't know if it happened the second time she won against Ronan or the third, but an unfamiliar feeling blanketed over me. Safety. And so much love, my heart could have burst from the sheer joy of it. There was still my Bond to worry about, yes, but I didn't have to look over my shoulder in fear of the chancellor's spies or worry if a liliach would rip my throat out. I wanted to freeze time and live in this moment forever.

"Can I borrow you for a moment?" Eoin said, tapping my shoulder.

"Yes. Please take me away from this miserable game." I threw the cards down, forfeiting before I lost yet another round.

Kalee laughed. "It's okay, Saoirse. Take a break. You must be exhausted after losing so many times. I'll take a turn at winning against Cillian for a bit." Cillian's eyebrows rose at the challenge, but he did not back down.

"I thought I might save you from Kalee's wrath," Eoin chuckled once we were down the corridor and out of earshot.

"It's nothing I'm not used to. I don't recall ever winning against her. But I appreciate the saving nonetheless."

Eoin led me out onto a terrace carved into the mountainside over-looking the courtyard where a squadron of witches trained. They practiced with brutal efficiency, some engaging in hand-to-hand combat while others mutilated wooden dummies with arrows and swords along the yard.

Across from the training area, sheltered in an aerie high in the neighboring mountain, was Órga. The black and gold dragon rested with her egg and was free to go where she pleased. I took to seeing her at least once a day, but she was in the skies for most of it, getting a feel for her freedom after being chained for so long and building up her stamina. My heart swelled. She would never be imprisoned again. I didn't know what us being anamcharas meant, or if we would ever solidify it, but at least she could live and raise her young as she wished.

"Will you miss her when you're gone?" Eoin asked, nodding toward the aerie.

My gut twisted. I hadn't told anyone I'd be staying behind. Too afraid to voice my plans lest the gods take them away. But I couldn't lie not even if I wanted to. The look on Eoin's face hollowed out my heart as if he knew what I was about to say would break his.

"Aislinn offered to let me stay in Ilythia with her."

"You can't be serious."

"You'd once asked if I could do anything, what would I do? There's a village near Aislinn's chalet where I can run a bookstore. It's what I've always wanted. We talked about it before we left to steal the cauldron. Aislinn said she would help me." The dream I clung to grew closer to a reality I'd never thought possible. I didn't dare to bring up Cillian's offer to take me back to the faie kingdom. No, I tucked it away into the box of never-happening-ever.

Eoin's brows furrowed. "What about the Shadow King?"

"You don't need me to stop Tenebris. You are a better fighter. Kalee is more knowledgeable than me. Cillian's magic is far stronger than mine, and now Ronan's is too." I shrugged. I was selfish for not wanting to see this to the end, but I was so tired of doing what others told me to do that I didn't care.

It was my turn to live.

"We do need you. *I* need you. Please come back—for me. I can hide you within the city. We can make this work if you try. I want *you*, Saoirse. Stay with me."

The offer was sweet, but...I didn't *want* to. For fifteen years, I lived by the whims of another. For fifteen years, I've had to look over my shoulder. If I returned to Centra, I wouldn't be safe.

"Eoin, I—"

"Please, Saoirse." His words were little more than a desperate plea. Eoin cupped the back of my head, threading his warm fingers through my hair, some of the pins springing loose. He held me there as he leaned in.

I held my hand up to his lips, halting his kiss.

"I thought you cared about me."

"I do, Eoin. But not—not like this," I grimaced. Over the course of our journey, whatever had sparked between us fizzled out and died. I tried sifting through the cinders to see if an ember still glowed, but there was only ash.

"Because you have feelings for the Hunter." His expression hardened, and the muscles of his jaw flexed.

I bristled. "He has nothing to do with this. I won't go back to Centra. I can't."

Eoin took a step back, shoving his hands in his pockets. "If you care about me at all—in any way—and yourself, for that matter, then think about it. Please."

Eoin turned away before I could speak.

Tomorrow.

Tomorrow, I would have the courage to tell him my mind was already made up.

CHAPTER FORTY-TWO

"Ready?" Aislinn asked from the entrance of the aerie. Her silver-streaked hair was woven into a tight braid that wrapped around her head. I nodded, though only my grip on the column kept me on my feet.

It's time, Órga said, sensing my hesitation. Her gold-speckled scales twinkled in the moonlight. A giant, molten eye bore into me—ancient and unblinking. Her eyes were not merely yellow but bottled sunlight, threads of amber and crimson entwined into them like an eternal flame. The obsidian slit down the middle was as narrow as any blade, cutting truth from lies and piercing straight to my soul. It was like staring into time itself.

Unlock your chains, halfling. A huff of warm air blew my braid over my shoulder.

What if it doesn't work? I asked.

What if it does?

A lump formed in my throat as I followed Aislinn out of the aerie. I threw a last glance at Órga, wishing she could come with us. Queen Petra, according to Aislinn, had a flair for the dramatics. There were mere hours left until the sun rose, and I would no longer be twenty-four.

"Nervous?" Aislinn asked, noting the slight tremor in my hands.

"What if something goes wrong?"

Aislinn stopped along the stone corridor, taking my hands in hers, smoothing out the tremors. "It will work," she reassured, leaving no room for argument. "I found the perfect place," she added, changing the subject.

"For what?"

"Your bookshop. There's a space that opened up next to Alice's apothecary. The previous owner was good friends with her and agreed to leave the space to you if you want." The light behind her pale eyes danced, thrumming with excitement.

"She would give it to me?" I asked incredulously. I didn't even know the witch.

"Well, she would sell it to you."

My heart sank into the pit of my stomach. "Oh, Aislinn, I don't—I don't have any coin." Disappointment lodged in my throat, but I swallowed it down. There would be other opportunities—a lifetime of them. I would find a way to earn a wage and save up for my dream. Maybe Alice would let me work in her apothecary.

"Did you think I didn't know?" A secretive smile spread across her lips. "It is of no consequence. Alice and I took care of it. It's yours."

"I can't let you do that," I sputtered.

She waved me off with a simple flick of her wrist. "Think of it as twenty-five, long-overdue name day gifts." The smile on her lips faded into guilt. "When your mother died, I assumed they'd killed you too. Words cannot express how sorry I am. I should have done more."

I laid a hand on her arm. I spent nearly half my life feeling guilty for something out of my control. I wasn't about to let her do the same. "There is no need to apologize. I don't blame you for any of it. You couldn't have known if I was alive or dead."

"If you wish to return with the faie to your homeland, do not hold back because of me, but I would love to have you."

I shook my head, my cheeks warming. "There is no home for me there."

Our gazes held until Aislinn felt satisfied I wasn't trying to appease her. I'd always been closer to my mother than my father. The only thing I inherited from him was my faie features. Maybe it was time to embrace the witch within me.

"Then Alice and I will be pleased to have you. Come," she said, guiding me up the stairs to one of the towers. "Let's not keep my sister waiting any longer."

THE TOWER WAS ONE OF THE FEW WITCH-MADE ADDITIONS TO THE Mountain Castle. Being the tallest point, it overlooked the entirety of Ilythia. By the way my legs burned climbing staircase after staircase, its height rivaled even the Ennisi Mountains.

"To be closer to the Triple Goddess," Aislinn said by way of explanation.

Tall, windowless arches lined the circular room, and a gentle breeze kissed the sweat along my brow. Candles of various sizes and shapes cast a warm glow over everyone inside. The only other source of light was the full moon hanging high overhead, seeping through the archways.

Queen Petranella sat inside a circle of lit candles with the cauldron in the center. Her long, dark hair flowed to the floor, and a simple crown of onyx jewels sat atop her head. Unsurprisingly, Niamh, Ahlani, and Flore guarded the queen, each posted in different areas throughout the room. Airi had returned and resumed his position at Niamh's side. The queen's raven perched on a rafter, its beady eyes making me unsteady.

My heart stuttered at the sight of the cauldron. The powerful object begged me to touch it, to wield it.

The queen's eyes flashed to mine as if sensing the cauldron's call to me. Eoin tugged on my elbow, pulling me away from her icy gaze. "May I have a word?" he said low enough so only I could hear.

Well, so only Cillian and I could hear if the way he stiffened in the corner was any indication.

"Can it wait a minute?" I asked, gesturing to the queen.

"No. I need to speak to you now, Saoirse."

"Fine," I sighed, deciding it would be better to give in now than argue with him in front of everyone. He led me out of the tower room, shutting the thick wooden door behind us.

"Have you thought about my offer?"

I nodded, the words too heavy on my tongue.

"And?"

"And I cannot go with you," I sighed, unable to delay the truth any longer. I hoped there would be more time to postpone my answer. But time waited for no one.

"Why not?" His voice rose with the growing anger in his features.

"Because I don't want to," I said, matching his volume. "I'm tired of doing what everyone tells me to do. I want to do something for *myself* for once."

We stared at one another. I would not break his gaze. He couldn't convince me to return to a place that made my life miserable. A place where I was unwelcome. Where I would be hunted and killed if the king ever found me again.

"Do I mean nothing to you? Do you think I cannot protect you?" He stepped forward, close enough that I could feel the heat of his body. This heat was not fueled by desire but anger. "You're going to let us face the Shadow King on our own?"

"You don't need me."

"Are you so selfish to walk away from this? To walk away from me?" He kept pressing closer until my back hit the wall, and we were nearly nose to nose with his arms on either side of my head.

"Is it so wrong to be selfish for *once* in my life? I will not have another person dictate what I can and cannot do, including you." I stabbed his chest with my pointer finger. "You have no right to try to control me the way you do. I've made up my mind, and if you care for me as you claim to, I suggest you accept it."

My shadows slithered under my skin, seething like snakes poised to strike. They crawled up my neck and spread along my jaw. He was too close, acting like yet another cage around me.

"The only thing you want is someone to control, Eoin. That someone isn't me."

I was foolish to believe he held any affection toward me. He didn't see me as an equal or a partner, but as someone to yield to in order to aid him in his mission. The faster he put an end to the Shadow King, the faster Ronan took over his father's seat, the sooner Eoin could leave. And while I wanted to see this change as much as Eoin, it wasn't my fight.

It was Ronan's.

Ronan held a position of power. Ronan had the skills, knowledge, and perhaps even the help of the witches to achieve his goals. He didn't need me. He never did, really. I was one person. Maybe I'd play a small role here, but there was no reason to believe I'd be someone of importance on this mission. Fate may have brought us together, but I was a step in his journey.

Surprise flashed across Eoin's features, and I seized the opportunity to shove him away, making him stumble. His shock was momentary until anger simmered back to the surface, twisting his handsome face into something more frightening.

Eoin shook his head. "You are wrong. You might not see it yet, Saoirse, but you will."

I scoffed at his back as he returned to the tower room. Cillian lifted a brow when I walked in, and I really, *really* did not feel like addressing it. The muscles in his jaw clenched. The last thing I needed was for him to say or do anything.

"If you're ready?" Queen Petranella drawled from her circle of candles.

I ignored Eoin as I stepped into the ring of fire and sat across from her.

"Now then." She handed Cillian and me a vial of something putrid-looking. Cillian's nose scrunched when he studied the cauldron's gray-green coagulated contents. "Drink," the queen commanded.

I sent a quick prayer to the Mother that this wasn't an elaborate attempt to poison us.

The concoction, thick and uneven, trudged its way down my throat. I held back a gag. The smell didn't help. Queen Petra rubbed her thumb over our brows with a powder once the vial was emptied. She tossed them into the cauldron, sending up a plume of green smoke. The queen then lit three candles separate from the ivory ones surrounding us: one red, positioned on the outside of Cillian; one white, placed next to me; and one black, behind the cauldron, creating a triangle between the cauldron, Cillian, and myself.

She murmured soft, lyrical words under her breath while she lit the three candles and again when she sprinkled herbs over them. Lavender, sandalwood, and jasmine filled my nostrils, calming my jittery nerves.

"A lock of hair." She held out her hand expectantly.

I unsheathed one of the daggers from the belt slung around my hips and fisted my braid, lopping off a considerable length, letting the rest unravel above my shoulders. Something akin to pride surged as I watched the silver braid shine in the candlelight and passed it to her. I was no stranger to a hair trimming. The weight would become too cumbersome once it reached a certain length. But now, I was handing over the last remnants of my previous life.

I was glad to see it go.

"I said, a *lock*." Regardless, the queen accepted it and discarded it into the cauldron.

I shrugged. "I've been meaning to cut it."

Cillian followed her instructions more meticulously than I under her warning glower.

"And now your blood. I will need *precisely* three drops from each of you. No more, no less."

We did as she instructed, discarding three drops of our lifeblood into the cauldron. The air hummed with energy as the cauldron consumed everything we gave it, and it was hungry for more. The buzz was intoxicating as the cauldron vibrated with power.

"Repeat these words exactly as I say them:
Of my blood, I give to thee.
For my bind to no longer be
Take this hair that's part of me.
Now let me go, my bind now free."

Cillian and I repeated each line in tandem, exactly as Queen Petra said them. When we finished, her head tilted up toward the ceiling, presumably toward the Triple Goddess herself. Eyes closed, a slew of strange words left her ruby-painted lips. The ends of her hair rose with her hands, hovering above the floorboards. When she finished her final line, the cauldron burned red, then green, hissing and fizzing until it died out.

At first, nothing happened. But as soon as the last of the fire flickered, something in me squeezed until I cried out. A horrid ripping sensation traveled along every nerve ending, my muscles contracting in violent waves that stole the very breath from my lungs and had me writhing on the floor. As if the king's Bond latched on so tightly—integrated itself so thoroughly—it refused to let go. I barely heard Cillian's cry echoing mine. The last of the Bond held a death grip around my heart. Unyielding, I thought it would cleave me in two.

And then it snapped.

I sucked in a breath as if I'd been held under water all this time. Coughing and aching, something swelled within me. I waited for it to settle, but it rose ever higher, coming from somewhere deep down I hadn't known existed. Like a dam breaking to release a catastrophic flood, a power I'd never felt before surged within. It was vast, it was darkness—

It was mine.

And I was free.

Chapter Forty-Three

The serenity of my freedom didn't last long before something more sinister took its place. Night stole my vision, as if the shadows spread across my eyes like they did along my skin. Shouts sounded from all around. I could feel them, almost taste their panic, while my magic ravaged the space, blotting out the candles and the moon.

It was pure chaos.

Amongst Airi's growls and the raven's squawks, the witches scrambled to protect their queen, trying to find a way to her. The magic coursing through my veins had never been this strong before. The power surrounding us felt dangerous and all-consuming. All those times I wished I could have lashed out with my shadows flashed through my mind.

What if they could?

My shadows tangled around the others, encircling them like a snake coiling around its prey.

Kalee's scream pierced the air, and I cried out. Her terror and pain shot through me as the shadows threatened to consume them. Her shouts were followed by Ronan's, then Eoin's. Aislinn's. Petranella's. Niamh's. Ahlani's. Flore's. All of them. In a body not my own, dark tendrils sprouted from me, snaking their way and wreaking havoc throughout the room. My magic had always sensed when I'd been afraid, and it had soothed me. But I'd never tasted someone else's fear so potent and putrid on my tongue. My magic didn't try to soothe them now. It used it against them. What the fuck was happening? I didn't know how to stop it. Didn't know if I *could*. I only witnessed their terror as darkness consumed them.

As *I* consumed them..

I fell to my knees. It was too much. Tremors wracked my hands. These weren't the comforting shadows I'd grown familiar with. This was something else entirely. I had no control. My lungs seized, and I couldn't breathe as the magic consumed me, too.

Images of my mother's broken body flashed through my mind. The chancellor's cane lashed at my back. The king's cruel sneer forced me to my knees to bow before him. Flashes of the teeth of the fomorii wolf prowled around me. Every nightmare I'd ever known played out, and the others' cries only grew louder as my magic plagued their minds with every horrible, rotten thing they'd ever been afraid of. I could see it all.

The lifeless bodies of Eoin's mother and sister. Ceana's frail form being shoved into a room, the door locking from the outside. I saw myself hanging limp in someone's arms. There were other memories, too—ones I didn't recognize. Petranella and Aislinn arguing. Word of mine and Ronan's mother's deaths. A young woman drowning in a lake. A man bleeding out. They weren't just fears. They were memories of the worst kind. The type that left a stain on someone's soul.

"Breathe, Saoirse," Cillian called over the screams. I tried, but I couldn't get enough air in. The darkness was suffocating. My hands and feet tingled with a sharp prickling sensation, and my head grew impossibly light.

"Focus on my voice," he said again, grabbing either side of my face. "Look at me."

I hadn't realized I'd shut my eyes against the dark cloud. When I opened them, it was not complete darkness that surrounded us, but a single light guiding me out. Cillian's warm skin glowed, acting like a beacon. This close, I could see the brown flecks in his emerald eyes and the slight stubble sprinkling his jaw.

"Good." He smiled. "Now, I need you to take a deep breath."

I did as he instructed, my eyes never leaving his. His thumbs caressed my cheeks. The frantic, fearful thoughts faded, and the pain of the others subsided.

"I can help guide you, but it is you who holds the power to stop this."

I clung to him, too afraid to spiral back into the place I'd come from. "Don't let me go."

"Never."

A tear slipped from the corner of my eye. The first I'd shed in front of another in years. I was fracturing, and Cillian was the only thing holding me together.

"You are so strong, little shadow. You just need to trust yourself," he whispered, and his words struck like a match. I shook my head. I'd never been strong. I survived all these years by sheer luck on the back of my mother's protection spell.

"You are," he said, "you may not see it yet, but I do. I've known it from the moment I laid eyes on you." His hands still held me there, giving me no room to avoid his gaze. "If you don't believe in yourself, then believe what I tell you is true. Now let *go*."

I focused on the hardness of the wooden floor against my knees, on Cillian's calloused thumbs stroking my cheeks. My hands squeezed around his wrists. He was the light ready to lead me out of the dark. His smile was warm and unafraid. And yet—

"It's too much," I whispered.

"Your emotions are tied to power, yes?"

I nodded. The shadows were always the most active when I was afraid or angry.

"You are overwhelmed by the sudden burst and are clinging to it. Ground your emotions. Think of something comforting and let your magic go."

I thought back to when my mother and I would pick wildflowers in the field next to our cottage. Of Kalee's maniacal laugh when we would sneak books from the castle library. The feeling of flying from Órga's back and sparring with Cillian until my nerves dissipated.

I could feel those thick tendrils again, which snaked around the room and slithered down the stairs, gripping me like a vise. Perhaps it was the other way around.

"Let go," Cillian murmured, and this time, I knew what he meant. Slowly, my muscles relaxed and light seeped in as darkness faded away, and soon, the tower room was back to how it was before.

A mixture of curiosity and horror filled the faces of those around me. Eoin hadn't composed himself enough to hide his appalled expression. Only Aislinn and Cillian hadn't flinched from my demonstration of power. Even Queen Petranella was awash with a type of curiosity that had me shrinking under her gaze. And when my eyes landed on Kalee's tear-stained cheeks, Ronan clutching her to his chest, my heart crumbled.

"Kalee—I'm so sorry. I didn't mean to."

"What did you do?" Eoin spat, his voice laced with terror.

"I don't...I don't know. There's something wrong with me." Maybe the cauldron gave me magic that didn't belong to me. I didn't recognize it.

"There's nothing wrong with you," Cillian said sharply. True to his word, he didn't let me go. His hand threaded in mine, sharing his warmth.

"Curious," Queen Petranella mused from her seat, still inches away.

"What is?" Aislinn asked, taking a step toward me. They might have been sisters, but Petranella was still a monarch, and I was in her kingdom. Something within me warned that whatever it was I had, she wanted.

"Do you not find it odd that you have never experienced this level of power before?" She tilted her head like a cat—a predator assessing a possible threat.

"Perhaps she was Bound before she came into her full power, stunting it before it had a chance to grow to its full potential," Ronan offered, still cradling Kalee. "Once the Bond broke, it could have come in all at once."

"I don't think so," Cillian answered. "I experienced a surge of power as well, though perhaps not as great as Saoirse's. As if a hold on my magic was finally released."

"What does that mean?" Eoin asked, pushing off the wall. His hand was resting on the pommel of the sword strapped to his hip as if sensing some other threat.

"It means," I said slowly, putting the pieces together, "the King of Centra has been stealing our magic through the Bond along with every other Bonded linked to him."

CHAPTER FORTY-FOUR

"How is that possible?" Kalee asked, wiping her tear-stained cheeks. I bit the inside of my lip, tearing off a chunk of flesh. I did that to her—hurt the one person who cared for me all these years. *I* frightened her.

"When the faie mate, one advantage is sharing power. The king must have found a way to manipulate and use it similarly," Cillian speculated, his eyes lingering on my face.

"What can he do with that magic?" Niamh asked. Airi nudged his head under my hand, lying at my side.

"Control us, for one," Cillian answered. "With a simple command, spoken or not, we are compelled to obey it. Anything else, I'm not sure. I've never seen him use magic before, but that doesn't mean he hasn't."

Flore crossed her arms over her slender chest. "Humans can't use magic."

"Humans can't produce magic," I corrected, thinking back to when Eoin unlocked the entrance to the Underground. He had said anyone could access it as long as they knew how. "But how he's Binding himself to osnádúrtha through magic…I don't know."

"The only way would be with a conduit unless someone else is performing them," Petranella answered.

"No, there's never anyone else. I've witnessed more Bondings than I'd care to admit." I shuddered. I hated it every time. Once it was over, you could practically see the light dim from Bonded's eyes.

"Where would he get a conduit?" Ahlani asked.

Everyone turned to Ronan.

"Don't ask me." Ronan held his hands up. "He claims his mission in life is to rid the world of magic. Even to me."

"Or harvest it for his own purposes," Aislinn mused, sharing a look with her sister.

"Or for someone else," Kalee countered. "We suspect the king is working with Tenebris. The seer said he was trapped within the Shadow Realm. Would he need magic to escape from it?"

Flore placed her hands on her hips, her fingers thrumming against them. "Tenebris is supposed to be a god. Surely he would have plenty of magic to spare."

"It is known that the God of Darkness was banished by the Nine. Only their power can release him," Petranella argued. "I am more concerned about the king in this realm storing magic that doesn't belong to him." The queen's perfectly trimmed brows furrowed, creating the faintest of creases between them.

"Would he be able to store it?" I asked despite not wanting to know the answer.

"If he has a conduit, which seems most likely, then all he would need to do is channel that magic into an amulet or object of some meaning to hold it."

"How would he know how to do that?" Ahlani asked.

"You forget he was married to my sister. I'm sure he learned something in their years together."

Ronan's face paled. "Regardless of my father's knowledge, we can assume he's draining all the other Bonded. Cillian, you said you felt like the hold on your magic was lifted."

Cillian nodded.

"How many Bonded belong to the king?" Niamh asked. She adjusted the strap of her scabbard across her chest.

"No one knows for sure. Fifty at any given time, if I were to guess." I looked toward Ronan for confirmation.

"There are many more. You're forgetting the Bonded on loan to other members of nobility. Not to mention those in his armies and others stationed along the borders. Including those serving in the castle, I would say at least three hundred. Not to mention those he's killed over the years are far greater."

Three hundred Bonded.

"I didn't realize there were so many osnádúrtha left in Centra," Queen Petranella said.

"My father has always claimed the osnádúrtha provoked the gods' wrath and used it as an excuse to attack them. But it's always been about control. He used the Reckoning to scare them, to cut down their numbers. And when they were too afraid and outnumbered, he used the Bonded's magic for himself until they no longer suited his purposes," Ronan said darkly. "I've never known how he's done it. I tried figuring it out for years until I finally gave up and focused my efforts on getting the osnádúrtha to safety instead."

"Do you believe it's possible he doesn't realize he's sapping power from his Bonded?" Eoin asked.

Cillian shook his head. "When a faie shares their magic with their mate, they know. He chose to make an imitation of the mating bond for that very reason—to take our magic, though he made sure his Bond is one-way, which is why we didn't know until we were released from it."

"We need to reinforce our borders," Niamh said to her queen. "We don't know what he plans to do with his stored magic."

Queen Petranella waved her off. "Ilythia has stood for far longer than that human or his lands. I doubt he'd even know what to do with it. Let him try to take what does not belong to him." A twisted, blood-red smile crept over the queen's flawless face, and a shiver threatened to crawl down my spine.

"He could be using it to protect Centra's borders." Eoin shrugged.

"The *Conqueror King* sitting on a well of stored magic?" I scoffed. "Do you honestly believe he isn't capable of wanting to conquer more lands for the benefit of Centra? He's picked off the osnádúrtha one by one for sixteen years. You know he practically decimated the merrows and forced them into submission. Are you so dense to believe he wouldn't continue to do so?"

Flore snorted, and Eoin's jaw flexed at my outburst, but he managed to rein in his anger.

"You plan to return to Centra, yes?" Queen Petranella asked Ronan.

"We do. I can only be away for so long before my father grows suspicious. As it were, it has already been too long. His patience must be worn thin by now. Plus, I will have to explain why his two favorite Bonded are no longer with me."

"Then, when you return, you must find the conduit and whatever he's using to store his magic in."

Ronan dipped his chin, looking more regal than he had in days. "For what he did to my mother and sister and the rest of the osnádúrtha, I will never stand with him. I want what is best for Centra and *all* its people."

"What will you plan to do about your father?"

"Whatever is necessary. Things cannot continue as they are. He has proven himself unfit to rule his people peacefully. Once I take his magic away, he will resign from the throne and face his crimes either by his own will or by force. My father will pay for what he has done." Ronan's expression steeled into someone I didn't recognize. Ronan was all laughs and jokes, but there was none of that now.

I did not envy Ronan for having to make such decisions. His father was cruel, vile, and wicked. I would not shed a tear for the man if he died tomorrow. And yet, the man was still his father, who once read him stories when he was frightened, who would chase away young Ronan's nightmares. He'd told us how there used to be love between them. I didn't care for the Conqueror King, but I did for the son who was forced to choose between the father he once loved and the monster he became.

The Witch Queen dipped her chin. Perhaps she recognized Ronan's decision and felt sympathetic toward the prince. Perhaps all she cared about was his assurances. "Ilythia will provide support should you ask in exchange that *you* take Centra's throne."

"I will see Centra return to its former glory as a peaceful kingdom that welcomes any and all who walk this earth. I have no intentions to take what does not belong to me. And," Ronan added, "I will find a way to break my father's Bonds. If he's using something to make them, then maybe that's the key to severing them."

My heart squeezed. I prayed that what Ronan said was true. The queen hadn't been keen on using the cauldron to break mine and Cillian's Bond, and I doubted she would consider using it for several hundred other osnádúrtha. But perhaps Ronan was right—they could be destroyed along with whatever the king used to create them. Or maybe they would break if the king were killed.

"Good. Then, keep a weathered eye on the horizon. Should you need to send word, Enya will assist you." The queen stoked her raven's feathers, and the familiar cawed. "We will be able to send communications through her without raising suspicions."

It was risky to align himself with a queen he hardly knew, especially one who once sought our deaths, but Ronan nodded all the same. If he intended to take the throne for himself, he would need the witches' help. Undoing years of hate the Conqueror King instilled into his people would not be an easy task. The price of peace and freedom for all would be steep.

"Have you come to your senses and changed your mind?" Eoin asked from the doorway of my room, his pack slung across his shoulders. A quick scan beyond the door told him all he needed to know.

"Have you decided to stop being an ass and support my decision?" I retorted, crossing my arms.

"You're making a mistake. You'll be safer with me than in Ilythia. Don't think for a second that because you share a drop of their blood, they will protect you. Not like I will."

I couldn't hold in my sigh.

"What makes you think I need protection? I've managed to survive long before I met you." I lifted my chin, though it wasn't entirely truthful. My mother shielded me from the king's soldiers before she died and kept me alive with her protection spell. But my powers had grown, and Cillian offered to help me understand them. I didn't need anyone to protect me now. I could do it on my own.

"You weren't even capable of speaking up for yourself when we met. What makes you think you can protect yourself from harm? Because you are no longer Bonded? You might be free of the king, but you are the same person who let the chancellor beat you. He didn't do that to everyone. Only the weak ones."

"That's a low blow, Eoin," I ground out, his words stinging more than I wanted them to.

"You're a coward, Saoirse. That's all you ever were and all you'll ever be if you keep hiding. You're the one who's walking away. *You're* the one who refuses to help stop Tenebris. If the king is harvesting magic, then we need to stop it. Innocent people—*your* people will die, or will become

Bonded. If you stay, you're no better than the king or anyone else who turns a blind eye."

I stepped back, tears pricking behind my eyes. How could he say such hateful things? He was supposed to be my friend. He cared for me once—helped me once. But now, when I no longer needed it, I was nothing to him.

"She's allowed to do whatever she pleases," Cillian said from behind Eoin, his arms crossing over his broad chest. The rolled sleeves of his tunic revealed corded bronze forearms. I shot Cillian a glare. He didn't need to defend me.

"I've made my decision, Eoin. You might as well accept it unless you plan on kidnapping me."

Eoin stormed off without another word, his heated steps stomping down the hall.

My breath turned ragged trying to keep up with the sickening pounding of my heart. I clenched my fists together to stop them from shaking. A sconce flickered on the wall.

"Saoirse," Cillian said, but I couldn't hear him over the blood pounding in my ears. Any sadness was quickly replaced by red-hot anger. Another flicker of the light. How *dare* he call me a coward. I was forced into a life of misery. I did what I had to survive. I might have cowered before the king to cling to life, out of necessity. If I had spoken up, I would have died. I refused to trade one captor for another. Eoin didn't own me. He had no right to dictate my life.

"*Saoirse,*" Cillian said again, his voice breaking through my thoughts. I blinked. Darkness was all around us. The only light was Cillian's, his fire glowing under his copper skin like a beacon. "As much as I would like to be wrapped in your shadows, I'm not sure everyone else feels the same."

Shouts and curses sounded beyond my room. I braced myself to feel their terror, to be flooded with their memories like I had in the tower, but none came. Witches scrambled and ran into one another, trying to figure out what happened to the lights. There were no windows this deep into the Mountain Castle. Without the sconces, we were plunged into an endless void. Heat crept along my cheeks.

Cillian took a steady step toward me. "Do not be embarrassed, little shadow. And do not let Eoin get under your skin. If you like, I can retrieve him, and we can learn exactly what those shadows can do now." He smiled, cruel and wicked like he was the Hunter once more. He would do it, too. There was no doubt in my mind. If I wanted to retaliate and hurt

Eoin the way he hurt me, Cillian wouldn't hesitate to drag him back to face my wrath.

But underneath the anger was something harder to stomach.

"What if he's right? What if I am a coward?"

"You have lived most of your life forced to serve another. You're allowed to make your own decisions. You are no coward, Saoirse Órlaith. To have endured being Bonded to the Conqueror King for over a decade? To have survived all this time? To risk your life to conceal the names of the smugglers when you could? You are the bravest faie I know."

Cillian wiped away my tears with his thumbs. For the second time, I cried in front of this faie. I couldn't bring myself to care; the action was so kind, it made my chest ache.

"The consequences of the king's choices lie with him," Cillian continued. "Do not blame yourself for them. You are the decider of your choices." Cillian poked the space above my heart for emphasis. "But now, you must also live with the aftermath of them, too. Whatever you decide, you have my support. I will still help you with your magic, whether it's here in Ilythia or in Centra or in another realm. You've had enough misery in your life. No one would blame you for staying. Just make sure that whatever you decide, you will not look back on it with regret."

EOIN'S WORDS ECHOED THROUGH ME AS CILLIAN AND I WALKED TO THE stables to see the others off after Cillian relit the sconces. He didn't judge my decision to stay like Eoin. I deserved this. I was finally free, and I deserved to live a quiet life where I could be happy, work on my magic, and tend to my bookshop. The selfish part of me was glad Cillian offered to stay. It was difficult enough to let Kalee and even Ronan go. I had Aislinn and Alice, but it wasn't the same.

I gave a wide berth between myself and where Eoin, Ronan, and Kalee saddled their horses, preparing to ride onto Alice outside of Wolfhollow, where they would change out their mounts before crossing into Centra.

"Please be careful," I whispered, squeezing Kalee into a tight hug. It was hard to imagine an existence where Kalee was no longer with me every day. We'd spent most of our time together for more than half my life. Though I knew I made the right decision to stay, it was as if part of my heart was departing with her.

"I don't want to leave you." Kalee clasped my hands, refusing to let go.

"You don't belong here. Your heart isn't in Ilythia. It's with Ronan." I nodded toward the prince.

"Then come with us, we can stay together. Finish what we started—together."

I shook my head, casting away the doubts.

"After everything we've been through, do you not want to see this through to the end?" Though her words were similar, her tone was much kinder than Eoin's had been.

Excuses formed and fell off my tongue. "My magic is too uncontrollable, and I need to stay here and train. Plus, I am not ready to leave Aislinn and Alice. Even if I wanted to go, I would be too much of a liability in Centra right now. The chances of me being caught are too high, and I won't risk being back in the king's grasp."

Kalee sighed. "You've endured more than most. All I've ever wanted was to see you free. But think of the others who are still Bonded against their will. Do you not want them to experience the same freedom?"

"Kalee," I gasped, doubt washing over me. Out of all people, how could she not understand? "I'm trying to protect *you.*"

She gave me a weak smile that didn't reach her eyes. "If you say so."

Without another word, she pulled me into an embrace. Our final goodbye was left with words unsaid. Did all my friends, aside from Cillian, believe I was a coward? What did they need from me anyway? Ronan said he would free the osnádúrtha. If he needed help, it would be Petranella's he sought.

"Send word if you ever decide to return," Ronan cut in, pulling me into a tight hug. "I'll do my best to keep you updated on our progress. I am proud to call you my cousin. I only wish our circumstances had been different."

"I'll keep searching for anything that may aid you in defeating Tenebris, but you'll be fine without me. It is you who will usurp your father and prevent Tenebris from returning. *You* were born to rule and protect, and you will do so brilliantly, cousin."

"I am glad you have so much faith in me, but you are an asset. Feel free to change your mind at any time." Ronan kissed my temple and shoved my arm in jest before turning to Cillian. "That goes the same for you. We can always use someone with your skill set."

Cillian looked at me as he said, "I will keep that in mind, but for now, I will remain here to help Saoirse with her magic."

Ronan clasped Cillian's forearm before pulling him in, whispering something into his ear. Cillian acknowledged Ronan's words with a silent nod.

"Of course, he's staying here," was Eoin's only form of goodbye before mounting the black-speckled stallion. I bit the inside of my cheek to keep from screaming. Anger once again reared its ugly head, but I managed to tamp it down and keep the shadows from swarming us. Maybe one day, he would understand.

"Be safe, be swift, be smart," Aislinn said, taking Ronan and Kalee into her arms. "Here's a map to avoid the Willows. Do yourself a favor and memorize it. It cannot leave Ilythia, understand?"

"Kalee's mind is like no other. She'll know it by heart before we reach Alice."

"Good. Give my mate a hug for me when you see her."

The three of them rode off into the distance. Guilt gnawed at my insides. I'd been so sure I was making the right decision until it came down to their departure. I only moved once they were well out of sight— their disappointment lingering like a foul smell. My heart clenched, but I shoved the feeling aside. Something else bloomed there, too: hope for a life I never thought I'd have.

Chapter Forty-Five

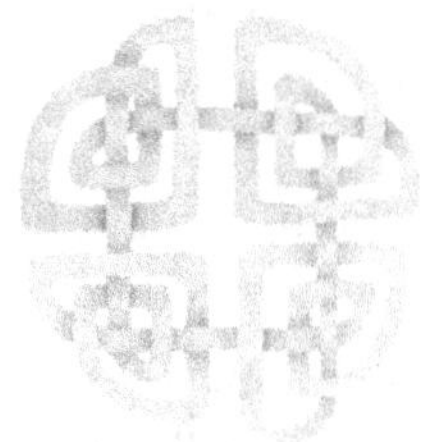

I stood in the empty training room—a dark, heatless flame engulfed my hands as Cillian had instructed. Never before had my shadows lived outside of my skin, and never were they black. Those that still swirled their familiar patterns along my body remained silver, but as soon as they left the confines of my immortal form, they darkened and shifted into a familiar nightmare.

"What if I can't control it?"

"You can and you will," Cillian said. He crossed his arms over his broad chest, his biceps testing the confines of his tunic. "Try again."

I rolled my shoulders, trying to dispel the tension, but the shadows wouldn't dissipate. Summoning them had been simple. They were always at the ready, especially in the natural dimness of the Mountain Castle. But they refused to let go, as if the king's Bond had disconnected us for so long, they couldn't bear to part with me now.

"Focus."

"I'm trying," I growled, my molars moments away from grinding into dust.

"No, you're not."

"Yes, I *am*."

"If you were, something would have happened by now."

I shot him a glare. The sconces in the room flickered.

"Well, that's something," he quipped, that incessant smirk twitching his lips. Gods, I wanted to strangle him. We'd been at this for nearly an hour, and I'd yet to yield any results. "Now, do it with control."

"You make it sound so easy!" I cried in frustration. "All I've ever known is how to conceal myself. What am I supposed to do with them like this?" I shoved my hands in front of my face, the black inching down my forearms, shielding me.

Cillian's smirk disappeared. He took a step toward me. Another. Until we were mere inches away. I clasped my hands behind my back, remembering the last time my shadows touched someone. Cillian cupped the underside of my chin, stealing my breath as he tilted my gaze toward him.

"You're afraid. Why?"

My magic hadn't just grown in strength like the others had speculated. It morphed into something new altogether. Something far too cruel—too familiar to the fomorii. Whether they could see memories like I could, I didn't know. But there was no mistaking their shadows and the fear they instilled. Sure, I could manipulate the darkness around me, but that was where our similarities had ended. Now the line between us blurred too much for comfort.

"You don't have to hide yourself. Not from me, little shadow. Now tell me so that I can help you."

"Back in the tower room, I did more than blot out the light."

Cillian didn't let go of my chin. He forced me to keep looking at him. To not shy away when all I wanted to do was hide.

"When my shadows touched the others, I felt their terror in my bones. It was as if my magic burrowed into their minds and yanked out their worst memory."

I waited for him to let go, to put more distance between us, but still he held me.

"Did you get to choose the memory?"

"No. Some I already knew about, but others were foreign to me." I'd recognized the memories of Kalee, Eoin, and Ronan as soon as I saw them—the others I could only guess at.

"This happened when you touched everyone?"

"Yes," I breathed. "Save you and the familiars. But the thing is, I don't know if they even knew I was in their minds."

"It's possible they were too distracted to notice. I agree with you, though. The queen would have had many more questions if she knew you had a front row seat to her memories. You said you sensed their fear. Which came first, yours or theirs?"

I frowned. "It wasn't until my magic touched them that I was truly afraid. Do you know what this is?"

"I don't, but everything is unknown until it isn't."

My hands shook, his words doing little to ease my worries. "The fomorii—their shadows look like this. Am I—" I swallowed hard. "Am I becoming one of them?"

Cillian stroked my cheek, wiping the tears that fell so easily around him. He touched his forehead to mine, our eyelashes kissing. "No. You are not a monster, little shadow. You are good and kind and brave. I'm not sure what this is, but you are not like them."

"What if I hurt someone?" The others had cried out last time, their fear overwhelming. What if I could cause physical pain as well?

"Touch me."

I reared back. "Did you not listen to a word I said?"

"I am not afraid of you. Touch me and maybe we can understand it better."

Shakily, I unclasped my hands, hovering them over Cillian's forearms. Seconds passed. Maybe minutes. What if he was wrong? What if I saw something he didn't want me to see?

"Touch me," he whispered, his words curling my toes.

My fingers latched onto his arms, and within moments, my shadows curled around him, snaking their way over his shoulders. At first, nothing happened, then—

"I see a field," I said, bracing myself for something horrifying amongst the flowers.

"What else?"

"A woman. Waving. She's—smiling?" It was a simple memory. Happy. A calm settled over me, soothing the tightness in my muscles.

"My mother," he said, a soft smile tilting his lips. "In a moment, I'll walk over to her and give her a hug."

"Can you tell I'm there with you?"

"I don't see you, but I may not be the best judge because I can always sense when you're near. Try to pull away from the memory."

"How?"

"Reel your shadows into you."

My brows furrowed despite the warmth radiating from the memory as Cillian embraced his mother. "I can't. They always return to the environment after."

"Yes, you can. You've been forced to rely too much on your environment. But this—" He looked down at my hands. The dark veins flowed and wrapped around him. "This is you. It's your magic. Yours to wield. We can use what's available and manipulate the element that calls to us, but make no mistake, it lives within you, too."

"That's how you're able to produce fire when there's none around," I said. "How are you so sure mine works the same?"

"Our magic may manifest differently, but all faie are created this way. My fire, much like your shadows, lives within me. I conjure and wield it at will." He placed his palm over my heart. "It comes from here. Think of it like a rope. You loosen the slack to release your magic, then pull it back once you're done."

Cillian opened his other hand, and a ball of fire appeared—a single flame glittering in the dimness. He clenched his fist, and it extinguished. "Before, when the king was siphoning your magic, you had to rely on the shadows around you. But look at you," he marveled, almost glowing with the endearment. His fingertips brushed the underside of my forearms, tracing the swirling silver. "They've always been with you. They've just been trapped for so long."

"How come you didn't have a problem manipulating your fire at will?"

He shrugged. "I'm not sure. Maybe it was because I knew how to control my magic before I was Bound, or perhaps it was because he hadn't been stealing from me for as long."

I took a fortifying breath and closed my eyes, searching for the tether to my shadows. They caressed Cillian's form as if my own hands ran up and down his corded muscles, savoring the firmness of them. With a strong hold, I pulled them back to me.

To my amazement, they obeyed, seeping into my skin. Black giving way to silver.

"Careful, or I might ask you to touch me with your magic again."

Nines, I *wanted* to touch him again, but not with my shadows. My fingertips twitched, aching to feel the warmth of his skin. The sharpness of his jaw. The softness of his hair. But the way he looked at me? It wouldn't be a mere fling, like with Eiric.

No. Once I welcomed Cillian Aodhán into my bed, there would be no going back. He would ruin me. Part of me wanted to let him, but gods, it was like he could see into my soul.

I was terrified of what he would find.

"Tell me one true thing," he whispered, his palm cupping the column of my neck—thumb ghosting a touch to my bottom lip.

There were a thousand things I could have told him. My doubts about controlling my magic. My fears of hurting someone. The guilt of letting my friends and family handle a conflict all on their own. That's what they were—family. I'd clung to the past, so focused on what I'd lost, I hadn't realized the connections I'd built along the journey, despite how dysfunctional we might be.

Ronan was my cousin by blood, and still, I let him go. I'd let them all walk away.

With every breath I took, the kaleidoscope of Cillian's eyes shifted—turned from grass, kissed with fresh morning dew, into glittering emerald. My favorite was forest green, deep and rich, hinting at the depth and complexity within. I could drown in his eyes, not because they were beautiful—though they were—but because when he looked at me, I came undone.

"I'm a coward when it comes to you," I whispered, the confession escaping my lips. My heart pounded against my ribcage, threatening to jump out.

The words hung between us, sharp as a blade unsheathed in the dim light of the training room. He didn't flinch, didn't blink as what I'd revealed threatened to cut me open.

"Why do you say such things?"

"Because you've risked everything for me, and all I'll do is disappoint you like I do everyone else. I'm not whole, Cillian." Images of Eoin and Kalee's faces flashed in my mind, dismay wrinkling their brows. The sad smile turning Ronan's lips.

I was too shattered, too damaged to be what Cillian wanted—what he deserved. Eoin had been right. All I'd ever known was to hide. To walk away.

Maybe it was all I'd ever do.

Cillian's grip tightened around my throat. Not threatening, but to remind me he was there, holding on. Not letting go unless I ask. My breath hitched, and gods, he must have heard it. Felt the way my pulse jumped beneath his fingertips.

"I didn't risk everything because I expected to find this perfect version of you. Nines, I hadn't sought out anything other than your safety. I left Arundell because I wanted to honor my king. But now? Now, all I want is you, whatever version. Rain or shine, broken or whole, I want *you*, Saoirse."

I didn't know what to do. His gaze flicked to my lips, and Mother help me, my tongue darted out as if it could taste him. I curled my hands into his shirt, gripping him closer until there was but a hair's breadth between us.

Without warning, my shadows wrapped around him, snaking up his chest and around his neck, pulling him closer. Heat flooded my veins as the sconces flickered around us.

Images clouded my vision—me.

I was the center of them all.

Chapter Forty-Six

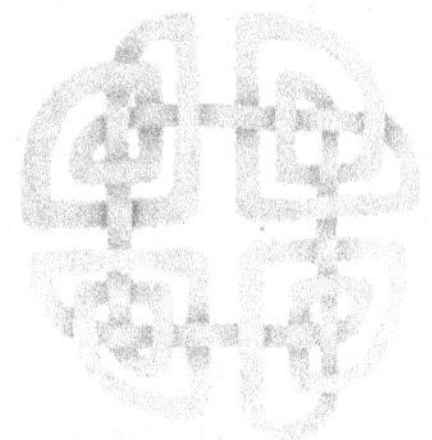

Cillian's desire entwined with my own. Years of teasing remarks and lingering looks played out as memories. From our first encounter, up to when he held me the night my Bond broke. Gods, there was so much longing it hurt.

Panting, I ripped my hands and shadows away, severing the connection.

"I'm so sorry. I didn't—I didn't mean to."

Cillian didn't push me aside—didn't shout at the invasion of his privacy. He only shook his head. "I've never tried to hide how I feel toward you. I won't start now."

"All this time?" I asked.

I'd written off every flirtatious comment Cillian threw my way as a bid to get under my skin, rather than genuine interest. Afraid to recognize it for what it was. But the want, the *need* that flooded my senses—there was no denying it.

"Since the day I laid eyes on you. But if you still harbor feelings for Eoin—"

I held a finger against his lips.

"I feel guilty for how we left things," I whispered, "but I haven't held any romantic sentiment toward him for some time."

Perhaps longer than I'd thought. Eoin had seemed like the better, steadier choice. Like most, I'd believed Cillian was a monster—too wild, too abrasive. He *was* both of those things, but gods, it was beautiful.

"Good." Cillian pressed his lips together, as if trying to keep them to himself.

"Good," I parroted, unable to formulate anything else.

For too long, I had denied how Cillian sparked something inside of me that Eoin hadn't. In the beginning, Eoin stood up for me when no one else would, but he gave me no room to grow. To change. Eoin wanted me in a cage—to be used to help him achieve *his* goals.

Cillian offered the key.

And now, I needed him to do something other than look at me. To touch me. Taste me. He could incinerate me with his magic, for all I cared.

"I told you, you would be mine one day," he murmured, smirking. The dimple that only showed itself to me dented his cheek.

"You're still a bastard."

"Ah, but I am your bastard."

Cillian's cards were all splayed on the table. It was my turn to make the next move. It was like the moment before lightning cleaved the sky—an unspoken agreement. Once we finally acknowledged whatever lay between us, there was no going back.

It was a consequence I was more than willing to accept.

My shadows knew what I wanted. They pulled Cillian into me, closing the distance between us. He didn't fight them.

When our lips collided, it wasn't soft, not that I expected it to be. It was weeks, no months of hunger shattering in a heartbeat.

I yielded to his silent request, opening up to him and letting his tongue sweep in to possess me. Cillian groaned into my mouth. One hand grasped my neck, tilting my chin up while the other threaded through my hair, discarding the pathetic strip of cloth that had held it together.

He gripped me as if he never wanted to let go.

Cillian's touch turned more demanding, exploring every inch of me.

I mirrored his movements, traversing his hair—feather soft, just as I'd imagined. Running my fingers along his jaw, sharp enough to cut glass. I lingered over the broadness of his chest. His face. Back, arms, abdomen.

He trailed his hands down my back, snaking them behind my thighs before lifting me against him. I gripped his shoulders, solid as rocks, and wrapped my legs around him. Savored the hardness of him.

Cillian pushed me up against the wall, pressing his body further into me—the evidence of his desire unmistakable. The pulse in my center grew stronger.

I needed *more*.

Pieces of me stitched back together as he met me where I was. Embraced me for who I am. Imperfect. Traumatized. Healing. Cillian never once walked away from my former self or the person I was becoming.

"Saoirse," he murmured, kissing my jaw, my neck, my ear—each touch leaving a fiery blaze in its wake.

My name on his lips was a prayer and a plea. His was my only breathless answer.

His eyes found mine. "If you would like to stop—if this is moving too fast, all you need to do is say so."

We shouldn't—not when anyone could walk in, but I was tired of doing things I was supposed to do.

"Don't stop," I demanded, holding his gaze.

His answering growl vibrated through me as he peppered my neck with more kisses. The sharp edges of his canines skated across the tender flesh. My legs quaked. Something unknown and intrinsic had taken over.

Cillian relinquished his hold on my thighs, guiding my feet back to solid ground.

I stopped breathing entirely when he found other areas to roam.

"I've wanted to touch you for a *very* long time," he murmured, his hands trailing over the fabric between us—circling my breasts, mapping out my abdomen—as if painting a picture of what lay beneath. My chest tightened. Would he be disappointed at what he found? I didn't inherit the genes that made the faie a picture of perfect grace. I wasn't tall and lean with ethereal beauty, nor did I have muscles sculpted by the gods themselves. My middle was soft. My thighs and ass far larger than my breasts.

"Fuck," he cursed. The torture—the hunger in his voice dispelled all of my thoughts. Cillian tugged at the collar of my tunic, tracing it before he followed the curve of my collar bone, trailing down my side. "These, I love." He lingered on the sides of my breasts, gooseflesh prickling in the wake of his gentle caresses. I grew molten under his ministrations, gasping for air as he ran his hands over my ribs as if he knew I couldn't breathe. "But this? I'd kill over this." Cillian smacked my ass.

I yelped.

"Cillian," I panted. Before I could pull him into me for another kiss, he grabbed my wrists, holding them above my head.

"I've had to wait ages to touch you, little shadow. I'm going to take my time." His tone was little more than a veiled threat. Cillian stole any argument from me as he slipped his thumb into my mouth. I sucked on it, hollowing out my cheeks. He groaned, releasing it with a *pop* before sliding it down the center of me, my wrists still bound above my head in his other hand.

Slowly—so fucking slowly—he made his way to my waistband, teasing the edge of it. My muscles spasmed. His deft fingers found the drawstring of my pants and loosened their hold.

More.

He chuckled. "Impatient, are we?"

At last, he dipped down, skimming my clit. His touch was electric, sparking more heat than I'd ever known. It was breathtaking. Exquisite. And still, I wanted more, greedy for the feel of him.

"Cillian."

"Gods, Saoirse," he moaned, the slick evidence of my desire coating his fingers with each passing stroke.

"Cillian," I pleaded. His movements were leisurely and deliberate. Every part of me fixated on his fingers teasing at my entrance. If he didn't comply, I was sure to burn to dust.

A feline smile graced his perfect lips. "Cillian, *what?*"

"Please," I begged. I'd do anything in this moment if only to get him to give me what I wanted.

"That's more like it."

He complied, slipping a finger inside me.

The moan that escaped my lips couldn't be helped as he stroked my insides. Another finger followed the first, the pressure and stretch a gift and a curse all at once. Each caress stoked the fire, and I was well on my way to ignition.

"Like this?" Cillian murmured, his teeth nipping at my earlobe, then down along my neck. His fingers coaxed me until I went taut, clenching around him.

I groaned, not caring if anyone heard. My hips moved in tandem with his strokes. He hissed and plunged deeper. Faster. Making sure I felt every inch he offered as he worked me.

My name on his lips was the only thing I registered before everything went black. Shadows consumed the room. The pressure built, growing rigid until it released, threatening to cleave me in two. I shattered around him. My legs wobbled as Cillian stroked me through my climax.

"Such a good girl," he said, barely visible in the engulfing dark. He slipped his fingers out of me and into his mouth—sucked on the taste of me—sparking my desire all over again.

I reached for the buttons of his trousers, needing to feel more. I wanted to know all of him and give him the same in return. His hands clasped around mine.

"I will not take you in a musty training room, Saoirse. Not for our first time." His hands dug into my hips. "When I have you, I want you open. Sprawled out for me. I want to take my time and savor every part of you."

I gulped.

"Now, instead of letting the shadows go back into your surroundings, pull them to you and keep them there."

"Really? You're trying to make me perform more magic after that?"

"You're the one who put them here. Do as you did before."

I groaned but shut my eyes and did as he instructed, searching for the invisible link to the darkness. Like the night in the tower, there was not one tether, but multiple. Shadows filled every nook and cranny from the ceiling to the floor. With a sharp inhale, I sensed what lay in the lightless room. A rack of weapons fastened on the eastern wall. Rolled up mats in the far corner. Training bags strung up in a line. I knew these things were here, but like I felt Cillian earlier, it was as if I'd touched them with my hands.

Could I move them?

Instead of pulling, I pushed, testing my hypothesis. When I was Bonded, I struggled to manipulate the shadows. I hadn't questioned it, thinking it was the way my magic worked. Now, it was nothing. Simple like breathing. It was mine. An extension of me. Willing and ready to do as I commanded.

A chain holding one of the training bags creaked.

"Not very good at following instructions, are we?"

I scowled, taking one of the tendrils and imagining it wrapping around his ankle so I could drop him on his ass. He sidestepped and denied me the pleasure of having him at my feet.

"Be a good girl and pull them in, little shadow."

I would have attacked him again, but his words shook my core. Instead, I grabbed each dark tendril in my hands and yanked them back into me. Back home. Firelight flickered as my shadows returned. My veins flooded with cool, liquid magic, and the silver shadows patterning my skin writhed, ready for more. Eventually, they settled, though the power was ready to leap to my fingertips.

"I did it," I gasped, clinging to him.

"There was never a question that you could."

"When we, uh—What I mean to say is, a moment ago, I didn't see your memories like I did before."

"Then perhaps that can be controlled, too."

Something in my chest lifted. When I'd lost control—when my magic shifted into something new, I was afraid I'd lose myself and become someone I didn't recognize. This small example of authority gave me hope that I would become strong, like Cillian. That I would make my mother proud in the Otherworld. Someone who my friends could depend on.

The king had taken more than my magic. There was no telling what I was capable of. Eoin was right about one thing: I barely scraped by in my time with the king. I *wasn't* protecting myself.

I inhaled a shaky breath, meeting Cillian's gaze and finding understanding and a fierceness that made my heart soar. I'd continue to train. Become stronger. Faster. I would never again rely on anyone else for my safety.

No one would ever take from me again.

Chapter Forty-Seven

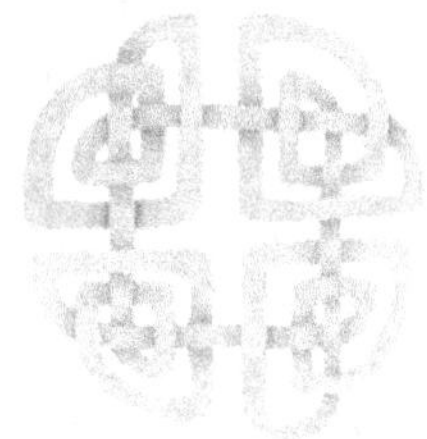

You wish to leave, Órga said, sensing my thoughts as I stepped into the aerie. She lay in the corner by the opening to the side of the cliff, curled around her egg, soaking in the sunshine. Vines crawled over tall pillars and wide arches. This section, the one Órga chose to call home, was the largest of them all. Even with its current occupant, loneliness clung to the air. The aerie was meant to house hundreds of dragons. Instead, it was a whisper of what it once was.

"I have no purpose in the Mountain Castle, but I'll remain in Ilythia with my aunt." I bit the inside of my cheek, reluctant to leave her here.

I can think of a few uses the Witch Queen might have for you. Her mixture of suspicion and curiosity coursed through whatever connection we shared. It didn't matter that Queen Petranella was technically my aunt. She shipped mine and Ronan's mother off to marry unknown kings. She stationed Aislinn at Ilythia's border to ensure her sister wouldn't challenge her throne. If I stayed, she would use my magic for her own purposes.

"I don't like the idea of leaving you," I said, but it was time to begin a new chapter—one without Bonds, demands, or choices that were not my own.

Do not feel guilty for living your life, halfling. You gave me my freedom. I will not hold you back from yours.

"Will you ever tell me who chained you?"

Steam hissed from her snout, warming the chilled air. *Before the witches and winged faie, dragons dominated the skies. We were the champions of the gods. When the war between gods broke out, dragons were on the front lines. We were the frontlines. Between us, the witches, and the faie, we held them well. That is, until the Dark God created something to rival even the dragons."*

My breath hitched. Tenebris. The image of the chancellor's tapestry of dragons burning down shadowed figures flashed in my mind.

"What did he create?"

His own version of my kind.

"How is that possible?" My stomach churned although I knew the answer before the question left my lips. Tenebris was a god after all. He created the fomorii, who were modeled after men and animals alike. A dragon wasn't so far-fetched.

Órga's eyes clouded, peering off to a place, a time, far away from here. *We held for a time, but the Dark God's dragons were adequate rivals. They knocked us down one by one. Most did not get up again, including my mate. I fell soon after. Before I awoke in the mountain, the last thing I remember was crashing into the ground.*

The smell of salt tinged the air. A tear slid down her scaled face, splashing down at my boots. I rested my hand against her leg as she told her story—one she'd been holding onto for a very long time. It needed to be said. She shouldered this burden by herself for so long. The least I could do was help her bear it.

In the mountain, shadowed demons poked, prodded, and tore into me. They studied me and how I worked. The Dark God had done this before to make his own dragons. They had pushed the previous one too far and needed a replacement so that they could keep building their army. Why they chose me, I do not know. Convenience, likely.

Her scales caught in the sunlight. Horrible, jagged scars I hadn't noticed before marred her body. Bile rose in my throat. The Conqueror King was cruel enough, but Tenebris? I couldn't imagine what horrible things he'd done to her.

I met the Dark God many times before my slumber, she continued. *He would inflict the worst sort of pain. His face still finds its way into my dreams, even after so long. The last time I saw him, he told me they were going to make their final stance. To end the war. To destroy the gods and either enslave their creations or end those who resisted. The Dark God had said he would be back before putting me into a dreamless sleep that must have preserved my body. You can imagine my surprise when I woke, especially when I discovered my egg.*

"Did you know?"

No. I must have conceived before I was taken. It can take decades for an egg to form, centuries before it hatches. She shifted her tail, wrapped around her egg as if checking to make sure it was still there.

"When did you wake?" Did the magic wear off after so long? Or was something else the source of her awakening?

I cannot say. I was asleep, and then I wasn't. I believe I arose in recent years although it's hard to tell. There was no one around. No one except the liliachs who grew too curious.

My heartbeat quickened. "Did they bite you?" What if the liliachs attacked her? Could she succumb to their curse?

Those rats with wings couldn't harm me. They were my food source. It wasn't the liliachs I was afraid of. I kept waiting for the Dark God to show his face again. To finish what he started. To harm my egg. But he never came. Aside from the liliachs, you and your friends were the first living beings I've seen in years.

"I am sorry, Órga, for what you went through." I shook my head, trying to find the words I didn't have. Nothing I could say would take back the pain and fear. No amount of apologizing or comforting words could erase her anguish. Órga nudged me with her snout, and I took the invitation to rest my forehead against her. She was warm like Cillian, as if her fire existed just beneath her scales.

"There is one other question I'd like to ask." I met Órga's stare now that we were eye to eye and tried not to fidget under her gaze. I hadn't forgotten Órga's strange words on the mountain, even if breaking my Bond had taken precedence. "What did you mean when you said Fate chose me?"

She blinked as if I should already know the answer. *You are my anamchara, Saoirse. By some strange design, Fate has intertwined our lives, and I will not ignore her. I am willing to accept this bond. Are you?*

"The bond is not already in place?" I pressed my lips together to try to keep from biting my cheek. My heart stuttered at the thought of another bond taking hold without my knowledge. Another choice was made for me. An all too familiar shake started in my hands. I clenched my fists together.

No, halfling. A true bond must be accepted by both parties. It is yours to accept or deny.

Suddenly, the air became too hot. I couldn't deny our connection, but my anamchara? *My* familiar? I barely knew what that entailed. The room spun, or perhaps it was the questions whirling through my head. I just escaped one Bond. I couldn't jump into another. The last one nearly took my soul with it.

Are you aware of the familiar bond between dragons and witches? Órga asked, distracting me from my racing thoughts.

I nodded. Both Alice and Niamh had explained it. "But I'm not a witch, only half of one." I stared out beyond the aerie, examining the snow-capped mountains. The tallest peak of the Ennisi Mountains rose above the others. "I'm not sure I belong anywhere. I wield my magic like the faie, but aside from my ears and teeth, I look nothing like them. Even my magic is different. A shadow wielder is unheard of. I suppose I resemble the witches more because of my eye color, but that's where our similarities end."

You and I are not so different. I, too, it seems, am the only one of my kind. Órga nestled her egg tighter. *There is, however, enough witch in you for the bond to appear. There's no denying we are anamcharas. I felt it between us the moment I saw you. It is a bond, but not like the one you freed yourself from. I shall never take from you, or you from me. We can share our strength to help one another, but we promise to do no harm.*

It was an effort not to touch the whisper of the Mark still etched into my skin. My flesh was scarred, the tissue raised, but the stark blackness of it was gone. The Mark no longer sprang to life when I acknowledged it. The king's Bond was placed to steal my magic—to command me to his will. But whatever was between Órga and me didn't feel sinister. Looking back, I was drawn to her. I wanted to help her. To protect her and keep her egg safe.

"How does it work?"

Accepting the anamchara bond will allow us to continue communicating as we do now—no matter how far apart we travel. The bond allows us to share our magic. To help each other when in need. But beware, the bond can have devastating consequences if one of us takes too much.

"Órga, you should know. When my Bond with the king was broken, my magic changed. I fear I may be somehow linked to Tenebris."

It's not about what you can do for me. It's about what we can do together. Perhaps this is why Fate brought you to me, because of whatever connection you might have to the Dark God.

"But why me? I am nothing. You deserve someone better. Someone strong. Whole." I was healing, but at the heart of it, I was still fractured. I didn't even have full control of my magic. How could I strengthen or protect her if I could barely help myself?

Saoirse, you freed me and my offspring. For that, I will be eternally grateful. More importantly, I sense what lies beneath. The goodness there. You may feel like you are all alone, but you are not. Let me change that. Let me be your ally.

Something in my chest cracked a fraction. "I am not good, Órga. I have done so many terrible, awful things I can never rectify."

Do you know how the bonds between witches and dragons came to be? she asked, ignoring my confession.

I shook my head.

You may know dragons were one of the first creations. Before witches, before faie, merrows, and humans, dragons settled in Ilythia long before anyone tried to lay claim to the lands. When the witches came, disputes over territory, and tensions between our kinds were high.

For years, we quarreled and killed one another. Each claiming to protect their own. Until one day, when the hatchling of the dragon leader was captured by creatures who no longer plague this earth.

I sucked in a breath. Something worse than Tenebris and his fomorii existed?

Dragons are fiercely protective of our young. She continued, shifting into a more comfortable position, her scales shimmering with the movement. *For you see, dragons do not reproduce often, and when the leader's line is threatened, chaos can ensue amongst dragonkind, disrupting our structure. If the heir of the taoiseach had died, civil war could have broken out among the clans, where they would have destroyed one another until a new taoiseach was established.*

"What became of the heir?"

A young witch by the name of Selene stumbled across her. She did not know who this hatchling was to us. She'd been taught to fear the dragons, to not come too close unless she wanted to be burned alive. Despite this, she chose to release Kaidah. To help the heir with no ulterior motive. When the taoiseach learned what Selene had done, she wanted to burn down her village, afraid Selene had somehow discovered the location of the den.

"What a horrible thank-you gift."

Órga chuffed in agreement. *Kaidah learned of her mother's plans and pleaded to spare Selene and her village. When the taoiseach refused to listen, the heir defied her mother and flew ahead in secret, searching for the village to spare them like Selene did for her.*

I sucked in a breath, hanging on the edge of Órga's story. "Did she save them?"

She did. But not before angering the taoiseach and the rest of the clan. When the witches saw a dragon on their doorstep, their first instinct was to attack. Once again, Selene risked her life to protect Kaidah, to stop her fellow sisters from attacking her. And when Selene was threatened by the taoiseach and the rest of the dragons, the heir stood in the line of fire. Both kinds witnessed their selflessness firsthand and were able to come to a peace agreement. They asked the Triple Goddess for a way to show appreciation to one another, and thus the anamchara bond was born of Selene's and Kaidah's kindness. From then on, dragon and witch kind swore to protect and care for one another.

"That is a lovely story, Órga, but what does it have to do with me?" I wasn't like Selene. I wasn't good. Or selfless. I let my friends go on without me. They would risk their lives to stop Tenebris, and I would be safely tucked away in Wolfhollow amongst my bookstore.

Don't you see, halfling? Not only was the bond present between us, but you chose to help me when you could have easily chosen not to.

"Well, it was either help you or be burned to a crisp," I jested, trying to cool the intensity of Órga's gaze.

Órga made a noise that resembled a laugh. *That may be true, but you made your choice nonetheless. You chose out of the kindness of your heart, like Selene did when she saw Kaidah trapped. I see the goodness and selflessness in you, even if you cannot.*

The lump in my throat was hard to swallow. I believed I was without a soul from what the Conqueror King made me do, from what the chancellor made me feel. For fifteen years, I'd been told I was worthless. I was nothing. But to hear I was good? To hear I was selfless after Eoin berated me? It was almost too much.

You chose me, Órga reiterated. *Now, I am choosing you if you will have me.*

"If I accept the bond," I said shakily, my heart already pulling me in the direction it needed to go, "will I have another anamchara, or do I only get one?" Alice had said witches get two anamcharas, but I was not a full-blooded witch. Maybe I was selfish for already thinking about another anamchara, but if I were only able to do this once…

There is more witch in you than you realize, halfling.

It wasn't an outright answer, but it was as much as I was going to get.

Since my Bond broke, I'd been determined to do things on my own. Perhaps there was a difference between being alone and doing things for oneself. One didn't have to happen with the other. Kalee had been there for me for so long, and when she could have used my help, I let her down. She would never say it, but saw in her eyes during our goodbye. I found friendship with Ronan, my long-lost cousin, and I let him bear the weight of the Tenebris on his shoulders for my own selfish reasons. And Eoin… perhaps I was so focused on my freedom, I neglected to help him achieve his.

I'd never thought I'd be willing to form another bond so soon, but this was different. I'd witnessed the love between Aislinn and Alice. Between Niamh, Ahlani, and Airi. Órga wasn't only offering strength or protection. She offered amity. Understanding. Instead of wanting to turn away, I wanted to run toward her. She was alone with no one but her egg. Loneliness and I were all too familiar friends.

As if on cue, a cool breeze flowed through the aerie—the winds of Fate itself urging me toward her.

"I will accept the bond. I want to be your anamchara," I said, squaring my shoulders.

A sound reminiscent of a cat's purr thundered deep within her. She looked me over, assessing me. *Lift your tunic enough to expose your side.*

I did as she asked, revealing my ribcage. The memory of soldiers holding me down as the king etched the Bond Mark into my neck flashed. My heart pumped with a sickening thud.

This will not hurt, Órga reassured. *Now look away.* I squeezed my eyes shut, and the air around us warmed enough to draw sweat. Blood roared in my ears, and I jerked back. Pins and needles prickled along my abdomen, but as Órga promised, it didn't hurt. And like Niamh described, it…tingled.

The connection between us glowed brighter, solidifying our anamchara bond. Then, I felt Órga's magic. Ancient and primal. I wasn't sure what type of magic a dragon possessed, but this was more of my own. The well of my power didn't just grow deeper like it had when my Bond broke; it was as if my shadows swirled in an endless void. I didn't explode like last time. It wasn't mine to take, but to access if needed.

The imprint on my side body was a miniature version of her. Delicate, glittering, gold and black scales almost shimmered along the markings. She made it so that her wings were outstretched as if she were soaring through the skies.

"I love it," I said, and I could have sworn Órga smiled. Amongst her black and gold scales, one turned the brightest silver in the area over her heart. Eyes watering, I brought my hand to it.

"I thought I'd find you here," Cillian said, leaning against the doorway of the aerie. "Nice work, Órga." If he had any reservations about the bond, he didn't voice them. There was no doubt Eoin wouldn't have held his tongue, likely saying I was careless for rushing into something I knew little about. Something told me Cillian didn't feel that way. No, Cillian's support seemed to be everlasting.

"I wanted to say goodbye," I said.

"Are you sure you wish to leave? We can stay if you want." Cillian's brows furrowed. I looked nervously at Órga. Would she think badly of me for accepting the bond only to leave?

Go and experience life for a time. Do not be afraid. I am only a short flight away. And since our anamchara bond has been accepted, distance does not matter. We will be reunited again. Órga nudged me with her snout. It would be impractical for her to come with us. There was no shelter for her in Wolfhollow. The aerie at the Mountain Castle would be the best place for her and her egg.

It had been too long since I had a place of my own to call home. Though now, the thought of a home felt empty without the presence of my friends. At least I still had Cillian and Aislinn and Alice. But it wasn't just a home. It was a life I only ever dared to dream of. I'd be a fool to deny it.

"Yes," I answered Cillian and placed my hand on Órga's snout.

"Are you sure she won't burn the place down with you gone?"

She huffed a plume of steam in amusement.

"This is the safest place for her egg, and her offspring comes first. Besides, she's just a short flight away." I shrugged with feigned casualness, repeating her reassurances. I didn't like the idea of leaving her, but she was safe here.

Cillian gave an affirmative nod. "The witches would sooner die than let the last of the dragons perish."

I picked up my pack from its place by the door. Thanks to Ahlani, it was filled with extra clothes and spare food as well as healing poultices courtesy of Flore. There would be no goodbyes to the witches. Queen Petranella already sent them off on their next assignment. I didn't know how long it would be before I saw them again. I'd grown fond of the trio. I would miss them.

We said our goodbyes to Órga and walked down the many steps of the aerie. Cillian gave me a sidelong glance. "Was it difficult to accept another bond so soon?"

"I know it was the right choice, but it was difficult to understand I was deserving of it. I'll still have trouble with that, I think."

"I'm sure Órga will continue to remind you that you are." His hand rested on the back of my neck, his thumb circling the remnants of the Bond Mark. His touch ignited sparks along my flesh, threatening to send me into an aching mess.

Aislinn met us in the corridor, bag slung over her shoulder and broom in hand. "Are you coming with us or returning to your homeland, faie?"

"A land doesn't indicate a home, but those who surround you," Cillian replied to Aislinn, but his attention remained on me.

Warmth flooded my face, remembering what happened yesterday in the training room. Any time I looked at him, I couldn't help but think about it. Breakfast had been a disaster. I couldn't recall what we talked about, having been too distracted by every little thing he did. When his hands threaded through his hair, I could only think about how soft it was. When he scratched the stubble along his jaw, I felt its phantom touch against my neck. All words died on my tongue, and I was a total, utter fool. Now was no different.

Aislinn gave me a look of suspicion before leading the way, and my cheeks flushed further, heat creeping toward my ears.

Cillian chuckled and rested his hand on the small of my back as we followed after her. He'd never been afraid to touch me before, but after yesterday, he found any excuse to brush my hair behind my ear. To rest his hand on me. To stand so close I could feel his warmth as if he couldn't bear to be apart.

You'll be mine.

He was laying claim to me. And gods help me, I'd let him. I'd gotten a taste of him and now I wanted the full meal.

Thunder boomed in the distance and lightning crackled, cleaving the gray sky in two. The fresh scent of rain was calming as I stepped onto one of the landing decks carved out of the mountain.

Aislinn mounted her broom and readied herself. Cillian dropped his glamour, letting his wings stretch wide, ruffling the mottled feathers. After a few days of stretching and flying, Cillian's wings were finally healed. Thunder rang closer, and its sister cracked close behind as the sky threatened to spill its contents.

"Do you think it's safe?" I called out over the gods' cries.

Aislinn surveyed the sky. Cillian didn't seem too concerned, no doubt having flown in similar conditions before.

"We'll outfly it. Stay low," Aislinn instructed.

"Ready?" Cillian reached out for me, and I gladly wrapped my arms around his neck, soaking up his warmth. His spiced, juniper scent was intoxicating. I nuzzled into him, receiving an answering squeeze in return.

"Be careful, little shadow," Cillian said low in my ear, "or we will have to make a stop along the way. I wonder what your aunt would think?"

"Are you so concerned about what she thinks of you?" I mused. I didn't think Cillian cared about anyone's opinion.

"No, I'm not." The threat hung between us. My core pulsed.

Cillian groaned before bolting into the air, following Aislinn's lead as if he was fighting to not make good on his warning.

We flew hard and fast, the landscape but a blur around us. We wouldn't stop at the cabin as we did before, easier now that there weren't so many of us. Instead, we'd go straight to the chalet so Aislinn could resume her duties at the border. I knew she was ready to return home to Alice. The thought of them reuniting brought a smile to my lips.

When we passed over Wolfhollow, my heart flipped. The small village outside of Aislinn's home was where my bookshop awaited. Anxious butterflies fluttered in my stomach. I couldn't wait to get started on it. There were so many things to do. So many books to read and share. Aislinn had talked about how she and Alice would help me collect an inventory to start filling the shelves. A jolt of excitement raced through me.

I scanned the town, hoping to glimpse where the shop might be. Aislinn said it was next to Alice's apothecary, but the tops of the buildings offered no indication of what they might hold inside. The village was as quaint as I imagined. Buildings lined the main cobbled strip, and a well stood in the center of the town. Smoke plumed from what must be a bakery. Children ran, chasing one another.

No. Not chasing. *Running.*

The winds turned, and I could smell the smoke now. Not from baked goods but from burning buildings. From a village about to go up in flames.

"Cillian," was all I could manage, too stunned at the sight now behind us.

But Cillian was already changing direction, having scented the horrors on the shifting wind. He yelled over to Aislinn, who now flew behind us.

A conflagration threatened to overtake anything willing to burn. Buildings that weren't ablaze were overrun by a black mass of shadows. Witches either fled or drew their makeshift weapons as a host of fomorii poured into the village, screams following in their wake.

CHAPTER FORTY-EIGHT

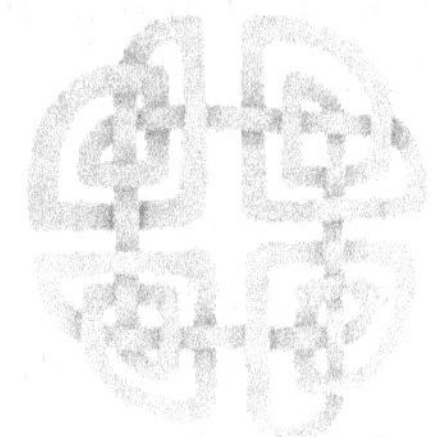

Fomorii were everywhere—more than I'd ever seen at once. Wolves like the one that attacked Eoin and me in the forest weaved between buildings. The more humanoid ones hunted the witches down with their shadows, cleaving them with their weapons without an ounce of mercy.

The flames sprouting from the buildings conflicted with the mass of black clouds, but the fomorii who weren't casting their shadows out like harpoons ran with torches, setting everything ablaze in sight—including the witches themselves. Screams pierced my ears in all directions as we landed in the heart of the town.

It was pure chaos.

Witches and witchlings alike scrambled in all directions. Shops succumbed to the flames, scattering debris throughout the cobbled road. Demons ripped apart those who stood their ground—a blur of teeth, claws, and weapons. Shadowed weapons took the shape of swords, daggers, and other deadly forms. They tore through their opponents with little resistance, their translucent armor shimmering, as if they were part of a legion acting on the orders of a higher command. I couldn't pinpoint the markings on their armor as shadows shrouded them. Several of the fomorii sat astride demon horses, trampling witches underfoot.

Some of fomorii ceased the bloodshed to grip the witches and inhaled whatever remained in a deadly kiss, their bodies morphing into husks before they were ash on the wind.

I vomited, chunks splattering my boots.

I'd seen bloodshed before, but not like this. And never had I witnessed the life, the magic, sucked out of another.

Movement out of the corner of my eye caught my attention. A man crouched atop one of the only buildings not aflame. Even from here, I could make out the broadness of his shoulders and the way his eyes glowed with the familiar red of the fomorii. It was improbable, but for a moment, we locked eyes, and I could have sworn he smiled—a general commanding his troops.

A chill skittered across my flesh.

"Saoirse," Cillian called, commanding my attention. "Use your magic to reel in the shadows while I take care of the flames. We need to try to save as much of the village as we can before it is too late."

My stomach knotted. This was too big a task. I'd just begun learning how to control them. I wasn't strong enough. "Shouldn't we worry about the fomorii instead?" I asked, taking the sapphire-hilted short blade Cillian extended toward me. Shrieks erupted from the black mass as if on cue.

"Choose, Saoirse. Either help them or they die," he said, slicing off the head of an oncoming fomorii with his long blade. The spray of its dark life's blood splattered across my face. It was an effort not to heave again at the feel and stench of it. My head swiveled between the fires threatening to consume the village, the rolling mass of shadows doing gods know what, and the horde of bloodthirsty fomorii with unnatural strength and an inability to register pain.

"Stop arguing and listen to him," Aislinn said beside me, finishing off her attacker. "You take out the shadows, pretty boy deals with the fire, and I'll keep you both alive and handle these vermin."

"There are too many of them." Even the townspeople who stayed to fight would not be enough. They were no warriors. Aislinn had said the town was made up of witches retired from the queen's service or witchlings too young to attend the academy.

"Do not fret. We have friends." Aislinn dipped her chin toward the other end of the street, where two men sliced their way through the crowd of demons.

Ronan and Eoin.

I let out a shaky laugh, but relief was temporary. If Ronan and Eoin were here, then where was Kalee? I scanned every terrified face, every remaining building, and there, behind us, Kalee led a group of witchlings away from the attack.

Why were they here? They should have been far from Ilythia by now.

Halfling? Órga's voice echoed in my head from miles away.

I'm alright, I reassured, speaking back down the strange bond. *There's a host of fomorii in Wolfhollow.*

I'm on my way. I could feel the determination in her voice. We were anamchara—she would come to my aid without hesitation, but—

Don't. You can't leave your egg unprotected. We can handle it.

You cannot tell me what to do. I am a dragon, for gods' sakes.

I pushed her retort away and prayed she stayed. *We're handling it,* I insisted, trying to convince both of us. My shadows danced along my skin, coming to life as fear threatened to consume me. I shook my head. I could do this. I *would* do this.

I inhaled deeply, centering myself as Cillian once instructed, and focused on the cloud of shadows crawling toward us. Tiny, rope-like tethers were haphazardly thrown throughout Wolfhollow.

Cillian was much faster than I. One moment, I thought my skin might melt from the sheer heat of the fire from the building closest to us. The next, it was gone, nothing but smoke remaining. Cillian gave me a nod of encouragement as he extinguished the other buildings without so much as breaking a sweat.

It was difficult not to stare at him. The sheer force the male exerted was breathtaking. I thought he'd been powerful when he was Bonded. But now with the king no longer draining him, he was unstoppable.

Cillian remained at my side, fighting off the fomorii with ease as Aislinn fought side-by-side with the other witches now that Cillian was no longer occupied. He switched between using his blade and his magic. Fomorii screamed their frustrations in his wake.

I shook out my hands, focused on the tendrils of shadows around us, and started pulling. They resisted at first, belonging to the fomorii, but eventually obeyed as they seeped into me, releasing their hold on their victims. I drank them in, absorbing them into my very being.

"Keep going!" Cillian called out beside me, though he felt a million miles away. Shadows continued to race toward me, shrieks ceasing as they did so.

My breathing threatened to turn ragged, but I couldn't stop when I was so close. Each tug on the magic grew leaden, adding more weight with each pull.

Time ceased for a moment as everyone in the village, witches and fomorii alike, turned to witness the black cloud covering half the town shrink into nothing. All eyes turned to me, surprise marring most of their faces. I had done it. *I* had done it.

I didn't know if I should be afraid of my show of power or proud of it. Maybe both. My knees threatened to buckle, but at least I'd managed to help. I didn't want to think about the fomorii. I didn't know if I had the strength to fight them.

"Little shadow," Cillian said calmly, "do you remember when your Bond broke and your magic lashed out around the tower room?"

"Yes," I managed between gasps. I would never forget the others' terror.

"I'm going to need you to do it again."

The general surveying the attack whistled with an unnatural sharpness that rang in my ears, shock and anger replacing his smug expression. At once, the fomorii pressed toward us, a battle cry on their lips.

My chest deflated. Though I'd absorbed their shadows, the well of power residing in me dwindled. It took most of my energy to steal them. What if I didn't have anything left to give? There was no time to argue, however, as the fomorii attacked with a fervor. I looked to Cillian. Determination set behind his green eyes as if knowing I had more fight within me. I pushed my boundaries further than I had before, testing my newfound strength.

This time, I didn't pull but pushed, flooding the fomorii with my magic. My chest tightened. How long would I last before exhaustion consumed me? There was the part of me linked to Órga, but her power was frightening. I didn't know how to tap into it, and I didn't want to risk hurting her.

I pressed forward, and my shadows moved with me. They raced down the line of shops—curling around the fomorii. I braced myself for their memories to overtake me, for their emotions to become my own. But none came. They were nothing more than pawns to be used, Soulless and without heart.

For a moment, I didn't know what to do. I didn't have a clear plan when I set my shadows loose, only acting on instinct. My magic curled around them, but they fought to loosen my hold. Fear threatened to take hold, and my grip slipped. I pushed it down. I wouldn't falter now. Maybe

I could hold them long enough for Cillian to lob off their heads. Gods, there were too many. I wouldn't last.

During the night the fomorii wolf attacked, there had been a moment —a heartbeat—where it was as if I tugged on its shadows instead of the environment's.

Without a second thought, I yanked on the shadows that made up the fomorii, pulling them toward me. My magic tore them apart, breaking down their very beings. One by one, they fell beneath my power and disappeared until only one remained.

"Well, that's useful," Cillian said.

Before I could verbalize the rest of my plan, he took off toward the general—a flash of gray wings. My knees gave out, and I barely had time to brace myself before I fell to the ground, hitting my elbow. Hard. I winced, searching the skies for Cillian. He could handle himself, but I shuddered to think what a fomorii general might be capable of.

Thunder and lightning greeted us once more. The storm finally caught up, releasing its contents in full. *Would have been nice a few minutes ago,* I chided as the torrential downpour worked to douse the smolders of the burning village.

Kalee rushed to my side. "Are you alright?" Her rich brown hair stuck to her face from sweat. Save for the long, thin cut slicing down her cheek, she appeared unharmed. The blue eyes of the witchlings grouped behind her widened as the shadows trickled toward me.

I nodded, but every muscle in my body barked in pain. A flash of movement caught my eye as Cillian chased after the general, Eoin and Ronan racing after them. Kalee helped me to my feet, supporting my weight against her.

"What are you doing here?" I asked.

"Eoin fell ill, so we stayed with Alice for a few more days. We'd just left when we saw a horde of fomorii headed toward Wolfhollow. It was like they appeared overnight out of nowhere." Kalee shook her head. "We stayed to help."

Bodies of the wounded and dead littered the street. My heart ached for the lifeless blue eyes staring off into the distance.

Alice ran up to us, helping Kalee shoulder my weight.

"It's good to see you again," I managed, my voice hoarse as if I'd been screaming for hours. Despite my exhaustion, I couldn't help but smile at the white-haired witch.

"I wish it were under better conditions." Her full lips pressed into a thin line as she assessed me, her healer's instincts kicking in.

"Have you seen Aislinn?" I asked, searching for her in the crowd along the street.

"A few nicks and bruises, but still alive, thank the goddess. Her boldness will be the death of her one day," Alice swore, but the corner of her mouth twitched upwards as she said it. My grin grew wider, and my shoulders sagged.

Under Alice's guidance, she and Kalee carried me to her apothecary. Somehow, the shop managed to get by with a few scorch marks on the exterior walls.

"Sit," Alice instructed before opening the cabinet closest to her, pulling out a vial of bright lavender liquid. "It won't heal you fully. You've exhausted yourself too much too fast, but it will keep you standing for a couple of hours longer."

I didn't argue as I took the vial from her. Even now, sleep threatened to consume me—my eyelids were heavy, and every bone, muscle, and fiber ached. I worried that if I kept pushing myself, I might fall into a sleep I wouldn't wake from. The potion, sweet on my tongue, instantly eased the demand for rest. I was still tired, but at least my eyes stayed open.

"How do you make these?" I asked, examining the empty vial.

She shrugged. "It's like cooking."

Before she could explain any further, the shop's bell flew off its brackets as Cillian, Ronan, and Eoin crashed through the door, the general writhing between them. I loosed a breath. Aislinn stomped in after them, her face dirt-caked and chest heaving. The general's black hair fell into his eyes, burning crimson, as they narrowed on us. Bands of fire wrapped around his torso, securing his arms against him. If he were human, his skin would have melted right then and there. But this was no human.

The fomorii general sneered down his crooked nose as Cillian pushed him to the ground, careful not to disturb Alice's various herbs, bottles, and vials filled with colorful liquids neatly organized along the shelves.

Eoin and Ronan forced the general into a chair, and Cillian added more fiery bands to strap him in place. They glowed brightly, but didn't burn the wood. Crimson eyes looked between us until the fomorii general settled on the silver shadows moving beneath my skin.

"Curious. You and I are not so different, girl," the general rasped, his voice sounded as though he swallowed a handful of broken glass.

No. I couldn't be like him. Even if I was connected to Tenebris, I was *nothing* like him. I was flesh and bone and heart and soul. The general looked as if he could slip away at any moment if he wanted to. If my shadows wrapped around him, I would feel nothing like I did with the others.

"Eyes on me," Cillian growled, and the shadowed demon complied with a lazy grin etched into his face. Despite the general's chilling words, Cillian's command sparked butterflies in my stomach. Heat bloomed beneath my cheeks as Cillian's gaze flicked to me momentarily before returning to the general, a smirk threatening his lips as if he knew exactly what those words did to me. My throat tightened.

"You waste your time thinking you can interrogate me. I was conceived from horror by Fear itself. Nothing you say or do will yield anything I do not wish to give freely."

The room stilled under the general's proclamation. Even the cries from the mourners and wounded seemed to die down outside. Kalee took a step closer to me.

"We can make the information worth your while," Eoin said, breaking the silence. My blood nearly boiled at the suggestion that we offer the general anything.

The general cocked his head, his crimson eyes gleaming. "There is nothing *you* can give me. I am merely here to deliver a message."

He was toying with us. We were pawns in a deadly game. A game that might be much more significant than we realized. If the fomorii decimated an entire village of innocents, what else were they capable of? Órga's chains flashed through my mind. Tenebris had no trouble wiping out the dragons. Had no qualms capturing and torturing Órga for his own purposes. No, the deaths of the innocents in Wolfhollow were the beginning.

"Let today serve as a reminder to those who resist. Tenebris, God of Darkness, King of Shadows, Wielder of Death and Despair, will not stop until every being who opposes him is either decimated from this gods' forsaken land or enslaved. There is no hope for survival for those who fight. Tenebris will usher in a new era. For too long, we have been banished to the Realm of Darkness, forced into our solitude. Now, we will snuff out the light. Ilythia is as good as dead unless the Witch Queen hands over the Cauldron of Power. Those who choose to stand with Tenebris will be granted mercy and, as a token of appreciation, will be given more power than their silly lives could ever hope to wield."

Bile burned the back of my throat. How could I have let my friends try to face such a threat alone?

"You are forgetting we won today," Cillian said smoothly, not bothered by the general's threat. "Why should we agree to give you anything when you are our prisoner?"

The general smiled. His beady eyes narrowed on me, assessing me once more. Eoin repositioned himself, blocking the general's gaze. Despite the relief from not being the focus of the demon's attention, I wanted to shove Eoin for thinking I couldn't handle myself.

As if I hadn't just saved all our asses.

"You have mere days before Tenebris's army marches on these lands to retrieve the cauldron. Either comply and live to see another day of your miserable lives or die an early death." The general pushed against Cillian's restraints, leaning to get a better look at me. "Tenebris would be very interested in you, shadow. Tell me, do you know which god your magic derives from? Come with me and I will tell you everything you need to know."

My stomach quivered. There was a part of me that wanted to know the answer to why I was so different from the others—what my shadows might be capable of. There was a link to Tenebris, as much as I hated to admit it, but I prayed some other unknown god was involved. I pushed Eoin to the side with more force than he thought I could muster, making him stumble.

"I'd rather die than go anywhere with you," I snarled. The king forced me to do evil, vile things before, but that didn't mean *I* was evil. I had a choice now. It didn't matter if I ever faced the truth of my magic; it wouldn't be used for malicious purposes.

"You'll come to us soon enough, shadow," the general sneered.

"Do not listen to him, niece. His time has run out," Aislinn said as Cillian drew his sword.

The general smiled. Before Cillian could deliver a killing blow, the demon vanished, leaving the chains of flame behind. He reappeared next to me, and I froze as the fomorii lunged. Aislinn pushed me away, putting herself in the path of the general.

Time stopped as he gripped her. A savage grin split his brutal face. There wasn't a second to spare to scream her name. Aislinn's face was one of resolve as she and the general evaporated in a cloud of smoke, leaving nothing but a dark stain behind.

Chapter Forty-Nine

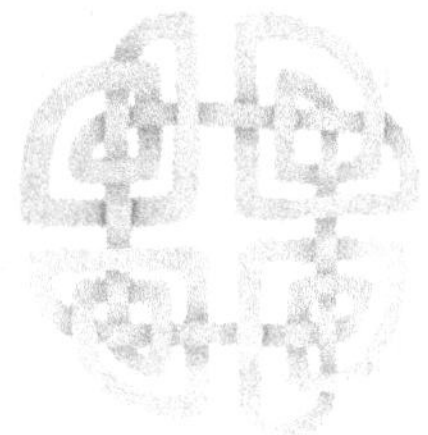

She was gone.

One moment, Aislinn defended me like my mother had. The next, she vanished like ash on the wind. And like my mother, I failed her. The fomorii demon took her to gods' knew where. He'd wanted *me*, and she sacrificed herself. Would he kill her? Torture her for the sheer pleasure of it? Endless horrors played out in my head. I was going to be sick.

There was no stopping the tremors in my hands. My heart pumped relentlessly until I couldn't breathe. No matter how hard I tried, I couldn't catch my breath. I was dying.

Aislinn was gone, and I was dying.

Steady, halfling, Órga's low voice rang in my head. Blood rushed to my ears.

You shouldn't have chosen me, Órga. I didn't deserve her. The anamchara bond was designed for protection, yet even when Aislinn was within reach, I was still powerless. How could I ever help Órga?

"Saoirse," Cillian commanded my attention by holding my face in his hands. I dragged my eyes over him, his features fuzzy. All I could focus on was how I failed Aislinn, how history was repeating itself. My chest rose and fell with rapid speed, but still, I couldn't suck down a breath. The world darkened around the edges as the last dregs of my magic pulled from the shadows of the room, trying to shield me from wide eyes.

"Saoirse," he said again, "listen to me. Breathe. I need you to take a deep breath." The concern in his voice fractured another piece of my heart.

I needed to run. To get away from eyes surveying me too closely. My magic could only do so much. I didn't need their pity or their blame. And gods, I couldn't look at Alice. Maybe not ever again.

I wrenched myself from Cillian's grasp and flung open the apothecary door. Eoin might have called my name. Or maybe Kalee. Not even Cillian could get me to stay. Nothing could erase what happened.

Aislinn was gone because of me.

Debris crunched under my boots as I stumbled over the rubble and passed bodies littering the streets. I walked until the stench of decay didn't linger in my nostrils, until the haze of smoke didn't cloud my vision.

Early signs of spring bloomed on the outskirts of Wolfhollow, untouched by the horrors of the fomorii. I took my first full breath, sucking down untainted air in greedy gulps. Tree branches swayed in the breeze, and fresh rain clung to my lashes.

Water soaked into the fabric of my pants as I sat on the sodden earth. I fumbled with my boot strings and yanked them over my heels. I needed to feel something, anything, other than the emotions threatening to take over. Damp grass squished beneath my bare feet—the action bringing back memories of my mother. Any time the world became too much, she would tell me to ground myself—to physically connect myself to the earth.

Let it calm you, she would say. It had been years since I'd done it, the action too close to her for comfort. But now, I needed her more than ever.

Wet earth leached into my back, a welcoming cold creeping over my body. It had been too long since I connected with the land. My tears mingled with raindrops. Scenes of Aislinn's capture and my mother's death played over in my mind, interweaving with one another. The circumstances were different, but the feeling of helplessness remained as they succumbed to their fate over and over. Memories of my mother's death engulfed my mind like a band of Cillian's fire.

Imaginary smoke hung heavy in the air, its thick fumes coated my lungs like they had fifteen years ago. Plumes of it sprouted from the rooftops, carrying the screams of the villagers, while my mother and I ran through the field behind our home. It hadn't rained in ages, and I could still feel the crunch of dried grass beneath my bare feet.

"I'm sorry, momma, I'm sorry," I cried, my voice small and high-pitched, once again a child, as she dragged me along. I hadn't meant to use magic. I didn't know I had magic. She told me my father had been faie, but because she was human, I didn't think I would get any. I didn't *want* any. I wanted to be like her. Human. Normal.

"Don't apologize, sweetling." Her voice was calm for someone running, still covered in blood from slicing a soldier's throat. He was the one who made my shadows appear, but it was too late. The other soldiers had already seen, and chaos erupted.

"Where are we going?" My legs hurt. I tried to run as fast as my mother, but I couldn't keep up. Despite being the fastest child in the village, I was no match for her. I slowed my mother down, too big for her to carry.

"To the tree line. We'll lose them in the forest." She pointed up ahead. It wasn't close, but it wasn't too far either.

Something whizzed between us, nicking my ear. I cried out at its sharp sting, but still we ran. An arrow protruded from the ground. A soldier on horseback followed us and nocked another into his bow. "Mom—"

"Faster, Saoirse," she urged, tugging harder. The trees were closer. "We're going to make it."

She tripped, letting go of my hand, as an arrow found its home in her thigh. The tip dripped red, the whole of the arrow still embedded in her leg. The soldier galloped toward us, his sword gripped in his hand.

"Momma!"

"Go," she urged. I grabbed her hand and pulled. She had to come with me. "Run, Saoirse."

"I–I can't." I couldn't leave her. She was everything to me. We only had each other.

The soldier was close enough to see the curl of his lip.

"Sweetling, I'll be right behind you. I need to stop the bad man first, okay?" She stood on shaking limbs. I didn't miss the wince she tried to hide.

"Okay." I nodded.

She kissed my cheek. "I love you, Saoirse. Now go and don't look back, I'll be right behind you." She spun me around and pushed me forward. I stumbled, catching myself before I hit the ground. My legs broke out into a sprint. I ran fast enough to make her proud. She didn't say where to wait for her, but she would find me. She always did when we played hide and seek.

I was steps away from the tree line when she screamed.

She told me not to look back, but I couldn't ignore the sound of her pain. It was too late. The Centran soldier's blade protruded from her chest. Without thinking, I ran toward her. She mouthed something, either "Go" or "No," I couldn't tell, but my legs had a mind of their own.

The whites of her eyes widened. She hadn't been afraid before, but when she saw me running in the wrong direction—

The soldier caught up to me in seconds. Blood poured from her chest as she reached toward me. The look on her face burned into me like a scar —the starkness of it fading over time but with me forever.

It wasn't long after that when I was bound to the king and forced to mourn her death in silence as he used my magic. I couldn't control it at first, but the king was interested in my shadows nonetheless. The king honed my magic by having his men hunt me down. If I were caught, I was punished. Once I gained a semblance of control, he sent me on missions. Small at first. Then they became more deadly over time.

A groan escaped my lips as I shoved the memories away. When my Bond was broken, I thought things would be different. I thought I'd be stronger. My hands dug into the grass. Soil wedged its way under my nails. Cillian said I wielded my magic better every day, but it wasn't enough to save Aislinn. Maybe I'd never be enough to help those I cared about.

You are hurting, halfling. Órga's voice flitted in my head.

I am broken beyond repair. I don't know why you agreed to be my anamchara, I said, the tremble in my voice apparent, even in my mind. *I don't deserve your comfort.*

Do not say such things. You think you are weak, but you are stronger than you realize.

I couldn't save her. I couldn't save either of them.

You speak as if she is already dead.

She's as good as.

So you're choosing to give up now when there's still hope?

No, I—I didn't say that.

You cannot change what happened, but you control what you do next. That's what defines us. You are quick to place the blame on yourself, but your aunt made her decision. She chose to save you.

How Órga knew the details—I didn't ask. Couldn't because her words sliced into me, burrowing deeper until they took hold.

Do not let forces outside your command control and shape who you are, she continued. *Forge your own path. You can succumb to that which threatens your collapse, or you can rise above it. In that, you always have a choice.*

Órga withdrew from my mind, leaving me to mull over her words. Cillian had said much of the same before. Their sentiments seeped into me like a steady drizzle of rain. Hardly noticeable at first, until I was soaked from head to toe. The gray sky shifted overhead and gave way to sunlight. Warmth tickled in, breaking through the cold of the damp earth. Perhaps they were right. With my mother's death, I was defenseless. Scared. A child, for gods' sakes. If anyone else told the same story, I wouldn't cast the blame on them. Wouldn't expect so much from a child.

So why, then, did I expect it of myself?

I shook my head.

No matter how strong I became or how much magic I had, I couldn't control what others did. Bond or no Bond, I couldn't prevent death. Couldn't take back what happened. All I could do was my best as I am now. Órga was right. Aislinn was gone, but there was still time to get her back. I lorded no control over Fate, but Fate be damned. I wasn't giving up.

HARDLY ANY TIME HAD PASSED SINCE I RAN OUT OF ALICE'S APOTHECARY, yet it was as if I'd been gone for days. My steps were sluggish from exhaustion, but my mind was clear. Everyone stood in Alice's apothecary, where I'd left them as if everything had ceased since that moment. As if all my problems waited for me instead of solving themselves.

There would be no running.

No one questioned the blades of grass clinging to my hair or the dirt wiped on my trousers. I returned Cillian's raised brow with a subtle nod. *I'm alright.*

"She is still alive," Alice reassured, though tears lined her eyes. "I can feel it."

I blew out a breath. We still had time.

"What do you mean you can feel her?" Kalee asked, her usual pristine appearance battered and worn. Alice must have loaned her more clothing. It wasn't the full skirts that the Centran women were expected to wear, nor was it the tight-fitting leathers of the witches at the Mountain Castle. It was somewhere in between. Her flowing skirt had slits on either side up to her hips, allowing for easy movement, and the fabric covering her legs appeared flexible and form-fitting. It suited her.

"She is my anamchara," Alice said. "I can feel her emotions through our bond. It's stretched too thin to communicate, but she's there."

Why does distance limit them? I asked Órga. She said we could communicate no matter how far apart we were with our bond. Why was it different for Aislinn and Alice?

I am a dragon, she said simply as if it were the only explanation I needed.

"What is she feeling now?" I asked, my voice hoarse as if I'd been screaming for hours.

"At first, there was anger, then confusion, and then it was as if someone threw a woolen blanket over our connection. She's a whisper to me now. As if she left Rúndaiaithe completely." Alice's brows furrowed in confusion.

Perhaps she has left this realm for another, Órga chimed in.

My throat went dry. *You mean to say she was taken to the Shadow Realm?*

"We have to get her back," I choked. I had only just found her. I wouldn't let her go so soon. If she were taken to the Shadow Realm, there was no telling what horrors she would face there.

Alice nodded. "We will, but first I must speak with the queen."

"But—" I argued.

"We do not know where the general took her or how to find her. We do, however, know where he's going and what he wants. He'll use Aislinn against us. We'll get her back."

"Alice is right," Ronan added. "We have a better chance at saving her with an army behind us."

An owl hooted from the rafters and flew toward us, landing neatly in front of Alice. A ring of dark feathers surrounded his tawny eyes. Different shades of browns and whites speckled his rounded body. Aislinn hinted at Alice's familiar when we first arrived, but I hadn't had a chance to see the animal. Quill and parchment in hand, Alice scribbled something down and handed it to the owl.

"Deliver this to Petra. I'll follow shortly." Alice's familiar puffed up his tawny feathers at her request. He studied me, twisting his head at an unnatural angle, waiting. Cillian opened the door, letting the bird fly off toward the castle.

"If the fomorii can disappear and reappear at will, we should assume they'll make themselves known directly at the castle." Ronan paced. "And if bands of magical fire can't hold him, then I fear we will need more than magic on our side."

"They won't be able to appear into the castle, not with the wards in place," Alice explained. "The wards are different around the castle than the willows bordering Ilythia. They were forged from the Cauldron of Power itself. The Mountain Castle is nearly impenetrable, and no unwanted creature may pass. They would have to break through them first. Even then, that would be nearly impossible."

"How come we were able to get into the castle?" I asked.

"You were escorted by a witch." Alice gestured to Ronan. "It allowed you to pass."

"But Aislinn–" I started, recognizing the fomorii's upper hand. Whether the general realized it or not, I didn't know, and I didn't want to find out.

"Aislinn would sooner die than risk Ilythia's stronghold."

The lump in my throat was hard to swallow. Alice's tone left little doubt. We needed to get Aislinn back before she was forced to choose between her life and her kingdom.

The windows rattled and glass vials clanked under a thundering boom. The earth itself shuddered under Órga's massive form.

"Nines, that's hard to get used to," Ronan muttered.

"Aislinn wasn't kidding when she said you found a dragon." Alice gaped at Órga.

I couldn't help the grin that broke my lips as a golden eye peered into the window.

"How is this possible?" Alice marveled, her mouth hanging open. Órga was breathtaking. Her scales glittered in the sunlight, the golden ones peppered throughout, sparkling as if they were made of the precious metal itself.

"Long story," I said before everyone rushed outside the shop to greet her, careful of her talons. Alice was too preoccupied with Órga to notice the lavender potions I swiped.

You are feeling better. Órga's snout dipped toward me once I stepped out of the apothecary. It wasn't a question. She said it with certainty, as if she could feel the small, rekindled spark.

Yes, thanks to you. Her snout was warm against my fingertips.

"Alice, this is my anamchara, Órga." Her lone silver scale glittered brighter than all the others.

"Anamchara?" Eoin asked, his brows furrowed. "When did this happen?"

"This morning, actually." I braced myself for Eoin's lecture, but none came.

"Anamchara? By the Goddess, I have many questions, but none we have time for." The wonder in Alice's gaze darkened. "If any of you wish to leave now, go. Fly to Arundell if you must."

Ronan stepped forward, resting his hand on Alice's shoulder. "What kind of nephew would I be if I didn't offer my help?"

Eoin gave a single nod, following Ronan wherever he would go until he was able to chase his own dream in life. No matter how complicated our friendship had become, I wanted to believe the best of him. He'd shown his loyalty over and over again.

Kalee took Ronan's hand, and I smiled. I adored the love my friend had found.

They all looked at me, waiting for my answer. Cillian hadn't given one yet, but my heart told me he would follow me to the Otherworld if I asked.

I surveyed the ruins of Wolfhollow. There wasn't much left of the village. The apothecary and a few of the nearby buildings were some of the only structures still standing. But there was one building I hadn't seen yet… My heart stilled for a moment.

The bookstore. *My* bookstore.

While the apothecary remained mostly untouched aside from a few scorch marks, the building next to it hadn't been so lucky. What had been my future stood in ruins. A lump formed in my throat as I choked my tears down.

Alice rested her hand on my shoulder as she awaited my decision. She was giving me a choice. I could keep running, find another dream, and finally experience my freedom. I was no longer Bound. Decisions were mine to make. But running would not stop evil from coming. And I would not let my friends—my family—out of my sight again. No bookstore, no dream of a peaceful life could bring Aislinn back or staunch my grief.

I lifted my chin, looking Alice in the eye as I said, "I am with you."

"You worry too much," Queen Petranella drawled, studying the parchment organized in neat stacks across her desk. An array of weapons and books filled the council room. She idly stroked the raven perched at her desk, unconcerned with the news of her sister. Niamh, Flore, and Ahlani all stood behind her, hands resting on their weapons.

"You do not worry enough, Petra," Alice hissed. "Did you hear nothing of what I said? They have her. They aim to take the cauldron, too."

"For Goddess's sake, Alice. No army, immortal or not, has ever breached these castle walls." Queen Petranella paused to glare at us. "Even if these fools made it through because they had a witch in their midst, the cauldron is safe. You know better than most that Aislinn can handle her own. And besides—" she shrugged, "we have a dragon. And her, it sounds like."

It was an effort not to shrink under her narrowed gaze. Petra was mistaken. I didn't know if I could use my magic like I had in Wolfhollow again. Even now, Alice's potion kept me standing. Her brew was potent, but I would eventually succumb to the exhaustion.

"They appeared in Wolfhollow with no warning. Not even the wards at the border alerted us." Alice tried to get through to the queen, but we had been in her council chamber for over an hour. Despite the fate of her sister, the queen remained unconcerned. Though stone-faced, I hadn't missed the flash of surprise from Niamh at the mention of the fomorii.

"If it will put your mind at ease, we'll strengthen the wards around the castle, but I assure you they are firmly intact. No magic can be used against them, and no trespassers will be allowed through."

"What if they use her to gain entry?" I asked.

"Aislinn knows her duty. She would die before escorting the enemy into her home," Queen Petranella said coldly, repeating Alice's statement.

"What about your subjects in neighboring villages? No one is safe." The general promised destruction. There would be no leniency, no mercy to those who opposed Tenebris. If the queen objected, then the whole of Ilythia would be caught in his wrath.

"They'll be notified, but I assure you, they can protect themselves. Not all of my subjects are as soft as those in Wolfhollow." Her biting gaze was as sharp as any sword.

Shadows swirled beneath me, and sconces flickered throughout the room. How could someone so ignorant be allowed to rule a kingdom? How could she refuse to help her own sister?

"Leave me," the queen commanded. "If you're so concerned, rest while you can before this army arrives. You, yourself, said it would only be a matter of days."

"Petra—"

"Aislinn will escape, Alice. Demons are of no threat to her; powerful blood runs through our veins. Or, if you wish, try to rescue her. It is of no matter to me, but my soldiers shall remain here."

"If she dies," I said, voice low, "her blood is on your hands."

Chapter Fifty

"Saoirse." Cillian snapped his fingers in front of my face, startling me out of my doze.

"What?" I bolted upright from my slumped position in the hardwood chair. Had the fomorii come already? I waited for the chaos of witches running down the halls, but there was nothing save for the rustle of parchment and the soft flicker of lanterns in the library.

"You're doing it again."

"I'm fine," I yawned, returning to the same paragraph I'd read at least five times. Cillian raised a pointed brow.

"You're allowed to sleep, Sersh," Ronan said, not bothering to look up from the parchments sprawled out in front of him.

"Not until we can find something to help her."

The witches had shooed us away from trying to prepare for Tenebris's army. No one could deny the fomorii's existence after the attack on Wolfhollow, but like their queen, they weren't nearly as concerned as I wanted them to be. Everyone seemed to share the belief that no matter what was to come, the castle couldn't be overrun, and Ilythia would prevail.

Even Petranella grew tired of my pestering and relinquished access to her private library. We hadn't found anything of use in the castle library that was open to the public before, but maybe we would have better luck here and discover more details about who we were up against.

"You're being ridiculous," Eoin said. "No one will think any less of you if you sleep."

"Nobody asked you, Eoin," I snapped. "Please, for gods' sakes, say something useful for once." I regretted the words as soon as they left my tongue. He hadn't had any bite to his tone—he'd wanted to help.

The silence was so stagnant that even Kalee peeled her attention away from her book.

Eoin's lips thinned. I winced as the legs of his chair screeched across the wooden floor before he stormed out.

"Eoin, wait," I called to his back. Our footsteps echoed down the empty hall as I ran after him. "Please stop."

He turned, nostrils flaring. "What do you want from me?"

"I'm sorry for what I said. I know you meant well. It was wrong of me to chastise you, and I feel guilty for how we left things. I want us to be amicable."

"Saoirse, I—" Eoin sighed, reaching out to touch me, but must have thought better of it because he pulled away. "I've replayed our last conversation since I left. I'm sorry for what I said. I was out of line." Eoin blew out a long breath. "I wanted to keep you with me so I know you're safe. Sometimes I can't help but lash out with my words. I know I don't handle myself as well as the others, and I'm trying. I care for you. You know that, right?"

"I know. I care for you, too, I do, but I need space to learn who I am without my Bond. I'll make mistakes and do things I probably shouldn't. I know I should get some rest before they come. But I *can't*. I can't stop thinking about Aislinn. I have to feel like I'm doing something, or else I'm letting her down."

Eoin's shoulders sagged. "I'm sure it must be difficult, but you can't help us find her if you're half-asleep." No one knew about the potions I snagged from Alice's apothecary, but he had a point.

"You're right. Just a little longer, and then I'll get some rest, alright?"

"Alright." The corners of his mouth turned up, his first smile at me in ages. I returned it, the animosity dissolving between us.

"Friends?" I asked. It wasn't what he coveted, but it was all I could give, and I wanted Eoin in my life, just not intimately.

"Friends," he confirmed, though hurt flashed in his eyes.

We walked back to the library together, content with the silence between us. Cillian's expression was wary, but his posture remained relaxed.

"Have you two finally made up?" Ronan asked, leaning back in his chair. Eoin flicked the back of his head in answer. "A simple 'yes' will do." Ronan rubbed the area, and I pressed my lips together, fighting a grin, as I took my seat next to Cillian. His hand found mine beneath the table, his touch feather-light until he squeezed, grounding me to him.

"I've got something," Kalee said, looking up from the ancient, fraying tome in front of her.

I twisted in my seat, leaning to peer over her shoulder. She pointed to an illustration featuring a fomorii with clearer features than we have encountered thus far. Fomorii were shrouded in shadows, but this man—this man was otherworldly. Flawless. Shadows as black as a starless sky swirled beneath his skin.

"Tenebris," I whispered. Like me, Tenebris's shadows lived within him. The fomorii were merely an extension of his darkness.

The Shadow King stared at us with cold, crimson eyes down his straight nose. Not a divot on his stone face save for the scar running through his brow. His black hair was longer and sleeker than Ronan's, coming down to his elbows.

Chills erupted across my skin.

"What does it say?" Ronan asked.

"It mostly confirms what the seer told us and what we found in the *History of the Gods*. But it also speaks of god-born objects," Kalee answered.

"As in more than the Cauldron of Power?" Eoin asked, coming to stand behind us.

"Four objects created by the Mother and gifted to her children as a show of appreciation. A cauldron to provide for those in need. A sword to cut through deception. A spear to pierce resistance, and a stone to validate the sovereignty of the land," Kalee read.

I rubbed my temple. "And where are these other objects?"

"It states that when the gods made their permanent home in the Otherworld, they gifted their objects to their successors in each region to help maintain peace and preserve the land. The stone to the north, the sword to the east, the spear to the south, and the cauldron to the west. We know the cauldron has stayed in Ilythia, so it's safe to assume the stone would be in Arundell, the sword in Sóngnahánn, which leaves the spear in the Barrens."

"There's nothing in the Barrens," I argued. "Lest it's buried under sand. And what about Centra? Were they not given anything?"

"You forget," Ronan interrupted, "Centra didn't exist when the kingdoms were first created. Centra was formed as a middle ground after the gods had already moved on. My great, great, great, great grandfather left all he knew in the Barrens to create a neutral territory for those who wanted to live in harmony."

Cillian crossed his arms over his broad chest. "Ilythia would have had to give up some of its land to your ancestor. Why would they do that?"

"Natural charm and charisma? I haven't the slightest idea." Ronan shrugged.

"So your great, great, great grandfather—" I started.

"Four greats," Ronan corrected.

"Great, great, great, *great-grandfather* would have taken the spear with him to Centra then."

"He didn't rule the Barrens. He established Centra with nothing but an idea and the clothes on his back."

"Ambition must run in the family," I muttered and gave Ronan an apologetic look. "If your father was able to gain more land and overpower other kingdoms, then we should assume he has at least one object. But which one?"

"This says not all objects were made equal, and some of the first rulers were offended by their gifts. For centuries, they fought over which was given to them and sought to collect them all. It wasn't until they learned of the objects' true potential for destruction that they decided to sign a treaty to end their bickering by keeping the objects in their original kingdoms. They tried to convince everyone to forget about the god-born objects. Whichever one the Conqueror King might have, he would have stolen it and would've been aware of its existence."

"Wouldn't it be for the best if everyone knew about the god-born objects?" I asked. People had a right to know what exactly their kingdoms and rulers were capable of.

"Not if they wanted to keep people from seeking them. Something like that could change who holds the power," Eoin said, his thumb and forefinger stroking his jaw. "But what if the king doesn't have an object? He hasn't made a move on any of the other kingdoms. Maybe one of the other rulers broke the treaty over the centuries and took it, or perhaps the spear is hidden in the Barrens."

I prayed Eoin was right. The king was powerful enough; he didn't need a god-born object on his side. But— "How did he manage to take Sóngnahánn's islands then? Or overpower the osnádúrtha?"

"My father has the spear," Ronan confirmed grimly. "I was only a boy, and I haven't seen it since, but I remember him carrying a spear when he left to take Sóngnahánn. I didn't think anything of it until now."

"Was that why he attacked Sóngnahánn? To get the sword too?" Cillian asked. "Furthermore, what's stopping him from going after another kingdom? It's been over a decade, and he's yet to make another move."

"I don't know. I'm not privy to my father's plans." Ronan shook his head and ran a hand through his hair, shaking the blonde strands. "Sóngnahánn actively rebelled against him after he started capturing and Bonding with merrows. I don't recall him carrying a sword other than the one he had long before the attack on Sóngnahánn."

"Kalee, does it say anything more about the cauldron?" I asked. The other objects were a problem for another day. We needed to save Aislinn now. Maybe the cauldron was our answer.

"Yes. It was intended to feed the land and provide for its people. The Cauldron of Power is arguably the strongest of the four objects. When in experienced hands, it can turn the tide of any battle. It can heal any wound, whether minor or fatal, as well as…" Kalee trailed off, her expression deepened.

"What?"

She looked up, her face pale. "It can also bring back the dead."

My heart stopped in my chest, my thoughts immediately going to my mother. What if I could save her after all?

Ronan must have read the idea on my face because he said, "Sersh… your mother…she wouldn't be the same." He gripped my shoulder. "Trust me, I would do anything to bring my own mother back, but nothing good comes from disturbing the dead. If I were to guess, they would be more like the undead soldiers who attacked us when we first sought the cauldron."

"I know," I scoffed, hiding my embarrassment. "It was stupid even to consider it. We don't have to bring them back, but that doesn't mean we can't use them to help Aislinn now."

Ronan ran another hand through his hair. "The cauldron may be too dangerous."

"What good is an all-powerful god-born object if we can't do anything with it?" The wooden legs of my chair scraped against the floor—an awful screech in an otherwise quiet library. I paced, needing to sort out my thoughts. "We will have to convince the queen this is our only option, even if she doesn't see it now."

"What if Tenebris comes?" Cillian asked, rubbing his jaw. "What happens if the fomorii are successful in helping him escape his prison? It says only gods may be defeated by their creations through the use of god-born objects," Cillian said, reading over Kalee's shoulder. "We only have the cauldron. We may need the other objects if we are to face him."

"If Tenebris wants the cauldron so badly, perhaps he needs it to escape his prison, and that's why he's sending his fomorii in his stead," Ronan offered.

"Then he cannot get it. No matter the cost." I scanned the text. "Because killing a god is awfully complicated."

Cillian nodded his agreement and pulled me into his lap. His warmth radiated, but did little to comfort me.

"If it comes to it, the seer said his blood must be used to defeat him," Kalee said, rummaging through the well of information we received. "But, according to the story of the Serpent and the Sparrow, Tenebris killed all his children."

"Maybe it's referring to his creations," I suggested. "Could we convince one of the fomorii to kill its creator?" As soon as the words left my lips, I knew the idea was absurd. The general was proof enough as to where their loyalties lay.

"I don't think the seer told us everything," Kalee murmured, her eyes moving back and forth as she flipped through the pages.

"Of course, the seer didn't," I laughed darkly, expecting Kalee to also find humor in the situation. But there was none. My stomach rolled at her wince.

"Tenebris did kill all his children—save one. A babe hidden in her mother's womb. His line lived on."

All of their gazes shifted to my silver shadows.

Bile burned in my throat as I looked between them at the implication that lay there.

"No."

But as much as I tried to deny or ignore it, the shadows living beneath my flesh said otherwise. I'd always suspected something tied me to Tenebris, but this… This was absurd. I couldn't be related to him by blood.

Kalee and Cillian only stared, then glanced at each other, a look of understanding passing between them. I turned to Ronan for help, but his gaze was glued on the parchment in front of him, his complexion paler than usual. Even Eoin, who always had something to say, offered nothing.

"It can't be me," I said. Fuck Fate. This wasn't happening. *I* wasn't destined to be the one to stop him. The world was doomed if this was to be dumped on my shoulders.

"If there's any consolation, it seems you're not alone," Ronan rasped, pushing the parchment he held toward me. Kalee peered over my shoulder. She gasped, comprehending it faster than I could. It was a list of names. A family tree. It meant nothing until—my mother's name, etched in neat script, her sister's next to hers at the bottom. Someone had taken the liberty of adding mine, Ronan's, Ceana's, and even my brother Bran's beneath them. I followed up the interconnecting lines until I reached the top of the parchment. Calista and next to it—

Tenebris.

"No. The parchment is wrong. Who keeps records for so long? It's inaccurate," I said again, as if I said it enough, it would become true. I snatched up the parchment again. "Look, Petranella's name isn't on here. It's wrong."

"All the records kept here are done so by magic," Kalee said, her brows furrowing. "Flore told me herself. There's a reason everything here is so well preserved. Think about it, Sersh. Your mother and Ronan's were both murdered."

I halted my pacing, whipping my head to her. "You think—"

"They were killed because of whose blood ran through their veins, and Tenebris is picking off the remainder of his bloodline one by one? Yes."

"Kalee," I pleaded. It was bad enough that they died, but this idea was preposterous.

"Why was the Queen of Centra murdered at all?" Her voice was steady, trying to get me to see the reason within her words.

"Why does Ronan still live, then? Why Aislinn or Petranella or myself? They are a part of this, too, if the line flows through them." The silhouette of my mother's protection spell whispered to me as if this was the reason it was placed. Not solely because of some faie squabble. But because perhaps she somehow knew there were other forces at work. Would Aislinn live for much longer? Alice had reassured me she still felt her anamchara, but in what condition? If what Kalee said was true, then Aislinn was in more danger than we thought.

Kalee shook her head. "I can't be certain. But I can't shake the feeling that the Conqueror King somehow figured out his wife was linked to Tenebris. Why else would he hunt for you and your mother, killing her and Binding you when he couldn't dispose of you because of your mother's protection spell?"

"It still doesn't explain why Ronan or Ceana still breathe!"

Both Ronan and Eoin were silent, offering no reason behind these inane theories.

"I don't know why we're alive," Ronan said at last. "But even my father cannot live forever. As far as Aislinn and Petranella, well, you know as well as anyone, Ilythia is shrouded in secret. Its borders are well protected."

"And now?"

"Maybe this is his goal," Kalee said, her amber eyes going distant. "To kill off any remaining descendants before he breaks free. Tenebris must be getting stronger if the fomorii are appearing more and more. Maybe all he needs is for them to steal the cauldron so he may free himself."

Ronan stood, turning his back to the parchment etched with our family tree—from the mantle that had been thrust upon us. "One thing we do know is that we're fucked."

CHAPTER FIFTY-ONE

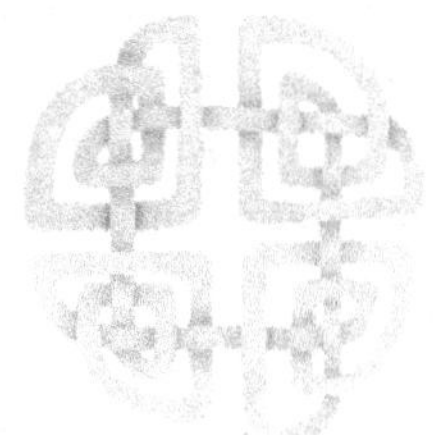

"If the fomorii are going to use Aislinn as leverage when they come, they'll show their hand before any fighting begins," Cillian said the following morning, leaning against one of the pillars in the aerie.

"That's where you come in, our scaly friend." Ronan splayed his hands as if there was no other obvious choice. For someone who'd been terrified to approach her, the prince had grown comfortable around my anamchara. It probably helped that I promised she wouldn't eat him as long as he behaved.

Órga huffed her response, her body warming the chilled air.

Am I only to swoop down and snatch her, or can I incinerate them, too?

"No fire," I said. "Unless Aislinn is out of harm's way, then burn them to ash."

An approving rumble shook the aerie.

After what seemed like hours, we finally settled on a plan to rescue Aislinn. Our best chance was Órga. She'd been left for dead on the mountain and they wouldn't expect a dragon. No one would.

"Then it's settled," Eoin said. "As soon as Aislinn appears, Saoirse will call to Órga—or whatever it is you do—and then Órga will take Aislinn to the southern area of the castle, where Kalee and Alice will meet them to help tend to her if needed. The rest of us will remain with the queen to handle the aftermath."

"I want to ride with Órga when she rescues her," I said.

"No. You can find her later if you want, but it could arouse suspicion if the general notices. The five of us and Alice need to be within the general's sight. Otherwise, he may suspect we're up to something."

I wanted to argue, to remind Eoin he couldn't tell me what to do, but he was right. And I wasn't about to risk losing Aislinn to prove a point.

"Assuming all goes well, we'll have her back in no time," Cillian added with a reassuring smile.

"That's a lot to assume," I grumbled. "We still don't know if they are oblivious to her lineage." Tenebris wouldn't want Aislinn alive, bait or not, unless they used her to get through the wards first.

"The general has no reason to assume who she really is. For all we know, Tenebris may be completely unaware he shares blood with your family," Kalee offered.

If Aislinn is there, it will go well. Órga's snout pressed into me, nearly knocking me over, but the gesture was comforting nonetheless. Even if I was quick to doubt myself, I didn't doubt Órga. As long as everything went to plan, Órga would rescue her.

I repeated the thought long after we left the aerie, chanting it over and over. If the gods had any business left in the mortal world, I prayed they would hear my pleas. At least this once.

"Faster, Saoirse," Cillian instructed. My shadows chased after him as he evaded my magic's grip. I flung tendril after tendril at him as I'd done in Wolfhollow. There was nothing left to do to prepare for Aislinn's rescue, and they couldn't sit around, waiting for the fomorii to show. I wanted to be ready.

After some much-needed rest, I begged Cillian for another training lesson, though this one was vastly different from our last. My gaze drifted to the spot on the wall where Cillian held me the last time we were here.

"Focus," he said with an irritating lilt in his voice. A tendril of my magic raced toward him and wrapped around his ankle. Before he had a chance to evade me again, I yanked, knocking him on his ass. "Much better." Cillian gave me an appreciative nod as I helped him to his feet.

"Let's try something else."

"What else is there?" I asked, wiping the thick sheen of sweat from my brow.

"The attack in Wolfhollow got me thinking." Cillian unsheathed his sword, and in an instant, the blade was ablaze with his fire. "Try extending your magic down your sword and hold it there."

I unsheathed Cillian's short blade from the standard-issued scabbard Niamh lent me from the armory. The cool blue hue of the weapon glimmered in the dim light, and within moments, my shadows surrounded it. Instead of making the blade invisible, it wrapped around it, the shadows alive and mobile, mimicking the way they moved across my skin. I beamed at Cillian; rarely did I get things on the first try.

"Excellent, now a shield." In his other hand, Cillian conjured a shield of orange fire. My lips parted.

"Why don't you do that more often?"

"Using magic takes energy. You have to know when it's best to conserve and when to use everything you've got. If you're without a shield and in a pinch, use it. Now, same idea as the blade. Imagine holding a shield, and let your magic take shape."

I tried to do as he asked, but it was harder to build something from nothing. My shadows wobbled, resembling a shield if you squinted hard enough.

"You have to imagine it's as sturdy as a real shield," Cillian instructed, surveying the magic. "I shouldn't be able to poke my hand through it."

"They're shadows for gods' sakes."

"They're magical shadows. The laws of nature do not burden them. Reinforce them."

I huffed out a breath and pictured the thickest, sturdiest shield I could conjure, and the shadows stiffened. Cillian swung before I could celebrate. I cursed, narrowly blocking his blade. The heat of his fire licked toward me, but my shield held, thank the Nine.

"Thanks for the warning, asshole."

"You won't receive one in battle." His green gaze narrowed, any trace of amusement gone. My heart pulsed once. Twice. Cillian attacked. He slashed, I dodged. I thrusted and he parried, dancing around me until I was panting. But still, my shield held, as did the shadows along my sword.

"You're a natural," Cillian said, finally allowing me to rest. "Your endurance is improving."

I took the proffered canteen of water and drank deeply. "Thanks."

"One last thing, and then we'll call it for tonight. I don't want you expending too much energy." Cillian handed me a bow from along the rack on the rear wall.

"Any arrows?"

"Make them," he instructed, and I did as he asked, picturing the sharpest arrow in the bow's notch. I pulled back, aiming at one of the training dummies in the far corner of the room. The arrow struck true before disappearing, but not before leaving a small hole in its place.

"You picked that up much faster than I did," he said, kissing my temple.

"So you admit I'm better than you?"

"Always," he said before sweeping me into a kiss. "Now, let's get you something to eat."

A male after my own heart. My stomach growled in agreement.

Chapter Fifty-Two

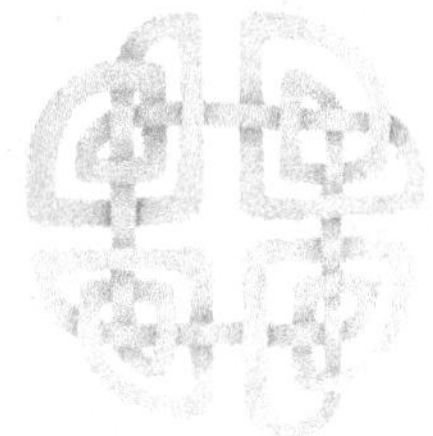

Warmth radiated from the blankets wrapped around me, from the pillow cradling my cheek—from the heat at my back. I anticipated the soft brush of pages turning, Kalee waiting for me to rise. I held my breath, dreading the moment when the Bond Mark would spring to life. But it wouldn't. Realization flooded in just as juniper and spice flooded my senses, something so unmistakably *him* filling the room.

My breath caught. Not only had I forgotten where I was, but I forgot I asked Cillian to stay—to chase away the thoughts that liked to stall sleep. I didn't open my eyes. Not yet. Not when the world outside seemed miles away. Especially not with Cillian's arm draped over me, his hand splayed over my stomach, holding me like he had the night in the tent. Tenderly. Possessively.

He shifted, his lips brushing against my hair.

"You're awake," he said, voice laden with sleep.

"So are you." The veil of sleep lifted, and reality, along with what we must prepare for, stumbled in. We needed to rise. To train. To see if there was anything left to be done.

"Don't go, not yet," he pleaded.

I didn't. Cillian tightened his hold, pulling me close enough for his heartbeat to thump against my back. Solid and steady. He trailed his hand up my side, running his thumb over my cheek.

"There is still time, you know. If you want to change your mind."

I stilled. "Are you asking me to?"

"I'm not Eoin. I won't force your decision to align with what I think is best, but I want you to have the opportunity to decide without an audience, knowing what we are up against."

"We have to get her back."

"I know," he whispered and placed a gentle kiss on my head.

"Do you think we'll succeed?"

"The queen believes we will. But something doesn't sit right."

"What are you implying?"

"Why warn us at all? Why allow us to defend ourselves when they clearly have the advantage of surprise?"

I bit the inside of my cheek. "Maybe the general is toying with us? Or he wants to scare the witches into joining them? Or what if they don't have a leg to stand on, and they're bluffing in hopes of compliance?"

"Maybe…or they're using this as a distraction."

"To get to the cauldron?" My brows furrowed, recalling what Alice said about the wards. "Do you think one of the witches will steal the cauldron for Tenebris while the fight ensues?"

"It's only a thought," he said, but his tone told me he'd been contemplating it for some time.

"We should go to one of the trio." They were the only ones besides Alice who took our concerns seriously.

"We will." He nodded. "I bet we can probably catch Flore preparing healing poultices. But first, how are you feeling?"

"I'm fine. Just tired." My stomach growled. "…and starving."

"I shouldn't have pushed you as hard as I did yesterday."

"No, I needed it. It helps me focus."

Cillian ran his hand along my arm as if he couldn't help but touch me. As if I would vanish at any moment. "Don't worry, we'll build your tolerance."

"How?"

"Think of it as like exercising. The more you train and use your magic, the better you get at it and the more you can expend. Just be careful of using too much too soon; you could exhaust yourself and lose control. It could be a sleep you don't wake from." He traced the silver shadows swirling on my arm. They wiggled under his touch, begging to play with his fire. "You're building your control quickly, but you could barely stand without Alice's potion the other day. It's my fault. I'm sorry."

"You knew I could do it, and I did. I was exhausted, still am, really, but at what point does the well of power run dry?" If I had the time and peace of mind, I could probably sleep for days, yet there was more power circling low within, waiting to be used. Not counting the part belonging to Órga, though I was still too afraid to go near it.

"It's hard to say. Each faie is different. I can disperse my power constantly over days, whereas someone else may only last a few minutes before it dies out. We can train all we like, but at some point, everyone reaches their limit. I've been around for many years, and all this time, I've never met someone like you."

"What do you mean?"

"No other faie has their power on display at all times. Or can wield shadows, for that matter."

"You think it's because of Tenebris's blood running through my veins?" I whispered. It was a hard truth to swallow, but there was no denying it. Not with the family tree linking me to him. The faie received their powers from the gods. Tenebris was one of them. Even though his kinship stemmed from my mother's line, my magic presented itself as faie.

Cillian turned me toward him, our bodies flush. My heart thumped against my ribs, threatening to break free. Save for our time in the training room, this was the closest we'd been. Even then, he'd been fully clothed. Cillian was bare now save for his sleeping pants, his upper body all packed muscle and hard lines. I forced my gaze to meet his eyes, trying not to ogle outright.

"It doesn't matter what blood runs through your veins or who your magic comes from. They are *yours* and you are extraordinary."

As much as worry tried to hold its place in my mind, Cillian's comforting strokes on my back dispelled any of it. Green eyes roamed over my face, down to the lack of space between us, and finally landed on where my hand rested dangerously low on his abdomen, my fingers, having a mind of their own, tracing the dip in his hip—a perfect v dropping beneath his waistband..

An audible rumble sounded, but it wasn't hunger I was consumed by.

"We should find you something to eat," Cillian whispered, his lips a hair's breadth away from mine.

"I've gone without for longer. I can wait a little while more," I said before I kissed him, not giving him a moment to object. Cillian tried to hold himself above me, but I used his momentum against him—straddling my thighs on either side of his torso, defined from years of work.

My unbound hair shielded us from the responsibilities we ignored. None of those thoughts crossed my mind as we kissed—a clash of teeth and tongues from desperation that seeded itself long ago.

I hadn't been able to stop thinking about what happened in the training room, hadn't been able to stop thinking about him. I cursed myself for denying what lay between us for so long. I did it out of respect for Eoin because I'd known him first. Felt like I owed it to Eoin to see if there was something between us. But now he knew where we stood, and there was nothing to hold me back.

Cillian's hands dug into my hips, guiding my movements as I ground against him. He growled into me—the evidence of his desire pulsed between us. I kissed him deeper, my hands roaming over his torso. Muscles twitched under my touch in the most delightful way.

"Little shadow," he groaned at another one of my teasing touches, gooseflesh prickling in its wake.

"What?" I asked innocently, running my fingers along the area right above the band of his pants, where his muscles contracted most violently.

"You tease too much," was my only warning before he flipped us.

Cillian's weight settled onto me, housing me in a shelter of his own making, his cock pressing into my groin. He locked my hands in a hold, lavishing me with kisses.

"You're one to talk," I gasped as his tongue licked up the column of my neck, fueling the flame already blazing within.

Cillian chuckled against me, and his breath shivered down my spine. "It's more fun when I'm the one to do the teasing." He held me in place to do just that until I could do nothing but squirm under his touch.

"Cillian," I growled.

"Not so fun, is it?" He laughed but released his hold, freeing me to begin my exploratory roaming once more. He shivered as I traced a scar that slashed down his left pectoral.

"What happened?" I asked. The wound must have been devastating if it was able to scar.

"A combination of youth and arrogance from defending my court."

"Tell me what the courts are like."

"Samhradh, the summer lands, is exactly what it sounds like—a land of eternal summer. It's always sweltering hot, but the waters are unlike anything I've ever seen. They're so clear, you can see straight to the bottom of the ocean."

"I've never seen the ocean before," I admitted, wondering what it would look like. Would the waters be colder than a river? Or would they be warm from constant sunshine?

"It's magnificent." Cillian smiled. "If you like, I can take you one day."

He spoke as if we had all the time in the world. As if there wasn't an army knocking on Ilythia's doorstep. He talked like we had a future. "I would like that very much."

"Then it's a date." He grinned.

"Tell me about your court."

"Fómhar?" He asked, repositioning himself to lie next to me, resting his head in his hand. It has a temperate climate, nothing extreme like Samhradh or Geimhreadh. The landscape is stuck in perpetual autumn. Some say Fómhar is half dead, but I believe the colors are vibrant with life. Earrach is beautiful with all its flowers, but it's nothing in comparison to Fómhar's rich shades. Though I could be biased."

"And Geimhreadh?" I asked, trying to disguise the longing in my voice. Before I knew of my past, the aes sídhe lands meant nothing to me. But now...I found myself wanting to learn more about the life I was supposed to have.

"Cold. Very, very cold," he laughed. "Yet beautiful in its own right. During Midwinter, there are these lights that appear in the sky every year. Your father used to invite all of Upper and Lowerlands to see them for their Midwinter celebration. If you thought it lasted long in Rothcek, it's nothing compared to Geimhreadh. The longest night of the year turns into days of celebrations. And, proper celebrations, mind you."

"Do you miss your home?"

Cillian shook his head. "A home is not a place. It is not a court or a kingdom. A home is found with the one who holds your heart."

"And who holds your heart?" I whispered.

"Only you, little shadow," he breathed, his lips skimming along my neck. I sucked in a breath, all thoughts of Arundell disappearing. His fingertips grazed the hem of my sleep shirt, brushing against my abdomen.

"May I?" he whispered, tugging at my shirt. I nodded, and slowly, he raised it over my head, his eyes never leaving mine as he revealed my bare skin. Heat flooded my body.

"Stunning," he breathed, drinking me in. His hands trailed along my breasts and down my torso. His fingers skimmed over the jagged scar that started below my sternum and ended right above my belly button.

"Fomorii wolf," I answered the unspoken question dancing in his green eyes. Cillian leaned down, kissing every inch of the scar before moving to my breasts, taking his time with each one with slow, torturous strokes I felt all the way to my center.

"Cillian," I pleaded. It was too much, the aching feeling too overwhelming.

"What do you want, little shadow?" he asked, not ceasing his slow, sensual torture.

"You," was the only word I could think of.

Cillian stilled, hovering over me. "No, tell me what you want from me because I want you, Saoirse Aíne Órlaith. Mind. Body. Soul. Day and night, you're all I think about, and I want everything you're willing to give. Say it to me now. Put me out of my misery if you must. If it's sex you want, what you need, I will live with it but know it'll mean more to me."

I reached up, brushing the stubble lining his jaw. For a heartbeat, there was only us. No war. No vengeful gods. No family in peril. I couldn't deny the constant pull toward him as if Fate herself nudged me. As if the gods granted me this small gift after everything I endured.

"I want you, Cillian Aodhán. All of you."

Chapter Fifty-Three

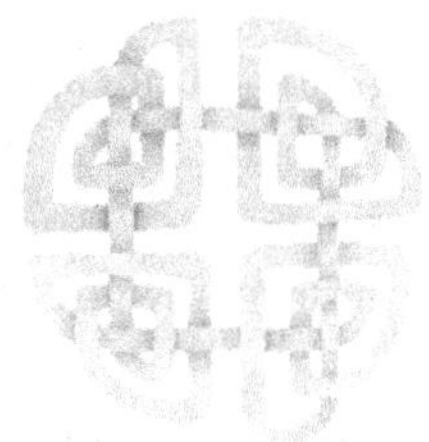

The last of Cillian's restraint dissolved just before he crashed his lips into mine. Cillian didn't kiss me with desperation—that this may well be our one and only time together if we didn't survive Tenebris's forces. No, Cillian Aodhán kissed me with reverence. Like he'd been waiting lifetimes to memorize the shape of my mouth, the feel of my skin beneath his touch. Like he waited so long to hear those words from my lips, he needed to taste the truth of them.

Cillian slid his hand to my waist, pinning me against the mattress. I threaded my fingers through his hair and tugged him closer. We kissed like the world outside didn't exist. Like the upcoming battle, the bloodshed, the anticipation of it all ceased—narrowing down into this one room, this one moment. I allowed myself to let go, to not worry about Aislinn. I pushed it all away until there was only him. Only us.

An approving growl rumbled through him. The vibration traveled to my toes. He broke our kiss to run his lips down my neck, my sternum, circling his tongue over my nipples and pulling them into his mouth one at a time. He brushed his mouth over the pink scar once more as if he could take away the memory associated with it. Cillian stopped when he reached the hem of my sleep pants—pausing—as if savoring this moment in time, trying to sear it into his brain.

His muscles flexed and bulged as he tugged my pants down, down,

down, his eyes never leaving mine until I was wholly naked. Cillian's emerald gaze raked over me, stopping where my knees came together.

"I told you I want you sprawled out for me," he said, his voice a low growl. Cillian tapped my knee, the touch shooting down to my center. "Be a good girl, and open up."

Heart in my throat, I complied, butterflying my legs. I'd never been so exposed to anyone else before. So vulnerable. And yet—I wasn't afraid or embarrassed but emboldened as Cillian looked at me like I was the most beautiful thing he'd ever seen.

"Fuck, Saoirse. You are a goddess reincarnated." Cillian bowed to me, his stubble rough against my inner thighs. A gasp tore from my lips as he lowered his mouth to my very center, splitting me with his tongue. Worshipping me as if I were indeed his goddess. I dug my heels into his back, pulling him closer.

"I had a taste before, but Nines, it's nothing compared to the source," he growled into me. His words alone threatened to make me spiral out of control. Cillian ate his fill like a man starved, his tongue circling my clit over and over again. My back bowed, hands gripping the sheets like my life depended on it. Shadows danced under my skin, and I could have sworn they played with heatless flames.

"*Cillian*," I sobbed, somehow managing his name. I was so close I wanted to scream, to beg for mercy and more at the same time. To—

Cillian slipped his fingers in me like he had before, stroking them in and out, curling them toward him, and I shattered. Release flooded through me like a wave of his fire with his name on my lips. He worked through the last of my climax, firing off more sparks before joining his lips with mine, the taste of me still on him. The hardness of his length was more prominent than ever, and my desire renewed.

"Watching you unravel has to be the single greatest thing I've ever witnessed," he murmured, his lips a soft caress, and gods, I wanted him more than I ever had before. Cillian, who had always seen me for who I am—not some timid girl, but someone strong. My body ached to be closer to him, to feel every inch of him, to know him more than anyone else.

We rose, meeting one another knee to knee, the mattress caving in where we came together. Cillian didn't rush me as I loosened the string around his hips. As I took my fill, tracing every hard line of him. A lump caught in my throat when I released him from the confines of his pants, ridding him of them. Fucking Nine. I was right. He *would* ruin me. In more ways than one, because gods help me, I was falling in love with

Cillian Aodhán. Or maybe, I'd been falling in love with him and now there was no undoing it. I was already in too deep.

Cillian brushed his fingertips along my neck as I ogled him, following the curve of my shoulders and down my back. He stilled when he reached my scars. My breath caught as our gazes met.

For the first time, I was afraid of what Cillian would say, what he would think. If he were to choose to cut his losses and walk away. I'd earned the scar from the fomorii wolf; it was a symbol of survival. But these—these were evidence of my weakness. Cillian had stopped the chancellor mid-attack before. He knew some of what I endured, but he'd never seen the full extent of it. No one had. Save for Kalee and the healers.

Most of my scars were minor from the bits of lead that had burrowed under my flesh. But others were gruesome. Thick and red from iron pokers. From being sliced open and forced not to heal. I'd seen the way the healer's faces twisted in horror, their eyes flashing with pity.

"Turn around," he ordered, his voice dark.

My heart cracked. "Cillian, I—"

"Turn. Around."

I wanted to run. To hide. It was stupid to be embarrassed over something I was subjected to. But it was lasting proof of my cowardice. I'd let it happen. And some part of me thought I deserved it because I wasn't strong enough to stand my ground. There was no denying Cillian, however. Not when he held my heart in my hands. And certainly not when he looked at me like that. I turned, baring myself, scars and all. I held my breath, preparing for his rejection. For his disgust.

Cillian brushed a kiss over my shoulder, peppering tender touches over my scars. A quiet sob tore from my lips. He stilled, if only for a moment.

"Did you think I would run from you?" he asked, lavishing my back with his gentle touches.

"I was afraid you'd be appalled. That you might think of me differently."

"There is nothing that would turn me away from you. I'd worship the ground you walk on if you'd let me." Another kiss to another scar. Tears threatened to cloud my vision. "Was there ever anyone else who hurt you the way he did?"

"It doesn't matter," I whispered. "I'm never going back."

"I will ask one more time. Was there anyone else?"

"No, it was only ever the chancellor."

"Good. Then there is only one person I need to kill."

My words caught in my throat. "There is nothing that can be done. He's miles away. I have no plans of ever going near him ever again."

"I never said you had to. His life may end with you safely tucked away in this castle for all I care."

My brows furrowed. "Cillian—"

He grabbed my chin, forcing me to look at him. "I would set the world aflame for you if you only asked." My breath caught in my throat at the absurdity of his statement, though the determination swirling in his green gaze told me he meant every word. "You are mine, Saoirse. And I am yours to wield however you want."

"I think I love you," I whispered. I hadn't meant to, but the words hung between us, threatening to wrap themselves around my neck like a noose.

Cillian kissed me, smiling against my lips. "Only you would proclaim your love for me at the promise of violence. I should have pledged to flay your enemies long ago."

I scoffed. "That is not why—"

He silenced me with a kiss. "I don't care what your reason is. You've consumed my every waking hour, your face fills my dreams, and I wouldn't have it any other way. I love you, S—"

It was my turn to interrupt him for once.

I crashed into him, muffling his words with a kiss. He gripped my hips, and my shadows laced between our bodies, circling before pulling us together. He shuddered under their touch. I braced myself to be flooded with memories, but none came. There was only us.

"You have me. I am yours, Cillian. And you are mine." *Mine.* He was. Even if I hadn't realized it before. I felt it in my bones. No matter what would happen, where the future would take us. He would be there. Solid. Steady. Safe.

I palmed the hard length of him, stroking his cock from root to tip.

"Gods, Saoirse," he groaned, his head falling back.

"I want you in me."

Cillian leveled his gaze with mine, bringing his hand to my neck, thumb brushing over my bottom lip. His other hand found my clit, stroking me into a frenzy until I was panting. "Then beg for me."

"*Please*, Cillian. I want *you.*"

My words shuddered across his skin, and he pushed me down onto my back. I bounced from the impact against the mattress, barely managing a breath before Cillian grabbed my calves and pulled me to him. He buried himself to the hilt, not sparing me a moment to adjust to the size of him. A ragged breath tore from my lips. Like I'd been drowning and just came up for air.

Cillian held my throat in his hand again, bending so his lips caressed my earlobe. "Remember how you begged for my cock when you scream my name—when you gasp for air, pleading with the gods after you've come."

Then he started moving.

Relentless. Mouth-watering pressure as I tightened around him. He drove into me, pulling my hips up to take me deeper. Hitting a spot that made me see stars over and over again. I cursed his name. My shadows ran over him, feeling every muscle, and he glowed. Actually glowed. His magic made itself known underneath his copper skin. He looked like a god sent straight from the Otherworld. Beautiful. Deadly. Mine.

"Fuck, Saoirse," he cursed. "There must be more witch in you than we realize," he accused. Cillian slowed, throwing his head back as if savoring the feel of me. This was worse. Infinitely worse. Unhurried, torturous strokes that had me pleading for more. Everything went warm. Tingly. My eyes rolled to the back of my head.

"Cillian," I begged, desperate for release.

He drove into me, knowing exactly what I needed, working me until I was on the brink of madness.

"Come for me, Saoirse," he said. It was a command I was more than willing to obey. His words threw me over the edge, my climax screaming his name, cursing the gods as I gasped for breath. Shaking. Cillian followed me over the ledge, finding his own release, spilling into me. He buried his face in my neck, breathing me in and leaving me boneless.

We lay there for a while, savoring each other's scents and the warmth of our tangled bodies. My stomach growled.

"We should find food," he said, voice low.

"I won't stop you this time."

He chuckled, sitting up. I cracked open an eye when he sat deathly still.

"What is it?" I propped myself up on my elbows, about to ask him again, when I caught sight of the marking on his arm. "What is that?" I followed his gaze—

"What the *fuck*, Cillian?" I yelled, looking at the new mark marring my left arm. Black Swirls ran from the center of my collarbone, travelling down the length of my arm until they reached my fingertips. Somehow, a mixture between my shadows and his fire, intertwining effortlessly as if they were meant to be together. I knew exactly what this was.

A bond mark.

I looked up, my gaze meeting Cillian's. My anamchara. My mate.

My. Mate.

My.

Mate.

"What did you do?" I whispered, thoughts spinning. I'd been bound out of my control. Again. Was this his goal all along? I scrambled from the bed, suddenly wanting to get far, far away from here. He reached for me, but it was too late.

"Saoirse, stop. I didn't know this would happen. I swear," he said, the muscles in his jaw flexing.

"But you knew we were anamcharas?"

Silence.

"You fucking knew we were *mates* and you never thought to tell me?" I shoved his chest and ran to the closest, squeezing into my leathers. Gods, these things were already constricting, but now they threatened to suffocate me. Or maybe that was *my mate* staring at me.

"I didn't want to overwhelm you. I wanted to wait for the right time." He shoved his legs into his leathers and pulled his tunic on.

"Before the bond was solidified would have been nice!"

Someone pounded on the other side of the door.

"I didn't know that would happen," he said again as if trying to make sense of it himself. It didn't matter. He should have told me. I should have known the risks of getting involved with him.

I will always find you.

It'll mean more to me.

You're mine.

Fuck, he did in his own way. But it honestly didn't matter. He should have outright said it.

More incessant pounding. I flung open the door. "What?"

Kalee's wide eyes met mine, bouncing between me and Cillian.

"They're here."

Chapter Fifty-Four

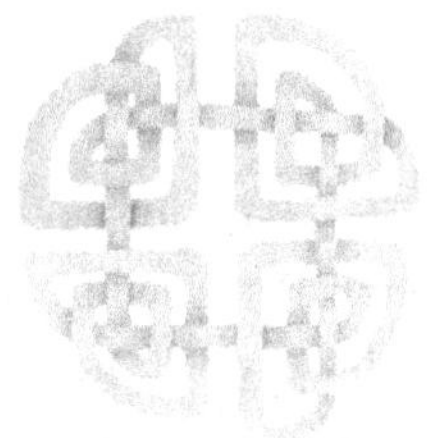

This day couldn't get any worse. The world spun and threatened to spiral out of control. Kalee's words echoed over me. The fomorii had arrived. They intended to destroy everything and everyone I cared for in one fell swoop. We could die tonight. Aislinn may already be dead. And I was bound again. Unknowingly. Cillian, my mate. Forever.

I was going to be sick.

"We need to find one of the trio," Cillian said, far calmer than I wanted him to be. "There may be someone in the castle who may try to steal the cauldron for Tenebris."

"Who?"

He shook his head. "It's just a theory, but I'd rather be over-cautious than not at all."

Kalee nodded and gave us both a wary look.

Witches rushed through the halls, a blur of leather and steel. It would be impossible to pick out a face in this crowd, but any of the three witches we needed were never far from their queen. We merged with the crowd, racing through the halls and up the winding stairs, and even then, all I could think about was the mark on my arm.

I swear to you I had no idea.

I gasped, and Kalee shot me a look. *Get out of my head, Cillian.*

I cannot stand how you're feeling. I want to make it better. His voice rumbled into me, skating across my spine, and gods help me, I felt his sorrow—his apology—in my bones.

Maybe should have thought about that before you fucking MARKED me.

Fools, Órga's voice flitted in. *You were both delusional, thinking nothing would have come of your promises of devotion and their consummation.*

The whites of Cillian's eyes blew wide when Órga's voice entered our minds. Heat scorched my cheeks.

Don't be embarrassed, halfling. You are blessed to have found both of your anam-charas so soon.

I groaned. Gods strike me down, I didn't need both of them ganging up on me.

Ronan and Eoin caught up to us just as we reached the tower door. The trio stood around Queen Petranella, Airi next to Niamh. Alice's hands clutched the railing as she peered out at the mass of black shadows outside the castle's doorstep. It was poetic, somehow. The room that birthed my freedom would also be home to my death.

Dusk whispered over Ilythia, sky bleeding from gold to violet as shadows stretched over the land. I scanned the horde of fomorii for Aislinn, finding the general instead and—

The chancellor.

My blood chilled. Flashbacks of every horrible, awful thing he did came bubbling to the surface, bringing me back into that low, dreadful place. Cillian's promise rang in my head. He reached for my hand, and I pulled away.

"Are mommy and daddy fighting?" Ronan asked, his blue eyes raking over me.

"Gods help me, Ronan, I *will* throw you from this tower," I threatened, my shadows bleeding onto the floor. He held his hands up in surrender, turning to Kalee. She shrugged.

The chancellor barked orders to the nearby soldiers—his face red with a familiar rage. If he were here with Tenebris's army, then Kalee was right. The Conqueror King was connected to this. The how and why remained a mystery, but there were no other Centran soldiers among the sea of shadows. There didn't need to be. The fomorii had the power to decimate us without the aid of humans or Bonded if Wolfhollow was any indication. The chancellor was here to observe and report. I ducked when he at last turned toward the castle, pulling Ronan and Eoin down.

"There is no sense in hiding, little shadow," Cillian said, rage coming off of him in waves. I suspected it wasn't only the chancellor who sparked his ire.

"He's right," Ronan said. "The time for secrecy is over. We make our stand now."

"Together." Eoin nodded. They rose, and I took Ronan's extended hand. I spent over half of my life shielding myself from the chancellor. It ended today. Ronan looked down between us, where our hands touched, where Cillian's mark tangled with my fingers. His brows furrowed. I pulled away and clasped my hands behind my back.

"The chancellor is a dead man," Cillian said before Ronan could comment on my new mark. The one Cillian also shared. *He* didn't bother to try to hide it. Despite winter's chill, the sleeves of his tunic cut off at his biceps. His marking ran in similar swirls from his fingertips and peeked above the collar of his tunic. Gods, I was going to kill him after this was done.

"He's mine," I said, my rage squashing any timidness. As much as I hated the chancellor, I'd never taken a life before. Not directly, at least. I'd brought many to the executioner, but I was never the one to deliver the killing blow. The fomorii were different. Unnatural. Soulless. The abominable creations of a dark god.

Killing the chancellor—that was a conscious decision, a vengeful commitment. I had no doubt he would slay me on the spot if our paths crossed. But if I sought him out, then it was *my* choice. *My* decision. *My* kill.

And I would have to live with that.

Despite the trepidation between us, pride radiated from Cillian down our newly found bond. Not because I was out for blood, but because I stood tall, willing to face my fears and confront someone who had caused so much pain.

"We started this together. We'll end it together, too," I said, giving a nod to each of my friends and extending a temporary alliance to Cillian. I was still pissed, but Aislinn, the safety of Ilthyia, was more important.

"If you wish to live another day," the general called from below, his voice as loud and clear as if we were standing next to him, "then surrender the Cauldron of Power now and pledge fealty to Tenebris, King of Shadows, God of Darkness."

Queen Petranella sneered, letting his words fall to a hushed silence. To their credit, none of the witches moved. They stood in solidarity. Not a moment of hesitation.

"Return to the hole from which you crawled out of or die where you stand," the queen replied, her voice brokering no room for uncertainty.

"You may want to take a moment to reconsider." Shadows swirled beside him, revealing Aislinn, bound and bruised. Alive. I blew out a breath. She was okay.

Now, Órga.

Petranella's hand twitched. "You could have ten thousand of my people, and still, I would not bow to you." There would be no surrender nor mercy to those who dared to threaten her kingdom. Airi howled, and arrows rained down upon the fomorii before I had a chance to take my next breath.

Like a harbinger of death, Órga swooped down from the clouds behind the army, flames igniting those in her wake. *I promised ashes for those who imprisoned me.*

Before the general could send Aislinn back to whatever horror he conjured her from, Órga scooped her up within her talons. Shadowed bolts pelted Órga, but they were nothing more than a nuisance, pinging off of her. Órga flew into the safety of the wards. Arrows bounced off the invisible barrier.

I loosed a breath. Finally, something had gone right. It was almost too easy, but perhaps Fate had blessed us for once. Alice and Kalee took off, running to catch up with Órga and tend to Aislinn.

"I told you she would be fine. Nothing ever passes these wards," Queen Petranella said, a smug expression plastered on her face.

"No thanks to you," I mumbled.

Despite Aislinn's rescue, the general made no move to retreat. He stood there, assessing. One by one, his army vanished, the witches' arrows striking true and making a dent in the legion before us.

The general raised his hands high above his head. Rock shook and sputtered until the earth split under the weight of the massive creature from some horror only the Shadow Realm might construct.

The arrows stopped.

"Is that a dragon?" I gasped, my grip tightening around my daggers. It wasn't a dragon, not truly. Its scales didn't glisten the way Órga's did. Its eyes were crimson embers. No, this dragon was crafted from Tenebris's shadows like the unnatural replica from Órga's story. Black fire spat from its mouth, curving around the invisible barrier protecting us.

Niamh cursed before barking out orders.

The fomorii dragon showed no mercy as it blasted the wards. Its screech was loud enough to ring in my ears.

"It can't get through, can it?" I yelled over its cries.

"I don't know," Niamh said, her queen silent in quiet horror.

We all watched as the wards finally gave way to the fire and then crumbled altogether. Thin, nearly invisible pieces floated about—nothing more than ash on the wind.

There was a moment of silence at the sheer disbelief at what had happened.

Then, the screams began.

Cries bellowed out as witches tried to outrun the dragon's black fire. Despite the coloring, I could feel the whispers of its heat from here. No one could get away fast enough.

Queen Petranella's face blanched. "Call for your dragon if you want to live," she said before running out of the tower room and into the fray with Niamh, Ahlani, and Flore in tow.

"Wait," I grabbed the queen's wrist. If it were under any other circumstance, I'd imagine she would have smacked me for the action. "The cauldron, we must use it."

"No."

"But if the wards are lost, then we have no other choice."

"You do not understand, girl. Magic comes at a cost. Magic from a god? The price is steep."

"You used it to break my Bond."

"Breaking your Bond is nothing compared to warding off an entire army created from a damned god," the queen spat. "Even then, the cost wasn't cheap." She indicated her hand—the black, rotten pink finger. I recoiled.

"So you would choose to sacrifice your people over yourself?"

"The cauldron is a last resort. Period."

"Wasn't it gifted by the gods to the rulers of Ilythia to protect the land?"

She laughed. *Laughed.* "God-born objects require god-born power. Anything less is life-draining. We were fools to think we could wield it as we pleased."

God-born power?

"No," I said, shaking my head. "It's because you are not Ilythia's true successor."

Petranella went deadly quiet. "What did you say to me?"

"The family tree. I saw it. You weren't there. That's why you sent your sisters away. That's why you didn't care if Aislinn lived or died. So she couldn't challenge you, for she would win."

The queen wrapped her hand around my throat faster than I could blink and shoved me into the wall. Stars pricked the edges of my vision. Cillian held a blade to her throat. Niamh to his. "You know *nothing*," Petranella spat. "I've ruled this kingdom for over a century. You have no idea the sacrifices I've made for this kingdom and for my family. Question my authority again and you'll be but dust on the wind."

Cillian growled, his blade pressing hard enough to draw a line of blood.

"If we can't use the cauldron, then at the very least, we must enforce the protection around it," I insisted. "With the wards gone, anyone can get inside."

"There is another set of wards to keep them from stepping into the castle. They're holding, otherwise, they'd already be here."

"For how long?"

Petranella stared at me, and I could almost see her debating ending my life behind her icy eyes. "Flore, enforce its defenses; bring with you whoever you must. Niamh, Ahlani, with me." The witch queen left without another word.

Órga, I called down.

I'm coming.

No, not yet. We need to protect the egg first.

It's safe. Órga's massive silhouette flew overhead, fire spilling from her maw. Her speckled golden scales sparkled in dusk's glow. Of course, she wouldn't run and take her egg.

The fomorii dragon shrieked at Órga's charge, the shadowed spikes around its head puffed out in warning.

I felt the boom all the way in the tower when the two dragons collided.

Chapter Fifty-Five

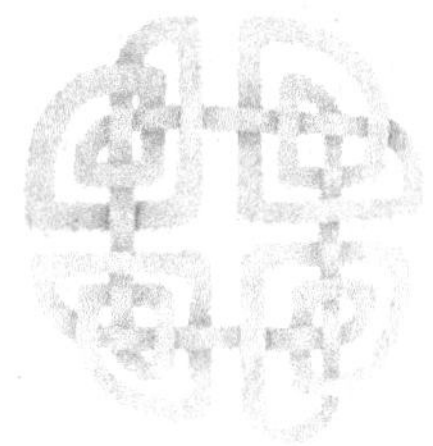

Another tower collapsed to my left. Debris stuck to my sweat-slicked skin thanks to Órga's constant stream of fire. The fighting leathers were thick and protective, but gods, they were hot.

Fomorii were everywhere. Most scaled the castle. Others made it past the archers and tore through the witches with ease. Órga incinerated as many as she could, but with the fomorii dragon on her tail, she was too preoccupied trying to lead it away from us. The covered battlement provided some reprieve from the chaos. Nothing, however, could block the cries and shrieks from fomorii and witches alike.

My chest was hollow as I knelt on the stone, firing arrow after arrow, aiming down at the demons who clawed their way up the side of the Mountain Castle. Another bolt notched into my bow pushed down any emotion threatening to rise to the surface. There was no time for thought or second guesses, only action.

Cillian was close by. I could feel his presence, and every now and then, I caught a glimpse of him out of the corner of my eye. His steel glinted in the light of the glittering moon, attacking those who made it past our arrows.

The fomorii soldier, paces beneath me, shrieked, its hot breath reeking as the sound threatened to blow out my eardrums. I reached for another arrow, but my quiver came up empty. The supply in the witches' quivers on either side of me was also dangerously low, though neither showed any signs of concern.

Cillian cautioned against using too much magic so soon after I exhausted myself at Wolfhollow. But the shadows called to me, begging to be released. I followed their lead.

I pictured an arrow in the notch of my bow. The shadows flowed through me, excitement sparking in my blood as a dark arrow fit perfectly in its rest. I drew the bowstring, muscles fatigued from repeated use, and sent the dart straight into the approaching demon.

My victory was short-lived as the fomorii was replaced with another, then another. They were too fast, and we were outnumbered. It was only thanks to the Mother and Órga that we had made it this far. But the fomorii dragon would have to be taken out if we were to see the sun rise again.

A flash of shadowed scales caught my attention, gut-wrenching screams from the witches following its wake. Their cries were a prayer on their lips: a plea for a swift and painless death. There would be nothing painless if the rows of its razored teeth were involved.

If the castle weren't carved from the mountain itself, it would have already fallen. I prayed those inside would remain safe, that we could hold the fomorii off and make sure they didn't overrun the castle. I couldn't imagine the terror of being trapped inside, hearing the battle around me. Kalee, Alice, and Aislinn should be among them. Aislinn would be in no shape to fight, and Kalee and Alice would tend to the wounded. I lost track of Ronan and Eoin long ago, but I knew they had each other.

In their chase, the fomorii dragon knocked Órga into the battlement. Stone shook beneath me. Its violent tremble shook my body—the all too familiar crack of breaking rock. I scrambled to my feet, but there was nowhere to run as the battlement crumbled apart. Those near the far ends might have a chance, but I was too far away to dare to dream it. The faces of the witches on either side of me were those of resolve, at peace with how their lives were to end—protecting and serving their kingdom.

"Into the darkness and out toward the light," the one on my left said, her rows of tightly braided hair still somehow intact, rock and wood raining down around us.

"May the Goddess bring us home," the other finished, giving her fellow witch and me a tight nod. I wish I'd known them under different circumstances.

Then we fell.

I twisted, trying to grapple onto something. To get a last look at Cillian. Despite my anger, I still loved him. He was still mine. I didn't like the way our bond formed, but I had meant every word I said.

I'm sorry, I said through the bond to Órga and Cillian. I blocked out their responses.

There was something almost peaceful about free-falling through the air. This is what having wings was like. Untied to the earth. Liberated. Air whipped around me, and I breathed in its wild scent, closing my eyes to ignore the bit of blood and dirt tainting it. Instead, I focused on the pine and juniper trees abundant in Ilythia, their fresh scent welcoming me..

I braced myself for impact. Would I feel every bone in my body break, or would the initial collision be enough to open the doors to the Otherworld? At least now, with my Bond broken and my final stance with which kind, maybe my mother might have been proud of who I was becoming. Maybe she could ignore the horrors of my past.

The crash came quicker than I expected, knocking the air from my lungs.

It *hurt.*

"Saoirse," Cillian's voice said as a cry of pain broke through my lips. In my distraught state, I imagined his arms around me, holding me to his chest. I was too afraid to inspect the broken mess to open my eyes. Was it too much to ask to die quickly?

"Saoirse," Cillian said again, grabbing hold of my attention.

We were still in the air, Cillian flying higher and higher—the ground several paces below—dodging chunks of debris raining down on us.

"Cillian," I whispered, not believing my eyes.

"Did you think I would let you fall?" He was covered in dust, rubble, and dark blood. A cut sliced along his temple, but otherwise okay. Alive.

I was alive.

A sob broke through my lips at just how close I came to meeting death. I shouldn't have made it. I should have died alongside the witches trapped on the bridge. Yet here I was. My chest tightened, searching for them. There hadn't been anyone to save them, though.

My chin quivered, and I was unable to stop the tears.

"I know," he said, holding me tighter. It only made me cry harder.

Cillian didn't let me go until we were inside the castle and at the triage area. I didn't have the energy to argue when he said I needed medical attention. Everything ached. I hadn't noticed the gash on my bicep, nor the one on my thigh.

Moans rattled the air. Some gasped for their last breath before they stilled. A metallic tinge hung thick in the air. It was a massacre. Blood, guts, and bone. Everywhere. I lost the contents of my stomach, which was saying something considering I still hadn't eaten.

It was all too much. Even with Órga, we didn't stand a chance. Not without the cauldron. I didn't care what the queen said. I would be the one to pay that price if I had to, if only to see those I cared for walk away from this. Consequences be damned.

"Saoirse," Kalee gasped, running toward me, supplies bundled in her arms. She knelt beside me, but I shooed her away.

"I'm fine. Go to someone else who needs you." She tried to argue, but I cut her off. "Where's Aislinn?"

"I'm not sure," she said, shaking her head. "She was here a moment ago. She's fine, by the way. As fine as she can be, at least. A few bruises and broken ribs, but no permanent damage. She might have gone to help Flore with the cauldron."

I blew out a breath. She would be alright. It was no surprise she was already doing something to aid her sisters, no doubt leaving as soon as Alice patched her up.

"Where do you think you're going?" Cillian asked as I rose from the floor on shaking legs.

"I need to speak to my aunt," I said, ignoring the biting pain shooting through my head. Stars sparkled in my vision, and a wave of nausea threatened to overtake me again.

"I'll go with you."

"No, you need medical attention more than I do." I hadn't noticed the large gash in his side. It was a miracle we made it so far.

"It will heal in a moment." He waved Kalee off, but Alice already noticed.

"Not a wound this large. You're lucky your insides didn't spill out with it. You'll need stitches if this is to heal properly," Alice said, her years of experience ending any argument.

"Fine, go. I'll catch up with you when we're done here," he said as Alice cut through the remnants of his shirt, needle and thread at the ready.

Before I could take a single step, however, white-hot pain burned through me as if melting me from the inside out. I fell to my knees, gasping for air as the breath was stolen from my lungs.

"Saoirse!" Cillian cried. Alice and Kalee rushed toward me, but there was nothing they could do. Physically, I was fine—but the source from which it came was not.

Órga.

CHAPTER FIFTY-SIX

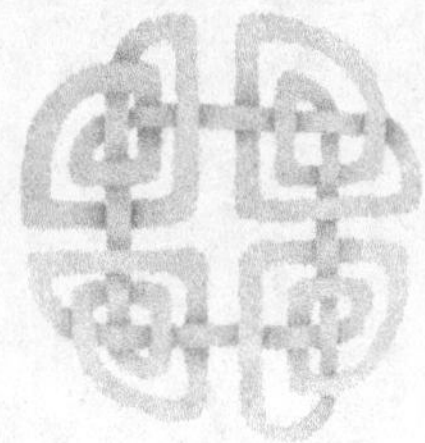

I sprinted toward the tower. Arms pumping and legs burning. I didn't know where Órga was exactly, but I didn't need to. I followed the tether connecting us, the link between our souls.

The fomorii dragon is too strong. Whatever it did to her, whatever made me feel her pain, weakened her. Her exhaustion weighed me down as if it were my own. Draining. Consuming. She kept flying, kept fighting, but she wouldn't hold out against the demon dragon for much longer.

I'm holding, she growled, and I could almost feel her gritting her razor-sharp teeth.

No, you're not. It's weakening you, Órga. Our bond was thinning, her strength waning. *Use my magic.*

No. I can handle it. We haven't had time to practice together and learn our limits.

Stubborn dragon. This is what the bond was for. To share magic when one didn't have enough. I hoped whatever magic I possessed was sufficient. *Stop arguing and take what you need. I trust you, Órga.*

I whistled, hanging out the window of one of the towers. I didn't know how sharing magic worked. If we needed to be near one another or if we had to make contact. But for Órga, I would figure it out.

She swooped overhead, circling the tower before gliding below the window.

Jumping out a window several hundred paces in the air and landing on the back of a living, breathing dragon was never something I envisioned for my life. Certainly not three months ago. There was a moment, right before I jumped, when I regretted my decision. What if my timing was off? What if I couldn't keep my seat? What if I impaled myself on one of her very sharp, very large spikes?

All reservations, however, stayed at the tower window as I free-fell into the air for the second time today. Cillian wasn't here to catch me this time, but Órga seemed to sense where I was as she tilted ever so slightly, moving those massive spikes.

I landed with a thud, gasping for breath while I grappled for purchase.

That went a lot smoother in my head, I groaned, inching my way up to the space between her shoulder blades. The contours and general landscape of her back provided the perfect space for me to cling on for dear life.

It takes years to properly mount a dragon. You did well for your first try. Do not worry, halfling, I'd never let you fall.

My victory was short-lived as the fomorii dragon, twice the size of Órga, came around the corner. Its screech rattled my bones.

Órga's growl reverberated through me as she propelled herself upwards, trying to put distance between us and the fomorii.

Where are you injured? I examined her back across the scales and spikes. They were their usual dark glittering sheen, the sparse golden ones still sparkling in the night.

My underbelly. I'm still resistant to his fire, but he is faster and stronger.

Órga rolled, narrowly missing the jagged teeth that lurched for us. I thought for sure I would fall, but Órga was true to her word. Whatever magic she was afforded kept me in place as we tumbled through the air.

Can you speak to him? Maybe he can be reasoned with. A life in the Shadow Realm, chained to Tenebris, didn't sound appealing to say the least. Maybe if we offered him shelter, a better home, he would reconsider.

All he seeks is death. Her breathing grew laborious as she struggled to outpace the fomorii. I'd known he was too much for her after the pain I felt. But now, seeing how difficult it truly was…Órga would lose this fight if she didn't have help.

You're tiring, Órga. Take my magic.

No, you are still recovering from Wolfhollow. You could die if I take too much.

Will it help you?

No answer.

If you do not take what you need, then the fomorii will kill us both. Take it. I dug my palms into her and willed what magic I had to the surface; my shadows bled out onto her. For a heartbeat, my vision swam with another day filled with destruction. A horde of fomorii dragons. Of other dragons, some brilliant in color, falling out of the sky.

Órga tapping into my power pulled me back to the present. Cool liquid seeped from my veins as magic flowed from me to her. My eyelids grew heavy. I should have downed one of Alice's potions beforehand, but there were only two vials left.

I had more magic now that my Bond with the king was broken and more stamina after my training sessions with Cillian. I prayed it would be enough. There was too much at stake to fail. Cillian. Kalee. Aislinn. Alice. Eoin. Ronan. Ahlani. Flore. Niamh. The list of people I cared for was ever-growing, and they all depended on Órga. On me.

Black fire spilled toward us. Órga rolled out of the way, but it was close enough to make my brow sweat. She dove, making a nosedive for the ground, moving faster now that my magic helped propel her. The fomorii dragon followed, his talons outstretched and jaw hinged open, preparing to scorch us.

Órga pulled up at the last second, narrowly missing the already broken battlement. The fomorii wasn't so lucky as he became tangled up in the rubble. Órga advanced on him, spurting out a bright flame tinged with silver sparks.

Her fire didn't burn the dragon, but the structure around him, making it more difficult to free himself. Órga swung out her barbed tail, slamming into the dragon's side. Dark blood sprayed us. My mouth tasted as if something had crawled in it and died.

"Watch out!" I cried.

The fomorii's jagged teeth grazed Órga's hindquarters enough to draw blood. She spun out of his reach before he could lock on to her. Pain hadn't blinded me like before. Whether it was because I was witnessing for myself this time or because the blow wasn't as deadly, I didn't know.

The fomorii dragon cried in frustration as he launched himself at us. Órga was prepared this time. She flipped upside down, letting the dragon pass above us, and latched onto his neck before he could react.

A tangle of teeth and talons, they slashed at one another, hurtling through the air. Órga's grip on his neck held steady as she punctured her teeth through scales, muscles, and tendons until a sickening *crack* splintered my ears. The fomorii dragon went limp under her hold. She released him, and he dropped with a smack, shaking the earth. Órga's victory shrill rang out over the land.

Órga's release on my magic was immediate. Relief flooded through me, though it was difficult to hold my eyes open with each passing second. My bones ached, my limbs almost too heavy to lift.

Cries and cheers sounded at the death of the fomorii dragon, but the army of fomorii soldiers still fought below. They wouldn't stop until they retrieved what they came for. The dragon may have been our biggest obstacle, but we needed a miracle to stop the army. There were too many of them, and I was too weak to try to dispel them like I had in Wolfhollow. We needed the cauldron.

Take me back to the castle.

You're tired, Órga fretted. *I took too much.*

I'll be fine, Órga. I fumbled for the lavender vile in my pocket and swallowed the overly sweet potion. One more left. I needed to make it count.

It felt like centuries had passed since we broke into the castle under Aislinn's guidance to steal the cauldron. I let memory guide me until the telltale pull of the god-born object tugged at my gut.

God-born objects require god-born power. Petranella's words rang through my head as I raced further into the castle. The phrase had struck me as odd, but I had been too focused on ensuring the cauldron's protection to give it a second thought. What if the faie had god-born power? Our magic derived from the gods; surely, that afforded us a bit of their power. Perhaps it had been diluted over the years. But Petranella was a witch; her magic came from the earth. Not only did she not have Tenebris's diluted blood running through her, but she didn't have his magic…I had both.

The abhorrent sounds of the ensuing battle died down the deeper I went. I would have sighed a breath of relief if it wasn't for the eerie silence in the depths of the Mountain Castle. Not even whispers of the host of witches guarding the cauldron. They could be quiet, but certainly, there would have been some sound to accompany them.

My steps halted when I rounded the corner.

Seven sentinels stationed at the iron doors lay lifeless on the floor, their empty stares forever fixed on an endless void. Among them—

Flore. The healer-turned-warrior lay dead amongst her sisters. My heart pounded in my stomach as I approached, checking to make sure the assailant hadn't lingered.

For the first time today, I wasn't upset about my bond to Cillian.

Something's wrong; find Ronan or Eoin. Or anyone who can help, I said. His shock at me speaking to him clanged down the bond, a hint of hope swirling around it, before worry took hold.

Wait for me.

But there was no time.

I put my ear against the door, hoping to get a hint at what lingered beyond, but the iron was too thick. Carefully, I cracked it open with a dagger in hand. Relief pulsed through me at the sound of Eoin's and Aislinn's voices. They were fine. They stopped whoever tried to steal the cauldron.

Relief was short-lived, however.

Eoin's iron-forged sword was pointed at Aislinn's neck.

Chapter Fifty-Seven

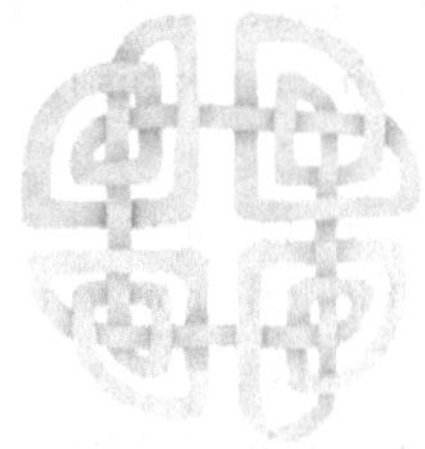

Eoin grabbed Aislinn at the sight of me, holding her in front of him, the edge of his blade pressed against her neck. Aislinn's face paled. She didn't look afraid, however. Something akin to sympathy lay amongst the bruises instead.

"Saoirse, I know what it looks like, but I assure you, I mean no harm," Eoin said. I wanted to believe him. I did. He was my friend. But he made no move to lower his weapon.

"Release her, and let's talk." I feigned calmness in the wake of pure terror. A familiar panic threatened to rise to the surface. Shadows swirled around me, beneath me, ready to pounce, but the blade was too close to her neck. One simple slip and she could die.

"I can't do that," Eoin said, voice solemn enough almost to make me believe this was a misunderstanding.

Almost.

Aislinn remained silent, pleading with her eyes for something I didn't see. To run? To fight? If I hadn't intervened when I did, would she be dead by now?

"Explain it to me, then. What's going on?" The room was the same as it was when we were here last. The statue of the Triple Goddess in the center of the room was gone. Only the plain, unassuming cauldron—save for the power thrumming within it.

"I'm stopping the battle," he said simply as if there could be no other explanation. "He wants the cauldron, and I'm going to hand it over. Once they have it, they'll leave."

"Then we are of the same mind," I said. "I've come here to stop this. Let me use it instead."

Eoin's brows furrowed. "I can't let you do that."

"I'll be fine, Eoin. Let me try. *We* can stop them. Together. You and I can put an end to this."

Eoin's grip on Aislinn eased a fraction. Not enough for her to slip out, but at least the blade wasn't so close. For a moment, I thought I had broken through to him, but Eoin shook his head. "You don't understand. I can't let you."

The world tilted. Realization crept over me like frost, cold and silent, until it settled into my bones. Coiled around my heart.

"You're working for him." My voice cracked—my heart with it. He was supposed to be my friend. We went through so much together, and his loyalty just changed? Was he ever with us, or was it all a facade?

"I made a deal," he said, voice hardened with resolve as if convincing himself he made the right choice. Aislinn stiffened.

"What kind of deal?"

"The kind that allows me out of this alive and onto a better life."

I recalled the dream he shared with me—to become something more. But this? After all we learned about Tenebris? I shook my head. "What about the others? What about Kalee and Ronan?" Eoin adored Ronan. Loved him. Ronan would never stand for this. Eoin had to know that.

"Once the fomorii have the cauldron, they'll retreat. They're on orders to do so. Can't you see? I am saving them."

"Break whatever deal you made—let's finish this the right way."

"There is no stopping him, with or without the cauldron, Saoirse. This *is* the right way. You just can't see it yet." Sweat beaded at his brow—the only sign of his nerves.

"You can't believe anyone willing to destroy innocent lives would let us live ours freely." I had to keep him talking, to keep buying us time. "How is it right for someone to destroy thousands of people? Because he is a god?"

Aislinn's stare turned misty. I prayed she communicated with Alice through their bond. That Cillian was on his way. I searched Aislinn's gaze for any hint of a plan, but her answering look provided no comfort.

"Does Ronan know?" I asked when Eoin didn't answer.

"No," he murmured, his hold on Aislinn faltering for a second before he regained his composure.

"The king?"

"He's fulfilling his own deal." Eoin didn't elaborate, but I could guess at the kind of bargain he made. Power was the only answer. How else would a human Bind himself to osnádúrtha if not through the help of a god?

"Why would you do this to us?" Eoin was loyal. Brave. He wanted to help people and better the world, not see it burn.

"I don't want to be second best anymore. I'm tired of living in the shadow of someone else. Not good enough for something greater. Not good enough for you," Eoin spat.

"I never said you weren't good enough. We're just *different*. But that doesn't mean you're worth any less. I understand what it is to feel like you're not enough, but this isn't the answer." It was hard to see past the blade at Aislinn's neck. I needed to get her to safety, and then I would help Eoin with whatever he tangled himself in.

"This is the only answer."

"This is wrong!" I cried. "What happened to the man who wanted to help the osnádúrtha and create a better world? What happened to the man who helped me?" My voice broke. He was the first person to show me any kindness besides Kalee. He helped bring me to Ronan and start my journey to freedom. He was the one who cracked open the door to me, believing I might be worthy of being loved. And now, he was the one who threatened to crumble it all.

"What Tenebris offers *is* a better world. He is the one true king, and he will eradicate this world of its faults."

"You're a fool, boy," Aislinn said, voice hoarse.

"Quiet, witch." Eoin tightened his grip around her, squeezing my lungs with it. A line of blood trickled down her neck.

"You're mistaken," I said calmly, trying to get him to see reason. "No world is without faults. No world he creates will be perfect." I shook my head. How had his perspective become so skewed? "You've witnessed the iron fist of the Conqueror King," I continued. "You know what it is for people to live in fear. People are imperfect. They will not fall in line because someone says so. They will question, and for good reason. It doesn't matter who sits on the throne."

"They will learn. Come with me so you can, too," Eoin pleaded, but he still held onto Aislinn.

"You know I can't do that."

His eyes drifted to the mark on my hand. He huffed a dark laugh. "I should have known. You've already made your choice."

There was no warning when he slit Aislinn's throat. Dark rivulets gushed from the wound. My mind didn't think, *couldn't* think, as I ran toward her, catching her before she dropped and applying pressure to the gash.

Eoin fled with the cauldron, the shriek of the wards blaring. But I would not leave my aunt during her dying moments as I had been forced to do with my mother.

"Aislinn, I—" There was too much to say, and there wasn't enough time.

How could I explain how much she meant to me? We'd only known each other for a short time, but she was my second chance at a family. I loved her, and now she was being ripped away from me.

Aislinn tried to speak, only to produce a horrid gurgling noise instead. Her eyes flashed from black to cool blue. A knot formed in my throat. Flore wasn't here to save her. No one was.

I shushed her and smoothed down the errant strands of her dark hair. "I will tell Alice you love her more than anything. And I hope you know I love you, too. I am thankful for every second we had together. I only wish I'd known you sooner." I couldn't mask the tremble in my voice. The quiver in my lip. It was the goodbye I hadn't gotten with my mother. I tried to be strong for her in her last moments, but I couldn't stop the tears.

In another world, another lifetime, we would be together. I would run my bookstore, Alice would have her apothecary, and Aislinn would be there to pester the two of us. We would be happy. It was a lovely dream.

But dreams were meant to be crushed.

She didn't try to say anything more. The squeeze of her hand on my wrist conveyed enough. She loved me, too.

"I'm sorry, Aislinn. I'm so fucking sorry," I cried, cradling her. I didn't want to let her go.

Her eyes fluttered closed as she drew in a shaky breath.

"Into the darkness and out toward the light. May the Goddess bring you home." I repeated the words the witches uttered, which seemed like a lifetime ago. I hoped it would provide her with some last comfort. The grip she had on my wrist went slack. She smiled up at me, and I knew she felt no more pain.

Aislinn was gone from this realm.

CHAPTER FIFTY-EIGHT

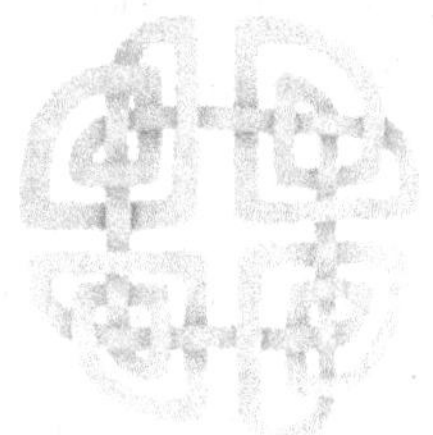

My footsteps pounded down the hall and echoed off the stone. Warning sirens added to the ringing in my ears, but unlike last time, no one came. Eoin couldn't have gotten far. I guessed at his escape route. There were only so many paths he was familiar with. Staircase after staircase, I flew toward the hidden entrance we snuck into together months before.

The door was left open carelessly.

Good.

He was afraid I'd catch up to him. Stars twinkled in my vision and threatened to overpower me as I raced toward Eoin, but I wouldn't stop. I wouldn't let Aislinn down. I wasn't able to avenge my mother's death, but I sure as Nine could Aislinn's. I would kill Eoin with my bare hands if I had to.

Chilled air greeted me, doing nothing to calm the fiery rage within. The battle still ensued. Its screams and cries raged on, though not as raucous as before. Órga's shrill pierced the air. I hope she incinerated all of them. I wanted to call her and ask for her aid, but I wouldn't stop her from helping the others. No, this was between me and Eoin.

Eoin's form was lost to the night amongst the thick trees, but the hum of the cauldron's power grew louder.

It was close.

Branches whipped and scratched my face as I closed the distance, pushing my legs harder than ever. His outline appeared ahead. The cool hilt of my dagger warmed in my palm. I hurled it as hard as I could—straight into Eoin's back. His steps faltered, grunting as he went down, the cauldron still in hand.

I didn't see my friend lying in the grass, reaching toward the wound. Instead, I saw red as I unsheathed Cillian's sapphire-hilted sword strapped to my back.

"How could you?" I screamed, vocal cords straining. His face glistened with a thick sheen of sweat, but I harbored no sympathy. Not after he killed Aislinn in cold blood. Not after he betrayed me. Betrayed all of us. He was supposed to be my friend. He was once my savior.

Now, he was my enemy.

"Do not blame poor Eoin for simply following orders," a voice tsked behind me, and my steps halted, heels digging into the grass. "Unlike you, Informer, Eoin excels at doing what he's told."

I whipped around to find the chancellor donned in black metal armor. My head bounced between the two: my past and present threats on either side of me.

"You can only choose one," the chancellor cooed, goading me into facing him.

"I don't think I'll have any issues getting exactly what I want." I flung my last dagger into Eoin's thigh. He cried out and dropped the cauldron, doubling over.

The chancellor huffed. "Is that meant to impress me?"

"Why would I want to impress you?" I asked, readying my sword.

The chancellor's bloodshot eyes gleamed at the sight of the azuline blade. "Now, where did someone like *you* get a blade like *that*?"

"The only concern of yours is what it feels like when it slices your flesh." Before, I didn't know if I'd be able to face the chancellor. But now, standing before him, I didn't see a human. I saw a monster.

The chancellor chuckled. "And where has that mouth been? I look forward to tearing into you again. This time, there will be no mercy." The red veins in his eyes grew black, as did those under his skin, slithering below the surface.

I sucked in a sharp breath. Nothing could have prepared me as the chancellor shifted into a fomorii demon. Gone were his human features. What once was pale flesh faded into a sickly gray, and shadows swarmed him. His red hair fell away, and his stout form trimmed down as if he were stripping himself of a costume.

"Surprised? Though I must admit, you're handling it better than Eoin or the false king across the border did."

"Who are you?" I breathed. This was worse. Much, *much* worse.

"My name is Amon, but it is *what* I am that should scare you, for I am Tenebris's right hand—his enforcer. And unfortunately for you, you are in my way."

The chancellor, Amon, flung out dark tendrils of magic. They wrapped around my leg and threw me against the ground. He smirked, prowling toward me, each step a slow, steady pace. Before I could sit up, he latched onto me again, tossing me in the opposite direction. Pain barked at my back when I collided with a tree.

Another tendril lashed out at me. On instinct, I drew a shadowed shield as Cillian had once commanded.

Amon faltered if only for a moment. "My my, what other things have you been hiding?"

"Only one way to find out," I growled, letting the shadows loose. I dug deep into the well of magic within me, finding what little I had left. I thought I was spent, but rage drove me forward. For a moment, I contemplated pulling from Órga's power too, but resisted. She was too weak. I wouldn't compromise her for the sake of my revenge, no matter how much I might want to.

Darkness ensued around us, our shadows clashing with one another. A cry broke through me as Amon slashed into my already battered arm. I didn't allow terror to consume me or for his memories to steal my vision. To falter my steps. Instead, I leaned into hope. Into the confidence I'd gained in myself over the weeks. Both of which I never truly had before. I heeded Cillian's advice, listening to the shadows.

I knocked Amon to the ground, not giving him a breath before attacking him over and over again. All the pain he'd caused me, I poured into him, turning my rage and suffering into his own. He cried out as the shadows tore into his back, replicating the markings on my skin.

So consumed in my own retribution, I didn't see Eoin get up. Pain exploded in my shoulder as his knife sank home.

"Gods," I cried out, the iron scorching as it ripped through flesh and muscle.

The face I once considered a friend sneered back at me. Any hope of his redemption died with Aislinn. Eoin knocked me down, the heel of his boot firm against my chest, his blade pressed against my neck.

"It didn't have to end like this, Saoirse," he ground out. Amon struggled to stand a few paces away. I wondered who would kill me first.

"Eoin?" Ronan stumbled around the corner, his eyes wide at Eoin's blade against my throat.

"Ronan. I—"

"Saoirse!" Cillian bellowed, the trees trembling against his wrath.

"Shit," Eoin cursed, dropping any attempt at an explanation.

My shadows tossed him off of me, using his momentary surprise to my advantage. Amon and Cillian raced toward me. Cillian's glorious wings were out, shining in the moonlight.

Amon was closer, though.

Eoin ran to Ronan, the cauldron gripped in his fist.

I flung out a tendril at him. His steps faltered, but my shadows didn't hold out for long. They were weaker now as exhaustion sank in and sleep threatened to pull me under. I fumbled in my pocket for a vial of Alice's potion. If the leathers weren't so godsdamned *tight*.

Órga, I yelled down our bond. The cauldron was too valuable to risk on my own. I needed her help. She was too drained to lend any magic, but she didn't need magic to stop them. Not when bone-melting fire or flesh-slicing teeth could do the trick.

I'm almost there, halfling. Her roar shook the earth.

Amon closed the gap, and I braced for impact.

He reached toward me, only to miss entirely, and grabbed Eoin and Ronan instead. Massive black shadows formed at his back, resembling makeshift wings. Ronan kicked and clawed in Amon's grip, but it was useless.

The shadows flapped. Once. Twice. They were airborne. Cillian shot upwards, chasing after them. Órga swooped down, claws outstretched. Cillian was nearly there, blade ready to strike.

I would have missed it if I blinked.

One second, they were there; the next, Amon and Eoin disappeared.

With Ronan and the Cauldron of Power in hand.

Chapter Fifty-Nine

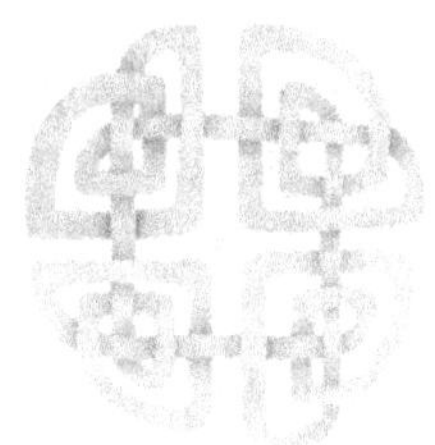

"They have him," I said through deep breaths. "Ronan and the cauldron. Eoin betrayed us. He's working with Tenebris and the chancellor."

Cillian swore, assessing my injuries. Órga landed close by, the ground trembling beneath her. The wounds inflicted on me were nothing in comparison to what warred within. I couldn't bring myself to voice what Eoin did to Aislinn.

I witnessed life leave her body. Saw it with my own eyes. Yet, there was a part of me that thought maybe if I didn't acknowledge it, it wouldn't be true.

It was, though. And Ronan... Gods, how was I going to tell Kalee? How would we get him back?

"The general," I said hazily.

"What?" Cillian asked.

"We need to get to the general before he disappears. He might know where they took Ronan." They already had the cauldron. Eoin assured me they would leave once it was in their possession.

"Let's go," Cillian reached for me.

With me, halfling. It will be faster.

Cillian didn't argue as he flew us up atop Órga's back. She leapt into the air, and like before, her magic held us onto her back.

I fumbled for the last lavender vial, the liquid sweet on my tongue.

I wouldn't fail Ronan as I did Aislinn. As I did my mother. There were too many people I'd let down. I couldn't bear to add Ronan's name to that list. Couldn't do that to Kalee. Doubt crept over me, Aislinn's face flashing through my mind. I shook out the thoughts. There wasn't time to dwell on my failures, not when I still had time to help Ronan. I couldn't control others' actions, but I could control my own. I'd be damned if I'd let my own self-pity keep me from getting to him.

My heart pounded under the potion's effects, or maybe the anticipation.

The fomorii numbers had dwindled significantly with their dragon dead amongst the broken rubble. Stragglers remained, ripping and tearing at the witches. But with the dragon gone, it was easier for the witches to hold their ground.

The general fought amongst them.

"There!" I cried out.

"We'll need to find a way to restrain him," Cillian yelled over the roaring wind. "I have an idea. Stall him as long as you can." He dove off of Órga's back, mottled wings flaring as he angled toward the castle.

Órga made a nose-dive for the general, casting out a stream of fire along the way. At first, I thought maybe we'd lose him right then and there, not wanting to risk going up against the dragon. But then, we locked eyes, and it was as if his resolve strengthened.

Don't kill him. We need him to find Ronan, I instructed as Órga landed, cratering the ground and blowing back dirt with her shriek.

It would be so easy.

Later, I promised. I wouldn't mind seeing the general go up in flames or succumb to her teeth. But Ronan was more important.

"Come to play, or will you hide behind your dragon?" the general yelled up toward me.

"I'm the one who sought you out," I reminded him, sliding off Órga's back.

"A mistake you'll soon regret," the general sneered, his crimson eyes tracking my every movement. He struck his magic out at me, sword in hand. I was prepared this time and blocked his attack with a shadowed shield, stronger now with the potion coursing through my system.

He struck, I defended. I whipped my magic out toward him. He repaired the gesture in kind. We took turns advancing our attack. The general was strong, but I was determined.

"Give it up, girl. You are no match for me alone." It might have been true. I might have had better luck if I weren't injured or if I weren't relying on a potion to keep me standing.

"No, I'm not," I conceded. "But I'm not alone."

The general's confusion gave me nothing but pure joy as Cillian flew up behind him and wrapped the fomorii in iron chains. They struggled until Órga lunged, Cillian diving out of the way before she clasped the general in her claws. Cillain winced, shaking out his hands covered in burns from the iron.

"Bitch," the general spat, squirming beneath the chains and talons.

"Tell us where Amon took our friend," I demanded.

"Which one? The spy or the prince?" He laughed. "The human swore he'd be able to get us the cauldron. I thought him a fool for promising the prince as well, but I guess he succeeded." The general smiled, and horror washed over me. Eoin had known him on the day of the attack in Wolfhollow. *Eoin* had been there each time the fomorii appeared. In the Ilythian woods, when Ronan almost died. In the Centran forest, when the formorii had said they were meeting someone. They waited for Eoin. We would have known if Cillian and I hadn't revealed ourselves too soon. The fomorii wolf that gave me my scar.

Eoin summoned them all.

He planned it. And worse, the general knew who Ronan was. Knew *what* he was.

"Both," I growled.

"It doesn't matter. You won't be able to reach them."

"Where?" Cillian demanded. The general squirmed, and Órga's talons squeezed tighter. His shadows withered under Cillian's fire as he wrapped the flames around the general's neck. He hadn't been afraid back in Wolfhollow because he'd known he could evaporate at any given moment. But now, with the iron wrapped around him, there was nowhere to go. No magic would save him now.

"The Shadow Realm," he rasped. "It is no use. You cannot access it."

"Take us there," I blurted. "You took Aislinn. You can take us as well." Any book that mentioned the Shadow Realm only described it as a miserable, dangerous place. I didn't care. Ronan needed help before it was too late.

"Release me from these chains and see where I take you," he croaked. The general could lead us straight to Tenebris. We'd be no help to Ronan if we were his prisoners.

"Let's make a bargain," Cillian countered. "You get us into the

Shadow Realm without notifying your master and bring us back at a time of our choosing. And we let you live."

"Fools," the general huffed, squirming under Órga's tight grip. "You think I value my life over my king's? My god's? You waste your breath. Save yourself the time and end me already."

"There are worse things than death," Cillian said, his face a hair's breadth away from the general. He looked more like the Hunter, more animalistic and otherworldly as he stalked his prey. "I will make you agree one way or another. How much you're willing to suffer before you do is up to you."

Chills ran down my spine. It was easy to forget how deadly Cillian really was. Even the general twitched underneath his threat.

"I have no doubt you are good at what you do, faie, but I am better," the general said before freeing his arm from Órga's grasp and slicing his own throat.

"No!" I screamed and scrambled for him. It was too late. The iron suppressed any healing magic he might have possessed.

Our chance at saving Ronan died with him. Then, as if I couldn't tether myself to this earth any longer, I faded into darkness.

CHAPTER SIXTY

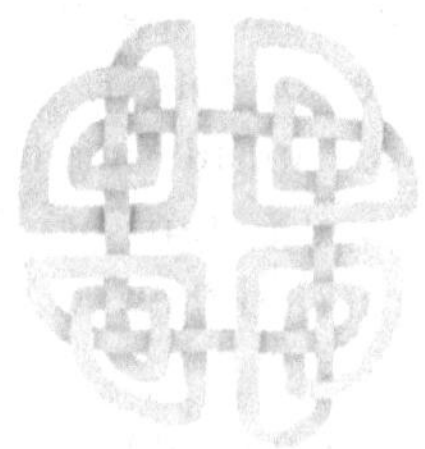

I was numb, body and soul, when I awoke again. Alice cursed me for stealing and relying on her potions to curb my exhaustion, saying I was lucky I hadn't died, unable to recognize when I was on the brink of a complete drainage. I couldn't bring myself to care. Waking only meant facing the consequences. I didn't know what was worse: Alice's cries or Kalee's when I recalled what happened. I failed them both. *I* had done that to them.

The goddess Cerri may have taken away the guilt from my mother's death, but no one, not even a god, could take this pain from me now. When my mother died, I was a child—I had no authority over my powers. I blamed myself for years over something I couldn't control. Now, there were no excuses. I might not have delivered Aislinn's killing blow or put Ronan in Amon's path, but I didn't stop it either.

I should have stopped it.

I was older now, stronger. I had no Bond to hold me back. I had a grip on my magic. I had a godsdammed dragon as my anamchara.

I should have fucking stopped it.

"Saoirse, you need to eat." Cillian shoved a plate of food in front of me. I glared at him. The dining hall was crowded with witches, though there were significantly fewer after the battle. Queen Petranella threw a feast in honor of the lives lost for Ilythia, though she, along with Ahlani,

Niamh, and Alice, were notably absent. This victory was pointless. Aislinn was dead. Ronan was gone. The cauldron was gone.

"You should eat," Kalee said beside me. Her red-rimmed eyes were still bloodshot.

Glazed boar, roasted vegetables, and a pink cake sat on the plate before me. It didn't even look good. There was no smell or taste to food as of late. Helping the witches clear the destruction was the only thing propelling me out of bed. Even then, I didn't sleep well. My nightmares returned, reliving Aislinn's death most nights.

"I've been thinking," Kalee continued, her fingers thrumming against the wooden table. "I believe we can still save him," she whispered.

My heart ached. I didn't want to hurt her, but I didn't want to give her false hope, either. "The general said there was no other way. We can only hope they bring him back."

Ronan was gone. There was nothing we could do for him. We didn't know Tenebris's plan. Even when Aislinn was taken, we were forced to wait and hope he brought her to us. Tenebris could just as easily kill Ronan because of his bloodline. It wasn't like they were going to use him for a bargaining chip, not when they had the upper hand.

Kalee shook her head. "I keep thinking of what Ahlani said about her classmate."

Cillian's brows knotted. "The one who died in the lake?"

"You think she was taken to the Darkworld?" I asked Kalee. Despite everything, I still couldn't speak with Cillian. Not yet.

"What do you mean?" Cillian looked between us. But Kalee, Mother bless her, ignored him. She didn't even know why I was mad, though I'm sure our new markings were enough indication.

"Ahlani believes her friend was dragged to the Darkworld. What if she were right and it was some kind of portal? What if it leads to the Shadow Realm, or what if there's another portal that can take us there?"

I could practically see the gears turning in her mind. The determination set on her brow. She'd thought about this a lot, it seemed.

"That's an awfully big risk for something we know nothing about," Cillian considered.

"I can't find any text that proves my theory." Kalee's shoulders sagged. I hated seeing my friend like this. I hated her not being able to get the answers she needed, but—

"What if we can prove it?" I blurted.

"What? Jump in the lake and see what happens?" Cillian's brow raised.

"No." I shot Cillian a look before I turned my attention back on Kalee. "The seer. If what you say is true, then the seer would know and could tell us how." If there were the slightest chance of finding Ronan, the seer would have the answers. Something sparked within me then. Suddenly, the world didn't appear as bleak and dull. There was something there—hope. It may be futile to go after Ronan. Kalee could be wrong, but there was still a chance we could help him.

And if we could find Ronan, we could find the cauldron.

I shoveled a forkful of food into my mouth, tasting all of the different flavors for the first time in days.

CHAPTER SIXTY-ONE

A knock came at my door. I wrung the water from my hair, the last of the dust gone from cleaning up the destruction. I was glad to be done. Glad to have another goal. Hunger gnawed at my stomach, and I prayed it was Kalee with food. We needed to talk about what we would do next.

I opened the door to find Cillian on the other side. I slammed it in his face.

Another knock. "I bring a peace offering," his mumbled voice said. He could have used the bond to speak to me, but he hadn't since I told him to stay away. That, he at least respected.

Cillian stood in my doorway, devastating as usual, plate of food in hand, the other tucked behind his back. Somehow, it hurt more when he looked at me like that.

"You took that from Kalee, didn't you?"

"I might have bumped into her."

"I'm surprised she entertained the idea."

Cillian winced. "That also took some convincing and bribery."

I reached out for the plate, but he swiped it away. "Some peace offering," I scoffed.

"It doesn't count as a truce if you don't let me in."

I left the door open and turned away, averting my gaze from the bed. Every time I looked at it, all I could think of was the morning we had together before everything went up in smoke. If it weren't for the mind-numbing exhaustion of helping the witches with the aftermath, I might have slept on the floor.

"You're still mad."

I pinned him with a stare, hoping it cut to the bone. I put aside my feelings during the battle, but the more I thought about it—about our bond unknowingly placed—the heavier the weight on my chest grew. And gods, it was so *stupid* because I had wanted to find my mate and had hoped to form a second anamchara bond. To be lucky enough to discover something like what Alice and Aislinn had shared. But this wasn't how I imagined it would be.

"Tell me, little shadow. Would things really be that different if you had known? I never lied about my feelings toward you. I know you didn't either. What's the difference if we're mated now or later?"

"The choice, Cillian. It was robbed from me. When I accepted the anamchara bond with Órga, she *asked* if I wanted it. I had a moment to contemplate a life-changing decision. *I* decided."

"Would you have said no if I asked?"

I didn't answer.

"Our bond wouldn't have solidified if either of us didn't want it," he said, his words soaking through my skin and down to my soul. He was right, of course. When the bond formed, it hadn't hurt like it had with the king. It was ecstasy like my soul opened up. Like I was whole.

"When did you know I was your mate?" I asked.

Cillian's gaze dropped to the food in his hand.

"*When?*"

"I told you, the moment I met you. I never lied to you, Saoirse. I came to Centra to free the daughter of my late king, to find some way to honor his death, but when we locked eyes—I was done for. I knew exactly what you were to me, and I couldn't do anything about it. Every day, for two years, I was so fucking afraid someone would find out. I can't imagine the unspeakable things they would have done to you if they knew. How they would have pitted us against one another." Cillian huffed a mirthless laugh. "Worse still, when we finally had an excuse to be close, to talk, your heart was skewed toward another. I had to watch that traitorous bastard worm his way to your good graces. I wanted to tell you *I* was meant for you. But I wasn't going to force you. I couldn't, especially not after what you endured. You deserved to live—to explore. To make connections with whoever you desired. To be free. When we left Centra, I knew neither of us was going back, and I decided right then and there that I would endure for you. Let your heart take you where you wanted to go, but I would always be there, waiting, until you chose me."

His eyes lifted back to mine, everything he felt—his regret, his sorrow, his love—tumbled toward me, beating against the barrier I placed between us. My bottom lip quivered. He was willing to sacrifice his own happiness for me.

"And when I chose you? When we kissed, did you not think to tell me then?"

"You had just been freed of the king's Bond. I didn't want to burden or scare you off. I was terrified you'd say no without giving us a chance. That the thought of another bond was so repulsive, you'd sever it before we could explore anything. When you accepted your bond with Órga, I planned on telling you after you settled into Wolfhollow, but everything went to shit."

All this time, he never said a word. Yet, the memories he shared of me in the training room conveyed it all; I was just too blind to see. Too stupid to recognize it for what it was. Would I have rejected him if he told me sooner? Would I have been too afraid to bind myself to another man?

Yes.

Only Órga's bond helped me see it was what it truly was. That it was nothing compared to the king's. Cillian's past was still a mystery, but I knew his heart. Knew his intentions were good, yet—

"I'm still angry," I whispered, part of my resolve fracturing.

Cillian set the food down on the table and took a step closer. Another. He held my chin in his grip. "Be mad. Be angry. Be whatever you need to be. But be mine."

Tears blurred my vision. Cillian hadn't tricked me into this; I had felt his shock mingling with my own when our bond solidified. My feelings hadn't changed; if anything, they'd grown despite my ire. He was closer now. I could feel him all around, nuzzled up next to my soul, right next to Órga. They were home. *Home.* When everything else crumbled around me, they still stood strong. Steady. Safe.

You owe me a lot more than a plate of food, I said down our bond.

The corner of his mouth twitched. *I will spend the rest of my life making it up to you, I swear it.*

He kissed me, and stars sparkled behind my eyes. The bond shimmered between us, pulsing and alive—a promise. We came together not just body to body but soul to soul. Real and raw. Broken and healing. We'd both learned how to survive, but now we had something to live for.

I was his.

He was mine.

I fisted my hands in his shirt, pulling him closer and savoring the familiarity of his scent.

I have something else for you, he said mid-kiss.

I pulled back. "You *were* prepared to grovel."

He chuckled. "It's more of a belated name day gift, but I'll allow it to count toward my penance if you will. We never had the chance to properly celebrate with everything going on."

My mouth went dry. Only Kalee ever bothered with name day gifts aside from Alice and Aislinn's generous gift that was obliterated.

"I would have given it to you sooner," he continued, "but they needed time to make it."

Cillian shifted his hand from behind his back, showing off a package carefully wrapped in brown paper, complete with a bow around its middle. It was heavy in my hands. Cillian's gaze bore into me as he waited. The anticipation mingled with nerves warred through me as I peeled away the wrapping.

A finely made leather scabbard as soft as any silk. My heart sank. "This is very kind, but I don't own a sword." I tried to hide my disappointment. I shouldn't be ungrateful for such a beautiful gift, but I had no use for it.

Cillian cocked his head to the side. "Of course you do. This belongs to you." He took the sapphire-hilted sword from where it rested against the wall.

My jaw slackened. "I—I can't take that. It's yours. I've only been borrowing it, remember?"

"It's always been yours. I'm the one who's been borrowing it." Cillian unsheathed it from its worn scabbard and ran his fingers lightly down the blade. "Your father had this made for you. It was to be a gift when you were capable of wielding it. They wanted to destroy it along with everything else of his, but I managed to save it."

A knot formed in my throat. "How did you find it?" There were so many questions running through my mind, but I couldn't focus on anything but the sword.

"I have my ways." Cillian kissed my temple and then set the blade in my hands. "Look at the inscription."

I held the blade up. I never studied it closely before. A large sapphire set in its pommel, the same color of my eyes—of my mother's eyes—black leather wrapped around its grip, and azuline veins ran in rivulets down the blade itself. Still, I never noticed the inscription of symbols down the center of the weapon.

"I can't read this."

"It's the old faie language. It's rarely used now; only members of nobility speak it." He grabbed my hand and ran my pointer finger along the symbols as he read, "For Saoirse, there is always light within the darkness."

My eyes stung. I had never thought—never hoped—that one day I might feel close with my father or even hold something that once graced his touch. And though my father had long since passed, his words remained. This was the most precious thing anyone could have ever given me.

"Thank you," I whispered, tears rolling down my cheeks. I didn't care how Cillian came in contact with the sword. I couldn't thank him enough for what he had done for me.

"What will you name it?"

I looked up at him. "What?"

"All the best swords have names."

"Zephyr," I said without another moment's thought. "It only seems appropriate to name it after him, so he is always with me."

"He's always been with you, even if you cannot see him." Cillian kissed my temple and sheathed the blade into its new home before dragging me into him, holding me until well after I finished with my tears, forgetting the food I'd been desperate for moments ago. My hold on him never wavered. In fact, I never wanted to let him go.

Cillian's heart beat steadily against my ear. His hand grazed up and down my arm—down my mark. "Little shadow?" he asked after a long while of standing in comfortable silence, drawing my attention to his face, his brows drawn in contemplation.

"Hmm?"

"Are you sure you wish to travel to unknown worlds? Tenebris is not done yet. The fomorii will return eventually. If he and the Conqueror King are in league together, he might give Ronan back to his father."

I considered him. I knew there was a chance Tenebris would bring Ronan back, but would the Conqueror King try to save his only male heir? Or would he let his son succumb to Tenebris's wrath?

"We still need the cauldron. Nothing good can come with it in Tenebris's hands. Petranella will try to get it back, but I don't trust her. Especially not if Ronan is in danger."

Cillian nodded. "And if we do find a way to travel to the Shadow Realm?"

"I will still go. For Ronan and for Kalee, I will go. Will you go with me?" I bit the inside of my cheek.

"Wherever you go, I will follow. Always."

"Even if it ends in peril?" I asked.

"Even if it ends in peril," he chuckled, kissing my forehead.

FAMILIAR FACES STACKED UPON ONE ANOTHER. THERE WERE TOO MANY OF them for separate pyres. Instead, they were organized according to their rank—a funeral fit for soldiers.

It took days to collect all the bodies strung out around the mountain. The witches refused to leave a single one of their sisters behind. Niamh and Ahlani clutched Flore's lifeless body until the flames flickered over her —another one of Eoin's victims.

I told them what I'd witnessed—who was responsible for her death. It wasn't only my trust Eoin betrayed. He fooled us all, leaving a slew of victims in his wake. I almost felt sorry for him. For if he were to cross one of the witches' paths, his death would not be painless. Eoin deserved the consequences of his actions and whatever came his way. If his end came at the hands of the witches, I wouldn't stop them.

Aislinn's pyre was the largest and brightest of them all. The flames reached up toward the Otherworld. A single tear slid down Queen Petranella's cheek. Did she finally regret not taking her sister's safety seriously? My jaw clenched, but I held my tongue. I prayed she felt every wave of guilt that came her way.

Alice sobbed into my shoulder, her whole body shaking. I held her, not knowing what else to do for her. I didn't stop Aislinn's death. I couldn't bring her back, no matter how much I wanted to.

Kalee stood next to me on my other side and squeezed my hand, reminding me I wasn't alone. I studied the bruises on her cheek. Despite every perilous thing we've been through, she survived. My closest friend, who had been with me since the beginning, was alive. And though Ronan was gone, there was still a chance we could save him. For her sake, I wouldn't stop searching for him.

All around were witches who held and comforted one another. Though they lost so much, they still stood. They carried on because that's what their loved ones would have wanted them to do.

Órga, my anamchara, my soul friend, let out a sorrowful shriek as the fallen witches burned to ash and returned to their Goddess. Her sorrow mingled with mine and Cillian's. But she was here, alive and breathing, the last dragon egg safe.

Cillian stood at my back as he always did. Always there. Never wavering. My mate whose love flowed freely down our bond. Who would always stay with me no matter what came our way.

I lost so much, but I was not alone.

Acknowledgments

Like any novel written by anyone ever, this couldn't have been without the amazing people at my side. To my husband, Seth, from the beginning, you have been my biggest cheerleader, even when I couldn't cheer for myself. Thank you for rooting for me from the sidelines, for taking care of our pups, and for feeding me when I forget to eat. Oh—and giving me your computer.

To Hannah Parker at Counterpoise Press, thank you, thank you, thank you a million times over for everything you've done to get AKOSS where it is today. Without you, it would still be sitting on my computer because my writer's block and imposter syndrome took over. I cannot express how grateful I am for the countless hours you've poured into my soul book. You know these characters as well as I do (if not more!). Working with you has been an absolute dream.

To Holly, Leia, Marissa, and Kam, who have had to deal with my pestering for years now—way before this book was conceived. Y'all's friendship means more to me than words could ever express. The Granny Smith to my apples, the butter to my cat (for levitating toast, of course), the ink to my tattoos (literally), and the shrimp to my cocktail sauce—there is a bit of each of you in this story. I hope you love it as much as I do.

To my parents, whom I've refused to share any information regarding this book, thank you for your unparalleled support. I love you guys so much. You have given me the world. I also hope you never see this because that would mean you've actually read it—don't say I didn't warn you.

Thank you to everyone who had their eyeballs on this book before it was brought to print—you guys rock. I'm still in awe that you all were interested enough to read it. To my friends in my writing group, your feedback, support, encouragement, and friendship are priceless. Amaya, thank you for taking the time to help me improve my craft. I hope I did you justice. Nicole, thank you for lending me your ear, your thoughts, and welcoming me into such a great group of people. Thanks to Kay for reading countless chapters and late-night writing sprints. To my friends on BookTok and Bookstagram, thank you for welcoming me into this community with open arms. I truly feel so lucky to have crossed paths with such amazing (and talented) people.

And to the reader, because without you, none of this is possible. I couldn't have asked for a greater gift. I am genuinely at a loss for words that you have taken your precious time to read Saoirse's story. I hope you love her as much as I do.